Books by Douglas Terman

First Strike
Free Flight

Published by POCKET BOOKS

FREE FLIGHT

DOUGLAS TERMAN

PUBLISHED BY POCKET BOOKS NEW YORK

All the characters in this book,
with the exception of certain Politburo members,
are fictitious, and any resemblance to persons
living or dead is therefore coincidental.

**POCKET BOOKS, a Simon & Schuster division of
GULF & WESTERN CORPORATION**
1230 Avenue of the Americas, New York, N.Y. 10020

Copyright © 1980 Douglas Terman

Published by arrangement with Charles Scribner's Sons
Library of Congress Catalog Card Number: 80-16635

ISBN: 0-671-42735-0

First Pocket Books printing November, 1981

10 9 8 7 6 5 4 3 2 1

POCKET and colophon are trademarks of Simon & Schuster.

Printed in the U.S.A.

To Seddon

THE HISTORIANS
September 1987

Aleksandr Slepov was an old man, his face disfigured by slick, pink scar tissue, his limp heavily pronounced. As he shuffled along the narrow corridor toward the Archives wing of Level Six, he had to use his right hand to steady his passage, letting his fingertips trail along the wall's surface.

Approximately every ten meters along the corridor, an overhead floodlight would flick on as he approached and the one behind would wink out. It was done acoustically, he supposed, a means of conserving the little energy available. But it produced within him the paranoia of being tracked, an insect pinned under the beam of a flashlight.

Slepov paused occasionally, allowing his heart and circulation to catch up with his exertions. As he rested, leaning against the wall, he could hear the muted vibrations of generators and air conditioners, the occasional sounds of steps in other connecting corridors, the opening and then latching of doors.

Why have I involved myself in this insane thing? he kept wondering, but the answer had been there from the start. *Because no one else will dare to—all the official histories will be a combination of distortions, half-truths, omissions, and lies. And without a surgical version of the truth, no one—not even far distant generations, will ever understand and learn from the tragedy of a blundered war.*

But it was a paradox—wasn't it?—that the identifiable and recorded precedents of past history's conflicts had never affected the course of future ones, that history was only a chronicle and not a teacher. Borisov himself had said, "If there is a history to be written of mankind, it will be summarized by one sentence: *He never learned.*"

The designers of this underground facility had cut it very thin, he thought, as he turned a bend in the corridor, stepping cautiously over rough, newly laid flooring. Even here on the sixth level, seventy-two meters below the surface of AW-4, there were fissures in the ten-meter-thick concrete that had only recently been filled with dirt and bridged over with a thin capping of concrete. Along the walls was evidence of recently spliced cables and hastily rigged air-conditioning ducts. It had been said that AW-4 could sustain a direct hit by a five-megaton weapon. The designers had been right—by a very narrow margin.

Slepov paused briefly, then resumed his shuffling progress down the corridor. His leg bothered him greatly today, which he put down to the air-conditioned dryness of the building, but still it hurt.

In the statistics, he was one of the lucky ones: a survivor. He had been away from the worst of it, up in Khatanga, researching the history of Soviet hydroelectric power and looking forward to a pleasant weekend with an old classmate from the Institute of Applied Sciences. The single-weapon attack on Khatanga had been a subsidiary affair, probably targeted on the aluminum-smelting plant twelve kilometers north of town. But the detonation had been great enough to sweep through the town with a wall of white-hot gas, cremating man and structure and machine with godlike indifference.

Slepov had survived only because he was in the subbasement of the Party Regional Records office, poring over molding boxes of files. The main building had collapsed, but Slepov had been saved from being crushed by the protection of a fallen beam. He remembered collapsing masonry and a fire, but that had burned itself out. Rescue squads had found him two days later, hanging on the thin edge of death, a folder still clutched in his hand.

Where the corridor intersected with three others, Slepov rested again, sitting down heavily on one of the metal chairs bunched in a row opposite the central computer room. As he rested, breathing heavily, he could watch the operators behind the large, fractured window.

Man has finally become the servant of machines, he thought. Absently scratching at the incessant itch of his scar tissue, he watched the operators load reels of magnetic tape into the machines and tend the printers, feeding them rolls of paper, then collecting the output.

Two women were servicing separate machines, but their actions were almost mirror images, the movements a precise technological ballet. It came to Slepov that man *was* the machine. The computers were only imperfect, subhuman replications of man's own commitment to mindless efficiency.

He thought about it. Ridiculous; growing old and more cynical, if possible. Seeing fault in everything that was not from the era of his own gentle beliefs. Was it something that his father had said, that the old get too caught up in their own inability to accept change? He filed the thought under "platitudes for geriatrics," and then got to his feet, moving toward the Archives wing.

It had been very difficult to get access to Borisov's diary. Men in the department who had seen it would not talk about its contents. An official history of the Seven Hour War was now frozen in concrete by those higher up. Stashinsky, who had now replaced Borisov as Director of Historical Studies, had fumed at the idea. One work was already published, another in the works. Why a third?

"Because Borisov was a contemporary and my superior," Slepov had answered. "Because I knew him well. Because I owe it to him to see that his work is faithfully rendered."

"Don't be too faithful," Stashinsky had replied, signing the requisition. "Personal touches, yes . . . but leave the factual body of the work for others." He had handed Slepov the slip. "Remember, I want no introspective accounts. The facts will stand as they have been approved and printed."

"There may be . . ." Slepov had started to object.

"There will be *no* revision of facts," Stashinsky demanded, slamming closed the authorization book. "None!"

The authorization desk, set in an alcove, was staffed by a woman in the mustard twill of State Security. Despite the severity of her uniform and hairdo, she was quite beautiful, with Nordic features and brittle-blue eyes. She didn't look up at first, still thumbing through a sheaf of papers, filing each in turn into a stack of wire-mesh baskets. Slepov watched her patiently as she stacked and sorted. She was rather like an ice-encased flower—something that, once touched, fractures and is no longer lovely. But he noted that her uniform had been skillfully tailored to show off her figure to advantage and that she had subtle traces of cosmetics around her eyes.

She finally looked up, her position of superiority now secure through calculated delay. "Your requirements?"

Slepov leaned against the counter, searching his pockets for the requisition. "I have a slip here somewhere. For files in Historical Division. It's section 13A material."

She nodded but made no response, keeping her eyes off his face. Slepov could hear her toe tapping in impatience.

"It's here someplace," he said. Still no response from the woman. At last he found the slip and passed it across.

She glanced at it and then looked up at him. "This requires also your security pass."

German accent, he thought. He passed the vinyl-encased document to her. As she picked it up, he noticed that her nails had some type of polish on them. Running the pass through the slot, she read off information from the cathode-ray tube, keyboarded in some numbers, then sat back as computers raced through records, trying to identify the necessity of Slepov's search for historical truth.

"The material you wish should be available," she said precisely, as if it was up to her discretion. With her polished fingernails she keyboarded into the terminal some data from the requisition form, and then waited as the printer clattered for a few seconds. ". . . down to the end of his corridor. Turn right, second door." She tore off a strip of paper from the machine. "Give this to the security monitor at the door."

Slepov mumbled some thanks, but she interrupted him, her voice now authoritarian, parroting something from memory. "This is state-controlled material," she instructed. "It falls under World Soviet Legal Code Twenty-one. No notes may be taken."

He objected, now tired of the woman, wanting to put her in her place. "These are Soviet Academy of Science archives. I am Deputy Director of the Historical Division. I . . ."

She looked up at him, full in the face. Her lips firmed for a second, then she said, "These are the rules." She turned away and occupied herself with the thin stack of papers, sorting and shuffling them into the wire baskets as if she were a somewhat slow but accurately programmed machine.

Slepov was very tired now and wanted desperately to sit down. He limped down the short corridor, now caught up in the idea that he would finally be able to see Borisov's personal diary. He had already read Borisov's official account of the Politburo's actions during the Seven Hour conflict, but he now suspected that the man's personal diary would reveal a great deal more detail. And if the diary conflicted with officially accepted "facts," to what purpose was all of this? Perhaps then it would be necessary to record as much as he could remember and leave it with one of his own trusted students in the hope that someday it might be printed. A vague hope at best, he thought.

The security monitor was a slightly built man with lieutenant's epaulets and drooping eyelids. He studied the printout and ushered Slepov into a cubicle that was a stark affair—a microfilm viewer and a chair. Slepov realized that the glass in the door leading to the cubicle was a one-way mirror—looking inward.

"I will load the film rolls," the man said in a thick Ukrainian accent. "There can be no taking of notes, according to . . ."

". . . Code Twenty-one," Slepov said wearily. "I have been informed."

"Sign in," the lieutenant said, handing him a clipboard. "Time, date, name, and authorization code. Signature on the last line." He tapped his pen against the form.

Slepov sank into the hard metal chair and completed the form, ending it with the scrawl of his signature.

The door closed. In the twilight of weak, indirect lighting, Slepov sat slouched in the chair, staring at the blank screen of the microform reader. From somewhere deep in the feed mechanism he heard a click, followed by the mechanical stirrings of the automated-loading sequence. A tongue of film appeared through the feed slot, ratcheted over pronged rollers, and disappeared into the takeup receptacle.

Slepov sighed and leaned back, watching the microfilm as it was projected onto the screen.

AW-4, Microfiche Files
Soviet Academy of Sciences, Historical Division
FILE SECTION: *1980–1990 (incomplete)*
FILE NUMBER: *SAS 86-05-1187/H*
SUBJECT: *Vassili V. Borisov, Personal Diary, January 1–May 12, 1986*
CLASSIFICATION: **HOLD IN FILE.** *No withdrawal or reproduction.*
ACCESS TO FILE: *Limited to persons with current Class 13A clearance.*
AUTHORIZATION: *By appropriate authority as per current list for subject file.*

Slepov hunched forward in his chair, advancing the microfilm, blurring through the early months of 1986. Occasionally, he froze the film advance and scanned a day in Borisov's life.

Borisov he had liked. A vain man, a little paunchy, with a taste for rich food and the perquisites of a party *vlasti*. One entry, covering the entire day of March fifth, detailed a lunch he had taken (at Soviet Academy of Science expense) with a visiting academician from Bulgaria.

But there was substance as well as shadow in Borisov's life—an obvious dedication to the rhythms of history, the curiosity of a man apart from the passions of the moment. And, perhaps above all, he had an incredible memory for detail and speech. It had been said that Borisov had recalled entire interviews with both Brezhnev and Zhukov without the aid of notes.

As he read Borisov's diary, Slepov began to revive his memory of the man as balding, shorter than average, with an occasional taste for cynicism. But for the most part, Slepov was a good-humored man, flexible and dispassionate.

The old man swept forward into March and April and May. He stopped the advance on May seventh, then began to read each page carefully.

May seventh, 23:30

Satisfying morning walk. Some indication of spring. Zoy will be pleased. Her crocuses pushing up. Twenty situps, and ran in place for five minutes. Heartbeat down to 73 after two-minute rest. Blood pressure 150 over 90. Might see eighty if I take care of this creaking old corpus of mine.

Z.B. joined me for breakfast—one poached egg, bun with English jam. Tea.

Z.B. and his economic blunderers full of gloom and doom. Why he tries to hang on my shoulder is beyond comprehension. Thinks, I suppose, that I can use my influence with the Academy's Institute of Economics to help protect his job. He seems to forget that I record history, not try to alter it.

While dripping egg on his suit, Z.B. told me that even with production counted from our "newly joined client state" of Iran, crude oil shortfall this year will be 11 percent. Grain also off badly, for third year in a row. What he doesn't know, of course, is that USSR gold production is nearly finished, due to short mine life. Unless we can obtain credits from the West, we will have no gold for subsitute hard currency reserves. Which means no foreign purchases of either grain or oil. Depressing.

Arrived at Center just after 13:00. Work going nicely on monograph of "Yugoslavian Assimilation, Part III." (Note: See to better quality of photo of Tito's statue on Manezhnaya Square. Have mixed-race grouping of Komsomol children at base with flowers. Zoy keeps reminding me that people photographed in the presence of inanimate objects lend both interest and dimension.)

Khmelnitsky on third draft of *Socialist States of the Caribbean*. It is flat and lifeless, something that generations of school children will probably be subjected to. However, I suppose that I shall recommend him for the obligatory Medal of Historical Merit, which will undoubtedly be awarded. And which Khmelnitsky will undoubtedly wear on his underwear, if not on his suit.

Late dinner with Zoy. Some kind of fish, which she masquerades as sole, in a lumpy sauce. Had one brandy and to bed.

As I write this, have just finished Z.B.'s report (internal circulation only).

This may be a worker's paradise we have created. At least the "worker's" part of it is right. This decade will be difficult.

For a man in my position I find it schizophrenic. On the one hand, we at the Institute produce the cheerful news of a worker's paradise for mass consumption. At odds with this are our summaries of progress (or lack thereof) for Politburo eyes only. For the 1990s I see only disaster. One sleeping pill and lights out.

May eighth, 22:20

No walk. Heavy rain, with sleet forecast throughout day. Run in place ten minutes, plus twenty feeble situps. Heartbeat a rewarding 72 after two-minute rest. B.P. 148 over 89.

Zoy gone shopping. Had breakfast of canned guava nectar and one orange. Tea. *Izvestia* claims good wheat forecast, "only slightly diminshed by late frosts." They should get together with Z.B. Dynamos take regional soccer championship. Must see playoffs if they make it!

Spent morning signing reports and requisitions that I haven't read. Paperwork incessant, even in my position. Would surely retire, if it didn't mean losing this villa and the Volga. Know that Zoy couldn't stand the step down in her group.

Midmorning, receive radiogram from Gregori. His weekend leave somehow canceled—no explanation. Had looked forward to fishing with him, but I suspect my son's glands are in need of exercising. As I recall, *it* is currently a nurse. If I know Gregori, she is probably 96 centimeters around the chest, with gray eyes.

Drove to Institute for an hour. Usual haggling. One bright spot, however. G.E.V.'s work, *Historical Implications of Disarmament,* a convincing document. His personal touches excellent. (Note: Have him review files for better photo of N. N. Inozemtsev.) Looks bilious in one submitted. *Why* do they always face to the right in official photographs? I swear there's probably a regulation to that effect.

Late dinner with Zoy. She had artichokes, a chicken in yesterday's lumpy white sauce, but a delicate Georgian wine, a Tetra No. 26, vintage 1983.

For a change, can barely keep my eyes open. Rain on the roof and wine will always do it. To sleep.

May ninth: 13:40 (on the way to airport)

Day started pleasantly. Clearing weather and a warm front bringing springlike weather up from the south. Zoy was ecstatic. She has gotten a shipment of Dutch tulip bulbs in through the wife of someone who thinks he owes me a favor. Frankly, I would have preferred Bols gin or some good Dutch cigars.

All my plans for a calm weekend have fallen apart. Marshal U. called me through the State Security switchboard at the Institute around noon. He says that there is a requirement for me to attend what he called "a meeting of great historical significance." I was about to beg off when he mentioned that it was at the request of the Secretary General, which I presume means a command performance. Instructed to take Soviet Air Force plane from Bryansk (about 50 kilometers from the Institute) to Moscow. One hour to pack and another hour holding onto the back seat of the Volga while an Institute driver gets me to the airfield.

May ninth: 23:40 (on flight south)

Flight to Moscow dull. The heating mechanism seemed to be malfunctioning, and only sticky sweets available. Sergeant–flight attendant says in-flight meals didn't arrive on time! Sometimes this is too much of a worker's paradise.

Disturbing conversation with major in Long Range Rocket Forces. Slightly drunk, he kept shoving a flask of cognac under my nose, complaining that he had had to leave Dodrisk after only two days of his planned leave of a week. Talked at great length about his wife. How they had planned this leave for over a year. I was bored and kept drifting off. Perhaps sensing that I didn't realize the full magnitude of his tragedy, he finally pushed me in the ribs with his elbow and told me that he was being recalled. "For what?" I asked. He shrugged, perhaps realizing that he had overstepped the secrecy of his orders, then finally turned away from me and stared out the porthole. I repeated my question and he just shrugged again. "My leave was cancelled," he repeated. No further comment from our brave Red warrior.

Arrive Sheppelov airport 16:10. Two GRU officers in plain clothes meet me at security control. My airplane companion sees this and gives me a terrified look. I doubt that he will sleep well tonight!

Overly rapid drive to unmarked building on the Ring Road. Marshal U. not there to greet me. Some subsecretary arranges meal—excellent! *Ikra, Syomga s limonom* and *kutlyety po Pajarski* with a bottle of *Palusookhoye*. Subsecretary keeps popping in every half hour to assure me that Marshal U. will be with me "momentarily." Fall asleep sometime around 19:00.

Awaken again at 20:00. Twilight just gone. U. steps in for a moment, dressed out in his impeccable uniform, loaded down with two briefcases. Very brusque, which is most unlike him. He informs me that I have been assigned "a duty of great historical importance." Period. No elaboration.

I suggest that we can get right to the matter after a decent night's sleep. (I have also wanted to set aside some time in the next few days to visit the GUM store for Zoy's love affair with Danish sweets.)

U. doesn't answer. His subsecretary and a couple of other GRU lackeys in plain clothes escort me and my luggage to a waiting van. We go to some military airfield east of Moscow and board an Antonov-72. Still no conversation with U. He confers with a rather burned-out-looking major who also has briefcases. Much discussion between them. So now I sleep.

May tenth, noon

As I write this journal of events, it is just slightly past noon. I am in a windowless room on the Eighth

Level of SW-4, a facility I have heard rumors about but have never been able to confirm, even in casual conversation with intimate friends in the Council of Ministers.

Marshal U. has told me it is near to Dobrekinov. It seems that SW-4 has been in existence since Stalin's era—a deep, multilayered concrete pit buried deep in the Urals. I do not know all the functions performed here, but U. says that it is a command and control center for use in crisis situations, a place that is all but invulnerable from American and NATO attacks by rockets. Based on the signs at different levels, it also seems to be a global intelligence-gathering facility and a storage depot for critical records that must survive any disaster.

Lunch, which is a name I hardly dare confer on the miserable rations provided me, consisted of a rather greasy assortment of *pirozhki* and warm beer. My room is minuscule—a cube of concrete measuring roughly five meters on a side, equipped with a surprisingly good bed, a metal clothes locker, a desk, and one chair. The toilet is some kind of an affair with pumps and valves and complicated instructions to match.

My function at these meetings will be to document historically the decisions to be made. Not even secretaries with the highest clearance will be admitted. I may use one tape recorder to supplement my notes, but the tape will remain in Politburo possession and will finally be destroyed. U. has stated that eventually an "official history" will emerge from my observations, fleshed out with background position papers that I will be allowed access to. The final document will be subject to Politburo "editing" prior to being granted release. In short, U. wants a "clean" history—one in which I show that the factors involved in the decision-making process were studied long in advance, that the meetings were harmonious, and that the final vote was carried unanimously.

My selection for this task is somewhat flattering. True, I know several members of the Politburo personally, but it is also a matter of my academic reputation. My latest biography, *The Brezhnev Years of Decision*, was well reviewed, even in some Western countries, and I would suspect that the thirteen men who now sit in power want similar generous treatment.

But it is to this diary that I will commit my real viewpoints. Our country has made great strides over the last thirty years, and someday we may even be willing to publish the truth.

Now close to 13:30. U. will be here in a minute. Time for a quick shave. More tonight on the course of our brave leadership.

May tenth, 23:30

Nearly midnight. When I first came back to my room, I sat on the bed and stared at the wall for what must have been an hour. I have a feeling of desperation and futility that I cannot dispel. Events are slipping over the edge of rationality, and I can do nothing, say nothing, only serve as the mute chronicle of madness.

We are to meet in six hours again, so there is little time to record what I have seen.

The Politburo has changed four of its members: Kirlenko, Suslov, Cherneko, and Kosygin are gone. No mention of their disposition was given, except that Andropov read a prepared text of denunciation, calling those men to account for "crimes of the highest magnitude against the State." Cherneko was particularly singled out as "traitorous—a servant of appeasement to the Imperialists."

Ustinov and Andropov have assumed copositions as Secretary General. So now the KGB and the Red Army have linked arms! Other new faces: Pavlovskiy, Gorshkov, Ogarkov, and Koldunov, all resplendent in medals and uniforms, each with a newly awarded Hero of the Soviet Union. It is my guess that the "disposition" of the former Politburo members was done very quietly; I heard nothing about it prior to now.

The picture that was painted, if accurate, was grim:

oil and grain badly off, with future projections even more devastating. (Z.B. should have been there—his forecast was cheerful by comparison!) There is great unrest in the autonomous republics of Kalmky ASSR, Bashkir ASSR, and in the Ukraine. The Islamic Brotherhood is gradually uniting and being fed arms from the Arab states to the south. Even Qadaffi is supplying them, that ingrate!

Perhaps the most serious political problem is intelligence gathered by Andropov that Rumania, Poland, and Czechoslovakia have conducted secret meetings at the highest state levels to discuss formation of a neutral socialist bloc, nonaligned with either the West or the Soviet Union. If this should occur, there would be no doubt that Hungary and Yugoslavia would join in. The Warsaw Pact nations, with the stroke of a pen, would cease to exist.

Contrary to my first impressions, I believe that there is great friction in the Politburo. I sense a certain posturing by two blocs—the minority "do nothings" and the majority "do somethings." Of course, the older members of the Politburo would seem to favor a relaxation of control on our own minorities, a degree of greater autonomy for our client states, with the overview that "things will work out."

But the "do somethings," largely men under sixty and the new military members, spearheaded by Andropov and Ustinov, seek a military solution. This has not been spelled out, but I envisage something on the order of Czechoslovakia or Yugoslavia. Except on a very grand and gory scale.

Toward the end of the evening, just after a sumptuous dinner of *ikra, gooryev skaya kasha,* and a rather sweet Sladkoye champagne, Ustinov launched off into what I first thought an irrelevant subject, the rearmament of the Americans and NATO. He first stated that we have strategic superiority over the U.S. in nuclear rockets, perhaps enough at present to reduce their missile fields to rubble with a 90-percent kill accuracy. He then detailed advances in antisubmarine warfare and cruise-missile interception. Although I was probably the only one in the room not to understand the complexity of the technical aspects, I gather that we are far stronger than the Americans. Ustinov, flashing a table of strengths and capabilities onto the screen, said quite calmly (if my tired eyes are correct and my notes accurate), "If we were to attack the American missile fields, their submarines at sea and in port, and their bomber bases, our computer projections are that we would reduce their retaliatory capability to under twenty percent of their present strength." He then went into a long, technical discussion concerning Soviet capability, which he referred to as SALT-free. It would seem that our Long Range Rocket Forces can reload our silos in a matter of hours and that some missiles not counted under SALT (because they have a published range of under five-thousand kilometers) can be quickly modified with an add-on rocket booster to achieve intercontinental range. From that followed an even more technical discussion by Gorshkov and Ustinov—names and numbers of new weapons systems that are now operational—a killer satellite, communications-jamming equipment, and an antiballistic missile device (apparently untested).

Like a simple university student taking notes, I almost missed the crux of what they were talking about—the unthinkable proposition that a nuclear war was winnable!

U. was there, all the time sitting behind Ogarkov like a pet dog. Ogarkov finally nodded to him and U. stepped forward. In that quiet, persuasive voice of his, he started to detail recent advances in American and NATO weaponry: the MX missile, the Pershing Two rocket, and details of the American cruise missile. He said this all very quietly and carefully, and the presentation had great impact. His conclusion was that within three months, these terror weapons would be deployed, cancelling our superority and throwing the world back into another period of hair-trigger tension. His final words—almost a plea—were, "We must act first."

The unspoken conclusion—the Soviet Union is dwindling in power. Our client states are reasserting their nationalism, breaking off into their own cooperative bloc. We have shortages of food and energy, not to be easily resolved. Coupled with this is the unrest of our southern borders and a growing, militant West. But is war the way to solve our problems? I count at least four Politburo members against such action. There is to be more discussion at 06:00 tomorrow morning before a vote will take place.

U. took me by the elbow as I left the conference room. He told me that regardless of what decision was reached, he had made arrangements to have Zoy moved to a "safe place." Thank God. To sleep—if that is possible.

May eleventh, 09:40

At 05:45 Marshal U. met me outside the conference room and drew me off into an empty suite, luxuriously furnished in what I call bureaucratic-modern: heavy dark furniture, velvet drapes, and a chandelier. I notice that there is luggage being packed by a KGB lieutenant. U. motions him out with a nod.

"Gorbachev died last night of a heart attack," he says. My hopes sink. Gorbachev was a moderate—one of the "do nothings," perhaps the strongest of that group—and only fifty-six years old, a man known for his dedication to rowing and hard exercise.

U. purses his lips. "One never knows when God calls," he says with a straight face. His only god, as I recall, is power.

He steers me by the arm back into the corridor, having shown me an empty room, as if that would confirm the cause of Gorbachev's death. "They are meeting in Special Sessions now. A new member is being elected to full Politburo membership."

I asked which one of the known candidates, knowing that there are six men permanently waiting in the wings, being groomed for the ultimate leadership task.

"None," he replied. "I am told that it may be Marshal Sokolov." Who I know to be First Deputy Minister of Defense.

We are finally allowed in. Andropov announces by unanimous decision the appointment of Sokolov to full membership in the Politburo. Sokolov is already there, smiling, as if he had been the first to lick the cream off the milk.

I look at the faces of the members of the Politburo. The "do nothings" have lost. Their eyes betray them, their hands fidget. There is a palpable sense of defeat and fear about them, as if they, too, wonder how long their hearts will beat should they dissent.

Andropov arranges a glass of champagne for all. And I have not even had tea as yet! There is a clinking of glasses. I should think that this scene resembles the desperation and ersatz good cheer that pervaded Hitler's last birthday party—those who think they can win, and those who know they can't. It is chilling.

From seven until eight thirty, a procession of pet marshals of the Soviet Union inform the Politburo of "war-winning strategies."

Hypothetically (as if these discussions were still abstract), Ustinov finally summarizes the plan. Soviet Delta and Hotel class submarines from the Red Banner fleet will launch missiles against American command and control centers, bomber bases, aerial refueling tanker bases, sub bases, and other strategically important targets. Time from launch to impact: eight minutes, average. At approximately the same launch time, 420 Soviet ICBMs will be fired against over 1,154 American missile silos. Each Soviet ICBM carries between six and twelve warheads. The projected destruction of American silos is over 90 percent. Time to impact: twenty-four minutes. Ustinov notes that since most of these targets are in unpopulated areas of the American heartland, only (only!) sixteen million Americans will die.

"What of the American retaliatory response?" Pel'she suddenly asks. Whether he has been prompted to say this or it is a real concern is uncertain to my mind. The man, at any rate, looks to be in a state of shock.

"We think that it's highly unlikely that there will be any American response," Ustinov answers. "Our computer predictions indicate that within twenty minutes of our launching the attack, the Americans will have lost 82 percent of their retaliatory forces. Six minutes after we launch, we shall start transmission of a ten-page Telex message via the hot line. This timing coincides with the first possible detection by American satellites and radar of our attack. We will offer the President and his council two options. The first is that if he responds with even one weapon, we will unleash the remainder of our armaments. With our silo reload capability and with the intercontinental range SS-20, we will actually be stronger than the so-called SALT II limitations. Coupled with this, we will have already launched our long-range bomber force. As you have seen from our presentations, the Americans have very limited capability to defend against an air attack. The devastation wrought by our attack would be total.

"On the other hand, we will offer the Americans the option of a lasting peace. They must, of course, dismantle their nuclear weapons under our supervision. NATO will be entirely disbanded. The Soviet sphere of influence will encompass Asia, Africa, Europe, Oceania, and South America. We will demand large percentages of American grain, oil, and industrial production. And, ultimately, perhaps within a year or so, the American government will be restructured under Soviet political cadres. We think the choice will be obvious—obliteration or peace under Soviet control."

"And what if they choose to strike back at us?" Pel'she asks.

Ustinov sighs as though dealing with a rude child. "If they do, the Soviet Union will take damage. But we have a well-planned civil defense program, an in-depth defense force of countless interceptors, surface-to-air missiles, and a new antiballistic missile. Over one million Soviet administrators, scientists, and citizens holding critical skills will be deep underground five minutes after we launch."

Ustinov thrusts his hands deeply into his jacket pockets and bends forward, as if addressing only Pel'she. "We are taking a risk, old friend. A huge risk. But if we don't act now, the Americans will soon catch up with us and perhaps even surpass us. Coupled with the great cost of our military expenditures, the internal problems facing us and the breaking away of our allies, we have no choice." He smiles. "But if we win, Pel'she, there will be a world under one rule, and that rule will be centered within this room. We will have peace and prosperity. Local insurrections, terrorists, and dissident factions will be put down by our military, and in a few short years collective socialism will unite the planet in productive harmony."

Pel'she matches Ustinov's stare and the silence in the room is absolute. "There is one situation we haven't discussed yet," he finally says. "In all of these presentations, you have assumed that the Americans will sit immobilized through our first strike and then select their response. But assuming that there is a lapse of approximately sixteen minutes between the time they first detect our incoming warheads and the time those warheads destroy U.S. silos, what is to prevent the Americans from launching? As I see it, our warheads might be falling onto empty silos as well as over a thousand U.S. rockets zero in on Soviet cities. Is that in your calculations as well?"

Andropov stood up, leaning over the table, his eyes boring in on Pel'she. "You're talking about the so-called 'Launch Under Fire' policy. The Americans abandoned that strategy in 1963. They have repeatedly reassured us that they would not employ such a strategy, because it placed the security of the world directly on the authenticity of a few signals received from orbiting U.S. spy satellites. Once we launch, we will either destroy or jam the American Argus satellite system. So I ask you, Pel'she—do you expect a national policy of over twenty years to be changed in sixteen minutes?"

Pel'she, whom I have known for three decades, sat back in his chair, his eyes on his hands. The room was silent for another minute, waiting for his response, but he finally just shook his head.

"I want," Andropov said very distinctly, the words strung out, "a vote. It has been our intent to present the factors underlying this decision as carefully as possible. There is risk, but it is minimal. There is also reward—the ultimate supremacy of a global Communist State under Great Russian control." He paused, looking down at a folder. "The timing of an attack is critical," he said. "Over eight thousand factors are constantly analyzed by our computer scientists. Some of these are unique, such as the movements of the U.S. President and his accessibility to communications. Other factors deal with the day of the week, the condition of weather in Europe, American defense deployment—far too many factors to name. But today is optimum—more particularly, within the next nine hours. We are prepared. I say that we vote and if, and only if, that vote is unanimous, we launch. Is there any further discussion?"

"By secret ballot?" Pel'she injected.

"Of course," Andropov replied. "As always."

Marshal U. passed around the cards. In less than a minute, each member came forward and dropped his card on Andropov's desk. Andropov quickly sorted through them. "It is unanimous . . ."

Pel'she was standing. "I voted *no*," he shouted.

Andropov thumbed through the folded cards again and then looked up. "You voted *yes*, Pel'she. There are thirteen cards and all voted *yes*." He nodded toward Koldunov. "Perhaps you should escort Minister Pel'she to his suite. The meeting has been a strain on him."

I watched Pel'she's face as Koldunov guided him out of the room. He made no further protest, his face blank. As he passed me he said quite loudly, "Put that in your history book, scholar." The door closed.

Andropov nodded toward Ustinov. "Check the computer updates. If the output is essentially unchanged, we will implement the Emergency War Order at 11:09. Otherwise, we will have to delay for twenty-four hours."

He turned back to the Politburo. "It was necessary that we reach this conclusion. We are obviously not at full readiness, but to have done so would have alerted CIA intelligence via their satellites. The American President is in Wyoming on a fishing trip. I doubt that he will be informed of the attack until it is over, or perhaps until he sees a glow on the horizon."

Ustinov called on the intercom—one word—"Go."

Andropov glanced up at the digital wall clock. "We launch at 11:09. Less than two hours. The meeting is adjourned."

May eleventh, 11:20

For the past hour and a half, I have watched from a booth overlooking the Central Command Post. Status boards, fed by computers, updated the progress of our launch. It would seem that even we are imperfect. Only 73 percent of our missiles got away on schedule and without difficulty. Some of the laggards are still in the process of launching, and over 9 percent blew up in their silos or shortly thereafter.

As I understand it, we destroyed three of the U.S. Argus satellites, but five more somehow resisted our attack. Jamming was commenced and U. says that it looks effective, though it is too early to tell. Just minutes ago, our submarine-launched ballistic missiles started impacting on airfields, military communication centers, and naval facilities. Damage assessment is limited as yet, but the attack seems successful to the present time.

I realize in writing this that I am watching an electronic game. It has no sense of reality. I cannot visualize half a million deaths signified by only the blink of a light or the printout of a computer. I have no doubt that ours is the right cause. It is historically inevitable that, without one country taking control, there would be ultimate chaos, both militarily and certainly economically. But it seems that we are cutting off a man's legs to remove a wart.

11:31

Watching from the booth, I have just seen a major change in the thing they call the Status Board. It is a projection of our northern frontiers, the Arctic and North America. Innumerable dots of light have spread like a wildfire across the northern tier of the United States. Much commotion on the floor among the console operators. Slowly—one or two at first—and then as with a rush, red lines arc across the pole into Soviet Russia. U., who has up until now been continuously on a telephone, turns to me and says in that ever-calm voice of his, "The Americans have launched their missiles before ours impacted. The computers have assessed their trajectories, and most of them are targeted against our cities."

I wonder whether Zoy is safe—whether she knows that I am safe. I even wonder whether it matters. Gregori is up in the Kola Peninsula with his squadron. This thing that Andropov and Ustinov have rammed through has caused a catastrophe. When was the last war in which mostly civilians died? Was there one?

11:50

There is no doubt now. Incredibly, the first response from the West was France's *force de frappe*. U. says that we can only assume that NATO elements launched minutes later. The U.S. Secretary of State was on the hot line already, talking about a negotiated peace —a cessation of hostilities. He surely did not know about the French and NATO response. Minutes later, the line went dead. And only two minutes after that, the Americans launched everything they had.

I asked him what we would do. "Launch everything we have left," he replied. And so we did.

13:10

I am back in my room. AW-4 has taken a near miss, and much of the electrical power is out. My room is lit by a battery-powered unit hung on the wall, and it is going dim.

I have no idea of the status of anything. I know only that a major war is in progress and as I write these words millions are dead and dying. How long it will go on, I cannot even guess. At last report the Chinese had joined in, striking at our eastern bases. Europe, I think, no longer exists, nor does North America. The Soviet Union has sustained major damage. There is nothing left to see or to speculate on. It is just a matter of degree—how great the damage will be.

Shortly after I got back . . .

13:30

U. came in rather unexpectedly. There has been further damage to AW-4. Fuel storage tanks on the Second Level ruptured and then ignited. U. says that the fire is under control and that they expect both air filtration and conditioning to be operative again by midnight.

Things are not going well, but U. wouldn't give me further information. He now lays the blame on Andropov and Ustinov, saying that they pushed too far and too fast. He claims now that he opposed the war!

Just as he was about to leave, he noticed my diary which I had shoved under a blanket at the foot of the bed. He pulled it out and flipped through the last few pages, then dropped it beside me. "I suppose it doesn't matter," he said, and left.

13:41

U. has dropped by again and just left. No news. All the microwave and satellite links are out. Only high-frequency radio is left, and that is unreadable, with heavy static crashes.

He has brought me a cold lunch—a bottle of Trishi No. 19 and some lukewarm *akroshka*. Not inspiring, but then again I have no appetite.

It is obvious that U. has been drinking heavily. I could smell the cognac halfway across the room. He assured me that Zoy was safe. All the wives of important persons were evacuated to small towns in mountainous country. She is in Prut, near the Rumanian border. Again—thank God. If there is one still left.

13:50

I have drunk half the wine and left the soup untouched. It is like a boiler room in here, and the light is nearly gone. Rumblings come from the levels above and the occasional sound of running feet in the corridor outside.

Very tired and depressed. Felt an indefinite pain in my chest, and respiration very high. I suppose that it is both tension and the physical conditions.

I have quit trying to think—about Zoy, myself and whatever world will still be left tomorrow. The unspeakable, the unthinkable has happened. My profession ceased today, because history ceased.

Thought just now about something I read years ago. A rhetorical question by someone whose name escapes me—but he asked (answered?) . . . will the living envy the dead?

Don't . . .

1

Mallen stripped off his belt, unbuttoned his fly, and stepped out of the mud-encrusted denims. He dropped them, along with his shirt, into the bucket on the porch steps and stood leaning against the railing, letting the sweat dry on his body as the sun dipped into the ridges of the Green Mountains.

The shadows were eating up the meadows; only the branches of the tallest maples were still pinked by the dying sun. Motes of dust above the path were illuminated and then gone as the sun set behind the ridge.

A cardinal called and Mallen listened for the return echo of its mate. The birds were beginning to come back, he thought. He scratched at his shin, waiting, but there was no reply.

The air, still through the hot afternoon, was starting to move, cooling first and then sliding down the slopes toward the valley floor. Humid enough, he guessed, for there to be fog in the early morning.

Turning, he reentered the cabin. On the shelf over the bookcase were two mason jars of tobacco. Roberts had told him that it was banned by the government. The only stuff he could get now was bootleg and badly cured, but it had been a crummy afternoon, so he chose the Borkum Riff that he had looted from one of the ruined towns in the spring of this year.

Was it Moretown, he wondered, or Middlebury? A day spent fruitlessly wandering through looted shops already picked over for more than a year. The dogs were running in packs, and he carried a crowbar to ward them off. He had seen one sallow-faced kid with open sores standing in an alleyway. Mallen had waved and the kid had run, panicked. "Definitely Middlebury," he said aloud.

He stuffed the pipe, lit it with the elegant cut-glass lighter Anne had given him, and returned to the porch. Darker now, the light was like ancient whiskey, warm and golden and smelling of age. He pulled at the pipe, enjoying the bitterness and the bite. There was still some of the wine left, but he rejected the idea. He would have to save some for Roberts when he came up for the shells tomorrow. Tomorrow was Friday? He decided that it was.

It was evenings such as this that made it bearable—the going-on part of it. He made a mental note to ask Roberts about another dog; maybe another pup from the same bitch. It had been pleasant with the terrier . . . evenings like this. The two of them would go down to the brook and sit under the overhanging branches and he would fish and talk to the dog, or sometimes just look into the silent pool, seeing his distorted reflection and fingering the long ridge of scar tissue that arched his forehead. There was no mirror in the cabin, a fact for which he was thankful.

But the dog was gone now. Mallen had seen notices posted in the fall of last year saying that the foxes had rabies, and he couldn't take the chance. He had killed the terrier in its sleep and buried it in the cornfield that same night. Perhaps another dog would not be such a good idea.

There was still plenty of twilight, but it was cooling off rapidly. He reentered the cabin and took a blanket from the rack, threw it over his shoulders, and returned to the porch, reluctant to see the light fade. The valley to the west was now in shadow. To the north, still in the sunlight of high altitude, a contrail was laid out like a chalk mark across the blue slate of an October evening. The jet was a barely visible spearpoint of metal heading north in polar flight. Men would be sitting in clean uniforms on the flight deck, moving controls and switches in a ritual of precise grace. And there would be muttered incantations between them in the dogma of numbers and pressures and velocities. Mallen could barely remember what it had been like. Except that it had been his life. God, I miss it, he thought. High thin air and the blue-black of altitude. The stars visible even at noon sometimes. It's finished, his mind said, and he pushed it from his fragmented memory. *Mallen Maxim number one: No thinking on the bus.*

He leaned against the railing of the porch, watching the light in the valley die. Naked except for the torn blanket over his shoulders, he shivered slightly in the cooling air. He turned once more to the north, eyes sightless and yet seeing, watching the contrail sublimate until it was finally gone. His shoulders ached and he realized that his muscles were tensed. Who was it that said that solitude was the balm of the troubled mind? He knocked the ashes out of his pipe. Perhaps someone who had never lived alone.

With the last vestiges of twilight and under a slipper moon, he walked the perimeter of his fields, checking the tripwires. Tomorrow would be better, he thought. Lots of stuff to mend and Roberts would be coming up mid-morning. And in the evening he would run up the aircraft's engine, provided, of course, that there was fog or a west wind to muffle the noise.

Remounting the porch steps, he paused and listened carefully for sounds from the valley and, satisfied, closed and barred the door.

Dinner was fresh corn, potatoes, and dried pork. He hated the pork, but it was going bad and he knew that he would either have to finish it or lose it. He lit the wood stove, carefully feeding pieces of pine into the chamber and then adding the larger slabs of maple. Setting out a pot of water to boil, he shucked the corn, tunelessly whistling something nameless. The melody was clear in his mind, and it bothered him greatly that he couldn't remember the words. Something Dylan had written, something that Anne had sung so often.

He paused in picking the silken strands from the furrows between the kernels, feeling his vision blurring.

"Shit!" he shouted, and threw the corn at the wall. He took down the jug of wine and poured himself a full tumbler, then drank it down in three swallows. Leaning against the wall, he closed his eyes and waited until the wine took effect. His heart slowed and he concentrated on breathing. "Shit," he said softly, and the thought passed and it was better. *No thinking on the bus,* he repeated in his mind.

As the corn was boiling, he shaved a few grams of salt from the cowlick and added them to the boiling water, then added more to the side of his plate. It would make a good winter project, he mused—build some sort of a salt grinder, the type that they had in good restaurants, where the waiter came around and did it for you. An elegant teak barrel with a sterling silver crank; crystal, and linen napkins. He grabbed the thought, holding onto it, remembering.

Sauces such as hollandaise on crisp vegetables, with little cups of sherbets between the courses, and clean glasses filled with white wine held up to the light, then religiously swirled and tasted on the tongue. All delightful bullshit, phony but pleasant. Anne had always worn the black chiffon for such dinners.

Humming now, Mallen took down the jug of wine, poured another full glass, and drank it down. He partially refilled the glass, set it carefully on the table, and then served himself, passing around the chair to the right, first setting the knife and fork with precision, then the mounded plate between them. He drew back the chair skillfully, not scraping the tile, and seated himself. As always, the food tasted of dirt, but the wine helped. Good year, he thought. Radioactivity makes the grape, if not the man.

After he finished the meal, he stacked the dishes in a bucket, wiped down the counter, and threw the corn husks and cobs into the stove. Keeps the roaches down, he repeated to himself. Not one in a year.

He fussed around the kitchen, putting things in place,

making it overly neat. And as he had done each evening
for the past two years, he opened the cupboard and
counted the remaining tins, checking off each item
against an inventory. Condensed milk, seventeen cans;
three-pound canister of chili beans; four jars of freeze-
dried coffee. Roberts had offered him three blankets
for just one jar!

He paused, the desire for a cup of coffee almost sex-
ual in its intensity. Twist off the lid and puncture the
seal—just like that. Hesitantly, he picked up a jar and
sniffed at the rim, as if that would release some of the
pungency to his nostrils. Disgusted with his own lack
of discipline, he slid the jar back into place. *Keep
counting.*

One hundred-pound sack of flour, wrapped in aluminum foil to keep the mice out, he hoped. No damage
yet. Cans of soup and fruit cup. Stale tea. Two large
tins of ham, both reserved for future Christmases. A
solitary jar of olives, with anchovies. Check.

The inventory, though unnecessary, was part of a
routine he kept to because it gave a reason and order
to his life. That was the hardest part, keeping up a
purpose. When Anne had been with him, it was easier.
She took care of things and he took care of her. But
after she died, he slid into mindless lethargy, leaving
dishes unwashed and the garbage unburned. The cock-
roaches came, and then the rats. One morning he had
scratched his head and found lice; since then he had
kept her faith.

Finishing the inventory, he locked the cupboards
and, with a final glance around the kitchen, took the
oil lamp with him and climbed the nine steps to the
loft.

He folded the blanket and crawled into his sleeping
bag, glad that the day was over. He resumed reading
one of the old Pynchon novels, *Gravity's Rainbow,* for
the third time. As he read, he subconsciously cataloged
the noises in the night: foxes barking and the wind humming through the tops of firs in an adiabatic whisper.
All safe sounds to his mind, and therefore unnoticed.

By eight he closed the book, after carefully marking his place with a straw, and replaced the book in its polyethylene bag. He wrote a figure in a tablet with the stub of a pencil, marking the one hundred fifty-second day in the second year since the war, blew out the light, and was almost instantly asleep.

2

On Friday, mid-morning, the tin-can tripwire alarm sounded. Mallen was expecting Roberts, but, as a precaution, he uncased the Winchester Model 94 and laid the scope's crosshairs on the path. Eventually, Roberts's body appeared in the sun-speckled shadows, laboring upward along the path. With Roberts foreshortened by the telescopic sight, Mallen had the impression of a man on a treadmill, slogging onward but gaining no ground, getting no closer. Mallen increased the scope's power, zooming up to twelve power.

Roberts's face was a ruin. The pouchy wrinkles beneath his eyes flowed to deep tributaries that spanned his cheeks. His nose, broken often, hung out over the face as a knob of rock would, projecting from an otherwise featureless cliff. His mouth was open now, sucking in the thinner air of the high country, and his teeth, yellow and misshapen, were those of an ancient horse.

Roberts broke cover and paused on the edge of the sunlight before crossing the lower meadow. He raised his hand in greeting, knowing that Mallen would be watching. Mallen could see him mouth the word "hello." Raising the rifle above his head, Mallen moved away from the edge of the cabin. The old man nodded to himself and moved upward, across the clearing.

He was carrying a large haversack and a metal canister of perhaps four gallons capacity. No easy load for a man of sixty-eight, Mallen thought, and he was extraordinarily pleased that this meant more gasoline for the aircraft. Mallen grinned in the sunlight. Four gallons would translate into 160 miles. He stuck out his hand.

Roberts took it and shook ponderously as if it were a ritual of lodge brothers.

"Good morning, Josh," Mallen said, leaning the rifle against the cabin.

"Gets steeper every time," Roberts said, blowing out his breath to prove it. "You come down next time. Too damn hard on my heart." He slung the haversack from his back and set it down on the doorstep, and placed the canister in the shade. "Nearly four gallons of good premium. Sally strained it through a chamois last night." Roberts stood awkwardly in the sunlight, shading his eyes against the glare, still panting.

"Come on in," Mallen said. "I've got some wine and it's still cool inside."

The two men entered the cabin, Mallen pausing to look back across the meadow.

"Jesus . . . you got books!" Roberts stood, arrested in step, scanning the shelves. He hesitantly moved toward the pine shelves, then turned back to Mallen.

"You had these all the time?"

Mallen nodded. "Some of them since I was a kid. A lot of them belonged to . . ." he thought of Anne ". . . to a friend." The best stuff, the classics and the histories.

Roberts examined Mallen's face as if he didn't believe it, and then turned back to the books, fingering the spines with cracked fingernails. "Jesus," he muttered again. "Are they stamped?"

Mallen shook his head and turned to look out across the meadow again. Nothing except a misshapen rabbit working over the lettuce. A mutant, he thought.

Roberts had withdrawn Conrad's *Mirror of the Sea* from its protective polyethylene bag and was thumbing through it, letting the pages flutter beneath his thumb like the wing beats of a small bird.

"This one would be all right. By Conrad. He was a Polack, wasn't he?" His forehead wrinkled. "Nothin' political in it, is there?"

"Not much," Mallen replied. "Sit down. I'll get you

some wine." Mallen returned with two glasses of the
New York red, setting one down in front of Roberts on
the packing-crate table. Roberts had the book open at
arms length and was slowly turning the pages.

"Really had a turn for words, didn't he?" the old
man said, not looking up. He ignored the glass of wine
Mallen had set on the table.

A little impatient now, Mallen said, "What do you
have this time?" hoping that Roberts hadn't forgotten
the spark plugs.

Roberts straightened up, looked once more at the
book, and closed it reluctantly with the brush of a hand.
The movement was one of surprising gentleness.

"I ain't read a book in two years," he said. "Not one
book."

"What do you have?" Mallen repeated.

Roberts sighed and set the book down. "The usual,"
he replied. "Matches. Six tins of canned fish. Dried
apples and a mess of punkin seed." He glanced down at
the book again, then looked up at Mallen. "I ain't
chargin' you nothin' for the seed. Government's givin'
it out free. I can get you some seed for radishes and
celery come spring."

"The plugs . . ." Mallen said.

Roberts picked up the wine and sipped. "The plugs?
Well, my son Hannel says he can git some over in
Duxbury. Fella has an old VW. Wants a bottle of
whiskey. A whole bottle."

Mallen shook his head. "It's too much. I'll give you
five shotgun cartridges."

"Eight," Roberts said flatly. "And I ain't promisin'
nothin'."

They argued for a while, just haggling, and finally
settled on six cartridges, which they both knew was
robbery.

Mallen dragged the haversack into the center of the
floor and carefully spilled the contents onto the rough
pine planks. The only alien object was a small plastic
box. Mallen nudged it with his boot. "What's this?"

Roberts downed the remainder of his wine and wiped

his mouth with his sleeve. "Radio. Just gets one station. Cost two *ochki*."

"*Ochik?* Mallen picked up the plastic box. What's *ochik?*"

Roberts took the box from his hand and held it in his palm. "*Ochki*, Mallen. O-C-H-K-I. Means *points*. I forgot you don't get the government paper." Roberts snapped on a switch and a woman's voice, strained and thin, talked about the prospects of a massive wheat crop being harvested in the Midwest, well above quota, for our citizens world-wide. Roberts turned it off and handed it to Mallen.

Mallen turned the small radio over in his hand, switching it off and on. "It only gets one station," he said.

"That's right. Doesn't matter. All the stations broadcast the same program, 'cept for local announcements."

Mallen handed it back to Roberts. "It needs batteries. I don't have any." *I want it,* he thought. *To hear another voice. Music. I haven't heard music in over two years.*

"Don't need batteries," Roberts replied. "Gets its juice from the sunlight. Sally just keeps it in front of a window and the damn thing plays all day. Solar cells and some kinda rechargeable battery. Permanent."

Mallen smiled and put the radio on the mantle. "Okay, Josh. I'll keep it. How much?"

They haggled for ten minutes, Roberts eventually settling on ten .22-caliber cartridges. As Mallen doled them out into a handkerchief Roberts had spread on the floor, Roberts said, "Make it eleven. One of the last bunch misfired. Lost me a rabbit. Wouldn't have been so bad, but it was a fat bastard."

Mallen sighed and put two more shells in the handkerchief. "One extra and one for the replacement, but next time bring me the dud shell. At least I can extract the gunpowder and the bullet."

Roberts shrugged and wrapped up the handkerchief. He ran his tongue over his teeth, thinking, then said, "About the books, Greg . . ."

Mallen shook his head. "They're not something I want to sell."

Roberts picked up the volume of Conrad and felt the texture of the binding through the thin plastic with his fingertips. "I was thinkin' that something like this would be swell for Sally's birthday. You know—college educated and all that. Would please her some."

Mallen thought about it. "I've got a few I've read a couple of times. What do you have for trading?"

The old man erupted in laughter, which dissolved into a hacking cough. He brought it under control finally and then took a sip of the wine, wiping his lips with the sleeve of his jacket. "God, you been too far out of it, man. That first winter—the first Peace Division that came through—they was issuing food coupons, but you had to turn in books, spare blankets, guns, stuff like that, or you didn't get the coupons. Couldn't understand why the hell they wanted books, but this yahoo said that they need the pulp for making newsprint. You figure that? I kept the guns hidden, but what the hell—food for books. You can't eat print, Mallen."

"You ever figure why they wanted the books, Josh?"

The old man thought about it, worrying at a pimple on his chin. He sat down on the couch and looked up at Mallen.

"Yeah, I know. Doesn't pay to talk too much about how they do things these days, but I figure that if someone out there that's running this wasteland wants to write a new history, they got to get rid of the old history. Some books okay, so they get stamped 'approved.' But the majority of them—gone." He carefully examined the rim of his glass, turning it to catch the light, sloshing the wine around in a nervous gesture as if thinking of what to say or how to say it.

"Look, Greg," he said carefully, "back then it was different—the whole society running sixteen different ways to Sunday. People were crazy. Leaping around, trying to turn a buck, always behind at the bank or with their goddamn taxes. Kids going wild on dope and sex. No sense in it. But times have changed. Them of us are left got to build on what we salvaged, which is damn little. But we eat, we drink a little juice, and the government don't bother us much. Fact is, things are more stable."

Mallen thought of cities devastated, a civilization gone, a history eradicated. "How do you figure that, Josh?" he said evenly.

Roberts let out a sigh, a mixture of impatience and fatigue. "Like they say that there won't be no more wars and that things are shared out equally. Like we're building a new era. Like people all over the world now get enough food. So *shit!* We get a little less now, but at least we live. And what's so bad about that? Same kind of life my granddad had: simple food and workin' the fields. Nothin' fancy." He slapped his stomach. "Sixty-nine in February and fit as a horse," and as if to prove the point he grinned, displaying the yellow, rotten teeth.

"I suppose," Mallen said, finding no other words adequate.

"They're gettin' organized now. Starting a survey," Roberts said.

Mallen was getting more wine from the crock. He walked back into the room. "What survey?"

"Survey of us people that's left," Roberts replied. "They're starting in the larger cities, workin' down to the towns. They got all the former records they could lay their hands on. Police, army, tax, motor vehicle, records like that. A lot of them are our own people. People that were in the old government—Americans."

"What is it that they're surveying?"

Roberts scratched at his chin, bringing a smear of blood from the pimple. He looked at his finger with disgust.

"What is it that they want, Josh?"

Roberts lifted his shoulders. "Just identification. What sort of work you do now. They take photographs and fingerprints. Give you ration books. Travel passes and work permits if you need that."

Mallen felt very warm suddenly. Then cold.

"Yeah," Roberts continued. "You need an identity

pass to do just about anything except squat." He showed his yellow teeth again. Then, more soberly, his smile faded and he said, "You'll need one as well. They ain't makin' any exceptions. And perticularly if you was an officer. They give you a special interview."

Mallen felt something crawling at the base of his skull. "What kind of interview?" he said.

Roberts sipped at his wine. "Talks with psychologists and stuff. Whether you feel hostile and that kinda thing. You go down to Albany for that. Correctional Clinics, they're called."

"You know anything about these Correctional Clinics?"

Roberts shook his head, eyes averted. "Guy down in Northfield had to go. He ain't back yet, but his wife gets a letter oncet a month. She told me."

Mallen sat thinking, feeling the world moving beneath him. "What do the letters say, Josh?"

"Nothin.' Just that he feels fine. Two or three sentences."

"You know of anyone who came back from Albany?"

Roberts shrugged and looked away at the bookshelf. "Nope. But that don't mean nothin'. Ain't many people around."

They sat for many minutes in silence, relieved only by the sounds of the cabin expanding in the heat of noon. Mallen wanted to ask more but was afraid to ask. He tried to bridge the silence. "You can have the book, Josh. I've read it five times. Just don't ever say where you got it."

Roberts nodded and took the book without thanks. He rose and arched his back, feeling his kidneys with both hands.

"Stiff as hell." He moved toward the door, then looked back. "You come down in a week or so. I'll get the plugs by then and you can stay overnight with Sally and me. Dinner with us. Do you good."

He picked up the haversack and slung it over his shoulder, then, as an afterthought, paused on the porch. "Greg," he said. "This survey thing. They got penalties

if you don't register. The radio says it's a crime against
the state."

Mallen was rising from the chair. The wine had
made him slightly dizzy. "Penalties like what?"

"Prison or more."

"More . . . ? What do you mean *more?*"

Roberts turned away, embarrassed. He shrugged his
shoulders and moved swiftly down the steps and across
the glaring bright meadow in a slow, steady gait, heels
digging in as he descended the grade toward the trees.
He didn't look back.

Mallen exhaled slowly, letting one long breath escape
his lungs. He watched Roberts until he was out of sight.

Mallen spent the rest of the afternoon working on the
northern approaches from the access road and on re-
pairing the tripwire that Roberts had unknowingly
broken. Tomorrow, he thought, would be a good time to
start a new latrine pit. And the making of snares for
rabbits.

He pushed the spade harder, working down into the
flinty Vermont soil. Man trap number seventeen. He
planned five more, six feet deep and lined with sharp-
ened stakes. He had seen them, and what they would do
to a careless man, in Southeast Asia. Mallen no longer
questioned their purpose. Constructing the man traps
had become part of a routine to evade madness or boredom. Whatever you called it; the same thing.

But, he reflected, the earth of Southeast Asia was
more the consistency of chocolate pudding than the
concretelike soil of the Green Mountains. He paused,
resting on the spade, day-dreaming. Roberts was just
trying to intimidate me, he thought. Almost two years
since the war, and no hint of trouble from whatever
government might have been organized. The whole
country was on an agrarian-barter society. What did
they have to gain with some form of registration? No
transportation left, no industry that he had heard of.
Certainly no organized resistance movement.

He was startled by a distant roll of thunder, thinking

at first that it was an aircraft. The light to the west was more yellow in tone, and between the trees he could pick out the towering cumulonimbus of a cold front, which meant rain.

He packed it in, dropping the spade. He had the pleasant agony of having worked well but without strain. Wth the plus of four hours of not thinking too much.

The angle of the sun looked about five as he walked back to the cabin, feeling the new wind from the north-west gathering in strength and cooling his naked torso. He avoided turning to watch the approach of the storm, because he wanted that pleasure to be from the shelter of the porch with a pipe and a glass of wine. And if the rain came with it, he could stand in it.

There was always the stream to bathe in, but it was like a memory of childhood to stand in a stinging bar-rage of rain, naked and singing, raising goose bumps and feeling his skin tighten. And the lightning and thun-der—that gave it a sense of adventure.

The wind was gusting hard by the time he made the shelter of the porch. He pulled out the pipe and the better tobacco, nagging himself for not asking Roberts about a resupply of wine. A couple of books would be all that Roberts would charge. Give him Balzac, he thought. I hate Balzac.

On the porch, he lit up and went for the wine but settled on cold water instead. Too much wine gone al-ready; too little left for casual drinking.

Leaning on the door frame, he watched the roll clouds approach, pregnant bellies swollen with moisture, churning over with black violence. The light was sucked up by the clouds and the wind was whining through the firs and pummeling the dead stalks of corn in the lower meadow.

The first drops of rain drove like steel nails into the earth, creating dark wounds. Then harder, and the steel became broad sheets of silver, tarnished in the gray light.

He put the pipe aside, stripped off his clothes, and

ran down into the rain. Beside the path, where the grass was soft and not too long, he stood with feet planted well apart and turned his face up to the wind and rain. It was falling torrentially, more water than air. He opened his mouth, letting the drops impact against his teeth and tongue.

He laughed with the passage of the rain, feeling young and free despite his forty years.

"Let the bastards come and get me," he shouted at the wind.

3

The rain had scrubbed the humidity from the October evening, leaving a clarity and brilliance to the stars. Orion was rising in the east, marking the dome above Mallen with a timeless familiarity.

He lay in the sling hammock, a net of canvas slung between two birches, and watched the night sky. Procyon there, with Rigel and Denebola going down in the west. He hummed, slightly off key, as his fingers traced out the constellations.

The radio was beside the sling on the grass, the music thin and watery. But it was Prokofiev's *Suite for Three Oranges* and the first music that Mallen had heard in nearly two years. He let the sound wash across his mind, but the thought kept nagging at him; Roberts was right.

Too many people knew of his existence. Roberts for one. The Hooper kids who had come to pick wild raspberries in the summer. And Franz Mosser, probably. Mallen had seen Mosser hunting with bow and arrow the previous fall. Mosser had ignored Mallen's wave. With a florid face and pot belly, Mosser looked like an inflated cupid, puffing through the woods with bow held ready. On tiptoes, for Christ's sake. Mallen had laughed and Mosser soundlessly mouthed an obscenity in his direction.

The decision would have to be either to register, which would roughly translate into a one-way trip to Albany, or to run. Staying was out of the question. Mallen could hold off one man; perhaps two. But man traps and a rifle were ridiculous; the answer was space.

41

It seemed fairly simple and direct. He would stay until forced to leave, but no later than the first light dusting of snow. From where the Sperber was hidden in the trees, the take-off run was across a six-hundred-foot-wide meadow on a steep downhill grade. The slope would shorten the run, but by how much he was unsure. Ideally, with the wind in the northwest, the takeoff would be successful, but there were trees to clear on the far side of the meadow.

He had been over the calculations many times and it looked marginal. The Sperber would break ground in seven hundred feet at sea level. Subtract one hundred feet for a ten-knot headwind and another hundred for the slope's natural rollercoaster effect; a margin of one hundred feet. In the end he had given up on the calculations and simply trusted his judgment.

But he knew that it must work. The plane, a visible symbol of escape, had kept him semi-sane through seventeen months of isolation. Once weekly, he had gone down at night and run the engine for ten minutes, taking care to ensure that there was either fog in the valley to absorb the sound of the engine or that the wind was westerly, blowing the exhaust noise up the valley slopes toward the desolate ridge that guarded his rear.

The load was a critical factor. With the cushions torn out of the back seat, there was room for the sleeping bag, tent, weapons, ten gallons of extra fuel, and food for two months. He had reshuffled the load several times, weighing it and then fitting it in the confined space. As it now stood, he would be taking off at 12 percent over gross weight.

Mallen had even considered cutting the crowns off the trees along his intended flight path on the far side of the meadow, giving him a margin of a few more feet of clearance on the critical climb out. But to crown off thirty-odd trees seemed a formidable task, so he stayed with the original plan: just get the hell out and hope everything works.

In the midst of his fantasy of escape, the music died

and the announcer told him that in ten minutes there would be a production of Asian folk music, followed by a discussion of camps for the aged. But first the news.

Mallen listened, fascinated, to the normality of plastic good tidings—wheat exports at record levels due to the volunteer efforts of Midwestern youth groups, production of a new methane-fueled bus, the Worker's Bus. A bit about a boy in New Jersey who had been awarded fifteen points for exceptional service to the state. There was no specific mention of what the service had been.

It was Mallen's first exposure to the new vocabulary, old words with a familiar ring but with different meanings: *Free seller, slipwork, night camp.* And then other words, which to Mallen had no meaning. Slavic sounding.

The news ended with an announcement concerning the establishment of registration centers. There was a delay and then the voice of a woman, locally produced, giving town names and dates for registration. The woman's voice had a hard, New England edge to it. Mainer, he thought.

Then there was a time tick, followed by distorted voices singing with a band of flutes and some unidentifiable percussion instruments. Mallen lay back in the sling, watching the stars wheel. Only one question yet to answer, he thought.

Escape to where?

Roberts had talked about it in the earlier days. And he had continued to peddle rumors, along with the provisions, over the past year—rumors cadged from men wandering through, from a few leaflets crudely printed on hand presses and, finally, from muted and obscure warnings circulated by the new government. Stuff such as the colony supposedly established on one of the Bahama out islands. An ex-navy CPO swore it was true. He was going there, he said, because women outnumbered the men five to one. Roberts had tossed that one off with a leer.

A more credible story came from a woman whose

brother was a radio ham. Guam, supposedly, had not
been hit. The men remaining there had wired the stock-
piled nuclear weapons into one switch and piled half a
mountain of coral on top of it. If attacked, they would
blow the whole thing to hell in a basket, contaminating
the planet. Doomsday and Strangelove and *Götter-
dämmerung* all in one slick fairy tale. Mallen didn't
believe it, and even if he could, the moon was just as
accessible.

He flopped over in the sling, curling into a fetal pos-
ture. The night was growing colder and dew was forming. He heard a dog barking down in the valley and the
sound of night birds. Now that he felt committed to
leaving, the cabin and the valley around him had
changed from prison to sanctuary. He disliked the
change. The cabin and the routine gave him some sense
of security, but now that he had to go he grasped how
alien the rest of the world might be.

He swung down onto the grass and trudged up the
path toward the darkened cabin, feeling the muscles in
his back pulling against each other from the work of
the afternoon. Slinging defiance in the teeth of the rain
was one thing; getting old was another.

In the loft, he lit the oil lamp and, finding that in-
sufficient, lit one of the few remaining candles. From a
stack of charts, he selected aeronautical sectionals covering Nova Scotia south to New Jersey and west to the
Great Lakes. From this point in Vermont, neatly drawn
radials splayed out to the north and west. Some were
bold and direct, strokes of blue pencil north into
Canada, seeking maximum range with the summers'
prevailing southwesterlies. Other lines in red crept along
river valleys, over mountain passes, avoiding fixed radar
stations and population centers that had existed little
more than a year ago and were now simply unknown.

Mallen picked at his teeth with a blunt fingernail,
worrying a bit of pork from between his molars. It was
a toss-up. Either north into Canada for the Maritime
Provinces, or strike west for British Columbia. He
doubted that the new government would penetrate the

remote parts of Canada for many years, and when they did he would just move deeper into the bush. Real Jack London stuff. Enough peace for a lifetime.

He picked up the cut-glass lighter and thumbed the wheel. It caught on the second try and he lit his pipe. He watched the flame for long seconds before closing the cap.

"Do you like it? Really?" She giggled and drank more of the Bordeaux.

He turned the ridiculous lighter over in his hands, letting its glass panes catch and refract the light from the slanting shafts of sunlight. Miniature rainbows wheeled around the walls of the cabin in the May twilight.

"God, yes," Mallen said. "It's elegant." He flicked the release a couple of times, producing a perfect flame of dimensions and breeding that would not be out of place on Park Avenue. "But why the hell did you give it to me? You're thinking of some gynecologist with blue eyes and a green Jaguar. Women always fall in love with their gynecologist, don't they?"

She punched him in the ribs, nearly causing him to drop two weeks of her probable salary.

"You're an ingrate, Mallen," she said, laughing. "I tramp all the way to this hovel from the civilized boundaries of New York State and I get zero for appreciation." She was smiling, hands on her hips, her pelvis slightly thrust out in kind of an upbeat woman's defiance—a woman who knows who she is and where she's going. And what she wants.

"Tiffany," she said smugly. "And if you want a reason, you won't find one. I bought it because it's useless. You can't carry it, you can't hock it. And it radiates beauty like a rose in the middle of a shit heap." She whirled around once, doing a little dance step. Taking a little bounce, she landed next to him on the sofa, then tucked her legs up under her tartan skirt.

"Seriously," she said softly, "you like?"

"Me like," he answered, kissing her forehead. Then

nose, then mouth. "Me like plenty. Cost much wampum, huh?"

She pushed him over, spilling the remains of his glass of wine.

"Next time, Mallen, you get glass beads or axe heads. You've got no culture."

Mallen poured them both another round and lifted his glass, gently touching her forehead. "To you, lady." They both drank and sat silently, holding hands, watching the sun go down.

"Seriously," he finally said. "Got a question."

"Shoot."

"What's the occasion? First date, first seduction, or anniversary of Gutenberg's first edition?"

"Nothing, you turkey." She pushed her hair back off her forehead, the individual filaments catching light like refined copper. It was something she did often, and it fitted her—a sort of statement that "I'm free, but catch me if you can." She lit one of those absurdly thin cigarettes with the lighter and then set it down carefully on the packing-crate table.

". . . Just fun," she said, "to come up here and be with you in this disreputable dump you call a hunting camp. I think, frankly, that all you bag up here are cases of beer and dumb secretaries."

He did his imitation of Donald Duck quacking "Who, me?"

"You!" she laughed, retrieving her cigarette. "And stop quacking. It makes me laugh so hard that it hurts my sides. Stop it!"

He went through his repertoire—the duck and Goofy, a character he called turkey legs, and a slightly dirty version of Pluto.

She was red in the face, her sides shaking, speechless with mirth, rolling on the rug.

Very simply he lay down next to her, and in the cooling wind of evening they made love.

They had franks, beans, and margaritas as a late, make-do dinner. Burning the paper plates in the fire, she sat back against the railing, watching the skyline.

"How many more days of leave do you have, Greg?" she said.

"Six. Five here and one to get back to Andrews. The squadron's flying UN missions next month. Mostly Middle East. I can't extend my leave."

"I wasn't asking for that," she answered, her voice flat, eyes averted.

"What were you asking?" A firefly blinked code and a dozen suddenly answered, all mixing in brief slurs of light in the lower meadow.

"I wasn't asking anything, no reason." She turned, just enough so that he could see her silhouette. "When is your next leave?"

"Look, Anne—I don't . . ." He heard the small edge of exasperation in his voice and calmed it. "They tell me when I can have leave. It might be two months . . ."

In the dim light he saw twin streaks of tears on her cheeks.

He sighed. "Annie, Annie. Let's not force it. We're friends. If it works, it works."

She turned away. "You're right," she said, her voice muffled by her hand. "Why spoil it? We've got a world of time to see if it works."

It turned out that she was wrong. Two nights later, as they lay in the loft, there was an incandescent flash that lit up the room—a light that, even in its reflection, scalded his vision. He pushed her from the bed, pulling the thin mattress over them.

The first shock wave hit, collapsing rafters and blowing in the windows. It was a continuing roar of destruction, of glass shattering and wood cracking and then exploding under the pounding of successive shock waves.

She was screaming and he held her, saying incoherent phrases, knowing that the unthinkable had happened.

When it subsided, the night was unnaturally quiet, as if all life were suspended. He threw the mattress off and, pulling on boots to avoid the shards of glass, went to the gaping hole that had been the window. The curtains were charred and smoldering and he ripped them off, throwing them out onto the grass below.

The whole valley was dark, the power lines destroyed, but pockets of flame blazed in the forests where dry timber had ignited spontaneously. To the northwest, a cloud of roiling red and luminescent cream boiled up into the stratosphere, animated by a light from within. "Oh, Christ," he said aloud.

She was screaming and he dragged her from the loft, pushing her down the narrow ladder. He snatched blankets and clothing and threw them down, following.

Pausing in the kitchen, he took canned goods from the shelves, filling jars with water from the hand pump, gathering anything that would be of value. She lay huddled on the floor, a blanket pulled over her, as if it would close out the obvious.

"What was it?" she asked, but her voice was detached, disinterested.

"It was Plattsburgh Air Force Base," he answered automatically. Was, he thought, is the operative word. Past tense.

Those next ten days had been spent living in a dugout pit beneath the cabin, eating canned goods and sucking air through crude filters he had fashioned from plastic milk jugs. It was a matter, he thought, of keeping the fallout inhalation to a minimum, although he had no way of assessing the effectiveness of the method.

Something about the Law of Sevens, he remembered. Radioactivity tended to halve every seven hours. Didn't sound right. It depended on the fallout pattern, the composition of fast- and slow-decaying material. Just survive, he finally decided. Drink canned fruit juice and keep under shelter, waiting. She screamed at night in her dreams and it was a bad time, a time that seemed to have no end.

On the eleventh day, he said that he would try to get enough gasoline for the Pinto so that they would have a crack at getting into Canada, away from the major fallout zones, and despite her hysteria he left, promising to be back in two hours.

Walking slowly down the dirt track that led from the cabin to the access road, he kept exertion to a bare minimum, breathing through a plastic tube he had glued into a gallon milk jug; creating a sort of Turkish water pipe. Right out of a head shop, he thought.

The Pinto ground through fifteen seconds of obstinance but then caught. As it warmed up, he realized the implication. No more Triple A, no credit-card calls for highway help, nothing. The electrical power was out and he grimaced at the thought of fifteen hundred in savings, probably electronically stored on a computer disk that had melted—no, more likely, vaporized. He thought also of the credit charges, Amex and Master Charge. Bytes, electronically stored, now dust. He started to calculate mentally his net worth and realized it was irrelevant.

The breathing filter was a problem, but he solved it by wedging the jug between the front seats with newspaper, allowing him to suck on the tube. For a weapon he had a Luger—something from the First World War his father had given him. He cocked it and lay it on the front passenger seat. It was a time, he thought, to venture forth into the brave new world. He dropped the Pinto into gear and started down the lane.

The trees were dying. Leaves, bright with the chrome green of spring, were already falling. And birds littered the ground, all dead. Twice, in fields of young corn, he saw deer, moving in senseless circles, stumbling. He slowed the car and realized that they were probably blind.

The dirt road led into the commons road and then down and over the covered bridge into Waitsfield. Shop windows were smashed and the village grocery was blackened with fire and still smoldering. No people at all, he thought, unless you counted the things that lay beside the road, bloated and distended, black with mayflies.

The Texaco station was a washout. Someone, undoubtedly in a frenzy to obtain fuel, had used an axe on the pumps, as if that would have released the store of hidden gasoline. Both the pumps and the car, an Oldsmobile with Massachusetts plates, were gutted from fire. Mallen turned away, sickened with the carnage. The passenger was nothing more than carbon in the charred interior; the driver unidentifiable.

In Irasville it was the same. The Mobile station was untouched except that both filler caps were removed from the underground tanks. Someone had used a hand pump and drained the tanks. Yankee ingenuity, Mallen thought bitterly.

Mallen shifted into gear, pulling out of the station. Off to his right he saw a man running across the empty parking lot, a rifle in hand, face masked by some homemade contraption for filtering the air. Startled, the man paused and waved and then ran. Fellow traveler in a strange land, Mallen thought, and waved back.

There were only two other gasoline stations in the valley, and it seemed likely that they would be cleaned out. But then an idea struck him—the airfield.

It was up on a plateau, well off the paved roads—something that only locals would know about. He turned left off the main road onto the dirt track that led to the strip, climbing the rutted lane, up through groves of birches and spruce, past horse-grazing pastures, then rounding the corner past the farm of David Graham.

Mallen remembered Graham well, the kind of man who gave rather than took, a man who kept his own counsel and tended his fields with care. Mallen looked for signs of life. The house was partially gutted from fire, but the concrete garage had newly placed plywood over the windows and an automobile was backed up to the door with battery cables running under the sill. Mallen smiled, knowing that Graham would be a survivor.

Beyond the dairy barns, the trees thinned into open meadows where cows had pastured. The cows were there now, bellies up, legs ramrod stiff, saluting the sky. The stench, even through the air filter, was nauseating. Mallen turned his eyes away, keeping them on the road.

Somehow he hoped that Graham had heard the car in passing and would know that there were others left.

The airfield was relatively untouched. Five planes were missing from their tiedowns, as was the avgas from the ten-thousand-gallon underground tank. The tank top was unbolted and two buckets with nylon line lay on the grass beside the tire tracks of a heavy twin-engined aircraft, probably George Gerrett's Beech Eighteen.

The few aircraft remaining were light planes, most with very limited range. Two had wing damage where axes or knives had been used to puncture and drain the fuel tanks. Stupid, he thought, because all of them had gas drains at the lowest point in the wings. Only a non-pilot would do that to an aircraft.

Mallen drove to the hangar, still with the windows rolled up. There wouldn't be fuel there, but he had a shopping list: tools, nylon rope, nails, soap, plastic jugs, and engine oil.

As he wheeled the Pinto into the recesses of the hangar, his eyes were slow in accommodating to the gloom. There wasn't much left. Halleran's Apache was gone, as was the Pitts Special. The only aircraft left were the partially rebuilt airframe of a Hiller helicopter and a couple of dismantled sailplanes.

Something I will miss, he thought. Driving a truck of a four-engined transport was boring. Sailplanes, which he had learned to fly after accumulating four thousand hours plus in the service, were a continuing delight, a reestablishment of the link between man and flight. He looked at the two gliders shorn of their wings. I will miss this, he thought.

The tool room yielded up most of what he required, with the exception of nylon rope. Moving back out into the hangar, he inspected the Hiller for usable goodies and fuel. The chopper was in the process of restoration and far from serviceable. But the circular fuel tank was partially filled, and with bolt cutters he was able to remove the entire tank.

He slung the tank in the back of the Pinto and was

about to leave when he noticed a canvas-shrouded shape in the back of the hangar. On just a whim, he worked his way through a clutter of stacked lumber and empty oil drums. Lifting the edge of the canvas, he looked at the glistening white paint of a sailplane's wing; almost a sailplane.

As he peeled the canvas carefully back from the aircraft, he recognized it: a Sperber RF-5. The aircraft was a hybrid—a sailplane in concept, with a small engine and a toothpick prop. Long wings, he thought, longer than fifty feet. The cockpit was two-place, fore and aft fashion with a bubble canopy.

A lot of it was coming back. Hutchins . . . Huggins . . . something like that, owned it. Pilot for Delta. Bachelor type who came up in his off time with an ever-changing lineup of off-duty stews. Mallen had known him only casually but had talked to him about the plane at a party. Huggins had said that it was a powered glider, one of the few in the country. Capable of six hundred miles' range on fifteen gallons of fuel. But with the engine shut down, it was a pretty good sailplane. Aerobatics? Mallen had asked. Huggins had shrugged Yes, not violent stuff, like snap rolls, but graceful maneuvers: Loops, barrel rolls, wingovers.

Mallen circled the aircraft, inspecting it. Although dusty, the Sperber was in good shape. The white paint was unmarred, slick and cool to the touch. Mallen experimentally thumped the wing and was rewarded with a hollow boom. He thumped again. Plywood. A thought crossed his mind: plywood wouldn't have nearly as much radar reflectiveness as an aluminum aircraft skin, nearly invisible to radar. Lovelier and lovelier, he thought.

The sailplane was deceptive in size. The vertical stabilizer, over six feet high, was striped in red and blue. He moved the rudder and elevator with his hand. Both moved easily, and he could hear cables sliding within the framework of the aircraft. Mallen suddenly realized that his inspection tour was a preflight.

The mud-spattered Pinto sat in the center of the

hangar, junk piled high in the back seat. I won't make that decision yet, he thought, but knew he really had.

Mallen opened the canopy and glanced inside. Conventional instrumentation, somewhat more elaborate than one would expect of a glider. Narco radio, artificial horizon, turn and bank—enough instrumentation for flying at night and in weather. The Winter variometer caught his eye. One of the latest types, it would measure the rate of climb or sink instantaneously, giving the pilot a precise indication of soaring performance.

A fitting in the lower panel caught Mallen's eye. A pressure gauge, it read 1,800 pounds. He bent down closer to the panel in the dim light and read the placard. It was a standard A-14 oxygen regulator. Feeling in the luggage compartment, he found two oxygen masks, fitted one, and plugged it into the console fitting. One-hundred-percent oxygen. Stale and dry, but clean of fallout. He sucked heavily on it, glad to be rid of the crude filter. Eighteen hundred pounds pressure would be enough for at least five hours, perhaps six.

Mallen didn't resist the decision to steal the Sperber. Huggins or whatever his name was probably was dead, and if he were alive, well . . . Mallen had no illlusions about driving the Pinto through devastated towns and cities. He had seen crowds out of control and looting in Southeast Asia. The evidence of violence in the valley was enough to show that Americans were no different.

He slid into the aircraft's seat and looked at the panel. Like most, it had a magneto switch that could only be turned with a key inserted. But unlike automobiles, aircraft were less likely to be stolen. Jumping the ignition would be easy, he thought. He felt around in the side pockets and found the key and flight manual. Thanks, Huggins . . . R.I.P.

Mallen read through the manual quickly and then, once again, with a more systematic approach, touched each control with his fingertips, then practiced the procedure with his eyes closed. A straightforward procedure, he thought, except for the landing gear, which seemed complicated. He decided to leave the gear down until he had plenty of altitude.

But he had no way of knowing whether the engine would start. He carefully went through the checklist, setting up the panel for engine start. *Brakes set. Choke on.* He smiled at this under the mask. The engine was almost pure Volkswagen. *Limbach* said the manual, but Volkswagen it was. He set the choke on full rich. *Throttle cracked one-half inch. Ignition switch on. Magneto on.* The panel was alive. Pressure showing on the fuel system and an electric fuel pump clicking away in the guts of the cowling. The fuel gauge indicated three-quarters full. He pulled the starter handle and the prop ground over two turns without a sign of firing. He rechecked everything, going through the procedure, the heat under his mask starting to generate perspiration. This time the prop swung through, fired, died, and fired again, stumbling into a rough idle. The sound of the exhaust, even within the enclosed hangar, was a muffled growl. He cut out the choke and the roughness disappeared into a steady beat. Mallen sat smiling under the mask.

It took him ten minutes to load the back seat of the Sperber from the Pinto. He discarded a few things and added aircraft tools to his hoard from the room in back, plus four more quarts of aircraft oil and a set of feeler gauges.

Before finally abandoning the Pinto, he read through the Sperber's manual once more: landing and takeoff performance tables, rate of climb, and stopping distances. It would be close getting it into the south meadow, and tougher still to get it off fully loaded. He would be able to take off downhill if he filled in the drainage ditch that bisected the meadow, but there was very little margin.

Flying the Sperber back would negate having the Pinto, and if he pranged the aircraft in, walking back from the cabin to the airfield to pick up the Ford would be an impossibility until the radioactivity had cooled off—two years? a year? Maybe just a series of heavy rains. He supposed that someone in some government would eventually get around to informing those who still survived that conditions were now favorable for survival.

He levered the Hiller out of the way, moving it to the side of the hangar. With each effort he ran back to the Sperber, sucked on the oxygen, than ran back, holding his breath as he worked. In the end he breathed naturally, knowing that the fresh spring air was clean smelling and lethal as hell. Strontium-90 probably didn't taste, he thought. Easy come, easy go.

The going was easy. He taxied the plane out into the May sunlight, steering to avoid the thousands of dead birds that littered the grass. Twice the Sperber almost bogged down in the soft ground, and he learned quickly to keep it moving with bursts of throttle. The wind was southwesterly, bringing more fallout up from the Hudson Valley, but also giving him a clean ten knots of wind right up the runway. At the end of the runway, he stabbed the rudder hard over and swung the aircraft around into the wind. With the brake still set, he smoothly applied full throttle, looking for any sign of trouble on the gauges. Oil temperature fifty and climbing; oil pressure high in the green, and 2,850 on the tachometer. All go . . . and he released the brake. The Sperber nudged ahead, agonizingly, sluggish in its acceleration. Nothing showing on the air-speed indicator, and the left wingtip drooping, he thought. Stick over and forward, trying to get the tail up so that he could see over the cowling. Better now, and he was surprised to find her drifting to the right of the runway. Left rudder, and the ASI flickered up to twenty knots. Thirty now, and the controls were beginning to firm up. Budding trees, some with blackened leaves, were no longer individual things, now blurs. Gear thumping along the rough runway and the engine picking up the beat, and Mallen felt that sensation that every pilot feels as the aircraft sheds the earth and joins the sky. The grass and trees fell away from beneath him. Trim nose down and pick up airspeed. Seventy knots on the

ASI now, and he banked out over the valley, climbing well, the engine and Mallen both singing at the top of their lungs.

The valley melted away and still he climbed, feeling the aircraft respond to the morning thermals that fed the fat cumulus, grazing like sheep along the eastern ridge. Rpms reduced and still climbing in the hot air, playing man-bird. He banked first one way, then the other, feeling the smooth silk of the controls, just poking his wingtips at the sun. Reaching the cloud base, he nudged his way through billowed valleys, still climbing higher until he was on top of the scattered cloud deck.

Mallen was laughing now with the sheer joy of it. The temptation was overpowering to keep climbing. To play and horse and clown in the light and shadow, and to smoke down through the cloud canyons at redline. And then back up again, converting airspeed back into altitude. He glanced at his watch. Two and a half hours gone now. She would worry, and he needed to conserve the thin supply of fuel.

He headed north along the valley, picking up Vermont state highway 100 and following it as far as Waitsfield, then banking to the east along the common road. The valley was rising under him, stacking up in layers of cultivated fields and meadows, then capped with a crown of timber and rock outcroppings.

When he spotted the access road turnoff, he pulled back on the power to idle and started to let down, following with difficulty the rutted road that led through the maple groves. As he descended, he eased back on the stick feeling for the control response of a stall, which he would want just at the moment of touchdown. There wouldn't be two thousand feet of paved runway to play with. "Just get it on in one piece, Mallen," he thought.

The nose was still coming up, blotting out the horizon, with airspeed in the high thirties. Then she burbled politely to indicate the edge of the stall and, satisfied, he dumped the stick forward and recovered, pleased with her good manners. No wingtip drop, and no mush, just clean and straightforward.

Just short of the ridge, he saw the meadow, impossibly small. One slow pass over the meadow to let Anne know and to look for rocks, and then he would give it a go. If he pranged it, he would be stranded, not even able to recover the Pinto.

He checked quickly through the manual, reading the checklist for landing. *Gear down with green indication lamp checked. Boost pump on. Cooling cowl open.* With a stroke of the spoiler handle, he started to throw away altitude, spiraling down for the approach. He checked the wings, making sure that the gates were fully extended, spoiling the flow of air over the wings, destroying lift. A bird flew past his canopy, startling him. A hawk, he thought—tougher than the rest of the smaller birds.

Not more than a few hundred feet above the trees, he closed the spoilers and added power, aligning the flight path with the center line of the meadow. Up the slope, he could see the cabin on the edge of the trees. As he watched, Anne ran out of the door, her face upturned and without the air filter. He rocked the wings and waved as she hesitated and then waved back. She had the Winchester, which pleased him, as there had been a long series of hair-splitting arguments on his part about postholocaust survival, countered by morality lectures on her part. He had won, as usual, and she had accepted the role of frontier mistress. "Just keep the Injuns at bay, babe," he had told her.

He made one pass at just above stall to feel out the strip, and then swung into final, carrier style, with a high power setting and cowl well above the horizon. He almost lost it over the trees, feeling the uncontrolled sink of an aircraft that has just quit flying, but he goosed the throttle and landed, tail-wheel first, with the main gear thumping down a second later, just clear of the fence. With the stick back in his lap, he walked the rudders, keeping her straight pumping on the brake. The Sperber stopped an easy brick's throw from the end of the meadow, and he swung her around and taxied back to the woman. The top buttons of her denim skirt were open and she was laughing. Crazy, happy laughter, her red hair streaming off in the wind, copper in the sunlight. "Welcome back, Mallen," her lips formed, and he cut the engine.

The candle was guttering now and Mallen blew it out. He put the Tiffany lighter back on the shelf, trying not to remember her. Anne had died and he had lived. No real reason, he supposed, except that he was stronger, and she had hated using the filter. The air tasted clean, she had said, and it had been impossible to convince her.

One day she had become sick and could keep nothing down. Her hair had started to fall out, and she wept constantly. Dysentery followed and she died quickly, without any will left to live. Exit Anne of less than a thousand days. He buried her up on the ridge on the evening of the day that she had died, learning that the mind can accept death only by first rejecting it.

Mallen sat for half an hour, watching the lamp's flame, thinking of the preparations. The sparkplugs were desirable but not a necessity. Still, Roberts said that he could get them. Maybe some more food, tinned stuff. Trade off the coffee. He wouldn't need the .22 caliber. Roberts would sell his old lady for three boxes of shells and the toy pistol.

He decided to go down into the valley tomorrow to get Roberts moving on the plugs and try to trade coffee and the .22 pistol for canned goods.

He would go north into old Canada, he decided— north first, beyond the populated areas, and then, if he could find fuel, swing west toward the Canadian Rockies. The new government would hardly bother that area, and the earth there wouldn't be nearly as contaminated by fallout. British Columbia, then, he thought. The name had a nice ring to it.

He found himself still tapping the edges of the sectionals, whistling softly between his teeth, the *Three*

Oranges thing. He stopped whistling and turned on the radio, sinking down onto the bed.

". . . building over the St. Lawrence Valley. Continued lower than seasonal temperatures will predominate in the Northeast for the remainder of the weekend. Frost expected in the mountain valleys of Maine, New Hampshire, and lower Canada. Free sellers are advised to protect their crops. Tomorrow fair and cold."

The announcer shifted to programs for tomorrow and then was displaced by a male chorus. A military marching song, he thought at first, then recognized it as the *Internationale*. He snapped off the volume control and stood up. Blowing out the lamp, he drew back the curtain and opened the window. The wind smelled of autumn, a dryness and pungency of things dying. The wild dogs and foxes were barking, a sound carried clearly on the wind. A time of bonfires and football games and brandy by the fire, he thought. Different world, long gone.

He lay down on the bed, still clothed, and stared at the blackness.

4

By early mid-morning, Mallen had traversed the three-mile dirt access road and started down the common road, sticking to the line of trees bordering the road. There was no evidence that the road was traveled by anything except horses and dog carts. There were no signs of heavy vehicles along the shoulder and no tire imprints on the dirt roads that left the pavement at right angles, just the occasional small wagon-wheel imprint.

The maples and birches were beginning to be singed with yellow in prelude to an early autumn. There were some strokes of scarlet and deeper magenta in the leaves. On days like this when he was young, he walked with his father in lanes such as these, throwing pebbles before him to make eruptions in the dust and exciting the collie to fits of barking. He remembered those autumn days and restrained the impulse to whistle.

Two of the farmhouses high above the common road were vacant. The grass was overgrown and the windows fragmented. Looted thoroughly, he thought, but they might be worth checking on the return trip. There really wasn't much that he needed, but if there was a pair of waterproof boots about his size it would be worthwhile. His own were wearing thin, so that he could feel the texture of the ground through his soles.

Surprisingly, the Mosser farm was intact. He had known Franz Mosser as one knows a remote neighbor, to wave at when passing on the road, never really to talk to. Mosser, Mallen had heard, considered anyone not born in Vermont to be city people. New Hampshire, though not being Vermont, shouldn't qualify as "city," but Mallen had never challenged him.

Mallen watched the farm for a long time, resting in the shade beneath an ash grove. The house was neat, with a well-tended look. One window upstairs was boarded over and painted green, matching the shutters, but it gave the house an unbalanced look, much like a face with a broken nose. He grinned and felt his own, and his fingers were drawn to the scar tissue that the axe blade had made when it had rebounded off a pine knot. Almost lost it there, Mallen, he reminded himself. Nearly died in the bloody snow for your own carelessness.

A movement near the house caught the edge of his vision. A woman, old and brittle, was moving slowly across the yard. In her hands was a wicker basket. She finally stopped beneath an overhead line, arthritically plucking washing from the basket to hang in flapping formation, secured by pins she drew from her apron.

Mallen watched her with pleasure, as if watching a vignette staged for his sole appreciation. Good setting: maples turning, green grass, laundry flogging in the wind with this Norman Rockwell character going through the motions.

It was just then that the man said, "Drop your weapon and lean against the tree . . . slowly."

Mallen, startled, began to turn. He froze at the sound of a shotgun cartridge being chambered with a meaty click. Using only his thumb and forefinger, he withdrew the .22 from his belt and tossed it gently to the grass beside him. He heard the slow expulsion of a breath behind him.

"Now against the tree, *durak*."

Mallen complied, spreading his legs and leaning against an ash. A hand at the extreme perimeter of his vision picked up the .22 and withdrew from sight. Mallen had the impression of a blue-cuffed shirt, buttoned at the wrist.

"Now what?" Mallen said, trying to be easy.

"Now we wait. Just relax and there's no hassle."

Mallen shrugged as best he could. Not easy leaning against a tree.

"Look, keep the gun. I found it in a farmhouse up the road."

"Yeah, I understand. Well oiled and with a round in the chamber."

Mallen listened to the man breathing easily. A farmer or the law. "What was the word you used?"

"You mean *durak?* It means idiot. Don't you read the standards?"

"Never get it. Hardly come down to the valley."

"Yeah, that's what Mosser said. He called and said someone was creepin' around up here. Thought it might be you. You're Mallen, heh?"

He nodded. "Yes. I'm Mallen. I live up on the ridge."

Two or three minutes elapsed in silence. Mallen could hear the other man settling down on the grass. Two birds flew through the ash grove, one chasing the other. I really didn't need the sparkplugs that bad, he thought. *Shitdammit.*

"Look," Mallen said, sighing, "do I have to stand like this? My back is beginning to ache. And what's the problem?"

"The problem, *durak,* is that you are carrying around a weapon. For starters. You have any interim papers? Transit pass?"

Mallen shook his head. "I don't even know what the hell you're talking about. I just live up on the hill. How about letting me sit down."

"Okay, Mallen. Sit down carefully, facing away from me." He paused and then said, "Sit cross-legged with your hands behind you, leaning back."

They passed another few minutes in silence. Mallen looked down toward the Mosser farm. The laundry was flogging away, dancing on the line, but the woman was gone. As he watched, a man came out the front door and moved across the lawn toward the ash grove. He was limping slightly, moving toward them along some invisible path that favored the grade. Mallen could see that it was Mosser. Round face, bunched-up eyes embedded deep in the fat of his cheeks. "Piggy, piggy, piggy," Mallen had heard the kids of the village calling after Mosser.

"*Kharasho' ootrom,*" Mosser said, standing well away from them, his face a sheen of perspiration. He had fieldglasses slung over his neck; a puffy Rommell.

"Yeah, good morning," the man behind Mallen said. "Did you call that number?"

"Immediately. They're sending a wagon up. I got your 'lectric plugged in down behind the house."

Apparently the man behind Mallen nodded, for there was no other answer.

Mosser seemed embarrassed, shifting from the game leg to the other, like a child about to wet his pants but too shy to ask to be excused from the room.

"You got him," Mosser said, rather redundantly, nodding toward Mallen. "I was dead right; it was him." He touched the binoculars, reassured.

"You can take off now, Mosser. You get your proper letter from the district officer. Probably about twelve points."

Mosser beamed, a moon forming in the fat of his lips. Mallen noted that Mosser really hadn't looked directly at his own eyes.

"Not every day you get twelve points, is it, Franz?" Mallen said, putting as much sarcasm into it as he could.

"City turd," Mosser snapped and turned away, limping down toward the house. Watching him waddle, Mallen thought that Mosser probably didn't need many more calories to top three hundred.

"Hey, Mosser," Mallen called after him. He cupped his hands and yelled, "Sowee, sowee, sowee."

Something thudded into his kidneys—not really hard, but hard enough. He sucked in a gasp of air, arching his shoulder blades backward.

"Don't move, Mallen. And no talking. Mosser was doing the right thing. He's local political administrator—keeps things on an even keel. Cooperation gets points."

Mallen gritted his teeth, the pain in his back receding slowly like a spent wave. I won't show it, he thought, swallowing. "You the law?" he finally asked. He had tensed his muscles, trying to distill the pain into a small point, then move that point off into space as if it didn't exist.

"Yeah, law. Eastern Peace Division. Corporal Bernshine." The man made a sucking sound, as if trying to extricate a piece of gristle from between his teeth. "You got *any* papers? Like travel passes or registration?"

Mallen could see Mosser limping along his porch, looking up occasionally toward the grove. A small vehicle pulled into his farmyard trailing a plume of dust, stopped briefly by Mosser, then pulled out, heading up the grade.

"No, nothing," he replied. "I didn't know . . ."

Bernshine snorted behind him and then rattled a paper as if he was unwrapping something. "None of them ever do, Mallen. None of them ever do."

The sun was more overhead now, hammering down through the thinning leaves of the ash grove. He could smell his own sweat. Definitely a difference between work sweat and fear sweat. One like the smell of baking bread, the other a sort of decay. He didn't hear the vehicle arrive.

"Get up slowly and turn around. Hands behind your back—clasped."

Mallen levered himself to his feet, stiff in the spine, and kidney still throbbing with pain. He turned around slowly. There were three of them now, all with shotguns.

The smallest one spoke; it was Bernshine's voice. Mallen was surprised at the age of his face. Weathered was maybe a better description. He had a large radiation burn on the side of his cheek.

"His name is Mallen, Greg C. A twenty-one oh one for possession of the weapon. No papers. Mosser says he's an ex-oh." The tallest of the three regarded Mallen as if he were an exhibit. The man was dressed in faded gray woolens without device or badge of rank. The uniform was a parody of a West Point cadet's, with stiff collar and of gray wool. Mallen liked his looks. His face was thin and sensitive, cleanly shaven with deep-set, widely spaced gray eyes. He looked as through he should be grading math papers, Mallen thought.

"You're an ex-officer? What branch?"

"Air Force. Cargo planes. I was on leave when it happened."

The tall one nodded. He turned to the third man, a thin youth with a sagging eyelid. "Get him in the back. Usual routine." Turning back to Mallen, he made a motion with his hand toward the truck.

Mallen walked over to the road. The truck was four-wheeled and built out of plywood over some kind of steel frame. The wheels were about the size of motor-cycle rims, and there was some sort of a chain-drive sprocket arrangement.

" 'Lectric?" he said over his shoulder, trying to pronounce it the way Bernshine did.

Something slammed into his spine, tumbling him forward into the truck. He sprawled awkwardly, unable to unclasp his hands in time to save landing heavily on his face. Someone shoved his feet in and slammed the door. The last thing he remembered was a hissing as of an aerosol spray and a sweetish smell, such as raspberries or blue ber . . .

"Tea?" the math teacher said, and pushed the tray across his scarred metal desk. He was smoking a brown-wrappered cigarette.

Mallen lifted his head off his chest and looked at the man. He was maybe early fifties. Lean and going white around the temples. Very kind gray eyes.

"Yes, one sugar and can I have one of those?" He raised his manacled hands together and pointed at the package of cigarettes on the desk.

The math teacher lit a second cigarette from the first and passed it over carefully. Mallen inhaled and was surprised at the smoothness of the tobacco.

"Virginia," the teacher said, showing a small break in the neat line of his lips. The teeth were very white. "Expensive and only at special stores."

Mallen nodded and settled back, holding the tea cup and the cigarette clumsily in his manacled hands. The room was early American footlocker. Besides the desk and the two chairs, there was only a cardboard file cabinet with dirty jars sitting on top of it. The floors were linoleum in a pattern that would probably have been described in the catalog as "moss green Morocco."

"It would be helpful to know your name and also the charges," Mallen said. His throat felt sore from inhaling the gas.

The teacher tapped the ash from his cigarette and watched Mallen steadily for some minutes before replying.

"Officer, grade four, McKennon. Eastern Peace Division. And you're up for firearms, unlawful possession of. Registration, lack of. There's more." He thumbed through a small stack of yellow pulp paper with tele-printer type on it.

"So what happens now?" Mallen said.

"I ask you some questions and you tell me no lies. Albany."

"And there?"

McKennon shrugged. "You'll be brought up to date. Maybe some correction. It'll work out."

Mallen finished the cigarette and dropped it in the half-finished cup of tea. There was a polite hiss.

"And do people come back from the C.C.'s?" Mallen asked, raising his eyebrows.

"Not my end of the job," McKennon said, looking down at his hands. "Only this part of it. The rest is up to other departments."

McKennon got up and went to the door and opened it, saying something muffled into an outer office. Some-one—it sounded like Bernshine—answered him. There was another noise in the background, a rattling of pots and pans and the smell of cabbage.

McKennon came back into the room and sat down on the edge of the desk. He lit another cigarette and looked down on Mallen. His uniform smelled of mothballs and cleaning fluid.

"This thing never pleases me, Mallen, but it's up to you."

"What's up to me?" Someone was coming into the room behind him.

"Relax," the voice said, and a brown leather band was slipped over his head, then down over his chest. With some fumbling and the clink of metal the belt was drawn tight.

"Too tight?" the voice said, and Mallen shook his head dumbly.

His legs were next, strapped in by individual cuffs of leather to the rungs of the chair. The kid with a dooping eyelid finished up and patted Mallen on the shoulder.

"That's fine," he said. "It'll be okay." The kid patted him again on the shoulder and left the room.

McKennon sat down on the desk again, facing Mallen. He withdrew a printed card and read through it. Standing up, he reached for the ceiling and drew down what Mallen supposed was electrical apparatus.

"It's standard equipment, you see," McKennon said, placing the equipment on the desk.

One object was a microphone. McKennon turned it over, looked at it, and flicked a switch. He tapped at the mouthpiece and blew into it. There was an amplified *tic-tic* and *poofff* from a ceiling speaker. McKennon gave the cord that suspended the mike a little downward snap and then allowed it to reel up toward the ceiling, finally setting it twelve or so inches in front of Mallen's face.

"Mike," McKennon said, unnecessarily. Then he rummaged around in the bottom drawer of his desk.

"Mallen, what size glove do you wear?"

Mallen shrugged. "I don't know. I can't remember." Perspiration was starting to run from his armpits down his rib cage.

"These should fit you." McKennon held up a pair of

rubber gloves, then came over and fitted them to Mallen's hands. From the desk top he took the two cables that were drooping down from the ceiling and plugged each one into a special fitting on the back of the glove. Then he tightened straps on the cuffs of the gloves.

"Try to keep the fingers of the gloves laced together. Like clasping your own hand. Some say it's better that way."

"Jesus, man," Mallen said. "You're American."

McKennon nodded. "Philadelphia. Founding fathers and all that crap. Just listen carefully, Mallen. This is all standard. Nobody ever dies. The mike goes to a machine that analyzes your voice. When you lie—*any* lie—there's a subaudible quiver in the voice. This triggers an electrical pulse to your hands. Each time you lie, the pulse gets . . . well, tougher. I don't have anything to do with it. The machine is programmed. I can't cut if off without having to write about fourteen letters saying why I did. The only justification is heart arrest. Understand so far?"

Mallen nodded, his tongue thick and dry within the cage of his teeth.

"Okay," McKennon continued. "So I go into the next room. That's part of the procedure. Impersonal. And I ask you questions, which you hear over the same speaker. I'll repeat it once, only once if you don't understand. Then you speak up distinctly and give me the answer. The true answer."

"How long does this last?"

"Until I finish the list of questions. It all goes on tape and becomes part of your permanent record. Nothing to worry about, Mallen. You tell the complete truth and you don't get a dose."

McKennon got up abruptly and left the room, closing the door almost gently behind him.

Mallen sat waiting for the speaker, watching the windowpane on the far side of the room. It was dirty in the direct rays of the forenoon light. A whole handprint smeared the pane. Beyond that there were maples and part of a brick wall.

"Toc, toc" from the ceiling speaker. "You hear me okay, Mallen?"

"Yes." A fly was buzzing against the corner of the windowpane.

"Louder, please."

"Yes, I hear you fine."

There was a shuffling of paper in the speaker. McKennon cleared his throat and said, "Give me your full name."

"Gregory C. Mallen." The fly was resting, just walking around slowly in a small circle.

"Where were you born?"

"Laconia, New Hampshire. Near there."

"And where do you live now?"

"Nowhere." The shock surprised him, causing his knee to jerk reflexively. Before he could think about it, the pain was gone, leaving an almost pleasant warmth in his chest.

"Again, Mallen. Where do you live now?"

"On the ridge. It doesn't have a name."

"Who else?" McKennon cleared his throat again.

"No one. I live there alone. It's a cabin that I built for the hunting season."

"Do you own . . ." there was a pause ". . . a Colt Woodsman semiautomatic pistol serial number three three four zero seven eight?"

The fly lifted off and started to batter himself against the glass.

"Yes," Mallen replied.

"And do you own other weapons? Bows and arrows included?"

"No." He swallowed. Nothing happened, and then the pain of a hot needle was in his spine, and his feet and arms and chest were convulsing. The pain stopped. The thudding was his heart, he realized. Again a warm tingle, but now not pleasant.

McKennon sounded impatient.

"Mallen, I can't help you. By the fourth dose it's pretty bad. Most people don't take it very well. Now again. Any other weapons?"

"Yes."

"Go on. The types. How many?"

"A rifle and a Luger." His heart was slowing back down but it was deafeningly loud. He wondered whether McKennon could hear it over the mike.

"Good. Much better, Mallen. We'll get back to the weapons later." A pause, then, "Have you committed any other crimes?"

"It's not a crime to own . . ." McKennon cut him off, irritated now.

"Mallen, the machine isn't programmed for discussion—just answer the question. If the machine doesn't measure a response as a truth or lie, it repeats the last level of shock dosage. Any crimes?"

"I smoke." True.

Surprisingly, McKennon took this in good humor.

"Bad for your health, Mallen. What else?"

The Sperber was taken before the present government took over; ergo, not a crime. "No," Mallen answered.

There was a pause and someone in the background, not McKennon, mumbled something.

"The reaction is indefinite, Mallen. I'll be more specific. Have you committed any violent act against the state?"

"No."

"Stolen anything?"

"No," but the cortex was denying that, and he knew it wouldn't work. *"Geeeeeeeeeeeeeeee!"* His body was lacerated with filaments of white-hot wire sawing through his jerking sinews. The sound of the scream was his own, but he couldn't hear it. The pain subsided and he sat gulping the stale air, his shirt saturated, muscles still strumming.

"Take a rest, Mallen. Think carefully. It's not worth it, and I can't do anything to help you."

The speaker clicked off and he slumped in the chair, as much as the straps would allow. His heart was tripping now, racing in syncopation, *didum, didum, didum. Buzz.* The fly echoed him, smashing against the glass. *Buzz. Didum, didum. Buzz.*

The ceiling speaker clicked back on. Mallen could hear the background noise. Someone was laughing and there was the sound of a typewriter.

McKennon spoke. "You're feeling okay?"

Mallen listened to his own voice, remote. "Yes," he whispered. "Dandy." *Just dandy.* His own hand was shaking uncontrollably and his mind was reeling, turning over and over in a blur of images.

The metallic speaker again. "That one was only eight hundred volts. The next stage is about fifteen hundred. Just take your time and answer it straight."

The sound of the fly buzzing was intolerable; loud applause. Isolation booth with the kleig lights. Suspense music and the MC with the smooth voice asking; *for sixtyfour thousanddollars name sixparts ofthe femalesexorgan.* Lots of sweat on his forehead; thinking. MC says again, insistent.

"Labia." *Correct!* Buzzing applause. "And cervix." *Wonderful.* Applause.

"Okay, Mallen, what have you stolen?"

"Vulva . . ."

A pause, then McKennon said, "Don't get smartass with me. I can't stop this thing. Again, . . ."

"Howaboutvagina . . . CUN . . ." and the scream ripped the word out of his throat and his body was thrashing like a fly with its legs torn off and his bowels voided, as did his bladder, causing the voltage to find a new path. He didn't know when the current was cut off—it was that bad—and he only registered one word that McKennon said, before the world shut down.

"Smartass . . ."

He woke up in darkness with just a trickle of light leaking in under the door. His clothes were gone, replaced by some kind of bathrobe. He fingered the material in half-wakefulness, trying to stop the earth from wheeling. He could definitely smell shit. His own.

"You awake?" The voice was agreeable, like his father's. Full and slow. Deep, with a blurred accent.

"Yes," Mallen said, sensing an aftertaste of blueberries.

"You convulsed. They gave you a sniffer. It's past eleven."

Mallen sat up on the cot, feeling very little empathy with his body. All the outlying senses were jangled. Only central control was working.

"Where am I?" he said, trying to rise and feeling a wave of nausea rise in his stomach.

"You mean generally, or specifically?"

"Both."

The other man hawked and spit. "Generally in Warren, Vermont. Specifically in what was the grade school. I don't know the name of it. Something like Ethan Allen."

Mallen massaged his wrists. The palms were burned and had some sort of sticky ointment on them. "My hands aren't in good shape. I can't shake. My name's Mallen."

"So I hear. Mine's Wyatt."

"So what happens now?"

"They start again tomorrow. From the beginning. It's best not to fool around with them."

Someone walked past the door and both men sat in the darkness, waiting for the steps to recede. Down the corridor a door opened, admitting scratchy music, then slammed.

"Christ," Mallen said, the nausea washing up a wave of acid in his throat.

"That's not on," said the voice from the other side of the room.

"What's not?"

"Christ," Wyatt said. "The standards say that he didn't exist. Or rather that he was just another prophet."

"The standards are . . . ?"

"Newspaper run by the government. Sets out new rules. Language study of Russian by cartoon characters. The official language worldwide in ten years, they say."

Mallen shook his head unbelievingly. "It's gone this far?"

Wyatt snorted in laughter. "Who knows. No news other than what the government puts out. No travel unless you're in government service. They're just starting to put civilization back together, Soviet-style. Where've you been the last two years, anyway?"

Mallen sighed. "In a cabin. I was on leave, duck hunting, when it happened. Had plenty of food stocked up there. And a lot of shotgun and twenty-two ammunition. I've been trading that for chow with a local farmer. Growing some food. It was all right." He paused, feeling the burns on his hands. "What are you here for, Wyatt?"

"Same thing as you, pretty much. Nonregistration. Stealing apples. I've been drifting for the last year. My wife and kid died. I've been moving north for Canada."

"What about Canada?" Mallen asked. "Any different up there?"

"Canada doesn't exist, any more than the States exist. It's all the same government. But some people say that it's better up there. Not as much damage and lots of abandoned farms to live on."

"So what happens now? To us."

Wyatt was silent for a moment. He cracked his knuckles in the darkness. "In four days they send us to Albany. To a C.C. You've got three more days of interrogation, Bernshine says. Me, I had four. I gave them the same story over and over. But watch out for McKennon. He's a bastard. He'll zap you with the full dose if he has a chance. Bernshine calls him the meat man."

Mallen lay back on the bed, the blankets rough beneath his skin. The room smelled of stale sweat and urine. "Is there any way out of here?"

"Feet first," Wyatt said.

"I mean otherwise. Escape."

"Not hard to get out. It's just an old school. Only two men on duty at night, both of them old farts."

Mallen sat up in bed, interested. "Then what's the problem?"

"The problem," Wyatt replied, "is where the hell we

go and how we get there. No public transportation without passes. No ration books and no points. Plus the fact that if we did get out, we'd have a squad of Special Forces types on our track by dawn."

"Special Forces being . . . ?"

"I don't know. Call them what you want. A paramilitary group, mainly Slavic or Mongols. Some Americans, though you'd never know, to watch them in action. They're used mainly to put down insurrections, riots. Keep things cool if the Peace Division can't handle it."

Mallen sighed. "So you're just willing to be shuffled off to Albany?"

"It wouldn't be as easy as you think, Mallen. Maybe you could make it on your own to Canada. I don't think we could do it together."

"I don't . . ."

Wyatt snapped on a bedside light. He was black. Purple black. The man was pure African, with deeply inset eyes of coal contrasting with distended rivers of red capillaries flowing outward from the irises into the whites of his eyes. His skin was deeply pocked by acne and the face was formed with rough panes of skin stretched over an angular skull. He smiled, the teeth even and white. "I might be noticed," he said.

"I didn't know you were black. It doesn't matter," Mallen said, now unsure.

"Yeah, it's a gas. The Wyatt name. Like I got rhythm. Vibes, man," he said, mimicking ghetto slang.

"Christ, I don't mean that. It was just your voice. Accentless."

Wyatt snorted. He leaned back on the cot, tucking one knee under his chin. "I paid over fifteen thousand plus G.I. Bill for that voice . . . accentless, as you say. Law school for five years. Specialized, woud you believe, in patent law."

Mallen looked more carefully at the black man who sat coiled neatly on the opposite bunk. He guessed that Wyatt would not exceed six feet, and yet there was a tension, perhaps, for want of a better word, about the man. The nose, broad and flat, disappeared into the face without the hint of a bridge. Mallen lowered his eyes, aware that he was staring.

"Not exactly from an old New England family, am I?" he said. Wyatt uncoiled from the cot and stood. "Do I pass inspection?" He grinned, insanely rolling his eyes from right to left and then doing a parody blackface shuffle with pink palms spread outward.

"Wayyyy down upon the Swaneee Ribber . . ." he sang softly, beginning to pluck an imaginary banjo.

Mallen stood up and faced him. "Knock off the bullshit. Nothing guarantees they won't send us down tomorrow. We make it out of here tonight. Together. I've got food, weapons, and transportation at my place, about five miles from here. So knock off the act. Can we get out of here, or not?"

Wyatt sagged down onto his cot. From underneath a rusted nightstand he withdrew a thin steel wire. He held it under the light for Mallen to see.

"Lock pick," he said. "Made it from part of the window shade spring. Tempered it with a candle flame and spit."

Mallen felt the wire. It was flame blue, with a slightly hooked point. "You tried the lock before?"

"Once," Wyatt replied. "Took me about five minutes. They're just standard locks. The P.D.'s just reversed the knobs so that the lock is on the inside of the room rather than in the hallway."

"Just like that—I mean five, ten minutes and we're out?"

Wyatt sat down on the bed, pulling a knee up under his chin, resting it there, watching Mallen carefully.

"Not that easy. Once you open the door, a light flashes on in their day room. Some electric switch in the recess of the door jamb. And, lest you forget, these guys have shotguns."

Mallen slowly expelled his breath. "So . . . ?"

"So we give it a go anyway." Wyatt got up and looked out through the barred window. "I open the door and slip out into the hall, then close the door. Their panel light will flash on and one of them will check it out. I'll be inside the crapper door opposite. He opens the door and finds you on the floor, puking. My bunk will be made up to look like I'm in it. While he's picking his nose trying to figure it out, I crunch him from behind."

"With what?"

"With these." Wyatt turned and held up his hands.

"And then?"

"You grab his shotgun to keep it from blowing me away. If I hit him right, he'll just drop the gun, but it might go off if it hits the floor. Then we get whoever else is on duty."

Mallen nodded. "They have a 'lectric parked out there?"

"Yeah, the small pickup. You can see it over on the edge of the grass. Usually plugged into the charger. It will give us about thirty miles, maybe less."

They rehearsed it a couple of times, Mallen playing the guard and Wyatt taking him from behind. Wyatt would try to snap the guard's head back with his hands while giving him a knee to the spine. He seemed to be sure it would work, but Mallen was skeptical.

"Where did you learn that hold?"

Wyatt grinned. "On the concrete sidewalks of New York, Mallen."

They made up a blanket in a roll and stuffed it into Wyatt's cot. It looked exactly like a rolled-up blanket stuffed into a cot. "It'll do," Wyatt said, shrugging. "He just has to hesitate for two seconds and I'll have him."

"What kind of equipment do they come after us with?"

"Choppers. Always choppers. And it won't be Eastern Peace Division only. Special Forces. They'll probably start looking at dawn after the shift change comes in and finds the mess."

"And our chances?"

Wyatt hunched his shoulders. "What chances? Maybe one in ten at the outside of getting away. But regardless of whether we're caught escaping or even if we just stay here and do nothing, it's still the C.C.'s and scrambled eggs for brains. I'd rather take the risk while it still exists, despite how damn thin it is." He paused, studying Mallen. "You up for this?"

Mallen looked down at his blistered hands, felt the churning in his gut. "I'm not exactly up for anything, but I'll give it a try."

Wyatt put out his hand. "Like a scene out of a Cagney Sing-Sing movie, Mallen. Everybody shakes before they start down the sewer on the big break. The black guy always makes it and the Italian kid gets two barrels of buckshot."

Using his fingertips, Mallen squeezed Wyatt's hand. "Only hope is—I'm not Italian."

". . . but you sho 'nough ain't black either, baby," said Wyatt with a lopsided smile.

Wyatt started working on the lock. In under five minutes he had it open. He was through the door and gone, shutting it softly behind him. Mallen caught the glow of a low-wattage light in the corridor.

More than a minute elapsed and Mallen heard nothing. Then a door opened, accompanied by the scratchy music. Footsteps down the hallway and a pause. Mallen jammed his finger down his throat. A little fluid, tasting of acid, filled his mouth. He gagged on it, choking, and forced his finger down his throat again. This time there was no vomit; only a series of racking coughs. A noise and he turned from his crouched position on the floor, wastebasket between his legs, to find a man, partly bald with a brush cut, standing in the door. The shotgun was held ready, cradled in both hands. The man's face was puffy from sleep, the bags beneath his eyes accentuated by the overhead bulb.

"How come . . ." he started to say and there was a snap, the sound of kindling being broken over a knee. In slow motion, Mallen watched the guard's head move backward within a necklace of black fingers . . . further back, until only the chin and the black fingers were visible above the guard's collar. The shotgun clattered to the worn asphalt flooring.

"Shit!" Wyatt hissed and grabbed up the weapon, chambering a round.

Someone called "Ziggy . . . ?" from the other room and there was the sound of a chair scraping as it was pushed back.

"Get his keys. Everything," Wyatt said between clenched teeth. "Dumb mother." He strung out the words in a curse.

Mallen still crouched stupefied on the floor, wastebasket clamped between his legs. The guard's face (how in fuck could this poor fart of a man ever be called Ziggy?) lay overlapping his own bare feet. The man must have been seventy, face unshaven with a day's growth of white stubble spreading over a flabby chin. The silver-framed eyeglasses he had worn were askew across his face, the right ear still hooked on but with the left lens sagging over the cheek. It picked out Mallen's reflection.

"Move!" Wyatt hissed. Mallen got to his feet and ruffled through the guard's clothing. Penknife. Key ring on a retracting chain. Wallet. The guard's boots were in good condition, about Mallen's size. He started to unlace them.

"Take his pants too. You'll need them," Wyatt whispered, and then they heard a door slam.

Someone said, "Ziggy . . . ?" in the hallway and there was a sound of shuffling footsteps moving toward them.

Wyatt inhaled deeply and swung out into the hallway, firing from the waist. Two shots closely spaced. The shock of the sound filled the building. Wyatt disappeared, running, and then reappeared seconds later. "That's the lot. Let's move out."

"I'm sorry," Mallen mumbled. "I screwed up. I should have . . ."

The black man looked at Mallen, eyes dilated, breathing heavily. "Yeah, you screwed up. Let's go."

The two men stripped the dead guards of boots and clothing. Moving to the day room, Wyatt lifted a third shotgun from the rack and then wasted several minutes trying to lever open the steel locker for additional cartridges, but finally gave up.

Mallen watched him, feeling useless. The initiative, if he had ever had it, was flowing to Wyatt. The man was decisive, instinctive. From the crumpled figure sitting on a cot, doing black-face mime, Wyatt had been transformed.

"Move your ass," Wyatt grunted. "Ransack those drawers for any type of form or transit pass."

Mallen checked the time on the wall clock. Twelve fifteen A.M. Six hours plus to dawn. He bent down and rifled the drawers. There were a multitude of forms, so he indiscriminately took four from each pile: yellows and grays, reds and whites.

"This way," Wyatt said, and Mallen followed him into a separate room. There Wyatt rolled Mallen's fingers over an inked pad and, with professional aplomb, rerolled them across the blank space of a pass.

"When do the vigilantes arrive?" Mallen asked, nodding toward the door.

Wyatt pulled the ghetto accent. "All de whate folk home in bed. Sheriff not comin' till dawn. Naght time fo' niggers, boy." He pushed Mallen in front of a camera. One flash, then another. "Polaroid. We'll paste them up to the passes later. Now you do me. Then my prints."

Wyatt made one final sweep of the building as Mallen stood guard near the front entrance of the school. He could hear Wyatt breaking things, overturning things, violating the building in lieu of the men who had violated him. He finally came down the stairs, holding a canister.

"Cleaning fluid," Wyatt said, grinning. In the day room, he used Ziggy's knife to pry open the wall-mounted phone box, then stuffed the white rag saturated with cleaning fluid into the guts of the instrument. With the remaining cleaning fluid, he saturated the furniture and the dead men. "Central Division in Albany rings them every morning about six. When the bell rings in the box, it sparks. This place will burn like a dried Christmas tree."

The stench of the cleaning fluid was making Mallen's eyes water. "Why this?" he said.

Wyatt moved toward the doorway, looking back. "Gives us a little more time, maybe. If it goes up like I think it will, they may think everyone died inside. Accident."

Wyatt led them out into the night. Surprised, Mallen could see the condensation of their breath. The smells were of leaves falling and spruce and maple. Clean. Not carbolic acid and sweat and urine and the stench of life leaking out of wasted bodies.

"I'll drive," Wyatt said, sliding into the 'lectric. He fumbled in the darkness, trying to fit Ziggy's numerous keys to the lock. "Fuckin' keys . . . there's got to be fifty on this ring. Looks like this is the one."

Time to level with him, Mallen thought. "Look, Wyatt, turn this thing around to the north. I'll show you the turnoff in Waitsfield."

"Think again, buddy," Wyatt said, looking ahead through the dusty windshield. Mallen looked up to see headlights approaching from the south through the village. There was a blue blinker flashing above the oncoming lights.

5

Mallen watched the blue flashing light grow larger, flickering through the night like a demented bug. The light was lost behind a curve in the road and then reappeared, coming directly toward them.

"No siren," Wyatt said softly, the breath easing from his lungs.

"No siren . . . ?"

"No siren, no problem. They always use the blue light at night. Priority traffic."

Mallen watched the headlights grow larger, sweeping up the short grade from the village. "I hope to Christ you're right."

Wordlessly, Wyatt shoved Mallen down onto the seat and then leaned over him, his head beneath the level of the windshield. Mallen heard the whine of the 'lectric decelerating, then stopping, just feet from their own vehicle. Noises: a door opening and a mumble, boots crunching on the gravel, and the soft sounds of voices moving away.

"They didn't plug in the recharging cord," Wyatt whispered, levering himself up to window level. "Which means they're not planning to stay long."

"How did they find out?"

"Didn't," Wyatt said. "Routine patrol. Stopping to bullshit and drink coffee. They're too casual for any kind of an alert."

Mallen gripped the cool metal of the shotgun more tightly. "Let's get going."

Wyatt shook his head adamantly in the darkness, the gesture absolute. "We can't," he hissed. "If we don't kill them both, those guys in there will be on the phone to Albany in another thirty seconds." He was already moving, taking a shotgun and opening the door. "Cover the front of the building," he said over his shoulder and was blotted up by the darkness.

Mallen felt infinitely tired, impossibly fatigued. He climbed down the 'lectric and chambered a round into the 12-gauge. He wasn't frightened, he realized, just something comparable to those last few seconds that one experiences as an airplane starts to come apart on you in a crash and you react in slow motion, watching the world spin, knowing that the metallic taste in your mouth is death, but still more curious than frightened. That comes later, when you live—the shaking and the incoherence and the triphammer heart.

The door of the schoolhouse was closed and the lights still burned evenly inside. Very normal. Late PTA meeting. Mallen propped the 12-gauge on the hood of the vehicle and held it closely against his shoulder. His breath made little clouds in the darkness, and it was getting colder. He wanted to chafe his hands together for warmth.

Sixty seconds had elasped, he calculated, no more than that. Still lights were burning in the schoolhouse. No outcry, no . . .

From somewhere in the back of the building there was the unmistakable roar of a shotgun. The echo rolled around the valley and was blotted up by the dying foliage, then it repeated—but this time he could see a flame of white light and the blast wasn't as muffled.

Someone was shouting from within the building, and there was a rapid exchange of shots, then the sound of a man's scream.

Mallen tensed, bringing the shotgun harder against his shoulder, watching the door. Two more shots came from within the building and one of the windows blew out in a shatter of broken glass. Dogs were barking in the village below and he wondered how long it would go on. Goddamn Wyatt, he thought, and lowered the shotgun long enough to wipe a trickle of sweat from his eye.

A dull explosion came from within the building, followed by a yellow flare of light, then a secondary explosion. Mallen's heart was starting to pound. He realized he was panting.

The front door of the schoolhouse slammed open and a man-thing staggered through the doorway, hair ablaze. The thing was frantic, beating at his face with his hands, uttering thin, piercing squeals so high in register as to be almost inaudible. And as a branch of pine that has been lying on hot embers will sometimes do, the thing's jacket burst spontaneously into an enveloping flame.

A shotgun blast from within the schoolhouse bucked the thing forward onto the dry grass. Mallen had seen the muzzle blast and another man emerged, running toward him. He raised the barrel but realized it was Wyatt.

"Shoot the fucker," Wyatt screamed across the lawn.

Mallen shifted his aim. The thing was on all fours now, its head lowered, crawling. The grass around it was beginning to catch fire. Mallen hesitated.

"Give me that!" Wyatt screamed, and tore the weapon from Mallen's hands, then turned and fired. The thing crumpled. Wyatt shot again and it was thrown backward into a heap. It didn't move now and, incredibly, the flame was extinguished.

"Let's go," said Wyatt. He pushed Mallen toward the far side of the 'lectric. "You drive. I took some damage. Can't see well."

Wyatt slid in after Mallen and pulled the door shut, still holding the shotgun in his right hand. He groped along the dash and turned the key. A relay under the hood chattered. Mallen stabbed at the accelerator, expecting nothing. The 'lectric bucked and leaped ahead.

"Easy," Wyatt said. "Do it easy. The motor doesn't idle. Push to go . . . and drop off . . . pedal to stop. No brakes much." He was starting to slur the words, his voice becoming fuzzy

Mallen turned carefully, trying to adjust his technique

to the machine. The U turn was ragged, overrunning the opposite side of the road, but he didn't want to risk trying to find out how to put the machine in reverse. He looked back at the schoolhouse, seeing it still whole but lighted internally by a white flaring light.

The 'lectric rolled noiselessly along the fractured road, no more than a box of wood propelled by batteries. Insanely, Mallen enjoyed it. Duster and goggles, he thought. The weak headlights probed into the darkness. Wyatt groaned by his side.

"How bad?" Mallen asked.

Wyatt didn't answer immediately, shaking his head, hunched over. In the lights of the dash, Mallen could see the dark wetness of Wyatt's forehead. Mallen drove on, past blistered picket fences in the outskirts of Warren Village, past the country store with gasoline pumps scrofulous with rust and disuse, past houses set back from the road, dark and silent.

"How bad is it?" he repeated. Mallen realized that he didn't know Wyatt's first name.

"Don' know," Wyatt said, almost inaudibly. "Glass shattered. Mother hit me with . . ." He slumped back against the seat, his breathing hoarse.

"I didn't fire on the guy that came out," Mallen started to say in explanation. "He was burning."

Wyatt nodded, barely moving his head. He turned with effort toward Mallen. "Burning . . . yeah, . . . that's why I shot him. . . . derstand?"

Mallen nodded. "I understand."

They drove over an iron bridge with a plaque that said it was the Mad River, and down past a farm that edged the two-lane asphalt road, walled tight on either side by dead stalks of corn.

As he drove, Mallen wondered how many of the people were left. Roberts rarely referred to it. Ten, 15 percent of the population left? The old ones and the children would have gone first. And the stupid ones. His mind nagged at him, telling him that he was avoiding a decision.

Mallen watched the twin probes of light jiggle over

the pavement, a pair of lead dogs in traces pulling them on. Where the lights go, we go. We. Wyatt was badly injured. It would be easy, he thought, with Wyatt gone. More fuel, less weight. And Canada.

He waited for a straight stretch and then looked closely. Wyatt's face and hair were covered with congealing blood, and his eyes were closed.

Curve. The 'lectric ran onto the shoulder of the road and Mallen wrestled it back, past a cluster of shops on the left, all dark. A sign flashed in the headlights: EGGS THURSDAY. It was written in chalk, barely readable. He thought of Roberts, always bringing eggs, which half the time were bad.

Down into Waitsfield now, with the buildings larger and more clustered together, humming by places that he had known in other years. Past the Ark Restaurant, which now had no name and no late lights and no swarm of drunken skiers in the bar, posing in the hearth light with tanned faces and white teeth. Past Andy's Cycle Shop and the Village Grocery, all familiar yet alien. Past the red brick ugliness of the Joslin Memorial Library where the St. Bernard had always blocked the door with his heaving body and a visitor had to knock first or suffer a growl and a hurt expression from the animal, and the librarian who owned him apologized if you were from out of town. The "Joslin" was boarded over with a wooden sign that said "Youth".

Mallen ignored the turnoff to the common road and kept to the main highway, carefully counting driveways on the left. One, two, past the open-air market and the old soccer field, then he swung left into a rutted lane. The 'lectric took it well, humming a little louder and slowing, but still moving up the steep grade in comparative silence. He crested the top of the small rise and then rolled down a shallow incline past a weathered barn. A sign on the rusted mailbox said Roberts.

The house was a clapboard affair of utilitarian boxiness, two stories high. The front-porch steps were missing. Cordwood was stacked nearly a story high on the north side of the house.

Mallen stopped the machine and sat in the darkness, listening. Wyatt's breathing was shallow and rapid.

A few minutes elapsed, then the front door opened and Roberts stuck his head out: a tortoise's neck, long and scawny, swaying from side to side. He carried an oil lamp that did no more than illuminate his own face.

"It's me," Mallen called. He heard Roberts say something over his shoulder and there was some kind of muffled reply from within the house.

"You got the Peace Division there? What for?" Roberts was coming out farther onto the porch.

Mallen switched off the lights and walked across the lawn into the dim illumination of Roberts's lamp. The old man held the lamp extended, looking closely at Mallen's rumpled, loose-fitting jacket. Ziggy's jacket.

"Jesus, mistah!" Roberts whispered, backing away. "Get the hell outta heah!"

Mallen caught the old man by the collar of his bathrobe and twisted it. "I am, but first you're going to help me. Tell your woman to keep off the phone. If they come, I'll tell them you helped me."

The woman came onto the porch carrying a little .22-caliber rifle. It looked like a toy in her hands, but she was pointing it toward Mallen. She stopped beyond the flare of the lamp, and it was impossible to read her expression, but her voice had the flat expression of hate.

"You're Mallen," she said. "Josh tells me about you." She stepped forward with the rifle aimed at Mallen's stomach. "One of them people that came to play in the valley. Sittin' up there on a ton of food and ammunition, squeezing us. And laughin'."

"I've got a sick man," Mallen said. "He needs help."

"And us down here," she continued, ignoring him. "We got to cooperate. Work for the government. Nine outta ten bushels of our corn goes to them. Barely enough to live on. And we got nine points accumulated, saved up for winter clothes." She was raising the rifle a little, but he could see that her finger wasn't on the trigger.

"Nine points for winter clothes and specials. And

even if they think we're not guilty, we'll lose them 'cause of you."

She moved forward into the lamplight, raising the rifle like a club. Roberts stopped the downward stroke with his right hand and shoved her away. She stumbled backward, tripped on her nightdress, and fell heavily to the porch. She sat there, crying, the little gun useless in her hand.

Mallen moved to help her up, feeling a sense of guilt and shame, as if he had watched his parents fighting. She swung the rifle toward him in frustration. He took it from her and threw it into the darkness.

"There's a man in the 'lectric," he said, turning to Roberts. "You have to help me get him inside."

"You're not leavin' him here," Roberts said flatly. The woman was still crying, her breath catching in her throat.

"No, but the sooner you help, the sooner we leave." He pushed Roberts toward the vehicle. Wyatt was dead weight and it took minutes to get him inside.

It wasn't as bad as he thought. Wyatt's scalp and neck were lacerated with particles of glass, and a lump bulged from behind his ear. Wyatt groaned a little as the woman irrigated the wounds with hot water. She had laid out an oilcloth on the linoleum floor of the sitting room, but the water, mixing with blood, had overflowed and pooled in the shallow depressions of the worn flooring.

"A mess this will be to clean up," she said under her breath. "The wound's as clean as I can make it and the blood's clotting, but I've seen worse." She mopped at the overflow with Wyatt's jacket.

"You have any antibiotics?" Mallen asked.

She replied too quickly. "No." She avoided Mallen's eyes. "He's the black man that we heard they caught last week. This is him, isn't it?"

Mallen ignored her, turning to Roberts. "You've got antibiotics. Get them!"

Roberts shrank under Mallen's stare. "Get 'em, Sally," he said, sitting down heavily into a tattered chair. He wiped the bridge of his nose, worrying at the mass of burst capillaries there. Reaching over to a table, he picked up a bottle and passed it to Mallen. "Have some, it's yours anyway. I ain't got the plugs yet."

Mallen took a slug, the liquor hot in his throat. Christ, it felt good. He took another. "What kind of antibiotics do you have?" he asked, passing the bottle to Roberts.

"Tetracycline. Way outta date. I don't know whether it'll be any good."

Sally came back into the room and gave a tube to Mallen—thirty capsules or so. Mallen pocketed them. "Bandage him up and we'll be going." She nodded.

Roberts drank and handed the bottle back. "What happened?" he wondered, nodding toward Wyatt.

Mallen took another belt, the whiskey smoother this time. He could feel it warming his stomach. He tried to belch, but couldn't. Roberts was looking at him hard.

"Not much. They picked me up yesterday. We got out tonight. We're heading south with the 'lectric."

"The medicine," Roberts said. "It costs."

"Take the twenty-two caliber shells in the cabin. They're in a coffee can on the rafter plate in my bedroom. Anything else I can leave?"

"The books, too," Roberts said.

"The books too," Mallen replied.

The woman came back into the room, tearing strips from a floral-printed sheet. She kneeled down and started to wrap Wyatt's neck and head. Mallen could see the curvature of her breasts exposed as her nightgown fell partially open. There was the suggestion of a nipple behind the fold of the lapel. Odd, he thought. I haven't seen a woman in two years and even this doesn't do anything. She couldn't be more than in her late thirties, and in some gray and tatty way she was attractive. He had the desire to look more closely at her face, to see whether there was any warmth in her eyes.

Clothes for the winter must have higher priority than

another man's life, he thought. How many points would she get for me right now? Four sweaters. A wool coat. Boots. Bernshine had said it. Doing right gets points.

"It's finished," she said, rising. "Now get out." There was no warmth in her eyes. She pushed her dull blond hair away from her forehead.

Roberts helped him get Wyatt to the 'lectric. It was decidedly colder now, the effort of their movements causing a fog of condensed breath about them. The night air was very still.

"You won't say nothin', will you?" Roberts wheezed. "About being here tonight."

Mallen shook his head. "Not unless you or your wife do."

Roberts cackled, flashing his yellow teeth in the darkness. "Wife?" he cackled again. "Ain't my wife. She's my wife's younger sister. My wife died two weeks after the war. Sally just came here and took over the bed." He chortled again, moving away in the darkness toward the house. Mallen heard the laughter even after Roberts had closed the door. I forgot the goddamn whiskey, he thought, but knew he couldn't bear facing Roberts again.

This time he kept the lights off. His eyes were accustomed to the darkness, and he kept the speed to a crawl going down the driveway.

He waited fifteen feet back from the main road, watching in both directions for any movement or lights. Nothing happened, no movement, except as stars and planets tracked through a fraction of an arc. He pulled out onto the asphalt highway heading back toward Waitsfield, trying to estimate the time, but gave it up. From the ridge he would have a better idea. Stars are the best clock if you can read them, he thought. Shock resistant, waterproof, ab-so-lutely guaranteed by their maker.

He turned off to the east, over the covered bridge. There was just the wisp of fog from the streambed lying like dirty linen on the road. He cut through it in electric silence, the chain drive singing a barely audible G below middle C.

Wyatt hadn't lost much blood, he reasoned. Concussion maybe, or just shock. The dullness was gone from his skin and he was moving a little, saying incoherent words. His breathing was slower now, and less shallow.

Mallen kept flipping coins in his mind, trying to decide whether he should take Wyatt or leave him.

Personally, he realized that he hadn't done a goddamn thing other than puke in a wastepaper basket. Wyatt had organized the whole thing and executed most of it. A good word, *executed*. But taking Wyatt was a real liability. It meant cutting down on the supplies to stay within the weight limitations of the Sperber, and, on top of that, Wyatt would have a better chance of survival if he could rest for three or four days. Assuming he wasn't caught. Which was unlikely.

If he did take Wyatt, he would have to pare down the supplies to a maximum of ten days' food, an additional five gallons of fuel, and the weapons, tent, and sleeping bags. Even that sounded as if it were too much. Still time to make that decision, he thought.

Mallen found the turnoff without difficulty and drove up the rutted access road past the first bend before stopping. Finding the switch on the dash, he turned off the 'lectric. A relay flopped into relaxation, and he could hear only the sounds of Wyatt's slow exhalations and the forest night trying to sound primeval.

Mallen opened the door and slid out into the blackness. It was quite cold now, colder than it had been in the valley. Turning his head up toward the sky, he could see marshmallows of white vapor from his own lungs. He tried blowing a smoke ring and succeeded in producing something that looked like a fuzzy milk bottle. Things were going *tickticktick* and *gezzzz*, but it sounded familiar—just basic Walden Pond noises.

He groped around and found a decent-size tree and urinated with relief against the bark, forming more clouds. First pee in twenty or so hours, but then again, come to think of it, he hadn't had anything to eat or drink.

He buttoned up his (Ziggy's) fly, noting that the buttons were wood. Capitalistic zippers banished forever, thus saving the masses from having their proletariat peckers pinched. Progress, comrades, is ours for the buttoning.

Mallen felt good, almost giddy. The tiredness was laying back, taking it easy. Still reserves as yet untapped. The alcohol, after all, had had some effect, but he needed food soon, and then he could face the other decisions. He walked forward, feeling for the ruts. Dry leaves fluttered under his shoes, and things sometimes ran across his path. Where the double set of birches bracketed the road, like apostrophes, he felt for the first tripwire. The wire was broken. Ziggy's uniform felt suddenly much warmer. Mallen moved slowly forward in a crouch, waving his hand in front of him, feeling for the second wire. The fact that he could have brought the shotgun nagged at him. Survival was no longer playing the "Hall of the Mountain King," picking nuts, and reading Conrad. Survival now was what Wyatt already somehow had known—cordite and reactions and planning even small things very carefully. The second wire was okay. He sighed in the darkness and the sound of a branch rubbing against another mocked him.

He went back to the 'lectric and removed the shotgun, feeding shells into his hand as he worked the pump. A total of five, with maybe eight more in the cabin.

Wyatt moved and said, "Where?"

"Almost home," Mallen replied, which sounded like a safe thing to say. "How do you feel?"

"Hurt like hell." Wyatt made a sucking sound between his teeth and tried to sit upright.

Mallen put his hand on Wyatt's shoulder. "Relax. We're out of the valley."

"How long before dawn?"

Mallen looked up at the night sky. Orion was almost

down in the west. Four hours, maybe less. "Enough," he said.

The 'lectric was surprisingly agile in the rutted lane, taking the ruts easily, with its high ground clearance. The giddiness was wearing away and being replaced by dull depression. Mallen was tired; his eyelids felt like blocks of lead. Two miles more.

The lane was arched over with maples, most with some foliage left. He decided that the risk of switching on the lights would be minimal now, so turned them on, startling a deer paused in the lane. A flick of its tail and the animal crashed off into the brush, pausing once to look back. We all run from something, he thought.

They broke through the trees into the south meadow and Mallen switched off the lights. Unlikely, he thought, that anyone would have staked out the cabin, but it was worth checking. He dropped to the ground, taking the shotgun, and worked his way up through the meadow and around behind the cabin. The alcohol was working out of his system, leaving in its wake a grinding headache. He listened at the back wall of the cabin but heard nothing except the sounds of the night.

The interior of the cabin was just as he had left it. First drawing the kitchen curtains, he lit a lamp, then shoved kindling into the stove. He added pages from an old magazine and kerosene, and touched a match to it.

They made their way up to the cabin, Mallen guiding Wyatt through the withered rubble of corn stalks and dried sunflowers. Wyatt was weak but he pushed on, running on some internal reserve of energy, uncomplaining. His teeth chattered in the early autumn frost and Mallen, in supporting him, found the bandage wet with blood.

They paused at the foot of the steps, Wyatt panting now, despite the easy grade. He wanted to sit down on the steps, but Mallen prodded him on, half carrying him to the kitchen.

Mallen moved Wyatt onto the cot, covered him with a blanket, and turned to the wood stove, feeding it splintered blocks of maple.

"How . . ." Wyatt began, moving his hands against the bandage.

"At my cabin. Get some rest. I'm making food soon. We can eat and then get going at dawn."

Wyatt mumbled something and lay back, mouth open, sucking in air. "Call me," he whispered.

"I will," Mallen said, knowing the decision had been made.

Mallen spent an hour loading the Sperber and checking it over in the dim light of an oil lamp. With the tanks topped off, he filtered some of the fuel Roberts had brought and filled a five-gallon jug, which he then lashed in the cargo hold. The oil supply was shy a pint and he added a quart, overfilling it slightly. The rest of the preflight was superfluous, checks he had made weekly for almost two years. After pulling the prop through three turns to get the oil circulated prior to start, he climbed back up to the cabin. That much was ready, he told himself.

Wyatt was sitting up at the table drinking coffee.

Mallen pulled down the skillet and set it on the stove. "You feeling better?"

Wyatt nodded, half opening his eyes. "I guess I did a fade on you after the fight. I wasn't out much. Just kept feeling dizzy and let it slide. Like falling off to sleep with a hangover already going."

"The head hurt?"

"Like a fuckin' bomb went off."

Mallen set the tube of tetracycline tablets down on the table, then added two tablets that he fished out of a jar bearing a label in Anne's handwriting, now long faded into illegibility. "Codeine," he said. "The ones in the tube are antibiotics. Two of each."

Wyatt pushed a snort of disgust out through his nostrils. "Yeah. Codeine I can use. The other . . . I doubt that I'm going to die of an infection."

Drawing a mug of cold water from the crock, Mallen set it down on the table. Without arguing, Wyatt took two of each, making noisy, gulping sounds.

The skillet was crackling hot. Mallen opened the tinned ham and cut off four slices, adding a can of mushroom soup over the top. The fat started to bubble and the smell of food that they could barely remember filled the room. Wyatt opened his mouth in a silent laugh, stroking the edge of his teeth with his tongue.

"You live right, Mallen."

"This is prewar. Stuff we can't take, we can eat." He flipped the ham over. Mallen had to swallow repeatedly to get rid of the saliva that filled his mouth. He poured himself a cup of coffee, adding some to Wyatt's cup.

"What's your first name?" Wyatt said between sips.

"Greg."

"Gregory. Good WASP name."

"A pope was called . . ."

"Gregory," Wyatt said. "Yeah, I know. Gregory the Seventh, 1073 to 1085. Also called Hildebrand." He paused, playing with a fork. "You planning to leave me here, Greg?"

"The thought had occurred, ah . . ."

"George. George W. Wyatt. The *W* stands for Washington. Noted slave owner. First in the hearts of his countrymen." He paused, feeling the bandage. "You're right, of course."

"About what?" Mallen flipped the ham slices onto two plates and set them on the table.

"About leaving me here. No good for either of us. I can't travel much with this wound. Couldn't walk twenty steps."

Mallen forked up a mouthful of ham and chewed. "Wasn't planning on walking out."

"Forget the 'lectric. Too slow and no range. Forget a car. It's been tried. You wouldn't get fifteen miles before you ran into a roadblock."

Mallen forked up another mouthful. "Plane," he said. "Two-place with five-, maybe six-hundred-mile range."

Wide-eyed, Wyatt stared at him. He flapped his arms a little and Mallen nodded.

Ignoring his food, Wyatt wanted to know everything.

Between forkfuls, Mallen sketched out the details, finally asking what Wyatt weighed.

Wyatt looked up, raising his eyebrows, fork poised in midtrajectory. "One sixty-six, maybe less after this last week. Why?"

"Trying to figure how much we can take."

"I can take all kinds of stuff on my lap. Pile it up on top of me if you like."

Mallen shook his head. "It's not space, it's weight. Too much and the aircraft will be tail heavy. There are some trees we have to get over at the end of the meadow."

"Where we going?" Wyatt asked, fishing a package of cigarettes out of a pocket. He offered one to Mallen.

"Northeast. With the wind from the southwest, it gives us maximum range and speed. Land anywhere we can up there, as long as there isn't much population. Hang tight for a week until they give up trying to find us, then head for western Canada. We'll have to scrounge fuel where we can find it."

Wyatt nodded. "Sounds okay by me. You've done the planning."

Using the Tiffany lighter, Mallen lit both their cigarettes.

"Gracious living," Wyatt said, nodding his head toward the lighter. He blew out a long stream of blue smoke toward the ceiling.

Mallen turned the lighter over in his hands, trying to see down through the depths of glass, seeing only fractured visions of the past. "From a friend," he said.

"Woman friend . . . wife?"

"Almost."

"She's gone?" Wyatt was watching his eyes.

Mallen nodded. "Gone." Upon the ridge under a pile of dirt. He set the lighter on the cupboard shelf beyond his range of vision.

They smoked in silence for some minutes, each keeping to himself. Finally Mallen stuffed out his cigarette and stood up.

"You get some more sleep," he said. "I'll wake you again just before dawn."

Wyatt kept his eyes on the ceiling, blowing smoke rings. Without preamble, he started to talk, keeping his voice expressionless. "It's not what you think, Mallen. I didn't enjoy killing those men. It was just something that had to be done." His voice was precise now, all trace of the affected ghetto accent gone.

"I didn't do much," Mallen said with a shrug.

"No, but you could have left me. You would have had a better chance by yourself."

"I thought about it. Thought about leaving you with the farmer. Maybe hoping you would just die." He stacked the dishes in the bucket. "But then I figured that I had to catch the rest of your act—the Mr. Bojangles bit."

Their eyes met and Wyatt smiled.

"You'll do, Mallen," he said. "You'll do."

6

Dawn had started to fracture the eastern skyline shortly after five by the clock on the instrument panel of the Sperber. Mallen paused beside the open canopy, watching the ridge, tinted by reds, grow distinct. Trees began to assume shape and texture. Outcroppings of granite, flecked with mica, glittered in the first light. It would be a fine day.

He made a check of the controls, the stick cold to his touch. Two years is a long time not to fly, he thought, and packed the remainder of the tinned food into the luggage hold.

One trip back up to the cabin. The batteries in the 'lectric were deteriorating rapidly and he reflected that Wyatt's estimate of its range was probably optimistic.

Wyatt was still sleeping on the cot, shotgun on the floor near his trailing fingertips. His face twitched occasionally in sleep.

" 'Bye 'bye time," Mallen said as he shook Wyatt's foot. He came awake almost instantly, as though he were a machine that had been switched on—no panic in his eyes, no confusion.

"What time is it?"

"Dawn. We're going."

Wyatt rose carefully, favoring his neck. The bandage was black with dried blood and Mallen could smell the taint of decay.

"I've thought about it, Mallen," he said, working the muscles of his neck. "You go without me."

"We discussed that already. You're going."

"Your chances are better without me. Just getting the plane off."

97

Mallen took him by the arm. "Shut up and let's go. It's my turn to pick up the tab."

They drove together to the grove, the fields frosted in glittering white. Neither man said much, thinking of the coming day. Mallen finally pushed it from his mind. Thinking too much destroys reflexes; the gut feelings were best. He glanced at the stand of high trees on the far side of the meadow. Too high, his mind said. Fuck it, his subconscious answered.

"Christ! I thought you said you had an airplane. This goddamn thing's a toy!" Wyatt walked around the aircraft, rapping his knuckles on the fabric-covered surface. He turned back to Mallen. "Shit! This thing is made outta tissue paper."

Mallen was enjoying it. "Fabric and plywood. What do you think they flew in the thirties?" He showed Wyatt the rest of the aircraft, feeling both amusement and pride. Clever, clever, Mallen.

It was then that they heard the choppers. The valley echoed with the sharp blat of their exhausts, and Mallen recognized the noise as piston-driven engines, not turbines. The Sperber was hidden in a grove of sugar maples half a mile from the cabin, and over the aircraft Mallen had nailed up panels of canvas to protect the aircraft both from weather and from casual, low-flying planes. But he wasn't so sure this cover would stand up to close inspection from a slow-moving helicopter.

"We've been had," Wyatt said, looking down the valley with his eyes shaded against the brightness. "I never expected them to come this soon."

Mallen was listening intently, trying to judge the number of choppers and their comparative size. Wyatt was still mumbling, and Mallen, turning to him, snapped, "Shut up and let me listen."

It sounded as if there were two, possibly three choppers, but they sounded like small ones, something that would carry three or perhaps four men. Excluding pilots, this might mean a maximum number of nine men in the strike force.

He caught sight of one coming in fast over the knoll.

The sun shone on the bubble canopy and the blades carved a sunlit swath in the blue autumn air. The chopper wheeled up in a turn and flew back toward the direction that it had come, doing a quartering search over the common road. The type of helicopter didn't look familiar in design—not Bell or Hughes or Sikorsky. Possibly something of Russian design. But the glance confirmed Mallen's initial impression that it was a light utility chopper. It held a pilot and three men. There didn't seem to be an ordnance rack on the belly, so its firepower would be limited to hand-held automatic weapons. Speed: probably in excess of 100 knots, but not much greater. The engine noise didn't suggest much horsepower.

Mallen got the rifle from the Sperber's back seat and took the Luger from its holster in the front. Wyatt's eyes gleamed at the sight of the telescopically equipped Winchester. He took it from Mallen and sighted it awkwardly from his left shoulder. Mallen shook his head and took it back, handing him the Luger.

"No good," he said. "You can't fire left-handed with that bandage. The Luger will be good enough."

Wyatt nodded. "Okay, what now? Do we fly, or not?"

"Yes, we fly. But not until we absolutely have to. There are two, maybe three choppers in the valley. They're probably carrying close to full loads, and they'll be using up fuel at a fantastic rate. What we want is for one or two of them to get low and return to base for fuel, probably Montpelier. That leaves one chopper left. Our chances are a lot better with just one to deal with, and if we get airborne and he doesn't catch us in half an hour, he'll be out of fuel."

"How much range does this thing have?" Wyatt pronounced *thing* as if the Sperber didn't quite qualify as an airplane.

"About five-hundred miles the way we'll be flying it. Possibly more if we can use lower power settings and get to high altitude."

"And the choppers?"

Mallen scuffed the dirt with his boot, thinking. "Two

hundred maximum. But they would probably be ten to fifteen miles per hour faster."

Wyatt stared down the valley, his eyes unfocused. He turned back to Mallen and said, "Well, if my math is right, we'll need about a twenty-mile head start. How much time does that take?"

"Twelve minutes, maybe. We'll be climbing at gross weight at not much more than seventy."

"She . . . it." Wyatt looked down at the Luger. "You'd better show me how to cock and fire this thing."

Mallen showed him how to work the toggle and the safety and change clips. "But don't use it unless they get really close in. We'll use the rifle for medium range."

By now the sun was well clear of the ridge. The morning was warming rapidly as it will after a cold autumn night. The choppers were occasionally visible farther down south in the valley as they worked outward from the village. Mallen could count only two choppers, one with a yellow tail rotor and the other coated in a darker shade of khaki paint, as if it was newer.

They opened a can of peaches and ate them with their fingertips, splitting the syrup equally. Mallen noticed that Wyatt took the tetracycline but not the codeine.

Wyatt, licking his lips, saw the glance and said, "Too much going on this morning, man. Don't want to be drowsy."

"How's the head feel?"

Wyatt cocked an eyebrow at him. "You're joking! Like a nuke went off inside my skull." He looked out over the grassy field. "We take off on that? I've seen bigger gardens."

Mallen nodded. "It's short," he conceded. "I've paced it off at just over eight hundred feet, but it's downhill, and that gives us some additional margin to get over the trees. There's a trench in the middle, but I've filled it in and laid some boards over the soft earth. We've got to hit it just right."

"You sure you can make it?"

Mallen puckered his lips for a second. "Nope. About eighty percent sure. It'll be close."

"But if you didn't have my fat ass in the back seat you'd make it?"

Mallen shrugged. "That isn't up for discussion. I've computed the thing as closely as I can, adding a fudge factor, and I think we can make it. We go together or we stay together."

Wyatt looked at him with a little smile of amusement. "They always told us that white people was dumb critters." He managed a grin. "But I doubt that we've got a choice." He nodded toward the Sperber. "How much warm-up time on the engine? If we have to get out of here quickly."

Mallen stood up, slinging the Winchester over his shoulder. "Two or three minutes. But relax. It'll be a while yet before they get low on fuel, and I figure they're combing the fields outward from the village. I'll be right back."

"Where you going?"

"Something I forgot to do." Mallen started toward the cabin.

Wyatt hunched down by a stump and shaded his eyes. "Don't be long, Cap'n, and whistle something like 'Dixie' when you start coming back through the trees."

Mallen walked carefully up along the perimeter of the woods, stopping and listening for the sound of voices or the crack of a branch beneath a boot. A crow cawed, but beyond that there was just the sigh of wind in the grass.

It was one of those mornings in late autumn that Vermont gives up with reluctance, with a pure white hot sun and a sky polished clean of haze. The fields were still wet with melting frost, clumps of rye grass barely nodding in the light wind from the west. Two squirrels disputed each other's territory, and there was a smell of permanence as if nothing had changed and alterations in the land were measured in centuries.

Instead of heading for the cabin, Mallen cut across

the corn field and climbed the steep escarpment to the ridge. Winded, he worked up the final slope, then sat down under the wild apple tree that shaded her grave. There were deer tracks on the ground and he could see where the grass was flattened from their bodies. Sighing, he lit a cigarette.

The choppers were still working over the lower valley. Like dogs quartering a trail, they cut back and forth, setting up a deep, metallic braying. It wouldn't be long before they were low on fuel. And then it would be time to go.

From the ridge he could see much of the valley, spectacular as it always had been in the fall. Flame colors in the higher elevations were licking down the slopes toward the valley floor, but one day soon, with the first of the equinoctial gales, the leaves would be stripped overnight, leaving the branches bare and knocking in the wind. Along the center of the valley, Mallen could see glinting reflections from the river and sandbars, prominent from the lack of autumn rain. The only scars were isolated brown areas where whole sections of spruce had burst into combustion.

He took one last look and stubbed out the cigarette.

Her grave was now just a shallow depression in the ground, marked by a field rock on which he had chiseled her name. There was nothing for him to say; no words that he knew, no prayer he believed in. Finally, he stood up and made his duck sound, flapping his arms a little, knowing that it was foolish, knowing also that she would have liked it. Then again, he realized, neither of us ever learned how to say good-bye.

The fields around the cabin were still empty. He paused in his movements coming back from the ridge, keeping to the trees, watching; but nothing yet.

"See anything?" Wyatt moved from behind the maple, the Luger held at his side.

"Nothing. All quiet on the western front. Both choppers still playing tag over the Waitsfield area. I think that it's about time to warm up the engine." He rested the Winchester against a tree and turned back to Wyatt.

"Keep a good lookout toward the lower meadow. If they come overland, they'll probably come from that direction."

Wyatt made a circle with his thumb and index finger and squatted down, chewing on a piece of dead straw as he watched the fields below. Hunched over as he was, he looked like a black, muscular gargoyle. And a damn tough one, too, Mallen reflected.

Rather than use the electric starter, he chose to prop the engine over by hand. The battery was starting to lose its punch, and it would be best if the engine was warm and the charge peaked when they finally had to go. He opened the choke with the magneto off, cracked the throttle an inch, and set the brake up hard. Keeping well clear, Mallen flipped the little wood Hoffman prop through two revolutions to prime the cylinders and break the adhesion of the sluggish oil. Moving back to the cockpit, he switched on the master electrical switch, fuel boost pump, and mag switch.

One quick pull of the prop was all it took to start the small VW motor. With its large, stainless-steel muffler there was only the suggestion of exhaust noise. Mallen watched the gauges for a few minutes and then, when the engine was warm, pushed the choke closed. The engine picked up a hundred rpms and the exhaust gas was now as transparent as October sunlight. He grimaced at the thought of the plugs—electrodes badly pitted—that would cause some loss of power. What I've got will have to do, he thought bitterly. Roberts had probably lied about getting replacements.

With the engine running, he didn't hear the chopper until it was almost overhead. Its shadow stroked through the foliage and it was gone, whump-whumping north over the meadow. He moved out from under the canvas to the edge of the trees and could just see it hovering to the south of the cabin. He didn't like it. McKennon was pressing the issue earlier than expected. Good tactics would have been to establish where Mallen and Wyatt were, then drop the troops in to encircle them. McKennon was pulling a frontal attack.

The amplified and distorted voice of a bullhorn howled along the meadow and echoed back from the granite ridge.

"Mall . . . en . . . en. Come . . . um . . . um. Out . . . ta . . . ta."

The helicopter hovered, swaying slightly from side to side in the roughness of the morning air. He could see a figure on the pilot's side hanging out of the aircraft and holding a weapon of some sort. The bullhorn repeated the message and there were some other words. Then, distinctly, he heard a laugh. It echoed back from the ridge and was swallowed by the forest.

It was then that he thought of the radio. Ass, ass, ass that he was. Dumbass. The choppers would be using regular aircraft frequencies to coordinate the search. If their frequency wasn't in the higher military bands, he would be able to find it and have firsthand knowledge of their movements.

The second chopper, Yellow Tail, flew along the ridge and angled west beyond Mallen's range of vision, probably assuming a similar position to the north of the cabin. He could hear its blades change pitch as it took up station.

Wyatt was moving through the trees toward him now, running low, his right hand holding the bandage but the Luger clenched in the fingers of his left.

"What now?" he asked, calm and not breathing hard, but Mallen suddenly realized that the game of leader was now his; Wyatt had relinquished the role.

"One shot with the rifle. Just one, and not to kill— just to worry." Mallen got the Winchester and set in five hundred yards on the elevation. Long, but the target was huge. If the shot was too good, he might bring the copter down, but that would put three or four armed men on the ground with automatic weapons and the options would be greatly restricted. Just one shot, close enough to make them cautious.

He rested the barrel in a crotch of a branch, chambered a round, and aimed for the aft section of the bubble. Breathe in, exhale a little and squeezeeee. The shot got off cleanly with no jerk. At first he didn't think he had scored, but in seconds the chopper dipped its nose and surged forward, its pitch changing. He lost it to sight.

He ran back to the Sperber and snapped on the radio, impatient now and blindly furious for his stupidity. He clamped on the headset and started to index through the channels, looking for their transmissions. He found them easily enough on 123.8. The exchanges were fast, professional, nonstop. . . . *teen and move back ovah section nine.* The voice was southern, flat as Alabama.

> *PD Nine back. Roger. We're sweeping the area south. Can't tell exactly where the shot came from. Springmaker's cut up by Plexiglas and shit. You want us to drop him back at ground control?*

This one was a young, mid-Atlantic accent.

A third voice broke in, unmistakably McKennon.

> *Both units, this is ground control. Drop Springmaker back down here. I'm taking his place. PD Five: Hold north of the cabin at five hundred meters or more. We'll be up in about ten minutes and then we'll pincer him. I've got ground troops on the way.*

PD Five acknowledged and, in the distance, the tone of an engine picked up, adding power for the climb. The other chopper was gone, pushing south for the valley floor.

Mallen rechecked the panel. Engine-oil temperature up to operating limits, everything steady on the gauges. Three or four minutes for the returning chopper to get to the valley floor, a minute for transfer, then maybe five minutes for the return flight. He checked the panel clock.

"Time to go," he told Wyatt. "Leave the shotgun. We don't have the room."

Two minutes gone.

Wyatt tucked himself into the aft cockpit, pulling the straps on the safety harness tight. He stuck out his hand and Mallen hesitantly took it. Wyatt squeezed. "You know, before the break. Old tradition." Mallen squeezed back and grinned.

Three and a half minutes. The second hand swept off increments of time. The chopper would be on the valley floor by now and McKennon would be there to meet it.

They still didn't know he had an aircraft, and he had to get rid of PD Five, which still hovered to the north, cutting off his escape. It was worth a shot. He picked up the mike and keyed it. *PD Five, this is ground control. You copy?*

Right back. The bastard was sharp. *This is PD Five. Say again your call sign?*

"PD Five, this is ground control. McKennon's on his way down to the pad. He wants you to swing down there and pick up some ordnance." Mallen was sweating, the mike slippery in his hand.

Ground control, this is PD Five. Reconfirm that we're to pick up ordnance.

Mallen gritted his teeth, trying to sound angry. "Roger, I reconfirm. McKennon said to get your ass down here." Too strong, he thought. Overplaying it.

Long silence. Four minutes and fifteen seconds gone. PD Five came back, the transmission broken. . . . *ta hell he'd make up his mind. On my way.*

In the distance, beyond the leaves, Mallen saw the chopper pitch forward, picking up speed for the valley floor. Four minutes and fifty seconds gone.

Mallen turned and looked aft at Wyatt. "You ready?" he said. Wyatt made a circle with his fingertips. "Put the headset on."

Wyatt nodded and slipped the band over his head. Mallen turned back to the gauges for one last check. Everything green. He pulled down the canopy and locked it, reducing the engine noise to a dim humming.

"You hear me okay, Wyatt?"

"Like you were shouting in my ear. Is this goin' out over the radio?"

"Negative. Just a straight intercom. I have to press the transmit switch up here for radio transmission. We're going in about thirty seconds. If we don't make it over the trees, I'll jettison the canopy once we stop moving. After that . . ."

Wyatt cut him off. "You're going to make it. Let's go."

Mallen fed in the throttle slowly, building up the rpms. Twenty-nine hundred and looking good.

"Here we go," he said and released the brake.

The Sperber slowly rolled from beneath the canvas shade into the sunlight. The main gear thumped over something, bottoming the strut. Every minor hump or depression in the ground was transmitted to the aircraft's structure and Mallen watched as the wings flexed in response.

The acceleration was agonizingly slow, even rolling downhill. Nothing on the airspeed indicator as yet, he registered, as his eyes flickered downward to the panel. Rpms climbing. Above the sound of the engine, he could hear the sound of his own breathing, coarse and ragged in the amplification of the headset.

The gear was bottoming heavily against the roughness of the meadow. The ditch flashed by, the Sperber rolling over the planked area. Controls starting to firm a little bit now. He had aileron control now and the wings were level, with just a touch of stick. And then she was airborne momentarily but settled back, slipping —and airborne again.

Mallen let her accelerate in the ground effect, picking up speed. His eyes flickered down to the airspeed indicator. Forty-five. Over three-quarters of the field was behind him and the trees were growing gigantic in the windshield, the tops well above the arc of the canopy.

He knew he wasn't going to clear it. No time to clean up the gear, and he could see the individual leaves. He horsed back on the stick and the Sperber reared up, buffeting on the edge of a stall, right wingtip dropping.

Scarlet and yellow and magenta leaves brushed the wingtip and a whipsaw sound rasped along the belly. They were clear then, but sinking, the Sperber well behind the power curve.

The slope fell away beneath him and Mallen eased the stick forward . . . sixty—and he knew that he was clear.

Depressing the safety lock, he tried to retract the gear, but found that he could not move it more than half its arc. The sound of wind hammering in the wheel well beneath him was proof enough that the gear was jammed.

He let it go for a minute and checked the gauges. Solid in the green, but the airspeed was low. The rate of climb was only about two hundred feet a minute, and to clear the ridge he would have to gain over a thousand feet. Five minutes. It wouldn't do.

"God," Wyatt breathed into the mike from the back seat.

"We got problems," Mallen said, banking toward the north. "I can't get the goddamn gear up and it's killing our airspeed. I think it's branches or crap stuck in the retraction mechanism."

"I got the chopper. Look, down to the south."

Mallen looked and at first saw nothing, but then, as the chopper banked in the sun, he caught a glint of light along the bubble canopy and a flash from the rotor disk. The chopper was banking toward them.

The chopper was starting to transmit something, the voice urgent, but Mallen overrode him. "Wyatt," he said harshly into the boom mike, his teeth gritting, "did you ever fly?"

"Yes, once when . . ."

Mallen cut him off. "Look, I'm going to try to force the gear up. It's going to take two hands. Just fly this thing straight. Keep the nose nailed on the horizon and keep the wings level. Don't use any rudder."

There was no hesitation. The stick moved under Wyatt's hand, erratically at first and then with smaller oscillations. The wings steadied in level flight and the nose held a bit low, speed slowly building up.

"Nose up just a bit. See whether you can keep the airspeed about seventy." The nose oscillated a bit and eased up, now climbing a bit. Good student, Mallen thought.

Mallen eased the shoulder straps so that he could lean forward. The gear-retraction mechanism was a three-foot-long handle that had to be pulled upward and aft from the cockpit floor to the locked position beside him. The unlatching mechanism was already released, but the lever was jamming halfway through its arc. Grabbing the handle with both hands, he yanked on it, putting his back and leg muscles into it. Under the pressure, he felt the scabs on his burned palms break open and it was as if he had picked up a red-hot poker. The thing budged through a small fraction of its arc and stuck again. Swearing, he gave it one last try, throwing his weight forward against the handle and then whipping it aft. There was a *crack* as the gear slammed home into the wheel well.

Leaning back, Mallen panted a little from the exertion. The Gear Unsafe light winked out and the speed began picking up, the sound of air flowing over the canopy now more insistent. "I got it," he said into the intercom, taking the stick and bringing her around more to the northeast, climbing for the ridge.

"The landing gear up now?" Wyatt said.

"It's up. You see the chopper?"

Wyatt grunted, turning to look back in the cramped confines of the aft cockpit. "No. . . . Yeah, I see him. Low and behind. Maybe three or four miles."

"Keep an eye on him. Let me know whether he alters his heading."

"I'll be the first to tell you. Can you outrun him?"

Mallen eyed the ridge, estimating the space and time. The Sperber was climbing well now, indicating four hundred feet per minute. He needed another six hundred to clear the ridge. A minute and a half. He flattened his climb, picking up air speed, hoping to just skim the ridge. The Sperber was efficient, clean, aerodynamic, but the engine was no more than sixty horses. He was competing with a bulky, inefficient helicopter, fully loaded—but with enough brute power to overtake them. Unless he could think of something, the twain would meet at some place in vacant space at a time appointed by pure mathematics.

"No, but I can outthink him," Mallen said.

The ridge ran north and south, one in a succession of green waves that rolled westward from the White Mountains of New Hampshire. The compass was steady on northeast. Behind, in the chopper, they would be staring at the bright speck of white fleeing for the ridge, watching for the slightest deviation in heading. And for the few minutes until the chopper cleared the ridge, the Sperber would be lost to their sight. Natural enough for them to think he would radically change course, once over the ridge, probably to the south. And natural enough for them to anticipate the evasion and try to cut him off. "I'm going to try to fake him out," Mallen said into the intercom. "As soon as we clear the ridge, I'll start a sharp bank to the right and push the nose down below the ridge."

"You mean back toward him?"

"Yeah, but just for a second. I *want* him to see the start of the turn. Once we're below the level of the ridge, I'll turn back to this heading. We've got a fifty-fifty chance he'll go for it. I may pick up another mile lead on him. If not, we'll have lost only a hundred yards."

"Up to you, buddy."

The Sperber was even with the ridge now, and Mallen leveled from the climb, letting the air speed build up. They swept in toward the crest, individual trees separating out of the blur of forest, then flashing in a green and gold and yellow wake behind them. One glance backward over his shoulder and then he slammed the stick hard right, feeding in right rudder. The Sperber reared over in a near-vertical turn, G-forces dragging at his body; then he pushed the stick back to the left with full rudder, and the turn became more shallow until northeast settled in the face of the compass.

"Think they saw us turn?"

"Don't know," Wyatt said. "Must have. You hear them talkin' on the radio?"

Mallen unconsciously shook his head. "No. Too preoccupied."

"It was Russian. Just one sentence."

The oil temperature was creeping from the green into the yellow. Mallen couldn't keep her at maximum revs much longer or the engine would overheat and possibly seize. He eased the nose down, picking up air speed, getting better cooling. More than a minute since the crest.

There was another transmission now and Mallen heard it clearly. A Slavic language; short insistent phrases and a response, the voice of McKennon. One minute thirty . . . forty . . . fifty . . .

"I see him!" Wyatt was pounding on his shoulder, pointing to the south. "Suckered the bastard right out!" Wyatt was nearly shouting in the mike, laughing.

Mallen looked to the south. Away, miles away, the chopper hung perplexed, beating the thin October air, no closer than a pinpoint. Five, six miles, he estimated, and smiled. Finally, the chopper must have seen them and turned north, but the advantage was his own now, Mallen realized. For there was another ridge and yet another, and the game with fifty-fifty odds could be played again and again, until the chopper had no fuel.

Mallen, this is McKennon. You hear me all right?

Mallen looked toward the south, trying to find the second chopper, McKennon's. The first was still coming north, riding the crest of the ridge but looking no closer. But no second chopper.

Mallen keyed the mike. *Fuck you, McKennon.*

There was a long pause, the static hollow in his headset. Then McKennon's voice.

You're looking the wrong direction, Mallen. I'm on your left wingtip. You ever hear of the squeeze play?

7

The chopper was less than a mile off his left wingtip, abreast of him and slowly converging. Grotesque and yet somehow beautiful, it looked like some prehistoric insect streaking for its lesser prey, intent on feeding.

You hear me, Mallen? McKennon again, confident. *Slow down. We're coming in closer. Any bad moves and you'll get a load of tracers.*

The oil temperature was edging into the red arc and the oil pressure dropping. Mallen eased back on the throttle, knowing that if he didn't, the engine would soon fail. The air speed slowly fell off, decaying to 90.

"How did he . . . ?" Wyatt asked.

"Anticipated our move," Mallen replied. "Went straight north while the other one cut south. They covered both options."

"You have any more ideas?"

Oil pressure and temperature coming back into normal limits. The clock on the panel swept through its arc. He didn't believe it at first. Twelve minutes elapsed since takeoff. It had seemed more like half an hour. Three or four more minutes and there would have been a chance—now, nothing. He slumped in the seat, feeling defeat eat into his gut.

"You have any more ideas?" Wyatt, insistent.

"No."

"You just going to let him close in and shoot us down?"

"He won't. Wants to get us to land. Much more likely."

The chopper was half a mile out now, faces in the

bubble almost recognizable. One figure in the right-front seat in blue-gray; the rest in khaki. Mallen watched it slowly converge.

Chopper pilots he had known: Cal and Pete; Bob Teising. Chopper pilots a very different breed, he thought. Proud and stubborn. Defensive about the weaker aspects of their craft, almost mystical about the stronger points. Compare choppers with fixed-wing, he demanded. Weak points are what? Short fuel range. High power-to-weight ratio. Ugly. What else? Not aerobatic. Not stressed for it.

The chopper changed course slightly, now paralleling the Sperber's course. Mallen estimated the range at five hundred yards.

Mallen, you hear me?

I hear you, McKennon.

We're all going to land at Montpelier. Take up a heading of . . . someone talking in the background . . . of zero six five degrees. Very slowly, Mallen. Very slowly.

Mallen sighed and edged into the turn, letting the sun drift across his canopy. Beautiful up here, he thought. Autumn in Vermont. Clear of clouds except a growing cluster of cumulus to the north. If he could reach them. Shit, if he could just reach them.

"You intending to land?" Wyatt said, his voice strained in the intercom.

"I don't think we have any other options. They got us on speed. Probably be able to climb faster. And I don't fancy a tracer up my ass."

He felt a cool, hard point of pressure on his neck. He knew what it was before Wyatt told him.

"Nine millimeter," Wyatt said. "I'm not going down there, Greg. No way, brother."

Desperate now, Mallen looked out toward the left. The chopper held station, matching his small fluctuations in altitude and air speed, keeping slightly above the Sperber and still a quarter of a mile distant. Smart cookie, that guy. Good field of fire and no risk of collision.

"What's the difference? McKennon's got us either way. Up here or on the ground."

"The difference, Mallen, is how we go. McKennon has other probes for his little electric chair. Not your hands. Something entirely different. And he can make it last for days."

The oil gauges looked normal now, in the low green, and the fuel pressure was good. The revs were steady at twenty-eight hundred, the altimeter at three thousand plus. The clouds were marginally closer on the northern horizon.

"You see those clouds, Wyatt?"

The pressure of the barrel was withdrawn. "Yeah, I see them."

"We get to there and I can lose them. Choppers like McKennon's usually aren't equipped for instrument flying."

"Which means?"

"Instrument flying—blind flying, if you want to call it that. And it's rough in there. We'll take a pounding. He can't. Choppers aren't stressed for it."

"I mean it, Mallen. You try to land this thing and I'll blow your brains out."

"I believe," Mallen said. "I believe."

Distances in the sky are difficult to judge on a clear day. The clouds were building in size and were definitely closer, fifteen miles or less. They were particularly heavier to the northwest, already humping up in popcorn texture, massing to form what would probably be thunderstorms in the afternoon.

Mallen keyed the mike. *McKennon, this is Mallen. What are your intentions?*

There was no immediate reply; then a voice said, *Stand by.* A pause, then McKennon was saying evenly, *Go ahead, Mallen.*

What are your intentions, McKennon? Clouds closer. Twelve miles and twelve light-years away.

McKennon actually laughed. The sound of the chopper blades wacking through the air filled in the background. *Intentions? You sound as if you had a choice,*

Mallen. You're landing in about three or four minutes. If you don't, you get shot down. How's that for a choice?

I have to talk this over with Wyatt. He says he'll kill me if I do.

He doesn't have the balls, Mallen. If he kills you, he kills himself. You'll both get a fair trial. The chopper started to edge in closer, converging noticeably.

Mallen added a little throttle and turned away slightly. He keyed the mike. *Don't get in any closer, McKennon. I can still ram you. Wyatt and I need some time to talk about this.*

A figure in the back seat of the chopper brought his weapon up to his shoulder, and Mallen tensed. Then he saw McKennon smash his arm down on the barrel. They were close enough in for Mallen to see the anger in McKennon's face.

You have two minutes, Mallen. After that you start to let down for landing or we shoot you down. Tracers make nice fires in airplanes.

Mallen tried to visualize McKennon's state of mind, watching the white aircraft off to his right. Working out a neat, precise equation of convergence and trajectory range. But it would be better for McKennon's record to get them alive, because the state would want some concise resolution rather than a sloppy ending.

Mallen keyed the mike. *Okay, McKennon. We'll work it out. Just five minutes.*

He was right back as if he anticipated a stall. *No five minutes, durak. Two! Starting now!*

"I mean it," Wyatt said. "You try to land this thing and your brains are going to be scattered all over this canopy."

"And what about you, hero?"

Wyatt made a clicking sound in the mike. "Me too," he said. "You just don't know McKennon. He's a fucking animal."

"There's one possibility." Mallen paused, thinking.

"Keep talking."

"Notice how the chopper stays slightly above us?

That's so they can fire on us without hitting their own rotor blades. If we sucker him in below us, we . . . you could possibly hit him with the Luger."

"Through the vent window?"

Mallen tried to visualize the field of fire through the small ventilation window in the aft compartment. "Won't work that way, but if we get him below us on the left, I can bank hard to the left, giving you a clean shot."

"How about firing through the canopy?"

"I think it would shatter. With no canopy, it would kill our air speed with drag. No possibility of escape then."

"What do I shoot at, the engine?"

"The pilot. If you don't get him, you might get a rotor blade. Engine is the last choice."

One minute left, Mallen.

"How do you sucker him in?" Wyatt hissed. Long pause.

Thirty seconds, Mallen. The chopper was gaining more altitude and edging in. This time, both McKennon and the man in the back seat had weapons to their shoulders.

Mallen squeezed the mike button. *All right, McKennon. We'll play it your way.*

Sensible, Mallen. Very smart. McKennon paused and then came back. *My pilot says Montpelier is in your twelve-o'clock position, about five miles. Pull back on your power and start a descent. You'll be landing to the southwest. Stay in the aircraft after you land. Any attempt to get out when you're on the ground and you'll be shot.*

Understood, Mallen said, putting resignation into the word. He eased back on the power and tucked the nose down a few degrees. Hot under the greenhouse effect of the canopy, he thought. The small of his back was soaked with sweat.

McKennon transmitted again, the closeness of the two aircraft distorting his voice. *Mallen, my pilot says to turn to a heading of zero three zero. Make it a long*

*downwind leg with a one-hundred-eighty-degree turn
onto final. Nothing fancy . . . no screwing around.*

Zero three zero was just a hair to the right of due
north. Mallen estimated it would bring the building
cumulus even closer. *Okay with me, McKennon. But
keep your goddamn chopper off my wing.*

The chopper drifted farther off to the left and gained
a slight bit of altitude. McKennon was playing it by the
book, retaining his options.

The two aircraft passed over a low ridge, then traced
a flight path over a descending slope. Ahead was a
lake, blue and ruffled in the morning wind. From north
to south, a four-lane highway flowed in a smoothly
winding ribbon. He could see no traffic on it, though he
was low enough to pick out the crashed hulk of a Greyhound bus overturned on the divider strip; probably
some who had tried to make it out of the cities. The
greyhound symbol was still visible, poised forever in
futile pursuit of an imagined rabbit.

Far ahead, over the nose, he could make out the
boxy outlines of a small city with a film of smoke layer-
ing above it. They would be heating by coal now, he
guessed, or perhaps just wood. Good morning to have
a fire in the hearth.

He glanced at the panel. Twenty-two minutes since
takeoff. Down to under two thousand feet. Eighty knots
of air speed.

Wyatt grunted in the intercom. "Down low . . . just
forward of the right wing."

Mallen craned his neck and picked up the shadow
first, then the chopper. It was Yellow Tail, the one
that had gone south, now streaking at treetop level for
the landing strip.

"He's low on fuel," Mallen said. "One less to worry
about."

Wyatt grunted something.

"Say again."

"When," Wyatt repeated. "Just tell me when."

Mallen nodded. The cockpit was really hot now,
baking under the clear autumn sky. He stole a glance

at the cumulus, not wanting to think about the intervening ten or so miles that he would have to bridge safely. It was an impossible distance. McKennon would nail him within the first mile. His sphincter puckered involuntarily at the thought of tracers.

Time was slipping by. Seconds passed. He knew that it would be essential to attempt the breakaway no later than the final approach to landing. McKennon was still perfectly positioned, flying high off his left wing, holding formation exactly. He tried to imagine McKennon's mental framework: probably confident of the capture, feeling in control. But also with his ass on the line for the escape last night and the four dead men.

Mallen, drop your landing gear and slow up to approach speed.

Landing gear, Mallen thought. McKennon's handed it to me on a silver platter. He unlocked the safety latch and bent down to pull the extension handle, making an obvious show of it. He extended the gear halfway and then held it.

Just the right degree of panic in my voice, he thought. *McKennon. The gear's jammed halfway down. I can't get it fully extended.* He said it very loudly, distorting the words.

Stand by. McKennon's voice had an edge of irritation in it.

Mallen watched the chopper edge in closer, easing down to his own altitude. The eager one in the aft seat had his weapon raised and he could see McKennon's face, partially obscured by the binoculars held to his face. The chopper pilot was saying something either on another frequency or in the intercom, and McKennon was nodding.

McKennon came back on frequency. *Mallen. Try retracting the gear and then extending it again. It looks like there's some leaves and stuff in the fork.*

Hunching over in the cockpit, Mallen made pumping motions with his shoulder and arm, keeping the gear handle firmly wedged with his knee. *No good, McKennon. Something's jammed. The goddamn gear is stuck.*

He wobbled the wings a little, pitching up slightly as if he was losing control.

The chopper dropped lower, edging in closer. Mallen could see every detail of the aircraft now. It was a foreign type, and he noted that the markings were in Cyrillic lettering. European design. Single exhaust stack. The blat of the chopper's exhaust and the whump of the rotor blades easily overpowered the noise of his own engine.

"Get ready," Mallen said in the intercom. "You're going to have time for about two shots. Lead him a couple of feet, but for Christ's sake keep the Luger out of sight until I start the turn!"

Wyatt said something not understandable, more of a grunt. One more thing to do, he thought. Check the runways to see what they've got. The airstrip was just off his right wingtip, only a few miles distant. The runways were deserted except for two choppers on the ramp. One was Yellow Tail, just landed, rotors still turning, with a fuel truck moving toward it. The other was larger but set back in a tiedown area with no activity around it.

Back on the frequency, McKennon sounded impatient. *Get this, Mallen. My pilot says to retract the gear if you can and land on the grass beside the strip. Keep your air speed a little on the low side and cut the engine just as you clear the fence. I want you and Wyatt in one piece.*

Mallen knew that they would be watching him in the binoculars, able to see every expression. He wanted them just a bit lower, in closer. Bending over, he pumped his shoulder and allowed the gear to move fractionally, extending it a bit further.

McKennon, he shouted, desperation now hard in his voice, *McKennon, the goddamn fucking gear handle is broken off. What's it look like now?* He wobbled the stick a bit and arched his head over against the canopy as if futilely trying to see what the problem was. The chopper edged in closer and dropped about twenty feet below his own path. He could see the faces looking up, now each one of them intent with the problem. The chopper pilot's face was white with anger, arguing with McKennon or someone on the interphone, protesting the idiocy of McKennon's commands.

Closer in, McKennon. Just a little closer. "Ready?" to Wyatt.

"Ready," Wyatt said softly.

"Now!" Mallen said, and slammed the stick over to the left, rearing up on a wingtip and exposing the chopper below. One, two, three shots hammered in his eardrums and he saw the chopper's canopy fracture. A face in mirrored sunglasses was upturned, mouth open, and then the chopper was gone. Mallen punched in the throttle, firewalling it, and slammed the gear up into the well.

"Bastard," Wyatt was yelling into the intercom. Another shot came from Wyatt and then a stream of tracers laced erratically beneath his nose.

The air speed was picking up. One hundred ten. He leveled the wings and then banked hard right, to the north. Revs now at redline and the air speed creeping up to one twenty. The cumulus to the north looked as far and remote as the next planet.

"Got him," Wyatt was saying over and over. "Got him."

"Where is he?" Mallen craned his neck, looking back over his shoulder.

"Can't see him, low. No . . . he's turning toward us. Coming."

"Shit," Mallen said to himself. One twenty-five knots on the ASI and the controls were stiff with the speed. He retrimmed for the pressure and concentrated on the northern horizon.

McKennon's voice was in his earphones, savage with anger. The background noise was much higher than it had been and there was someone yelling, the voice distant and distorted.

Goddamn you, Mallen! I'll . . .

Mallen switched off the radio, not wanting to hear.

"How far back, Wyatt?" he said. Cumulus looking closer.

"A mile. He's gaining. I didn't lead the bastard enough."

"You did great. It's going to give us time."

"Enough?"

"Enough," Mallen lied.

The oil temperature was creeping up again, the engine overrevving. He pushed the nose down a little, inching out two knots more speed on the ASI. The panel was vibrating heavily, the engine shaking in its mounts. Go, you mother. Two more minutes.

Wyatt let out a sigh in the intercom, a long explosion of breath. "No good. He's starting to close in on us."

8

The shattered canopy of the Klistov helicopter was breaking away in the slipstream. McKennon hunched down, getting little protection from the instrument panel. The sound of the engine was magnified to a rolling thunder, making it difficult even to think.

"Something wrong!" the pilot shouted into McKennon's ear. "Vibration and the oil press . . ."

"I don't give a good goddamn." McKennon screamed back. "Get this thing around to the north and keep after him. Everything you've got." He pointed toward the white cruciform shape of Mallen's aircraft climbing more than a half-mile distant toward the massed cumulus on the northern horizon.

The pilot, ashen faced, nodded. He slowly added power and flattened the pitch, angling into Mallen's flight path. "I don't think this thing will hold together."

McKennon's face was black with anger and he leaned over, shouting, saliva flecking the pilot's face. "Don't think, *durak!* Just get me close enough so that I can fire a burst before he gets to that wall of clouds." McKennon pulled back on the loading level of the Kalashnikov AK-47 and chambered a round. He switched the selector to Full Automatic Fire. Two hundred yards would be close enough, he decided. Smash Mallen's prop or engine, forcing him down. That would just be the beginning, something to look forward to. He picked up the mike and thumbed the transmit button. *Goddamn you, Mallen! I'll nail your ass to the wall!* There was no reply, just the empty crackle of static in the headset.

The Special Forces corporal in the aft seat was still screaming. McKennon looked over his shoulder and was almost sick. The kid was making high, piercing sounds, tearing at his face as blood pumped from the jagged mass of bone and teeth that had been his jaw. McKennon turned away quickly, feeling only revulsion.

The shape of Mallen's plane was growing larger. A thousand yards and closing. He fired a test burst and saw the tracers curving away and downward. Still too far. The cloud mass was closer. Hard to judge distances, he thought. If Mallen reached that, it would take hours to find him again. McKennon realized that the kid had the spare ammo clips and turned in his seat, looking for them. The kid lay prone now, the stump of his jaw slowly working. The flow of blood was blacker, a sluggish surge from the open maw of the wound. McKennon pushed him onto the floor, taking the spare clips. The boy's blond hair whipped in the wind through the fractured canopy, and his eyes were still open, staring up at McKennon. One more that I have to answer for to Brinkerhoff, he thought. Brinkerhoff would be thumbing through the morning dispatches by now, finding McKennon's name and the bare bones of the escape. And smiling as he realized that McKennon had screwed this one up royally. It's more than just Mallen and Wyatt escaping, McKennon thought. It's Brinkerhoff or me.

He hadn't noticed the alteration in the sound of the engine. Mallen's aircraft was tantalizingly close now, less than six hundred yards, but the pilot was pulling back on the power. "What's the problem?" McKennon yelled. His vocal cords hurt from the strain of shouting.

The pilot tapped the oil-pressure gauge, and as he did the needle slumped. "Losing oil somewhere. Pressure's falling and the cylinder-head temperature is outta sight!" His lips set a tight line and he kept his eyes on the panel.

"I don't give a damn!" McKennon screamed back in desperation. "Keep going."

The pilot nodded and added power. Gauges on the

panel began to blur in a dance of vibration. The whole airframe was responding, shaking, tearing itself apart as the engine began to seize.

The range was now five to six hundred. McKennon fired a burst. The tracers looped upward and fell wasted, still short of the aircraft. Close. McKennon slammed in a new clip. "Give me another thirty seconds," he muttered. "Thirty seconds . . ." The clouds were a massed wall before him, gray on the vertical faces and clustered upward into the sunlight with mounded tops. "Twenty seconds," he said to himself, his lips just moving. The Kalashnikov felt like an extension of his will, of his mind.

The vibration was bad now, and pieces of the windshield were shredding away as cracks speared across the Plexiglas. McKennon registered the sound of shrieking metal above the noise of the rotors, and then there was a heavy shock as the airframe shuddered, staggering in flight. The shrieking intensified, with the sounds of metal grinding on white-hot metal; then there was a detonation and the chopper slewed sideways, beginning to tumble. McKennon was flung outward, slamming his head against the side of the canopy rail. On the edge of his vision, he could see the pilot's hands dancing over the panel, shutting down the engine, activating a red T handle on the center of the console.

"Engine seized," the pilot screamed. "I'm turning back."

"We're . . ." McKennon said and didn't finish. He caught one last glimpse of Mallen's aircraft, then the horizon wheeled across his vision.

The sound was less now, the engine silent, and only the flow of the wind through the cockpit made speaking difficult. McKennon watched as the pilot shallowed his bank and rolled out on a heading with the bleak concrete mass of the airport before them, thousands of feet below.

"Get yourself strapped in and see to the kid in the back," the pilot said.

McKennon nodded but did nothing. "Can you make it?"

The pilot nodded. "I think so. Wind's behind us. It'll be hard landing. And get rid of that fuckin' thing."

"What?"

"The assault rifle! I don't want that thing spraying us when we land. Or put it on safety."

The chopper's air speed was picking up and the rotors were a blur of light and sound. Freed from the engine, they picked up speed, forming a black disk above the canopy. McKennon stared in fascination, watching whole farms become fields, become segments of fields. He could now see individual trees and boulders and then a roadway. A man on the road was looking up, mouth open. A house on the perimeter of the runway slid under the nose of the chopper, too close, the disused TV aerial nearly at cockpit level. The airport was underneath them and the plunge became almost straight downward. McKennon could only watch, immobile with fright.

The chopper pilot timed it well, changing pitch from flat to coarse at the last minute, using the flywheel effect of the rotor and the pitch change to create enough lift to soften the landing. They hit hard, collapsing one skid, and the Klistov settled, rocking down on the opposite skid. The pilot slumped back in his seat, breathing heavily.

McKennon unstrapped, grabbed the AK-47, and headed in a dead run across the ramp for the second chopper, which was coughing to life, blue clouds of oil smoke erupting from its exhaust stack. He turned, momentarily, jogging awkwardly backward, watching the diminishing speck on the northern horizon. He stared a second longer and the speck was gone, swallowed by the wall of cumulus. "Shit," he spat out to no one.

A sergeant, fat bouncing beneath his gray tunic of the Eastern Peace Division, met him on an intersecting path, stubby legs pumping, looking more like an inflated plastic toy. Farther up the ramp toward the disused terminal building a group of men in similar gray uniforms were running toward him.

McKennon grabbed the man by the arm. "Look," he shouted into the fat man's face. "Get Eastern Division Directorate in Albany on the radio and tell them to launch choppers along the old border. Montreal to Trois Rivières. Anything else they can put up. And have them alert all substations for an aircraft watch. He's heading somewhere between northeast and northwest. We'll use two forty-one point eight five as a new working frequency. Mallen's monitoring the old one."

"Sir . . ." the man started to say, but McKennon pushed him aside and sprinted for the yellow-tailed Klistov. He turned again, shouted over his shoulder, "Two forty-one point eight five."

The man nodded, his head bent down as he wrote on the back of his hand with a pen.

McKennon reached the chopper as the blades were beginning to reap the air in long, scything strokes, slowly building up speed. The pilot was hunched over, transmitting into his mike, intent. He barely glanced at McKennon. Another man in khaki fatigues was already climbing into the aft compartment. He carried with him a tubelike weapon with a shoulder mount and sighting device. McKennon acknowledged him with a curt nod and pointed toward the cumulus to the north. The man, a Latino, smiled back and patted the tube. In thirty seconds, the chopper had lifted off and turned to the north.

McKennon settled in, strapping on the seat belt. The pilot—Baines, the name tag said—nodded toward a headset clipped to the overhead bracket. McKennon fitted it on, thankful to be rid of the unbelievable racket of the rotors and engine.

They were gaining altitude gradually, Baines concentrating on getting up to maximum speed. The town below flashed under the nose: odd buildings, the blur of a shopping center, the remains of a Kentucky Fried Chicken shack burned to the ground, with bricks and rubbish littering the empty parking lot.

"You see him?" McKennon asked, still breathing hard.

Baines shook his head but said in a flat drawl, "Mother's up there somewhere. We'll get him." His cheeks were working hard, chewing on a quid of tobacco. McKennon watched Baines's face for a second. It revealed nothing, no emotion. His eyes were caged behind yellow-tinted lenses, making the irises black. He ignored McKennon, his eyes quartering the horizon ahead.

Professional. McKennon liked that. "How much fuel do you have?"

Baines reached down and tapped the gauge. He turned slightly, his eyes still ahead, and exposed a dirty row of teeth. "Full. Two hours' worth. Relax, McKennon. It'll be a while."

The man in the aft compartment was buckled in now, leaning back with his eyes closed. The weapon he held was cradled across his knees. McKennon worked out an appraisal: Probably Cuban, Special Forces warrant officer; Ethiopian and Angolan ribbons stenciled on the khaki fatigues; two more beneath that for the South African campaign; commendation ribbon from the Western Peace Division. McKennon looked back up to his face and found the man studying him through slitted eyes.

The Cuban smiled. "Santilla," he said in the intercom.

"How many rounds for the SA-7?" McKennon asked, nodding toward the weapon.

The Cuban held up three fingers. "Heat seeking," he said, with a Spanish inflection. "One will do." He closed his eyes again, the smile now just a thin compression of his lips.

McKennon turned away, satisfied. One will do, he repeated in his mind. A two-mile effective range delivering a 3.5-pound shaped charge. The heat of Mallen's engine would provide more than enough return for a good lock-on. But if he had the chance, McKennon knew that he would still try to get close enough for a burst with the AK-47. The missile launcher was a choice of last resort, something that would deprive him of getting Mallen and Wyatt alive.

He settled back, trying to relax. The fields below gave way to wooded ridges as they flew north. Isolated farms with overgrown fields edged disused lanes. So few people left, McKennon thought. A whole country grinding down to a survival economy, populated by sullen people scratching to live. The New Era, the state radio called it. The Stone Age, McKennon thought. He tried to keep his mind from returning to Brinkerhoff, but it kept coming back.

In the Rochester riots of one summer ago, Brinkerhoff had made a balls-up of it, losing forty-one of his own men. McKennon had nearly been number forty-two. Eastern Division in Langley convened an inquiry and, rather than support Brinkerhoff, McKennon had carefully engineered a package of half-lies and hearsay, damning Brinkerhoff for ham-fisted mismanagement. For that, McKennon had become one of the seven district commanders under Brinkerhoff, personally selected by Georgi Antonivich, the Eastern Division Commander.

Since that time, McKennon had carefully spread points and favors to the right quarters and played on Brinkerhoff's failures. More riots in Troy and Ithaca. Supposed criticism of Antonivich by Brinkerhoff. A few more months, McKennon reflected, and I would have had Brinkerhoff's job. Georgi had already personally suggested it.

But the trouble was, McKennon thought, that Brinkerhoff knew who was doing the talking. And Brinkerhoff had laid back, taking his own sweet time, just waiting to nail McKennon. In a sudden realization, McKennon realized that Mallen might be the nail and that time, or lack of it, would be the hammer.

They were beneath the cumulus now, which boiled up in the morning sunlight, fed by moisture over the warming ground. The air was turbulent, and McKennon felt slightly nauseous. He checked his watch and found that it was barely past eight. In the periphery of his vision, he watched Baines moving methodically, in tune with the controls of the chopper, grinding the quid of tobacco with relentless precision.

"Any trace of him?" McKennon said in the intercom.

Baines stared straight ahead, shaking his head. "Nah. Bastard's probably up on top of this. Which way now?"

"If you were him, which way would you go?"

Baines shrugged. "Your show, McKennon. Ah just fly this thing."

The turbulence was stronger now and the chopper shuddered in the gusts. The sunlight was blocked out by the towering cumulus above them. McKennon felt worse, slightly sick. Blue sky showed to the north and beyond that more rows of cumulus.

"Go northeast, then," McKennon said. "And let's get more altitude."

Baines, who had come from what used to be Texarkana before it took five megatons, eased in more power for the climb, nodded, and said "Dumbass Peace Division," just loud enough for McKennon to hear.

9

The Sperber was buffeting heavily in the turbulence, banked over at 45 degrees and climbing as though it were an express elevator. Mallen's eyes flicked momentarily to the variometer and watched the needle banging up against the stop, registering a more than 1,000-feet-per-minute rate of climb. Beyond the rain-streaked canopy the world was a gray-black void of tumbling violence. Wyatt was coughing in the back seat, the sounds amplified in the intercom. Getting sick, Mallen thought. Small wonder. He settled deeper into the seat, pulling the lap belt as tight as possible with his free hand.

For Mallen there was no up or down, no left or right, beyond the thin Plexiglas of the canopy. From the first second that he had penetrated the cumulus, the horizon had been obliterated. He held the Sperber's stick carefully now, watching the artificial horizon on the panel and then flicking his eyes over the air-speed indicator, altimeter, and rate of climb gauge. A gust slammed the Sperber, banking it ever farther into the turn, and Mallen used both hands, forcing it back. He wondered how the wings were standing up to the shock loading. And he remembered Rudi Meyers.

Mallen had met Rudi on a soggy April afternoon. The wind whipped in from the northwest over the Green Mountains, bringing scud and showers. Mallen watched him for a while: a man in his early sixties dressed in chinos and an ancient leather jacket. The man's face was square and unlined, except for the mass of wrinkles that radiated from the corners of his eyes, as if he had spent a lifetime squinting at the sun. What hair was left was combed back repeatedly by a scarred hand, only to be lifted in the gusting wind.

Mallen walked up alongside him, nodding toward the wind sock. "Not a great day for competition soaring," he offered.

"Nor tomorrow," the man said. "Or the next." He pulled out a pipe and stuffed it, but made no attempt to light it. Turning to Mallen, he stuck out his hand and said, "Rudi Meyers."

Meyers's prediction was confirmed in the late afternoon. The contest director told them that the 1974 Region One Soaring Contest would be put off for a few more days because of stationary cold front. Men shuffled out of the briefing room, back to campers, hotel rooms, and bored wives.

Mallen met Meyers again on the steps of the terminal building. "You were right," Mallen said, lighting a Pall Mall.

Meyers shrugged. "It's my business," he said, poking a pipe stem toward the low overcast. "Knowing weather." He pulled his leather jacket up tight around his throat and zipped it with the disfigured hand. He turned away and took two steps toward the parking lot, then turned back. "You'll have a cognac with me," he said, more statement than question.

Meyers had been one of the German *Wunderkind* of soaring in the thirties, the gifted children of a new Germany who were pressing against the known boundaries of flight. The Treaty of Versailles had forbidden a new German air force, so pilots of the still-secret Luftwaffe trained in gliders of designs that were still competitive twenty years later. Money and technology were lavished from obscure sources on the growing sport. Meyers showed Mallen a faded photograph of Hermann Goering presenting an armful of flowers to a beautiful girl who sat smiling in the cockpit of a gull-winged sailplane. "My fiancée," he said.

They had two more cognacs and coffee. Meyers

looked out the window of the restaurant across the valley at the cloud-cloaked ridges on the eastern side. "A lot of us died doing stupid things in those days," he said, lighting his pipe. "We didn't know much about weather."

"You're a meteorologist?" Mallen asked. He sipped at his coffee, waiting, knowing that Meyers would get to it.

"In a sense. I own a firm that makes instrumentation for meteorological studies." He blew out a cloud of blue smoke. "No, you're right. Meteorology is my study, particularly clouds. The rest is incidental."

Meyers wound slowly and carefully into the early days of soaring flight . . . tame soaring along the windward sides of ridges, sustained by a gentle cushion of upward-flowing air. And then the thermals. How cumulus clouds were thought to be formed by a rising column of warm air, and how pilots finally learned to circle like hawks in the invisible thermals, using the newly developed variometers to plot the rising air.

Meyers pushed his chair back and put his leg up on the low window sill, still looking out over the valley. "We found that the thermal was strongest at the base of the cloud. Some of us believed that the thermal continued straight up through the center of the cloud, becoming weaker as it got higher. So we decided to find out." He looked directly at Mallen and smiled. "I lost fifteen pounds that day," he said, tapping his leg. Only then Mallen realized that Meyers used thumbtacks for garters.

It had been a hot afternoon in August 1935. The Bavarian Alps filled the southern horizon. Three sailplanes were prepared and launched. The agreed-upon plan had been for each pilot to choose a separate cumulus cloud, penetrate it, and record as best he could the strength and characteristics of the internal mechanism of the cloud.

"It sounded all so very scientific at the briefing," Rudi said dryly. He sucked on the pipe, now gone cold. "But what no one counted on was that we were all young Luftwaffe pilots, ready to make a name for ourselves." He tapped out the pipe and restuffed it, his gaze unfocused, staring out across the valley. He turned to Mallen and met his eyes. "We each chose the same one—the largest. Horst penetrated first. He had the best ship, a Möwe 7A. I was second with Eric just behind me." He lit the pipe and then threw the match into the dying fire.

"I remember very little. Turbulence and rain. Then hail. Hail the size of apricot pits. There was a core of rising air, as we had suspected. But there was also a sheath of falling air surrounding the column. Where those two interfaced was a brick wall."

Meyers's controls froze solid somewhere around nine thousand feet. The storm cell spit him out the side, minus most of the fabric covering on the tail section. The canopy was shattered by hail. He was found unconscious in the wreckage of his sailplane. Horst's Möwe was crushed in the anvil of the storm and no recognizable part of the aircraft remained. Its pilot free-fell from well over twelve thousand feet, his parachute shredded.

"The third man?" Mallen asked.

"Eric. . . . He was my best friend, and the brother of my fiancée. Somehow he got out of his aircraft and deployed the chute. He was carried much higher, then spit out near the top and came down, only to be reingested by the core's chimney." Meyers played with the coffee spoon, pushing it carefully to the exact center of his placemat. "They think he made at least five trips up through the cell. He had been dead a long time before he finally landed. Frozen solid. Most of his skin gone from hail damage. The report called it a 'cyclic purgatory.' " But this storm cell had not looked mature, Mallen told himself. Just a young stud bull of a cell, looking virile and taller than the lower cows of cumulus that grazed beside him. Now it seemed otherwise.

A momentary rattle of rain slashed across the canopy and then was gone, leaving only fractured grays and blacks beyond the perspex. He pulled the power back to idle, trying to keep the air speed in the low seventies. Fly attitude and forget air speed, he told himself. He scanned the panel, pulling information from each indicator, air speed needle vibrating, erratic, and the altimeter pumping, showing a higher altitude with every second. Up through eight thousand and then nine. More rain now, sluicing across the canopy, deafeningly loud. The canopy seals were leaking, water streaming in rivulets along the sills and over the panel.

The turbulence was bad now, the worst he had known. He was alternately slammed heavily into his seat and thrown upward against his shoulder straps, the whole airframe shaking as though it were a toy in the mouth of a dog. The instruments were beginning to blur into unreadability. He caught the altimeter reading for a fraction of stability—thirteen thousand and something, with the vario still on the peg. His ears were howling from the pressure change and he began to wonder whether they were up through the freezing level, picking up ice. Couldn't tell, he thought. Heavy condensation on the canopy, almost fog in the cockpit from the sudden temperature change. Rattle of hail and then rain and hail again. Heavy stuff, he registered, and then the aircraft reared up on a wingtip, buffeting heavily in a high-speed stall, uncontrollable. . . . going over. Mallen slammed the stick forward, pulling negative G-forces, and countered with full aileron and rudder and the air speed was building up and then *slam,* he was back in the core again, overcontrolling, trying to keep the thing upright.

Wyatt was retching in the aft cockpit, incoherent. Mallen felt bad, vertigo overlaying his senses. Confusion chewing at the corner of his mind. Panic not far.

More hail, lighter, thank God. The canopies had shattered under hail. And then he was into a blinding, burnished, crystallized fog of ice particles, with the sun a pale headlight.

"Jesus," Wyatt was saying, then coughing and vomiting.

Mallen steered for the sun, and burst out into blue

space and calm air at 16,580 feet. He added power now, a little at a time, keeping the air speed low. His heart was pounding and the air felt thin in his lungs, but the aircraft was whole. Banking, he kept to the edge of the cumulus, ducking down the valleys, probing the canyons, then turning back to retrace the same path. It was safe and private. He flew carefully, trying to relax the tenseness his body had accumulated. A clear glazing of ice slowly melted in the sunshine, then slid off the wings in sheets and patches. It hadn't been too bad, he told himself, knowing that he would forever leave it to the Germans.

The vomit smell was beginning to get to him and he felt slightly sickened, but he also felt the exhilaration that comes from pushing against the limits of luck and winning one more time.

"You okay back there?" he inquired.

"Sick. I'm all right now. What in shit was all of that back in the clouds?"

"Just heavy turbulence. Hail and rain. We're fine now."

"You sound like you do that all the time."

"Nothing that rough. And it's not as noticeable in a large aircraft." Mallen banked through 180 degrees, moving back toward a blue valley between the thunderheads. "Can you do anything about the puke?"

"I've got it cleaned up the best I can," Wyatt replied. "With one of your shirts. What do I do with it?"

"Stuff it out the vent window. Just a bit at a time." Mallen picked up the oxygen mask and took a pull of 100-percent oxygen. It cleared his mind, his vision expanding. Even at 16,000-some-odd feet, oxygen starvation was insidious, something that nibbled at the edges of your consciousness, destroying vision and judgment. He took a second long drag and turned the regulator off.

There was the sound of the shirt flapping in the slipstream as Wyatt fed it out the vent, then just the groan of wind past the open vent. Wyatt shut it and the cockpit was suddenly very quiet.

"McKennon?" Wyatt asked in the intercom. "What of him?"

"You've seen the altimeter? Sixteen thousand plus. He's way below us. No chopper in the world is going to come up through that stuff. We're okay for the time being."

"What's the routine? And for Christ's sake, turn up the heat. It's freezing back here."

Mallen sighed. "Not that easy. The heater in this thing isn't that efficient. It's barely keeping the canopy from fogging. It'll get worse, not better." He paused, thinking. "Look, Wyatt, this is the situation. We can make a direct run for Canada from here. But that's exactly what McKennon will expect. He's got two choppers down there and probably he can call up more north of here."

"Which leaves us . . ."

"Which leaves us with either turning and going east or even south, into more populated areas, or just staying here."

"Staying here seems stupid," Wyatt said.

"Which is why we do it." Mallen pulled the power back to idle and retrimmed for best soaring speed. "This is a sailplane with an engine, understand? McKennon thinks of this as an airplane. He's expecting us to go *someplace;* north, probably. But if I shut the engine down and work the lift, we can stay up for hours, just tooling around the edges of these clouds. McKennon will expend his efforts on searching north of us. The more time we spend here, the farther north McKennon will search."

"How about radar?"

"Don't know, but remember two things. This aircraft is made of wood and fabric. Which means almost zero radar return. And also, these thunderbumpers around us have a lot of precipitation in them, which plays hell with radar. I don't think they'll look for us to stay here, and if they do, I don't think radar will be able to identify us."

"But, eventually, you still have to go north?"

"Agreed," Mallen said. "The surface wind was from the southwest. These clouds are drifting northeast. We stay with them and keep them as cover for maybe another two hours. Then we make a dash to the northeast, staying as high as possible. We should get maybe five hundred miles out of her at over a hundred miles per hour. If he doesn't see us by sundown, he'll figure that we're still south of him. And by tomorrow, he'll have two or three times as many planes and choppers in on the search."

Wyatt laughed into the intercom. "You sound like you're trying to convice yourself."

"Maybe. But it makes sense." Mallen watched the variometer carefully—some sink but a lot of lift, enough to stay up. He pulled the throttle back to idle and switched off the magneto. The prop swung through three or four turns, then stopped. Mallen switched off the electrical system and pulled the engine cooling cowl closed. The air speed decayed to forty-five miles per hour and he retrimmed, working lift along the leading edge of a cloud face.

"You can restart this thing?"

Mallen nodded, suddenly aware of the silence. He took the headset off and hung it from the clip. "The manual says so." They flew in silence for minutes, losing a little, gaining some.

Beautiful day, he thought abstractly. Great towering cauliflower clouds on all sides, with the blue-black dome above him. He banked carefully, tracing the edge of the cloud face with his wingtip. Beneath him, he could occasionally see an indistinct blur of brown between riffs in the cloud deck. Three miles down, he thought, and smiled.

"What are you doing?" Wyatt said.

"Trying to stay in lift. The stuff that took us up through the cloud; the stuff that most pilots regard as uncomfortable bumps." The variometer was well on the plus side and he watched the altimeter slowly inch its way higher.

"So how do you know you got lift?"

Mallen scratched at his two-day-old beard. The flying took concentration, the plane was unfamiliar, and this wasn't purely for fun. "Look down at your panel," he said. "The instrument in the center. It's showing one hundred sixty feet per minute on the plus side. In still air, this aircraft sinks at one hundred eighty feet per minute. But we're in an up-welling air mass that is rising faster than we're sinking. Bingo . . . we get a net gain in altitude. The vario shows how much that net gain is."

"So I assume that there are also pockets in the air that drag you down."

"Not pockets," Mallen said. "Call it *sink*. Some air is rising, some sinking. Fly into sinking air and you go down like a Simonized brick. The object is to stay out of the sink and in the lift. The variometer shows what's happening."

The cold was starting to penetrate the cockpit. With the engine off, the heater was useless. Mallen could hear Wyatt moving around in the aft seat, trying to keep warm. Seventeen thousand feet on the altimeter. Little tracers of crystalline frost laced the edge of the canopy, and Mallen could feel the beginnings of hypoxia. He took a couple of pulls on the oxygen and immediately felt better.

Mallen craned his neck around to see Wyatt, who had his feet tucked up on the seat, his jacket pulled around him. He grinned back at Mallen. "Cold, massa." He rolled his eyes.

"Get one of the down-filled sleeping bags from the cargo hold. Wrap it around you, but don't get it tangled in the controls."

"Anything else, mother?"

"We're high. Over seventeen thousand. If you get dizzy or a headache, take a couple of drags on the oxygen mask."

"How about you?"

Mallen lifted his eyebrows. "I'll be all right. If it gets too cold, I'll start up the engine and turn on the heater.

I'll use oxygen as I need it. But it's all we've got. So conserve."

"One thing," Wyatt said. "Serious."

"What?"

"Don't let McKennon get us. He meant it."

The clock on the panel swept through thirty seconds. More feathery ice slowly formed intricate patterns on the canopy. It was peaceful, quiet, remote, as only high altitude can be.

"Meant what?" Mallen asked softly, not wanting to know.

Wyatt didn't answer.

Wyatt was asleep now, the bag pulled up over his head. Mallen turned and checked him, but he hadn't moved in over an hour. Turning back to the panel, Mallen checked the air speed, vario, and altimeter. Losing a little, he thought. Down to fifteen thousand. Away to the northeast, across a span of open blue, was a build-up of cumulus. Just a few scattered puffs along the way. He decided to span it, hoping that the buildup would provide more lift now that this lot was decaying rapidly. Tired, he thought. And cold. There was the temptation to quit the hide-and-seek game, start the engine, and head north. Go for it. But of course that was what McKennon was expecting. And McKennon would have to be disappointed. Mallen took a long, slow pull at the oxygen mask and turned northeast, building up air speed to cover the opened sky as quickly as possible. No one would see him more than two miles above the earth, he told himself.

One man saw the Sperber, or at least thought he did— Eastern Peace Division corporal George Phengal, while standing in a runted garden patch near Kidderville, New Hampshire.

Phengal had spent the morning stirring the ground with a spade, mulching the remainder of his tomato plants into the tired earth. The year's crop of tomatoes and corn had been good, considering the early frost. Marjak, the barracks commander, got two-thirds of the crop, but both men agreed that it was a fair exchange in return for Phengal's pulling the easy night shift. And Phengal was given the occasional use of Marjak's horse and cart.

The sun was high, starting to slide down to the west. Phengal stood up and worked the small of his back with his large, lumpy hands. He looked toward the northwest, where thunderheads were building. It was a fair bet that there would be rain in the late afternoon. He started to turn away, then turned back, hesitantly, shading his eyes wih cupped hands and staring toward the cloud buildup. He stood motionless like that for some time, then turned and started down the path toward the barracks in a labored trot.

Sergeant Magrill looked up as Phengal thudded along the barracks porch and slammed the door open, allowing it to bang heavily against the wall. Magrill threw down the language standard.

"What's the problem, George?"

Phengal was panting, his plain, moonlike face flushed to a bright pink. "Aircraft . . ." he said. "Aircraft heading northeast."

Magrill looked at the wall clock and noted the time: twelve eighteen. "What color, how high?"

"White . . . ah, silver-colored, maybe. It was too high to really see." Phengal sat down heavily on a chair. "But it was an aircraft, just like Marjak briefed us on during shift change."

Magrill wiped his face in exasperation. "Phengal, you left your glasses on the desk. You can't see shit without them. You expect me to call this in?"

"It was an aircraft," Phengal said flatly.

"You hear the engine?"

"Yes," Phengal lied.

Magrill sighed, picked up the radio handset, and said, "Give me the Megantic Barracks. I have some information for McKennon."

McKennon reread the pink slip a third time, folded it twice, and slipped it into his breast pocket. He stood straighter, flexing his shoulder blades back, and looked to the south. One sighting, he thought, and not very reliable at that. But it slowly fitted in with what McKennon understood of Mallen. "Not as dumb as I thought," he said aloud. "But not very fuckin' bright, either."

McKennon stood apart from the rest of the men on the chopper ramp, watching the storm clouds pile up. He ran a hand through his gray hair, suppressing the desire to scratch his scalp and spoil the neat grooming. His uniform clung to his back and the sweat had dried, leaving a tacky feel to his skin. It would be good to have a shower before the refueling was completed.

So Mallen was still south, he thought. Baines had said that the Sperber was some kind of sport plane, maybe a motorglider. Probably able to stay up on a very low power setting, possibly even stay up with the engine off, if the conditions were right. It fitted together nicely.

A hand touched him on the shoulder and McKennon wheeled. Santilla stood there, smiling, the rocket launcher still cradled under one arm. "Radio for you," Santilla said, grinning. He didn't say "sir."

McKennon started to form words in his mind to cut this little greaser down, but he checked himself and turned away, striding for the barracks. He had no control over Special Forces, regardless of rank, something that Baines had made abundantly clear. Special Forces was here to pull Eastern Peace Division's fat out of the fire.

He passed the three choppers, being fitted with long-range tanks. Baines stood with one leg propped up on the airframe, working out a loading list from the items that McKennon had ordered from the Megantic warehouse. He didn't look up as McKennon strode past, but he said, "Thirty minutes and we're ready," then hawked and spat in the dust. McKennon nodded.

The barracks was cooler inside and fitted out with decent equipment. The barracks commander had a glassed-in office off to the side of the day room. McKennon supposed that this had probably been a Royal

Canadian Mounted station or maybe something that had belonged to Fish and Game. Solid furniture and desks were all fenced in by an oak banister with swinging gates.

McKennon followed a corridor that led back to the radio room. There were corridors leading off at right angles, with cells beyond.

The radio operator, a red-headed kid with acne, handed McKennon the handset and turned away to scribble in a log. He knew that the kid would blab everything that was said, and then the whole station would know. He turned to the kid and tapped him on the shoulder. "Get out," he said. The kid shrugged and left.

"EPD Officer McKennon here," he said, and flipped the receive switch.

A woman's voice, unctuous and impersonal, told him to wait. McKennon could feel the sweat beginning to dribble down the back of his neck. He waited for over five minutes, knowing that Brinkerhoff would do this intentionally. A photograph of the First Secretary glared down at him from behind a fly-specked frame. A photograph of Antonivich hung slightly lower. In the photograph Antonivich was smiling, with one eyebrow fractionally higher than the other, as if about to ask a question. McKennon couldn't think of any answers.

"You have him yet?" Brinkerhoff said in the handset. He had probably been listening all the time.

McKennon could imagine Brinkerhoff sitting there in a heated office in Albany, playing with a pencil, using it to comb the hairs of his moustache. "No sir, he's south of us . . ."

"You *think* he's south of you, McKennon," Brinkerhoff said sarcastically. "You don't know, do you?"

"All right, I think he's south of us. We've just about finished refueling. We'll launch in about half an hour. He's heading north . . ."

"You *think* he's heading north." There was a noise in the background as if Brinkerhoff was talking aside to someone and then he said, "Pull your head out of your ass, McKennon. You've screwed this one up all by your little self. And for the record, we don't get any radar returns of aircraft traffic near Kidderville. You got the word of one old fart with bad eyesight. Use a maximum of three choppers. Nothing more than that except ground troops. You got a maximum of ten days to get those two guys. If you don't get them, then you can plan on coming down here for a little personal interview." There was a snapping sound as if Brinkerhoff had broken a pencil between two fingers. That would be part of the message.

McKennon laid down the handset just as the kid radio operator opened the door, which had been left ajar. He was half-smiling as he took the handset up and settled down into the desk chair.

Turning to McKennon, he said, "You're finished sir?"

McKennon wanted to punch his face in, knowing he had been eavesdropping the entire time. "Don't ever get transferred to my district, kid," he said, and slammed the door behind him.

He stopped in the washroom and splashed cold water over his face. The water was bed-rock cold and smelled of sulfur, probably pumped up from a deep well. He blotted up the moisture from his face with a filthy rag and combed his hair again and again, trying to spread the part through the distinguished gray patch. He inspected his face carefully, looking for any sign of the contamination of failure, but there was none. He switched on a medium-warm smile, adjusted his jacket, and walked steadily back down the corridor. Fuck them all, he thought. I'll have Wyatt and Mallen by nightfall.

McKennon moved confidently back into the day room, keeping his spine straight. Baines and two other Special Forces pilots were leaning over a deal table, an aeronautical chart laid open before them. Besides Baines, McKennon recognized only the chunky German pilot. The other was an Australian, from the sound of his accent. The three of them were arguing, but Baines shut them up with a muffled curse, then drove his finger along a red-penciled line.

McKennon approached them, looking over the German's shoulder at the chart. All three stopped talking and looked up at him. Baines muttered something that McKennon was unable to hear and the three pilots leaned over the table and resumed talking, excluding McKennon from their circle.

Pouring himself a cup of coffee from the hotplate, McKennon moved over to the window. The choppers were now fully loaded. Santilla was sitting on the concrete with two other Special Forces troops, both probably Cubans. They were all laughing. One made an obscene gesture to Santilla and Santilla shoved the tube of the rocket launcher at him, knocking him backward onto the concrete. All three laughed at this.

McKennon pushed the curtain back and sipped at the stale coffee. He was less than sure of his position now. One sighting was a fragile thing to hang his career on. Mallen would be heading somewhere between northwest and northeast. If the Kidderville sighting were for real, it would mean that Mallen would cross over the old border somewhere along a seventy-mile corridor. Three choppers to cover seventy miles was spreading it a bit thin. He decided to try to concentrate two of the choppers in the eastern segment, because that was the direction Mallen had consistently been headed.

Baines came up beside him and said, "We're ready." He pulled the words out like putty.

McKennon nodded. "I want you and the German to hold more to the east. I think he'll come up through that sector."

Baines shrugged. "Your show, McKennon. Let's get movin'."

McKennon held him back by the shoulder. "Hold up, Baines." He hesitated and then said, "Do you think he would move west?"

Baines smiled, wrinkles forming in the flab of his jowls. "He goes west and you, not me, are in deep shit. I don't think nothin'. I just work out a search area based on what you told me. If it's wrong . . . tough titty."

"You're a sweetheart," McKennon said, moving toward the door.

In eight minutes, the choppers were airborne and fanning out over a seventy-mile corridor, waiting for Mallen.

10

The sun was well past its zenith. Mallen rechecked the time on the instrument panel clock and made a scribbled notation on the margin of the chart, placing his position just north of Caribou Mountain, Maine, at 13:09. The old Canadian border would be just below. Scanning the horizon trying to pick up secondary checkpoints, he saw a lake off his left wingtip, much larger than the rest. Lac Megantic, the chart said. Before him and to the northeast were the corrugations of worndown mountains speckled with small lakes and mantled with heavy timber; the wilderness typical of northern Maine. Beyond those mountains the land dropped in tiers to the coastal plains and farmland of the Gulf of St. Lawrence.

The altimeter was edging down through twelve thousand feet. The lift was weakening and those areas he could find were not as widespread, making soaring difficult. He found a small pocket of lift and circled, gaining back two hundred feet then losing it, making a third turn through heavy sink. He sighed and booted the Sperber back to a northeasterly heading.

The cumulus were thinner now and not building to full development. Between major buildups there were long patches of blue sky, promising nothing but dead air. He stuck to his heading, paralleling the border.

Mallen checked the sleeping form over his shoulder. Wyatt had been sleeping for several hours now, cocooned in the sleeping bag, feet drawn up beneath his legs. The sharp, acrid smell of vomit was still there, despite the cold. Mallen turned back and took a deep suck of oxygen, noting that the pressure was still over eighteen

146

hundred pounds. He doubted that Wyatt had used any oxygen at all. A good man, Wyatt. The pain from the wound would probably be hell, and the codeine was limited. He regretted again that he hadn't kept the bottle of whiskey Roberts had offered. Without it, there would be nothing to clean the wound with, and Mallen was worried about infection. Probably just the least of his worries.

The altimeter was winding down through eleven thousand feet and a clear path of blue lay ahead of him before another line of cumulus scalloped the horizon to the northeast, promising more lift. The vario indicated sink averaging a little over two hundred feet per minute, and Mallen felt that was acceptable. Five minutes would lose only another thousand feet and would put him five miles closer to the new patch of cumulus and a possible regain of altitude. He decided that, regardless of soaring conditions, he would crank up the engine by 14:00 and head northeast under power.

McKennon was flogging the brush to the north, he reasoned. Mallen had seen nothing of the choppers since the encounter at Montpelier. McKennon would project out Mallen's maximum possible range and search along that perimeter. He switched on the master and checked the fuel quantity. Probably five hundred miles' range left, Mallen calculated, provided he kept the power setting within reason. And the soaring had won him well over a hundred miles toward the northeast. The sum of those two distances would put him beyond McKennon's wildest estimates.

"How we doin'?"

Mallen turned in his seat. Wyatt was leaning forward, down sleeping bag wrapped around his body. "We're getting there. How's the head?"

Wyatt smiled without conviction and leaned back. "Like a truck hit me. I just took two more codeine."

Mallen pointed a finger down toward the northeast. "Maine up forward. Canada off our left wingtip. We've made about a hundred miles without the engine."

"I didn't know these things could get that far."

"The record's over one thousand miles, Wyatt. Some guy did that along the Alleghenies. Same thing in New Zealand a couple of years ago. They're not toys."

"Obviously." Wyatt was moving around in the back, trying to get comfortable. "I suppose you can't crank up some heat?"

"Not yet. I'll start the engine in about fifty minutes and then we'll make the dash straight north. It'll be better then."

"McKennon?"

"No trace of him. Haven't seen an aircraft since we left Vermont."

"You got any idea where we're going to land this thing tonight?" Wyatt asked. He struck a match and lit two cigarettes, passing one forward to Mallen.

"Not particularly," Mallen said, inhaling and blowing the smoke out toward the cockpit vent. "A road, a field. This thing doesn't need a great deal of space. I figure we start looking about half an hour before darkness. Land, then get off first thing in the morning. Farther north. From there we can start to relax, get more fuel and head west."

"You really think we ditched McKennon?" Wyatt said.

"It looks that way. I'll be able to give you a better answer in a couple of days."

Wyatt snorted from the back seat. He finally finished his cigarette and opened the vent to stuff it out into the slipstream.

"You want me to fly this thing for a while? Flew with my college roommate and he let me handle the controls." Wyatt chuckled. "God—I think of the number of times we'd flog that old, battered Cessna four hundred miles to get to some hick town where his girl friend lived. I could keep the thing straight and level, at least."

Mallen half turned in the seat and looked back. "Not yet. Not as long as we're soaring. But once I crank up, you can spell me. By the way, where in the hell did you get these cigarettes?"

"Found 'em in McKennon's drawer. Got six packs. Good trading material."

"Not at the rate we're smoking them." He turned back, checking the instruments, checking the sky. "What's this thing with 'points'? Some sort of ration coupon?"

"More or less," Wyatt replied, yawning. "Initially ration coupons for stuff like fuel, cigarettes, boots. But since your local friendly Peace Division is responsible for distributing them, they became something you got only if you cooperated. Snitch on your local free seller, pass the word on somebody putting the government down, inform on strangers passing through, and you get points."

Mallen shrugged. "Roberts, this guy that I traded with, never mentioned them. We just swapped stuff— ammunition for food."

"That's the other half of the economy if you can call it that; pure and simple barter. Roberts probably never told you but owning a gun would bring an automatic death penalty. The ultimate form of gun control. Always hated the damn things."

"You handle one pretty well."

A long silence, then Wyatt said, "You learn fast, Mallen. You have to in this goddamn savage world."

There was another long silence, Mallen thinking back over the past days. "Get some sleep," he finally said. Wyatt mumbled something and was silent.

Glancing back, Mallen saw Wyatt was already curled up, the sleeping bag pulled over his body. Best thing for him, he thought. Combined with the cold and lack of oxygen at high altitude, he would sleep more readily. Have to get that wound cleaned for Wyatt this evening. My hands too, he thought; palms raw from the burns. Great thing to start off into the Canadian boonies with. They'll get easily infected if I don't care for them.

The wind was a dim whisper, flowing over the canopy like a transparent fluid. Mallen shifted his grip, holding the stick between his thumb and index finger, feeling a little lift burble past the wing, pushing it up. He countered and rolled into it, keeping the bank shallow, through a full turn. Less than fifty feet of altitude gain. Hardly worth it. He rolled out onto a northeasterly heading, determined to hold it.

Wyatt, he thought. Slick, funny, tough, strange. Know nothing about him other than a few basic facts. Two very different personalities: half ghetto black and half accentless patent lawyer. And then something more in between, maybe the real Wyatt. Perhaps, he thought, it was just that the hidden core of the man had allowed him to survive and remain sane.

Checking on Wyatt, he noticed that the opened pack of cigarettes was wedged between the canopy reenforcing strut and the Plexiglas, matches neatly jammed in beside them. He pulled two out, pocketing one and lighting the other, trying to fight off boredom and weariness. The events since he had first been captured seemed like a movie run at high speed and blurred by an unfocused lens. Images of Bernshine, McKennon, Wyatt, and Roberts. Pain and tension and then waiting. And fear—a lot of fear.

He flicked the ash from the cigarette into the vent window, watching the glowing tip intensify in the slipstream. Where's it end? he wondered. Like a cigarette—just consuming itself until it smolders out. The thought shook him, the idea of death. He realized that he had been half dozing and sat upright, stuffing the cigarette out the vent window, watching it flick away into the slipstream. I'm alive, he told himself. Living. And that's something I'll try very hard to keep on doing.

His eyes fell to the instrument panel, scanning in sequence. Air speed forty-seven; a bit fast; he eased back on the stick, trickling off speed and trimming for forty-five. The altimeter was down to eighty-seven hundred feet, with the vario registering a relentless two-hundred-feet-per-minute rate of sink. Mag heading northeast. Cockpit temperature probably below freezing, he thought. The canopy was slightly hazed, with frost on the shady side.

Beyond the cowling, the cumulus was closer, growing

taller in the midafternoon sunlight. So much taller that the development had begun to reach that stage of growth where cumulus become cumulonimbus: great, growing towers of condensed vapor rising majestically through the autumn light into the stratosphere, cox-combing on top into feathery ice crystals. Mallen knew that later there would be heavy rain and/or hail, with lightining playing between the cells and thunder re-bounding between the low hills of southern Quebec. Mallen swept the horizon twice from left to right, quar-tering his search into five-degree increments. Nothing there. He had a blind spot directly behind and below; something that caused an uncomfortable feeling be-tween his shoulder blades if he thought about it. Mallen felt uneasy and craned his neck as far around as the shoulder harness would allow, but the sky was empty. He fetched the other cigarette out of his jacket and lit it.

How easy not to smoke and then start again. The pack was plain, without markings, and the cigarettes were a very dark leaf wrapped in brown paper. But the taste of the cigarette was smooth, almost narcotic.

He thought of Wyatt again, the odd passenger on the bus. Mallen analyzed his thoughts, triying to formulate some opinion of him. Without Wyatt he would have twelve more hours of fuel in the back seat plus more than enough food. But then again, without Wyatt he would be frying in McKennon's special chair with the matched set of rubber gloves and the polished elec-trodes.

Scan again, panel and then horizon, looking for a speck that would grow in the windshield to a deadly form. Below him he watched a sun-burnished lake slide beneath his wingtip more than a mile below. Eighty-one hundred feet and still sinking. He set his mind back to small, fragmented thoughts, keeping a basic level of awareness synched to the flight of the Sperber. Thirteen thirty-one on the clock; a long way to sundown.

He took off his sunglasses and rubbed the bridge of his nose, then put them back on. Just a little longer.

Then start up and get some heat in this thing. Wyatt could fly it—spell him every fifteen minutes . . .

A lance of white sound broke against his ears as he saw the flame track of the missile bisect the horizon in front of him. The missile continued a few thousand feet higher and then burst in a black-pink puff, fragments trailing smoke and flying out in looping trajectories. The shock wave of the explosion hit him seconds later and the Sperber shuddered violently. Mallen instinctively racked the Sperber into a sixty-degree bank, slamming the throttle to the firewall, forgetting in his panic that the engine was dead.

Wyatt was fully awake now, cursing in his confusion. Mallen kept the Sperber racked over, completing the 360-degree turn, scanning desperately for the source of the missile. He almost missed it, down low and far behind. He caught the chopper as the sun reflected off its canopy.

"Dammit, what?" Wyatt was yelling.

"Missile," Mallen said. Checklist: magneto on, choke on, boost pump on, master electrical switch on, cowl open. Mallen reached for the starter switch.

"What kind of missile?"

"Shut up, Wyatt! I'm getting this thing started." It dawned on Mallen that what Wyatt was asking was critical. Wht kind of missile? Radar? Not likely, from a hand-held unit on a chopper. Free aimed? Negative. Only two other types: wire controlled, the type used in antitank work, but he knew that would be stupid, impracticable for air-to-air combat. So it had to be heat seeking. And they had fired it because they just assumed he had an engine running, a high heat source. And starting the engine would give them a target. He shut down the panel.

"What kind of missile? Where from, Mallen?" Wyatt was yelling at him.

"Heat seeking. The chopper's very low on your right side."

"The engine doesn't start?"

"Christ, man, I can't start it yet. Engines produce

heat." Mallen pushed the nose down, gaining air speed. The cumulus were spotty; small clusters on the outlying fringe of the large cumulonimbus. Still very far, it seemed.

"I see him," Wyatt said. "Low but climbing fast."

"Keep an eye on him. He fires again and you let me know. I can turn this thing inside out. Without a heat source they got damn little chance of hitting us."

"Bullshit, Mallen. If they got automatic weapons, they'll nail us from three hundred yards. You gotta start this thing some time!"

"How many missiles you think they'd carry?"

"Three, maybe four."

Mallen nodded. "Four. I don't think more than that. McKennon would probably expect to get us on the first shot. The Cong had those things in 'Nam. About ninety-percent probability of kill on the first shot. Four would be more than enough."

Wyatt made a hawking noise. "We wait through four shots? They'll be flying up our ass by then, Mallen."

The cumulus were no closer. Mallen estimated carefully and guessed five miles. Five minutes at sixty. He stuffed the nose down a fraction, waiting for the air speed to stabilize. "How far are they back there?" He could hear Wyatt moving around, his head banging against the thin canopy.

"Mile at most, maybe less."

"And they haven't fired again?"

"Nothing. I'm watching."

Seconds ticked by. Very quiet except for the noise of the windstream.

"Nothing yet," Wyatt said, breathing heavily. "Still there, just trailing us. Getting closer."

Pock. The minute hand measured one increment. Four minutes, give or take. Mallen felt the sweat streaming down his rib cage, despite the cold. His mind seemed to be unable to focus on anything, unable to hold onto a coherent train of thought. Then he realized that McKennon had fired the first missile without a lock-on, assuming that the missile would pick up the heat source when it was close enough. McKennon was back there, sighting through the tube, puzzling why there was no heat return.

"You still have a full book of matches?" Mallen asked over his shoulder.

"Two. One almost gone. Another full one."

Pock. Another minute gone. Mallen altered for a valley between two smaller cumulus, still minutes away. He breathed in and then out, slowly. Get it right in your mind, he thought.

"Listen carefully, Wyatt. You screw this up and we'll be dead."

"I know what you're thinkin', Mallen. I light a match and throw it out. Give them a phony heat source to lock on to."

"Not enough. One match won't do it. Open the storm vent and then light the whole book. Get rid of it as soon as you're sure it's burning. And tell me when they shoot."

"Light it now?"

"Shit no . . . eat your lunch first!"

Wyatt snapped back, "Now, dammit?"

"Yes, *now,* dammit, and keep your eye on them. They'll shoot almost immediately if I've guessed right."

Pock. Mallen watched the second hand sweep through twelve and the cumulus come closer, boiling up. He refined his course for the valley between the outlying cumulus. "You get that thing going yet?"

"Match blew out . . . I'm tryin' it again."

Mallen's hands went through the checklist automatically this time, setting the engine up for start. Nose down a little . . . more air speed. There was a flare of light and the sound of the storm vent banging open against the stops.

"It's gone. Burned my hand."

"You still see them?"

"See them? Jesus yes! Three men in it. Can't tell whether it's McKennon, but . . . they fired!"

Mallen pulled up sharply, sucking the stick back to its full limit of travel, G-forces dragging down at his cheeks. Glance at the panel—air speed decaying rapidly, nearly vertical—and he slammed the stick full left with left rudder, shuddering over the top of a ragged roll, holding it there as the horizon snapped inverted, holding it as the nose fell through, coming back around . . .

The missile's rocket motor flared past the canopy, no more than a wingspan away. Mallen saw it as an incandescent corkscrew of light turning away clockwise with the horizon. Wings coming level, with the nose down, and air speed nearly redline. Up and to the right he saw the warhead detonate in a white flame, and the shock wave rattled the Sperber a second later.

The altimeter was winding backward like a clock's works gone berserk. Mallen held steady back pressure on the stick, flattening out the dive, allowing the air speed to decay gradually. Down through six thousand, then fifty-eight hundred. Air speed down to one forty.

"He's still there," Wyatt said. "Closer."

Pock. Less than a minute to the closest tendrils of cloud.

"I'm starting the engine. We need the power."

"You said heat-seeking missiles would home on an engine." Wyatt's voice was strained.

Mallen pulled the starter switch. The prop swung through two turns without firing. Cursing himself, he pulled the choke full on and hit the switch again. The toothpick prop ground through a slow arc and then the engine fired, the arc becoming a blur.

"What about the heat!" Wyatt yelled, leaning forward, his face inches from Mallen's ear.

Mallen slammed the throttle wide open and the engine stuttered and backfired, then caught. "Takes time for the engine to get hot. I need the power now. Strap in tight, 'cause I'm heading into the clouds. Keep me current on what McKennon's doing."

Mallen had felt the feeling before. Coming down a mountain road in Colorado on ice, the tires broke loose; the Buick started a slow rotation toward the shoulder, which had no guard rail. He had tried everything, steering into the slide, tapping the brakes gently—but nothing slowed the slewing convertible. Finally, Mallen had just sat there, relaxed and calm, waiting for the inevitable. The tires somehow grabbed in the gravel of the shoulder and Mallen braked to a stop, one tire hanging in free space over the crest of a boulder-strewn canyon.

It was that way now, flying toward the wall of the first scattered cumulus, engine straining at its highest power setting, seconds ticking past on the panel clock, nothing more to do than wait. Mallen reasoned that it would take McKennon a short time to reload and aim. The Sperber's engine would still be cold, but was gradually building up heat. The exhaust stack would give the greatest return. He had seen in-flight movies by Hughes Aircraft of one of their heat-seeking missiles flying straight up the tailpipe of a turbojet-engined drone aircraft. Half smiling, he visualized a rectal thermometer.

Pock.

"We're holding our distance," Wyatt shouted from the back seat. "I can see better now. It's the yellow-tail chopper. I'm pretty sure it's McKennon in the front seat."

"You see any rocket launcher? Something looking like a tube?"

"Nothing like that. The guy in the back seat must have it."

The first cotton balls of cumulus swept past his wingtip like outriders to a herd. Seconds now, he told himself. He wanted to watch the panel clock tick the seconds off, to be distracted from the agony of waiting. Panel okay, oil pressure high, and oil temperature barely off the peg. The engine would be taking a beating, starting from cold and being run flat out at redline.

"I can see the launcher now!" Wyatt screamed. "Guy in the back of the chopper is leaning out with the thing up on his shoulder . . . looks like he's having trouble with the thing. Wind's whipping at it . . . he ducked back in."

Mallen arched his head back, trying to see the chopper. Shocked, he realized that it had made up ground on them and was no farther than a thousand yards behind them, probably less. As he watched, the chopper pulled up, gaining altitude and slowing. The figure appeared again in the opened hatch, restrained by a beltlike device around his chest. The launcher was at his shoulder, and this time the air speed of the chopper was slow enough not to wind-blast him. Seconds now before he would obtain a lock-on.

Mallen snapped the magneto off and dumped the nose into a near-vertical dive. The engine backfired, detonating despite the absence of ignition. The prop was still windmilling and he advanced the throttle, letting raw fuel cool the engine. The air speed quickly built to redline and beyond. Clouds were in front and to the left. He eased the stick back, not knowing whether the wings would take it. He grunted against the G-forces squashing him down in his seat. Instruments blurred, vision going gray, the perimeter of his sight contracted as the blood drained from his head.

He was through a ragged wall of cloud and back into the open. The Sperber was nearly level, speed bleeding off, and his vision cleared as quickly as it had gone. In front of him was another wall of cloud so close that he had only enough time to switch on the instrument lighting and level the wings before he swallowed in blackness.

Rain drummed on the canopy, then lessened to a light hissing. Mallen concentrated on the attitude indicator, moving the controls in small increments to keep the minature aircraft in level flight behind its glass cage. His eyes slowly adjusted to the darkness. A pocket of brightness was off to his left and he eased into a shallow right bank, trying to find the core of the cumulus, but there was no organized lift, only light turbulence. His heartbeat was slowing. He slowly exhaled, realizing he had been holding his breath.

"You all right?" Mallen asked.

"I guess. Where'd you learn to fly, Mallen?"

He smiled. "In Waco, Texas. Courtesy of the Air

Force. They used to tell us it cost them one hundred thousand dollars per student."

Wyatt blew his nose and said, "They got their money's worth. What now?"

"Stay in here if we can find enough lift to keep up. He can't find us, and as long as the engine is off we shouldn't give off a heat return."

"You ever figure that McKennon is probably calling up more choppers? The fact that he found us wasn't pure chance. He's probably got five or six more strung out in a line."

Wyatt was right, of course, Mallen thought. He made up his mind quickly. "We're running out of options, buddy. So you're part of this decision. I say we swing southeast, at right angles to the direction we were going, hold that four, five minutes with the engine off, then crank up and head northeast again under power. Any better ideas?"

"You're flying this thing. Have at it."

Mallen kept the Sperber through one more turn and then leveled on a southeasterly heading, praying that the cloud structure would give them cover. In less than two minutes they broke out into blue air. Mallen jogged his flight path to take advantage of small, scattered patches. McKennon's chopper was absent from the vacant sky. Two more minutes. Wyatt passed him a cigarette. Inhale. Exhale. The packages used to say something about smoking being dangerous to your health. He thought about all the nonsmokers who must have been pissed off when they died from fallout. I would have been too, he thought, and inhaled again.

Five minutes. "You see him?" Mallen asked, setting up the panel.

"No."

Mallen hit the starter and the Limbach caught on first swing, stumbling into a rough idle. He held southeast for another two minutes, letting the engine warm, then slowly applied power, swinging to the northeast.

"Nothing yet," Wyatt volunteered.

They climbed for ten minutes, stacking up altitude.

Beneath their wings, Mallen watched the dark green forests of Maine creep by under a scattered lower deck of stratus. In places, the stratus layer was a white iridescent snow field, then it would be broken again, revealing the terrain below. Cumulus were still piled in clusters, but they were thicker in the north. Mallen realized that the colder westerly air mass was wedging under the moist coastal air, and the stratus was the result. He wondered whether it would be safer to get down into the deck, but discounted it. There were still mountains down there, and the peaks would be embedded in the stratus.

Eight more minutes eroded from time. Mallen counted each one, scanning the horizon. Wyatt was whistling between his teeth, the tune flat and monotonous.

"Nothing?" Mallen asked.

"Nothing," Wyatt replied. "Clear, blue sky . . ."

Mallen never heard the detonation of the warhead. But he felt the concussion, felt the hammer blow of the steel ripping through his arm, felt the Sperber stagger in the shock wave of the explosion, and felt the impact of the shrapnel tearing through the airframe. Instinctively, he hauled back on the stick. The Sperber pitched up, shuddered, and fell off on a wing, starting to spin.

"We're going," Mallen said, eyes closed, feeling only numbness. The sound of his voice was distant in his own headset, as if someone else had said it. He opened an eye and saw the horizon wheeling past the canopy, heard the sound of wind screaming. Two more turns through the spin and Mallen watched, doing nothing, comprehending nothing. Something was nagging in his mind. Something about rudder. He pulled back on the stick harder, but it was back to the stops. *Rudder* kept coming up in his mind. He could visualize it clearly, but nothing more.

"*Mallen!*" Someone yelling. He heard it over the sound of the wind and the engine. Something hitting his shoulder. He leaned forward, trying to get away. Just tired, he thought. "Stop it," he said in a whisper.

The pain was starting to come to his arm. He opened both eyes and looked at the jacket sleeve, torn away in shreds. He wiped at the blood with his right hand and fresh blood welled up. His hand and the side of the cockpit were both red. His mind dwelled on that. "Made a mess," he said aloud.

"*Mallen!*" He recognized it as Wyatt; yelling from the aft cockpit. The sound was an agony in his headset and he replied, "Shut up, shut up, shut up!" Something about rudder. Important. He tried to think. Both eyes open now, watching the earth turn beneath him. Turning right. Opposite rudder. Mechanically, he pushed against the left rudder. The rotation slowed. One turn. Another. The rotation stopped and then started slowly in the opposite direction. He released the rudder mechanically. No rotation. He giggled.

"Mallen, you hear?" Wyatt said slowly.

Mallen nodded.

"Release the stick."

Mallen released the stick and leaned back, his eyes open, watching the blue of the sky above. He felt nauseated and concentrated for a time on keeping his bile down. His mind started to clear and the pain in his arm became intense.

There was another light explosion overhead, thousands of feet above him. Mallen started counting as his father had taught him; four times seconds equals miles, from the sight of lightning to the sound of thunder.

"Which way?" Wyatt said. Mallen looked down at his arm. It was a black-red mess with bits of fabric and splinters of plywood embedded in the wound. "Which way?" Wyatt repeated.

"Which way what?" Mallen said. the pain in his arm was thudding so that he could feel every pulse of his heart.

"Which way do we head?"

Mallen realized that Wyatt was flying the aircraft, keeping it straight and level. He didn't remember letting go of the control. "Northeast," he said.

"Dammit, I know northeast. You got a compass

back here. It doesn't say northeast. It just says numbers."

Mallen made the translation in his mind. Hard to think. "Steer zero four five."

"Chopper," Wyatt said. "Not McKennon's. This one has twin rotors. He's way down on our right."

Mallen leaned against the canopy. He saw it almost immediately, the helicopter a tiny insect thousands of feet below. "I'm hit," he said. "Can you keep this going?"

"How bad you hit?"   ....

"Bad enough. I'm losing a lot of blood." Mallen checked the instrument panel. Blood was spattered in flecks across the gauges. The air speed read eighty-five. "Get your nose down a little. Hold about a hundred."

Unbelievably, Wyatt said, "Roger." Mallen found that he could still smile. He laid his head back, trying to clear his mind.

"You seen the wing?" Wyatt asked casually.

Mallen turned his head, looking at the left wing. "What's wrong with it?" he asked, slurring his words.

"The right wing. Is it going to stick together?"

Mallen turned and laid his forehead against the cold perspex. His eyes felt tired against the glare of the sun. He slowly counted five, six, eight punctures in the wing—and one was large, as big as a brick. But they were all mostly near the trailing edge, except the large one next to the spar. "No problem," he lied.

Seconds accumulated into minutes and minutes accumulated. Mallen waited for the final missile, his thoughts drifting. More cloud cover now, he registered. Wyatt doing a good job, snaking his way between the white battlements. He tried to look over his shoulder. Too much effort. A look down at the panel. Oil pressure good and temperature a little high. Fuel . . . his eyes came wide open. The gauge registered a quarter full, and as he watched the fuel low-pressure warning light flickered on, then off again. "You smell gasoline?" he asked.

"No. We leaking?"

Mallen pushed himself upright, gritting his teeth with the pain. He tapped the gauge. Same reading. "I think so. Gauge reads almost empty. They might have hit the tank in the right wing."

"How much more time?"

"Five minutes, maybe less." He watched the needle slump a fraction. "You see the chopper back there?"

"Still there. Not gaining on us. It seems slower than McKennon's. A lot bigger in size. I figure he's about two miles back."

Mallen eased off his belt and wrapped it three times around his arm just short of the elbow, then clinched it in an overhand knot. He took the controls and told Wyatt where the medical kit was. It was pathetic by any standard, but it had tape and compresses. Wyatt found it with difficulty and passed it forward, then took the controls while Mallen applied a compress to the ragged wound and wrapped it in tape.

Still waiting and a little lightheaded, Mallen leaned back in the cushions and closed his eyes a little, just filtering out the sun. "How close?" he asked into the intercom.

"The same." Wyatt sounded frightened. "What happens now?"

Mallen didn't want to think about it. Peaceful flying in the high, thin air. Arm bothering him, but not as bad if he didn't move it. "Keep going, I guess. We don't have any more options."

"Fuck you, Mallen. You're dying. I'm still living. Get me down on the ground."

He wished Wyatt would go away, leave him in peace. "Sure," he said.

"Sure *what?* Sure you're dying? Sure you're going to get this thing down on the ground? Sure *what?*"

Out ahead of them, Mallen could see more massed cumulus ahead. If they could make that.

"Sure that I'm going to get this thing down, Wyatt," he said. "Try, anyway. Keep this thing headed toward the clouds . . . a little more to the right."

"And when we get there?"

"The chopper down below doesn't know that we're losing fuel. Probably would reason that we'll go straight through. Or turn to a new heading. But I don't think he'll figure on us going down."

"To land?"

"Trees and lakes and mountains down there, Wyatt. I'll put it down the best way I can. You fly it until we reach the clouds."

"How much fuel left?"

Mallen tapped the gauge. It was down marginally, but not empty. "Enough," he said. "Leak must be in the side of the tank, not the bottom. It drained down to that level. I don't think we're losing more." Mallen slid back in the seat, head resting against the canopy. It was pleasant to let his mind slide away, the pain now just a dull ache. Only one thing to do, to get Wyatt down in one piece. Then he could rest. Lakes and timber below. He tried to visualize how he could put it down. In a lake, he thought. Near shore so that Wyatt could swim or wade. Water would be cold this time of year. Still good fishing. Muskies and perch. Ducks going south now. Pleasant to remember hunting with his father. Coffee in an enameled pot and flapjacks in the dawn. Just sitting still at sundown and listening to the wind in the pines and the fish breaking the surface of the lake . . .

"What now?" Wyatt was asking him a question, but he wanted to roll over and sleep some more and Wyatt was asking again, "What now?"

Mallen rolled up the lid of one eye and saw the towering pillar of salmon-white cumulus before him and sat straighter, forcing his eyelids open against a weight of tiredness that he computed to be massive.

"Say something?"

"We're to the clouds, Mallen. It's been about five minutes. You better take it from here on in."

Mallen felt lightheaded, finding it difficult to keep his vision in focus. First glance at the panel. Blur. He studied the clock and watched the numbers, meaningless, swim in and out of focus. Experimentally, he closed his eyes and reopened them. Same effect. Wyatt was saying something, voice distant and muffled. Mallen nodded dumbly and took the stick in his right hand. He tried to raise his left to trim but found the pain overwhelming. The needles of pain lacerating his arm brought his senses to immediate awareness. Pain is the answer, he thought. "I've got it," he said, and took the stick. "You see the chopper back there?"

"He's there. Plus another one. Both following and the small one is making time on us. You think you can handle this thing?"

Impossible to know, he thought. Hard seeing anything clearly. Bones functioned all right. For the first time, he saw splinters of plywood embedded in his upper thigh. The entry point of the shrapnel had been down lower, under the panel. He couldn't see it, but he felt the in-rush of cold air. He remembered the chopper sergeant in Viet Nam who always flew sitting on a sewer lid, afraid of losing his balls. A real complex about it. He smiled at the thought; an aging gunship sergeant, tough as nails, lugging his sewer lid across the flight line. He closed his eyes again, seeing the man giving the finger to his buddies, telling them . . . and Wyatt was pounding on his shoulder and he looked up to see that he was sliding off in a bank, losing altitude. He leveled the wings and nosed up, heading back to northeast. Left arm up for a fresh surge of pain and the consciousness that it gave him.

They were moving into an area of more densely packed cloud mass. Deceptive from a distance, the cumulus was not one homogeneous mass but rather isolated cells with clusters of lower clouds herding in close to the real growlers. He picked a patch between two towering cells; a narrow V-shaped valley of blue between white bulging cliffs. Scuffing the wingtips against the walls, he added power to climb as the valley climbed, unwilling to commit the Sperber to the more violent cells. They crested the col and Mallen pulled the power back to the stop, sliding down the opposite valley, losing altitude rapidly.

I can't put it off indefinitely, he told himself. Fuel damn low. Must be sloshing it out of the tank in the turns. "Get your straps tight," he said, surprised at the clarity of his own voice. "We're going down through the clouds. When we land, keep your straps tight until we stop. The canopy release is on your right side—the red lever."

"I got that," Wyatt said. "Still clear back here; no choppers yet."

Mallen nodded. Feeling better now. Vision cleared.

The wall of cloud was close enough to see the texture of condensed moisture forming and reforming, rolling under and swelling out. He thought briefly about possible damage to the wing spar. The engine must be running on fumes now. He switched on the instrument lights and boost pump. And then he penetrated the wall—out of sunlight and shadow into grays of wool twilight, with rain smearing across the canopy in small rivulets. He turned up the instrument light to full brightness and locked his eyes onto the attitude indicator. Still very dark, he thought, and with a curse flung off the sunglasses. Better now. Good accommodation. Some light turbulence was jarring them now, but not enough to make it difficult. He glanced at the panel clock, estimated an elapsed time of two minutes since penetration, and eased into a shallow turn to the left. The miniature airplane in the attitude indicator mimicked his actions as he held the bank to a shallow fifteen degrees.

More turbulence now, with rain driving in gusts against the canopy. He completed the first circle and held the bank, going into the second. *Down now,* dammit, he thought, reluctant to give away the altitude. He eased back the throttle to the stop and watched the rpms fall away to a slow idle. The fuel gauge was bumping on Empty and he knew that he had to have enough fuel for an approach to a cleared field or a road. He pulled out the spoiler handle and heard the immediate drumming of the wings as the airflow over them was blocked by the gates of the spoilers. The Sperber started to sink now, the rate of descent building up.

He glanced once through the gray muck to either side, to see that the gates were fully open. The arm ached— badly, just holding the spoilers open. He pulled back his left leg and crammed it against the handle and let the arm rest in his lap.

Two times around now. Heavy turbulence. Wyatt was saying something, but it didn't register. A brief shotgun rattle of hail, and then back into rain. He concentrated on the attitude indicator and the altimeter, stealing glances at the air speed and fuel. Down through 4,900; to 4,650. Then into really heavy rain and the canopy seal was leaking buckets and he panicked a little, wondering whether it would be this all the way to the ground.

Three times around, or was it four? The compass was dancing and the instruments were a blur from the turbulence. Thirty-nine hundred! Black like hell, and he manhandled the stick, trying to keep the aircraft upright and told himself just to fly attitude . . . just fly attitude—and they broke out beneath the cloud in a shower of light rain.

"Mother of God," Wyatt said distinctly.

Mallen leveled the aircraft and, flinching with pain, closed the spoilers. He goosed the throttle a little, clearing the cylinders of exhaust gas, and the engine gave a sick little cough and died.

Frantic, he pulled the cowl full closed and set the choke to rich. A pull on the starter handle and the engine coughed, backfired, and stumbled into a slow gallop, firing unevenly. Boost pump On. Dumb shit! Engine smoothing out, and he switched the choke off. Still running; sort of.

Seconds now, he thought, until she runs dry. The fuel gauge was dead on empty. Got to land. Now. *Now, now, now*.

The terrain below was a dull mixture of greens and grays. Unbroken tracts of forest and swamp. No roads, not as far as he could see. Lake. Off to the left. He rolled left and aligned the lake over the cowling.

It was shaped like a cat, he thought. Long tail, probably a stream feeding into the main body. Cove to the north, which resembled a head. Main body maybe two miles long.

Down through twelve hundred feet and the glide wouldn't make the lake without help. He fed in throttle slowly, getting alternate surges of power and dead windmilling. The fuel was nearly finished. At least there would be no fire in a crash, he thought

He told Wyatt that they were going into the lake, along the edge, and that he would jettison the canopy. No time to say much further. He estimated that he was less than a mile short of the lake, with enough altitude to glide it in. He cut the ignition and then the master switch and gave a final tug on the fuel cut-off switch. The prop windmilled to a stop.

The lake was much closer now, light feathers of wind on the surface, still basically from the southwest. A straight-in approach in smooth water, he thought. Unless he was careless, the aircraft would stay in one piece. He reached for the gear and dropped it in one smooth stroke and locked it down with the safety pin. And then remembered that it should be up for ditching and . . . to hell with it. Too close now and too low and too slow.

He lined up parallel to the shore and maybe twenty yards off, wanting to keep it close to land. For the first time he noticed that the shore was sand and scrub with marshy areas of black-green.

Without knowing why, other than his trust for solid land, he sideslipped into the shore and flared, using the spoilers to get it down. Two separate rocks, tall as a man, slipped by the left wing in a blur. He touched once on the main gear and bounced and settled again and was down and rolling in a shower of soft sand and the left wing whacked through some scrub pine and she started to slew to the left, digging her wing in, and that was all he remembered. Nothing more except the pain, and then even that was gone.

11

Mallen woke to the impact of cold rain splattering across his face. Pain washed against the perimeter of his consciousness, surging hard, breaking and then retreating. He tried to sit up, using his elbow for leverage, but a wave of nausea broke over him and his mind easily traded awareness for oblivion. His only vision was that of a black man standing over him. How strange, he thought, and passed into unconsciousness.

Much later, Mallen awoke still in darkness, and groaned. The rain (had there been rain?) was gone, and as he opened his eyes he could see stars between the breaks in a low mass of ragged cloud. The stars disappeared, and at first he thought that this was what it was like to be blind, but then they reappeared and he concentrated on watching them, to be sure that they weren't gone forever from his vision. One star, brighter than the rest, was flickering orange-red. Sirius, he thought. Dog star.

"How is it now?" Wyatt asked.

Mallen wanted to speak but found his tongue swollen and sore. "Water," his lips formed.

Wyatt moved on the periphery of his vision, a black shadow on black, disappearing and then reappearing with a canteen. He lifted Mallen's head and fed him small sips, spilling most of it. Mallen coughed, gagging, and then, using his right hand to steady the neck of the canteen, took three long swallows. The water was cold and tasted of aluminum. He swallowed more and the canteen ran dry. He wiped his lips and said, "More." Wyatt nodded and took the canteen.

168

Clouds crossed the stars three times while Wyatt was gone. Mallen concentrated each time, patient and now sure that they would reappear. The vision in his left eye seemed to be imperfect; dull and somewhat obstructed.

Wyatt brought back the refilled canteen and this time braced Mallen up against a boulder. Mallen noticed now that he was covered with the down sleeping bag and was sandwiched between two boulders that had some sort of a tarp spread between their tops to form a rough shelter. A small fire, more embers now, burned in a pit that had been scooped out at the base of one of the boulders.

"Welcome back," Wyatt said, handing him the canteen.

Mallen drank and drank again. "What time . . ." He found his own voice a coarse, foreign sound.

"Doesn't matter. Sometime after midnight."

"The landing . . . ?"

"Not bad. You hit your head against the canopy sill. I got you out, brought you over here, and cleaned you up. You'll survive."

Mallen looked down at his arm. It was bandaged in blue denim and the flesh was swollen tight against the dressing. His left cheek seemed abnormal, blocking out some of his vision. He touched it experimentally with his hand and found it the size of a bird's egg, tender and sore but with the flesh unbroken. A tooth seemed to be fractured, edge ragged against his tongue. I'll live, he told himself.

"McKennon?"

Wyatt fished a package of cigarettes from his pocket and lit two from a burning twig. "No McKennon as yet. Heard a chopper toward sundown somewhere to the north. It was loud and then soft and then loud again, like they were working back and forth."

Mallen watched the clouds moving for a moment, blinking stars off and on. He could hear the sound of wind moving in a forest of unseen trees, and he saw the faint reflection of starlight on the ruffled waters of the lake.

"And the plane?"

"The plane is okay. Some damage. You'll have to be the judge."

"What damage?"

Wyatt snorted in disgust. "Get some sleep. I'll wake you before dawn." He took the cigarette from Mallen's fingers and threw it into the embers. From his shirt pocket, he took an envelope and shook out tablets. Handing Mallen the canteen again, he said, "Codeine and tetracycline. Swallow."

Mallen nodded and took the tablets, drinking heavily. He eased back onto the ground with Wyatt helping him move his shoulders and body.

"Night-night," Wyatt said, smiling, the teeth iridescent in the black void of his face.

Trying a smile, Mallen slid back into unconsciousness, hearing the wind in the trees and Wyatt's boots scraping on the sand.

He woke again into a gray world with not enough light to distinguish form. Wyatt was beside him, propping up his shoulders.

"More medicine," Wyatt said softly, feeding him alternately with pulls from the canteen and tablets. The process, awkward with both of them fumbling, went on a long time. Mallen noticed a fetid smell of decay, as if he could smell meat going bad. The pain in the arm was somehow less.

Finished, Wyatt rocked back on his haunches, his shoulders supported by the opposite boulder, and lit a cigarette. He pulled on it, arching his head back, and blew the smoke between his teeth, the cigarette still clamped between his incisors. "We're all set," he said, taking the cigarette from his mouth and tapping the ash against the rocks.

The light was getting noticeably stronger, gray going to misty cream. Mallen realized that there was fog over the lake. A mosquito hummed, hovering in the dead air between the boulders.

"How are we all set?"

Wyatt tapped the ash again, unnecessarily. "For Mc-Kennon. If he comes." He wiped his hand across his face and Mallen realized that Wyatt had been up all night. His eyes were bloodshot and the face hardened in fatigue.

"You've been working on this all night?" Mallen said. The cigarette tasted curiously sweet.

Wyatt nodded. "It's not that much. I've pushed the plane as far back into the trees as possible. Smeared mud over the top surface to cut the contrast, then stacked cut branches of pine around it."

"How about the tire tracks?"

"Swept them over with branches. The rain did the rest. Looks like virgin soil." Wyatt smiled.

Mallen returned a tired smile. "There any more cigarettes?"

Wyatt lit him one and filled a saucepan with water and placed it on the embers. "Coffee soon."

The eastern horizon was fractured in reds and oranges, needles of light like chrome spokes on a wheel radiating from the hub of a still unseen sun. The eastern shore was a wall of treetops, rising above the mist of the lake. Mallen remembered other lakes in other years, when he would wait for the ducks at dawn with a 12-gauge and rum-laced coffee.

They sat in silence, both tasting peace. It was hard to believe that today, as yesterday and perhaps tomorrow, might be their last. Mallen wanted to reach across the small space and touch Wyatt, both in thanks and reassurance. Their eyes met briefly. Mallen said it silently and Wyatt nodded his head fractionally. A third person, witnessing the scene, would have never noted the gesture.

Wyatt poured the hot water into aluminum drinking cups and added a small measure of coffee. "You think McKennon will come?"

There is no use in lying, Mallen thought. No deception. McKennon would come with ten or twenty or a thousand more. He nodded.

"How do you think he'll find us?"

Mallen avoided his eyes and blew across the hot mug of coffee. Probably no definite thing. McKennon would have searched to the north and the south. No further sightings would come in from ground stations. He shook his head. Still avoiding Wyatt's eyes he said, "McKennon will come. Or someone else. They can't afford to let us go. Too many men killed, all cops, or whatever Eastern Peace calls themselves. . . . They'll come."

Wyatt moved his head in agreement. "I think so too. But if they can't find us right away, how long can they keep looking? Not indefinitely. We just hold on and then fly out."

Mallen drank the coffee in slow sips, pushing Wyatt's words around in his mind. How long is long? Food for ten days. Stretch it to fifteen. And then there was the matter of gasoline. "Two weeks is about the maximum we can hold out here. It's October. Snow soon."

Standing up, Wyatt stretched, hands on his hips and arching his back. He looked over the lake. "Yeah, snow soon," he said, almost to himself. Turning to Mallen, he looked down at his boots and scuffed at the sandy earth with a heel. "You think we can take off on this stuff? Enough distance along the shore."

"I don't know how long it is. Yesterday afternoon I would have guessed about a thousand feet. Maybe less."

"More," Wyatt said. "I paced it out. Four hundred and sixty paces. Which I figure is about fourteen hundred feet. Enough?"

Mallen nodded. "Enough to get airborne, but maybe not enough to clear the trees. I'll have to look at it. And there's a small matter of fuel."

"Yeah, fuel. That five-gallon jerry jug. How many hours is that?"

"Enough for takeoff and maybe another hour and a half of flying time. It's no good. We need full tanks to get far enough out of the populated areas."

Wyatt picked up a plaque of shale and threw it out over the lake, watching it skip twice and sink. "How about fishing camps? Hundreds scattered all through these woods. A lot of those places stockpile food and fuel. Probably any one of them would have a wood stove. Make it through the winter easy . . ."

"Eating what, for Christsake?" Mallen spat. "And you think all we have to do is walk two hundred yards in any direction and find a deluxe-edition, Sears and Roebuck equipped shack in the woods? If we were lucky enough to stumble across any, they'd probably be stripped bare." He drank the remains of the coffee and leaned back.

"Look, Wyatt," he said. "We've got fewer than ten days of food, a busted airplane, and, most important, almost no fuel. And the first snows are only days away. I see it this way—we wait a few days and walk out of here. There's a lot of farms to the north of here over the old border. We get food and split up. We got this far, at least."

Wyatt leaned down and glared at Mallen, his face warped in anger. "You think I buy that, prick? After I worked the goddamned night to hide that airplane? You think I don't hurt, white man? I hurt like hell, but I figure you're my ticket out of here. Thought you had the smarts to fix that thing I've got stashed in the bushes, and get fuel for it somehow."

Wyatt wiped his face in frustration, leaving smears of dirt. "So all right—you're probably right about fishing camps. If we found one, it probably wouldn't have enough food to make it through the winter. But sure as hell, you're going to fix that damn airplane, and sure as hell, we're going to get fuel for it. 'Cause even if you don't, Mallen"—he thumped his chest, his voice rising —"even if you don't, I want to live. We try walking out and they'll have us in two days. We got to make like Superman and leap from *here* . . ." He drove his heel into the sand and took two paces, driving it down again, splattering sand across Mallen's body, ". . . to *there!*" He was shouting now, face drawn back, exposing his teeth.

He's right, Mallen thought. Christ knows, he's right.

We make it together in that airplane or we probably won't make it at all. And he's exhausted and he's done more than I could ask and I owe. A lot. Mallen looked up at Wyatt, his face composed and serious. "Don't shout, Wyatt," he said softly. "You'll scare the fish."

Wyatt's eyes wrinkled for a second, and then he smiled and laughed. Laughed on the fringe of lunacy, with the noise of his voice rolling across the lake; laughed so that he lay down on the ground with tears running from his eyes.

And Mallen laughed with him and told him that, somehow, they would get out of this goddamn place together.

They spent the forenoon covering up the traces of the camp between the twin boulders and then set up a second camp deep behind the fringe of trees bordering the lake. Mallen chose the site in a grove of pines, away from the hardwoods, which were shedding their leaves in red and golden showers. Wyatt stripped saplings and arched them together, binding them at their apex to form the crude framework of a hut, over which he placed the tarp.

Mallen watched as he lay on the down bag, dozing in the sun. Wyatt obviously was a woodsman of sorts, working without hesitation and getting the hut up with a minimum of fuss. Sweating heavily, Wyatt stripped away the flannel shirt. Beneath that was a khaki green T-shirt with the letters *EPD* stenciled in faded ink.

"The letters stand for what I think they stand for?" Mallen asked.

"Eastern Peace Division," Wyatt replied, not raising his head as he pried stones from the ground for a fire pit.

"Nice of McKennon's people to give you one."

"They didn't give me this."

Mallen probed the edge of his teeth with his tongue, feeling the rough edge of the fractured incisor. "Which means . . . ?"

"Which means I was issued it."

"You worked for those bastards?"

Wyatt nodded, averting Mallen's stare. "Legal branch." He sat down heavily against the stump of a pine, slowly blew his breath out, and looked up. "I forgot that I had it on. Not mine, actually. Sort of the spoils of a private war. But yeah, you're right, Mallen, I worked for them."

Mallen had pushed himself upright, a wave of dizziness contracting his vision. He squinted hard, trying to focus. "You didn't . . ."

". . . say anything about it?" Wyatt finished the sentence for him. "No. Why should I have? You wouldn't have trusted me."

"What happened?"

Wyatt lit a cigarette and looked down at the burning tip for a long time before answering. "Lived in a little town in upstate New York. You know, local smart nigger makes good. Not much patent law, but a good little practice. Wife, two kids, a dog—the whole disaster. Loved the shit out of it, Mallen. People said hello and invited us over for drinks. Easy to forget being black in some of those small towns. And then one May night, the night my oldest kid had her first date, the power went off and never came back on. I listened to the car radio—remember how they used to have those thirty-second spots about how this was a test to check out the alerting system in case of disaster? Never said what kind of disaster. Well, man, there wasn't anything. *Not nothin'!* Except static. Al's Cash Market, the only gocery in town, got wiped out by looters the next morning. Shit, Mallen—people you *knew,* running down the aisles with five shopping carts and a gun in one fist, sweeping crap off the shelves. Not lookin' at each other, except to scrap over a can of this or a box of that. Al whatever-has-name-was, who owned the place, tried to stop the first looters, and somebody wrestled him down and there was a shot and, man, that was the end of your American-style law and order. Local cop right in there with the rest of the good folk. Christsake, Mallen, that pig backed his police cruiser up to the storefront and broke the plate glass, then shoveled cans of food into his trunk."

Wyatt handed the cigarette to Mallen, who drew on it and handed it back. "Got to conserve," Wyatt said. "Not that many left." He took a last long drag, then flicked the glowing tip off with his index finger and pocketed the stub.

"So what happened?"

Wyatt ran his tongue over his teeth, grimacing a little. "Probably what happened in most towns; who knows? As far as I could see, that was the end of it. People either left in their cars or headed for the cellar. A few strangers stumbled into town—no gas left, no food. Would try to force their way into a house and normally either blew off the head of the owner or got their own heads blown off in return. Open season, it was, man. But the strange thing was that damn few people died of fallout. Whether we were lucky or what, I don't know. Town thirty miles away got plastered with enough radiation to light up Forty-second Street."

Wyatt arched his back, looking up at the sky as if he expected to see the orange-green cast that had characterized heavy ionization in dense fallout areas. "No fallout—residual stuff only. Ten roentgens per week for the first twenty weeks, but not heavy stuff."

Mallen wanted to ask questions. He had seen none of it, hadn't know how it had really been, except to see the aftermath. But he kept quiet, letting Wyatt work it out of his system.

"Oddly," Wyatt continued, "it seemed kind of nice at first. People stopped coming to Klinesberg. Gasoline was gone, a lot of people gone. No radio, no TV. And people there, sort of by common unspoken consent, didn't talk about the past—the looting and panicking. Dead subject. Summertime, so most people had small gardens. Plenty of milk at first. Farmers came in with more milk and eggs than we could consume. What they had shipped away before, they had to sell locally. They sold salted horsemeat and pigs. Strange how we don't understand the basics of survival. Salt, Mallen—with salt you can keep just about anything. And people suddenly found that you could preserve with dehydration. And canning—shit, I helped Joy, my wife, lay away fifteen, maybe twenty dozen jars of beets alone. People tore up their yards and planted."

"What did you use for money?"

"Money, at least at first; then anything that had real value: tools, blankets, firewood. I rigged up my Pontiac's alternator to a propeller that I carved and, with some fiddling, got it to put out enough for some lights. People came to me with their car alternators and I set them up with electricity. We used lightbulbs from car taillights and interior lights. It almost seemed by the first winter that we'd make it. Rough, most people agreed, but we'd make it. In that October, we had a town meeting and elected officials. I was a coon, Mallen, but they elected me vice-mayor and justice of the peace—the legal background, you understand. The city founding fathers must have done barrel rolls in their graves with a spade holding down an important slot. And then just about the time of the first snowfall, the flu started."

"Jersey plague?"

"I later heard it called that. Local doctor said it was a mutant strain of influenza. The mortality rate was over eighty percent. From a population of about four hundred, we had seventy-four left by Christmas. Joy and my kids died. She . . ." Wyatt trailed off, turning away. Both men sat silent for a while, Wyatt fooling with a stick, drawing squares in the earth. He finally turned back.

"In the spring, the first administration cadres of Peace Division came by chopper. Checked the place over with radiation counters and declared it a fuckin' paradise. Grow crops, they said. Man, they brought in the first tractor. Turned out to be the first, last, and only tractor, but we thought it was pure witchcraft—hearing that diesel run, tearing up the earth. P.D.'s told me that I'd be assistant administrator. That was when there was still some concept of justice."

"What nationality were the P.D.'s?"

Wyatt shrugged. "Two American, one Hungarian. It was okay, at first. People worked, man, like they never worked before. No work, no food. Simple formula. And they brought in more people from other towns to help work the land. In the first year, any soil that wasn't badly contaminated was worth its weight in points."

"You think that all this had been preorganized by the Soviets—the administration cadres, P. D.'s et cetera?"

Wyatt shook his head slowly. "Who knows, but I doubt it. Had one interesting conversation with a Pole about a year ago. Agronomist type, working out means of decontaminating soil. You know how these stories start up. One guy tells a guy who tells another guy. His story was that initially the war was limited. The Soviets tried to take out only our strategic-missile bases. NATO jumped the gun and struck back while the United States was still on the hot line trying to work out some sort of compromise. The Soviets then went all out— launched everything—and the United States did likewise. Recorded history stopped at that moment, and who the hell can tell now? I expect that none of the decision makers are alive to write their nifty little memoirs.

"Everything I saw in terms of administration seemed to be ad hoc—manuals printed by hand, guys being appointed on the spot for specific jobs. The Soviets did send out these cadres, and they sure as hell set up both Peace Division and the Special Forces. But it's not neat and tidy. I see it as a loosely organized socialist society backed up by a police state. But the horrible part about it—something you could see right from the beginning— is that the Special Forces are regional, and they're setting themselves up as little feudal states. As an example, this guy McKennon is a Peace Division type, but he's been pulling strings to get Special Forces status and the equipment that goes along with it. Given a year or so, he could carve out his own territory."

"You still haven't explained how you quit Peace Division."

"Quit, hell, Mallen. You don't quit, because you

don't eat unless you work. And when you were as high up as I was, you got special privileges, bonus points, the whole lot. Remember, too, that at first it was okay. The Soviet policy seemed to be that we could run our own show. Everything was regulated within existing statutes. Then I got in a ninety-page book, printed in five languages. I read through it in one sitting, and wept. It was like law and justice had been set back a thousand years. No freedom of speech, no public assembly, no right of appeal. Then local Peace Divisions added regulations on top of this, and, finally, Special Forces amended it. The result was a hodgepodge of law. Regardless of what a man did, he somehow or other violated the law. And I was the bastard expected to administer it within our region. More appropriately, Mallen, I was the hanging judge. I helped put away my share of poor, suffering bastards. On piddling stuff: minor thefts of food, traveling without documents."

Mallen settled back into the ground, watching clouds move between the curtain of branches. "What made you get out?"

Wyatt snapped a branch off an overhanging spruce and stripped the needles, then used it as a whip, slashing at weeds. "One night . . ." he paused, thinking. "One night I went down to the barracks. Two guys on duty, Zannick and Schofield. They had been interrogating some dumb kid who got caught stealing a spilled bag of rice off the railhead platform. Think, Mallen! Interrogating a kid for simple theft. The kid was caught with his drawers down, already had pleaded guilty. He would have been given sixty days of field decontamination labor in a hot zone. But these sadistic bastards were still interrogating him. They forced a water hose down his throat. The kid died—at age eleven, for stealing spilled rice. I went over the edge. I took Schofield's 12-gauge and blew them both away. Since then, maybe seven or eight more. I've lost count."

Mallen stared at him for a long time. "Just working alone?"

He nodded. "By myself. But looking all the time for

some of the organized resistance units. There are groups all over. No contact with each other, but still you hear rumors of a raid now and then. If anything, it gives Special Forces a reason for being—a sort of mobile strike force to fly in and put down a situation that the local Peace Division can't handle."

Mallen propped himself up on an elbow, fascinated. The idea of resistance was something he had not thought possible. "These resistance groups," he said. "What are they trying to achieve?"

Wyatt threw the branch away, chucking it like a spear, and turned back to face Mallen. "Achieve? Most of those poor bastards probably started out in the classical guerrilla mold of trying to repel the invaders. But who the hell are the invaders? Eighty percent of the P. D.'s are Americans. Special Forces—mostly Eastern Europeans, but still plenty of Smiths and Joneses. Most of the resistance groups are no more than bandits now, grubbing for food, raiding and looting, trying to stake out safe territory." Wyatt shook his head slowly. "Mallen, you're trying to make some kind of sense out of it all, and you can't. The closest you can come is something like Europe in the fourteenth century after the plagues. Feudal lords, bandits, poverty, and death. But no organized pattern, man. Just chaos."

There was a long silence between them, Mallen trying to absorb it, Wyatt evidently sick of the subject.

"Did McKennon know about your background?" Mallen finally asked.

"He knew. My picture's been posted for over three months. But he wasn't allowed to lay a glove on me. Albany is hot for my body. Guy down there by the name of Brinkerhoff—heads up both Eastern Peace Division and Special Forces for the northeast. He and McKennon are somehow rivals. Even though McKennon is basically small change in the system, he has some friends in high places. That's the one basic reason McKennon will bust his ass trying to find us. He loses us and his career is screwed."

The sun was hot, lulling Mallen into drowsiness. "Where does it all end?" he asked.

"It took two centuries to restore order to Europe." Wyatt said it evenly, as if he had thought a great deal about the future.

"Jesus Christ," Mallen said softly.

In the early afternoon, they heard the sound of an aircraft—not just the flat whump-whump of a chopper but a jet aircraft much higher. The trees obscured their vision at the camp, so they moved down to the edge of the trees, getting a clear view to the east. They never saw the chopper until it was right down on the surface of the lake, less than two miles away and moving fast. It was unlike the type that McKennon had used, much larger, with twin rotors and painted gray. It was too far away to read any markings, but it was obviously a troop carrier. It pulled up at the southern end of the lake, made a ponderous turn, and came back over the western side of the lake at a lower speed.

Both men crouched behind the scrub pine at the tree line, waiting for the chopper to land, but it passed by the spot where the Sperber lay hidden, without any hint of detection. Mallen could clearly see the faces of men looking from the cockpit. One man leaning against a chain across the loading hatch wore mirrored sunglasses and held an automatic weapon.

They waited breathless until the chopper was gone. The blat of its exhaust echoed over the still lake for a long time, and when it was gone the silence seemed louder.

"You think he saw anything?" Wyatt asked, standing up, moving out of shelter, and looking away to the north.

"Not sure," Mallen said. "If they did, we'll find out in a few minutes."

They ran back to the camp, took the Luger and the Winchester lever action, and crawled painfully up a stone-filled gully to the crest of a ridge, and waited. Though they could hear the sound of the chopper, perhaps more than one, the sounds were distant in the still October afternoon. Far above, contrails were laid down in a crosshatch by a jet at high altitude, and Mallen inwardly speculated that the aircraft was a photo-reconnaissance type. It seemed to him that the heavy tree cover would render photos useless.

The sound of the choppers persisted through the late afternoon and Mallen worried about it. The area that McKennon should search would be vast, running several hundred miles in any direction from their last contact in the sky over the old border. But the choppers were persistent, quartering back and forth over the gray-green forests, never farther than the range of hearing. Wyatt worried too, and asked Mallen, who just shrugged his shoulders. It was beyond his control.

They lay in the sweet grass and pine needles on the small ridge all through the autumn afternoon. Mallen dozed off under the influence of the codeine, his mind fluttering sometimes on the edge of consciousness, mixing the reality of the sound of the choppers with the fantasies of uneasy sleep. Wyatt watched him without expression, feeding and ejecting cartridges through the magazine of the Winchester, impatient for something to happen.

Toward sundown, Mallen woke and took more tetracycline tablets, but rejected the codeine. They worked their way back down to the camp and to the edge of the tree line bordering the lake.

There were still contrails etched across the stratosphere, and it was all too probable that the damn thing was a reconnaissance aircraft. Their fire had been banked and smothered with water when the camp was broken between the boulders. Without any other source of heat and with the cover of the trees, both infrared scans and photography woud be inadequate. But still the choppers quartered the hills around them.

Wyatt lit a cigarette, drew heavily on it, and handed it to Mallen. "The last one we have."

Mallen looked at him with irritation. "There were more," he said flatly.

"There still are," Wyatt answered. "I had them in the aft cockpit, but the rain got to them when I was dragging you out of the aircraft. They'll dry out, but they always taste like shit after they've been wet."

"Not exactly the worst of our worries," Mallen said, and Wyatt nodded, making a sucking sound through his teeth.

The chopper must have come from upwind, because neither of them heard it until it was down low over the lake. It came down the middle of the lake at high speed, then slowed and stopped in mid-air, hovering twenty feet off the surface of the water, thrashing up foam-streaked waves beneath it. It hovered there for over a minute, turning slowly through 360 degrees as if it were some curious, dull insect.

Mallen took the rifle from Wyatt and sighted through the variable-power scope. He caught McKennon in profile, binoculars to his eyes, searching the north shore. As the chopper turned toward him, Mallen chambered a cartridge and laid the crosshairs on the third button down on McKennon's tunic, inhaled, exhaled, and started to squeeze the trigger. Nothing happened.

Frantically, Wyatt dragged him down into the scrub, smashing the rifle to the ground.

"You dumb shit, the safety was still on!" he said in a hoarse whisper, teeth clenched.

"I know," Mallen said, lips touching the earth. "I knew it. But I wanted to kill him. Just to know that I could blow his chest open. To get it over with."

"No good, Mallen. We're going to live. McKennon or not."

They both watched the chopper turn through a second circle and slowly pitch forward, picking up air speed, moving to the south. They waited for minutes until the sound had died in the distance.

"He knows that we're here, doesn't he?" Wyatt picked up gravel from the earth and threw it down again in frustration. "He's just playing, right?"

Mallen shook his head. "I don't think so. He probably just duplicated another chopper's search pattern, or saw something that looked interesting. There are a thousand little lakes up here. They're looking for places that we could have landed on, like logging roads or lake shores. The jet begins to make sense now. Look," he said, and bent down to the ground, brushing away rocks and pine needles. He drew with a twig on the moist earth. "The choppers work over the roads and the lakes. The jet recon plane takes strip photos of the whole area and brings them for analysis. Thirty, maybe forty people work over those photos looking for the shape of a plane in the trees . . . much easier to see if you're looking straight down." He thew the stick away and turned to Wyatt. "It probably doesn't seem possible to you, but every year, planes would get lost up in the northern parts of New England. Searches would go on for weeks that included the Air Force, Civil Air Patrol, volunteers, rangers, the whole works. And more often than not, they wouldn't find it. Maybe later, sometimes years later, a hunter or forester would stumble over the wreckage. It's just too big an area."

Wyatt turned away and stared back toward the camp. "McKennon knows," he said over his shoulder.

With some twilight still remaining, they walked down the edge of the tree line to the Sperber. Mallen stumbled into it before he saw it. Stacks of fir branches covered the fuselage and wings, and the surface beneath was heavily coated with black mud.

"What do you think?" Wyatt asked, hunching down against the fuselage. "Could McKennon or the other chopper spot this from the air?"

Mallen shrugged. "I don't see how, unless it looks unnatural because of the density of growth." He pushed some of the branches aside and opened the canopy. The smell of sweat and hydraulics, vomit and blood was overwhelming. Mallen switched on the master, and the panel lights and gauges came alive. Battery still good, he thought, and switched it off.

Together they traced the fuel lines, looking for the break. In the growing darkness it was impossible, but

Mallen guessed that it could only be the main lead from the tanks to the fuel pump.

"We'll work on it more tomorrow morning," he said, sliding out from beneath the fuselage. "It can't be much more of a job than putting a sleeve over the severed portion of the line."

In starlight they unloaded the aircraft, sorting it on the ground by feel and then returning the unusable items to the luggage hold. While Wyatt humped the equipment back to the camp, Mallen probed the ragged holes in the wing's fabric, looking for damage to the structure. He found one severed rib, a metal shard of shrapnel still lodged in the plywood. Beyond this he could find no other major damage. The fabric holes were of little consequence; they could be stitched with fishing line and taped over. Whenever. Add tape to the shopping list.

Their meal was cooked over a low fire, well shielded from all directions. Mallen and Wyatt conversed in monosyllables, eating tinned sausage and stale crackers. They agreed to stretch the coffee, so the result was flat and tasteless. They finished it with cigarette tobacco that had been dried on a rock near the fire and rolled into a piece of toilet paper. It was too harsh to smoke, and Wyatt threw it into the fire in disgust.

"Let's discuss," Wyatt said, leaning back against the trunk of a fir.

"Discuss what?" Mallen ate at the edge of a cracker, trying to imagine bread. Image of a communion wafer.

"Discuss how the hell we get out of here. Get fuel. Get whatever you need for the aircraft. And what happens if McKennon and company drop in?" He paused, wiping his hand across his face.

"McKennon's finding us is the easiest one to answer," Mallen said tiredly. "He comes, we fight and we probably die. There wouldn't even be any point in running. In our condition and with four or five men tracking us, we'd last three hours if we were lucky."

"Okay, then what about the rest?"

Mallen sorted through the pile of gear, drawing out

the aeronautical chart. He noticed that there were dried specks of blood on the reverse side. Mine, he thought. O-positive.

Wyatt peered over his shoulder as he traced the probable route of yesterday's flight. From the last encounter with McKennon, they could be on any one of thirty small and poorly charted lakes. None of them even vaguely resembled a cat, but then again, the scale was minute.

"It puts us in this box," Mallen said, moving his finger in a rectangular motion, touching the borders of Canada and moving through desolate Maine countryside unmarked by town or paved road. "A box twenty miles on a side," he added. "We have the choice of going deeper into Maine or crossing the border."

"Which way?"

"No choice. Into old Quebec. There has to be fuel and supplies there. We can't chance stumbling around in the Maine woods without shelter or food. Besides, if they search, they'll work deeper into Maine, is my guess."

"And McKennon's guess?"

Mallen spat into the fire. "McKennon would guess Quebec."

"Why, for Christ's sake?"

Mallen peeled the sock from his right foot. The stench was nauseating. He peeled off the left one. Thinking.

"Because," he said. "Because McKennon seems to know what we're doing. Because he understands us like a hunter understands a rabbit. It doesn't matter either way, because we still have to go north into Quebec."

"When?"

"Two, three days. They've searched this section. We're relatively safe. If we move now, we may move into an unsearched section. Let it die down. And besides, we're both too weak to move in heavily timbered country. We'll spend the next couple of days working on the plane and getting our gear ready." Mallen looked toward Wyatt for a response, but he was asleep, head rolled back against the trunk of a tree, mouth agape. Mallen woke him and in a dumb stupor, Wyatt crawled into his sleeping bag and fell asleep again in seconds.

Long into the evening, Mallen sat awake, thinking of the last three days. There was a certain surrealistic quality to it. Violence and fatigue smeared like oils across a canvas. He found trouble in remembering what day it was and, confused, counted days on his fingertips. Roberts had come on Friday. Saturday McKennon had him . . . then this would be almost Tuesday. And then he thought that it didn't mean anything. Time was just relative to a supply of food or the distance you could travel on foot or the remaining span in your life. He pushed the thoughts out of his mind. *No thinking on the bus.* On to Mallen Maxim number two: To live, you have to survive.

He heated lake water in a pan until it boiled, then unbound the bandages on his arm. Wyatt had done an effective job. The wound was clean, with a puckering star-shaped tear in the flesh that should have been sutured. The edges of the wound were pale white and dead, crusted with clotted blood. He washed it gently with warm water and sprinkled it with two crushed tetracycline tablets, not knowing whether they were of any use. Tearing strips from the soft blue denim shirt, he rebound his arm. Next he washed his bare feet, using sand as a substitute for soap. It would be good to bathe in the lake, but he rejected the idea; both from the standpoint of tracking up the beach and the fact that he was too damn tired. Bodies at rest tend to remain at rest. Whose law—Newton's, or mine? he wondered, and lay down next to the fire. The heat felt better than the touch of a woman, and he fell asleep by the dying embers, grateful still to be alive.

Twenty miles north and eight miles above the earth, a war-scarred MIG-25 Foxbat made the sixth and final sweep of its assigned search area; from the Bay of Fundy in the east to Lake Erie in the west, searching overlapping sections along the old border.

The pilot, a veteran of the Seven Hour War, was Rumanian, short tempered and at the moment very tired. He locked the autopilot onto a westerly heading and settled deeper into the ejection seat. Two of the six missions had been a washout. Faulty equipment. Inadequate coordination from ground radar. Two missions and ten thousand liters of fuel wasted.

He fumbled with his oxygen mask, lifting it and resetting it against the bridge of his nose, which was raw from chafing. He could feel the stubble of his beard grating against the chin section of the mask. These pissant missions weren't going to advance his career, he thought. Far better to take your chances in the Chinese Pacification Front. Promotions by the numbers with your name stenciled on the canopy sill of a new YAK-36 and the Order of Lenin at the end of a tour. He mused on, grinding his teeth while the infrared scanners swept an area forty-eight miles in width, looking for the slightest trace of man-made heat.

Five and a half hours later, McKennon examined the prints and smiled, circling the western rim of a nameless lake near the Tumbledown Mountains. He put the chinagraph pen down and lit a cigarette; the long kind with the fine Virginia tobacco, which you bought in Special Stores.

12

For two more days, Mallen and Wyatt kept to the shores of the lake. The leaves of the maples were falling now in golden profusion, hurried on by snapping frost and bitter, overcast days. The fire was kept burning continuously. Mallen worked on the plane during daylight while Wyatt gathered dry firewood and made the meals. Wyatt had gone sullen, mumbling at meals and turning inward on himself. Mallen shrugged and continued to tend the wounded Sperber.

The work would not have been difficult had there been tools. The fractured rib was not critical to flight. Mallen repaired it as best he could, splicing a strip of seasoned pine along the edge of the rib with copper wire he stripped from the electric system. He used stones to sand the edge smooth and then stitched the fabric with needle and Dacron surgical thread. Vinyl tape, when and if procured, would seal the raw edges.

But it was the fuel system leak that was the real bugger. Lying on his back, reaching up into the guts of the fuselage with his good arm, Mallen felt the shredded rubber hose, perforated in several places as if a dog had gnawed on it. Tracing its path with his fingertips, Mallen felt two brass end connectors on the hose and then spent the next three hours with a pair of rusty pliers, undoing the fittings until at last the whole hose assembly was removed.

Turning the thing over in his hand, he marveled how more than even one-tenth of the fuel supplied to the hose had gotten through to the engine. It was irreparable, for even if the punctures were taped, the gasoline would quickly dissolve the tape's adhesive.

Repair it how? he wondered. Both end fittings were threaded and had small stubs of copper tubing projecting out, mated to the rubber and protective fabric covering of the hose by a complicated compression fitting. Jamming the hose between his knees, Mallen worked till twilight stripping off the remains of the rubber with the dull knife. Even with the hose removed, it took him another twenty minutes to pry off the compression fittings.

"How's it hanging, Mallen?"

Turning, he saw Wyatt standing there against the growing darkness, more shadow than substance.

"Possible," Mallen answered, holding out the two fittings. "There's enough of the original brass fitting to slip a hose over and cinch it down with hose clamps."

"So where do you get the hose and clamps?" Wyatt scuffed over and sat down next to Mallen, letting out a sigh.

"Any truck. Even a car woud have a rubber hose like this, possibly in the brake line or fuel system." He held up a short section of hose. "External diameter not too important, but it has to be pretty damn close to this interior diameter to get a leakproof fit. The clamps will take up any slack."

Wyatt grinned back at him in the darkness. "McKennon's jugular about the right size?" He lay his arm across Mallen's shoulder.

Mallen laughed and pocketed the hose section. "Wouldn't you love that," he said. "No, Wyatt. What we've got to do is find the hose and clamps, about fifteen gallons of premium fuel, and carry it back here. No shooting up Peace Division—no messes."

Wyatt heaved himself into a standing position, grunting.

It was almost totally dark now. Mallen realized how weary he was, from just a few brief hours of work. "How's the neck?"

"Passable to middling fair. It's infected, but I think

it'll work itself out. Give it a few more days." He started back toward the camp. "Don't be too long. I've got some bread cakes, and a duck that couldn't paddle faster than I could throw a rock."

A flood of saliva filled Mallen's mouth. "Truth?"

"Would I lie to a honky, Mallen?" Wyatt laughed. He walked away into the darkness, silent as he had come.

As a last act, Mallen removed the magnetic compass from the aft cockpit, working by feel. It would be awkward to use, but it was the only thing he had for direction finding. Before closing the canopy, he stood beside the Sperber, feeling the upholstery, touching the controls. It had been so close, he thought—so close to making it. He realized that he had underestimated McKennon's tenacity and now he would have to pay for it. On foot.

Wyatt had spitted the duck; then packed mud over it and roasted it on the coals of the fire. In a tin can he had made a stew of the heart, lungs, and liver. They both ate in silence, stripping meat from the bird and then sucking what flavor remained from the bones.

"I figured we'd be going tomorrow," Wyatt finally said, wiping his hands and leaning back. "I got most of the stuff packed."

Throwing the debris into the fire, Mallen edged up closer to the fire, warming his hands. "You feel well enough?"

Wyatt snorted. "Good enough. I figure we wait much longer and it'll be even tougher. How about your arm?"

Flexing it, Mallen felt the length of the wound. "It's healing well. I can move all right with it. And you're right—I don't see much point in hanging around here with the food running out and nights getting colder." He pulled the stack of charts out of his rucksack and laid them out on the ground.

They worked it out together, generally to walk north, keeping to the ravines and valleys where possible, until they crossed the final ridge of low mountains marking the old border. Then down into the St. Lawrence Valley, keeping to the fields, moving only at night.

"What do you think our best bet is?" Wyatt asked.

"You mean where we have the best chance of finding the stuff?"

Wyatt nodded, yawning. "Yeah. I'd figure outlying farms."

Mallen thought about it and rejected the idea. "No good. Outlying farms would probably be the marginal operations." He traced over the map with his finger, moving north, deeper into the St. Lawrence Valley. "Probably better if we get into a really small community, something of about five or six houses. We increase our chances of finding fuel in a small area. They'd probably be sharing some type of engine-driven farm implements." He pointed to a small hamlet labeled St. Sabine. "Someplace like this."

Wyatt shrugged. "General area looks okay. We can play it by ear. Might be lucky enough to get a couple of horses to pack our stolen goodies back with." He pulled a long face and said in an artificially deep voice, "You Lone Ranger, me Tonto. Gettum ponies and go-juice for great white bird."

Laughing, Mallen pulled his sleeping-bag zipper open and started to crawl in. "First a gourmet dinner and then a supper club comedian. I'll put a big tip on the bill."

"One other thing—seriously," Wyatt said hesitantly. He pushed another branch into the fire and watched it take hold, thinking. "You given any consideration about what we do *if* we get the parts and fuel and then *if* we get that great white bird of yours out of here?"

Mallen hunched his shoulders. "Go north first, I suppose, as planned. Eventually get to the Canadian west—British Columbia."

"How long you think before we'll be ass deep in snow?"

"You're perhaps suggesting Miami Beach?"

A grin split Wyatt's lips. "Yeah. Why not?" He stirred the ashes of the fire and sobered. "No, Mallen. We need something better. A house with a fire and some women and food for a long winter." He turned and faced Mallen in the firelight, shadows deepening the lines in the corners of his eyes. "Ontario. More accurately Lochrane, Ontario. I have family there. A small farm and what used to be a tire-recapping shop on the outskirts."

"You know they're still alive?"

"Nothing north of Sault Ste. Marie was hit. Knowing them, they made it through."

"And you're suggesting . . ."

Wyatt rubbed his nose, looking up at the gray night sky. The temperature was in the low thirties and growing colder. "Cold as a nigger's ass. That's what they used to say, isn't it? Well, it's true. Snow tonight." He pulled the aeronautical chart over and pointed to the northern edge. "Yeah, I'm suggesting. Suggesting that we fly north over the St. Lawrence River and keep north of the major cities. I don't think it's more than five hundred miles from here. Less, maybe."

Mallen watched his eyes. Dark and brilliant and hard. Just spots of reflected firelight. "How do I fit in?"

"You fly me there. I get you more fuel so you can go west or you stay with me through the winter."

"Just like that?"

"Just like that. We'll get papers, or fake up the ones we plucked out of McKennon's office."

Mallen fumbled with the zipper of his sleeping bag. Getting colder rapidly, as if someone had kicked the blocks out from under the thermometer. He blew a long stream of condensed breath. "So who are these kin of yours?"

"Uncle and assorted wife, brats, cats and dogs. They'll cover us."

"I'm not the right complexion," Mallen said, avoiding Wyatt's eyes.

"You'll pass," Wyatt said, smiling. "In-tee-grated community. Fewer than fifty or sixty families spread over twenty square miles. I'll teach you to milk, shovel shit. I spent my summers there when I was a kid."

Mallen rummaged through the tote bag and pulled out an en route chart. It looked reasonable: north across the St. Lawrence and then west, leaving Quebec City and Montreal to the south. Desolate country.

"It's worth a try," he said. "It depends on fuel and weather. Five hundred miles may be stretching it a bit, particularly if the wind is from the west. Does your uncle have a large pasture, something about a thousand feet on a side?"

"Something better," Wyatt said, sliding deeper into his sleeping bag, "A dirt road about a mile long. Runs in from a country road as straight as a die. I know, because I used to walk it to get the mail from the letter box. No farms within half a mile. Grove of trees shields the farm from direct view."

A large wet flake of snow fell through the firelight, and then another. There wasn't much time left for them, if this was going to be an early winter.

"We better get some sleep. First one up wakes the other," Mallen said.

Wyatt grunted and rolled over, his back to the fire.

Mallen stayed up a lot longer, eyes unfocused, listening to the low-register moan of the wind in the treetops. Nothing to lose, nothing much to gain. Just keep moving. As he fell asleep, he thought he heard the distant rumble of a jet at high altitude, and he dreamily envied the man far above the earth looking down on blackness but with stars above him.

McKennon stared out across the withered lawn of the Megantic Barracks and watched fat snowflakes drift down through the floodlights. If the snow stuck, tracking would be easier and Mallen would have to keep a fire at night, he thought. Met was forecasting clearing and cold for tomorrow, with no cloud cover to hamper infrared scan.

"Six days left, McKennon," Brinkerhoff said, lounging back in a canvas chair. "Six days." He picked at an earlobe with a fingernail.

McKennon breathed heavily, fogging the window. He

turned back to Brinkerhoff and met his stare. "I've got them," he said. "They've got to move with the cold coming on. . . . Sir," he added.

"You're full of shit, McKennon. You fuckin' well don't know. Men and equipment wasted. Go in and get them *now!*" Brinkerhoff lit a cigar without offering one to McKennon. He threw the burned match on the floor.

McKennon watched the man. Thick and tough. Gray everything: tunic, moustache, hair, and face. Running to fat, but the eyes . . . ferret's eyes. He decided that Brinkerhoff was running scared. "I'll get them," McKennon said evenly. "But if I do go in, I'll lose men, which is exactly the way you want it, isn't it, Eric?"

The fat man shrugged. Avoiding McKennon's eyes he said, "I don't give a shit." He tapped ash onto the polished pine floor.

"Your 'I don't give a shit' is pure bluff," McKennon spat. "You want to see me screw up so bad that you can taste it. You're the one that screwed up, and Antonivich hand picked me as your replacement."

"Have it your way. I'm here officially to oversee the capture. The report goes to Antonivich with my recommendations. It'll reflect that you were unwilling to go in after them." He arched his head back and pulled on the cigar, blowing smoke at the ceiling. "These aren't some dumb farmers stealing feed, McKennon. Antonivich and I want them bad. You let them walk out of your barracks. Five dead and one badly injured so far. How do you explain that?"

McKennon turned away and looked across the lawn. The snow wasn't sticking, but it was getting colder. All he asked for was two inches of wet snow. Damn Mallen and Wyatt! He turned. "You're the one that has to worry, Brinkerhoff. Two riots you failed to put down. And a resistance group working in the Adirondacks. You haven't gotten one of them yet."

"Who says a resistance group, McKennon? Power lines down, a railroad trestle burned. What's that mean, a hundred fifty guys in sheepskin coats and carbines ridin' ponies? You read too many books." He tried for a smoke ring. It was a perfect zero. "Doesn't matter," he said. "If it's a problem, it's my problem. We're talking about your problem. Antonivich says that if you lose any more troops, you're shit canned."

"Which is why I'm not going in until Mallen and Wyatt start to move."

Brinkerhoff stuffed out the cigar on the arm of the chair and tossed it for the wastebasket. He looked up at McKennon and smiled. "You never learn, do you? Mallen and that nigger are out there in the bush. They're going to move deeper into Maine. These guys've been living in the boonies for over a year. They've got weapons. Why then should they come down into the St. Lawrence Valley?"

"They'll come down," McKennon said softly, his breath condensing against the window pane. "One of them is hurt, or they'll need supplies. Something. But they'll come down, and when they do, we'll have them in open country."

"How about the plane?"

"Nothing. We've checked every lake and road within fifty miles of where we've got the heat return. It's either crashed in timber where we can't see it or sunk in a lake. If he had it, he'd have flown out."

Brinkerhoff made a show of checking his watch. "It's past midnight. Five days now, *durak*. And I'm telling you—if you don't get Mallen and Wyatt, you would do well to die trying." Pushing himself up, he moved toward the door. "See you, McKennon," he said, and softly closed the door behind him.

McKennon stood for a long time, watching the snow flutter down, flakes sticking together in the windless night. Brinkerhoff's chopper barked and blades whacked through the floodlights. McKennon watched as Brinkerhoff scrambled up into the chopper, pounding a ground crewman on the arm in phony camaraderie. Popular. Tough and mostly competent. Also ruthless, very ruthless. If I don't get Mallen and Wyatt, he'll get rid of me as painfully as possible and no one will question it, he thought, watching the chopper lift off and swing south, building up speed. But if I win, Brinkerhoff will die, and Central won't ask questions. They only want results, and a little infighting keeps the slacks out of the operation. Brinkerhoff would look good on a meat hook. McKennon drew one in the condensation of the window and added a man hanging from it.

Come down, Mallen, he said softly, looking out across the blank white. Come down.

They headed ten degrees west of north just after dawn. Mallen led, sighting over the aircraft compass, chart tucked under his shirt. Wyatt stumbled after him, carrying the bulk of the load.

The wind was from the northwest, glass brittle and cold as tempered steel. Even in the dawn light, the sky was blue-black and cloudless. A light haze of snow clung to the naked branches of elm and maple and fir, thumping down in showers as they pushed on their way beneath the laden branches.

Under the trees, very little snow had accumulated; just a dusting on the pine needles and fallen leaves. But in the open patches, where dead rye grass fluttered in the crevices of rocks and on flinty soil, the accumulation was more than four inches. They first kept to the trees, but the additional mileage was time consuming, so they decided to keep as straight a track as possible, relying on drifting to cover their footprints.

Mallen called a halt in mid-morning and they brewed coffee over a quick fire of birch bark and maple twigs under the lee of a stone outcropping.

"What's beyond that ridge?" Wyatt asked, pointing to a white-frosted bulge on the northern horizon.

Mallen consulted the chart and said, "Another ridge. And another after that, but then we're in Canada."

"Was Canada," Wyatt corrected.

The going was erratic most of the morning, with Mallen taking frequent bearings on prominent hills and marking their azimuth on the chart.

"I thought you said you didn't know where we were,"

Wyatt grunted, laboring up a long-strewn ravine behind Mallen.

"I'm not sure," he replied. "These bearings could match three or four locations. But once we hit something recognizable, I can compare our track and find out where we were. For the trip back," he added.

"And gasoline. How many gallons do we have to lug back?"

"Ten gallons minimum. With the other five we have, that will give us about five hundred miles range."

"So how much does ten gallons weigh?" Wyatt said, breathing hard on a slope.

"Sixty pounds plus the containers. We may have to leave some of this stuff behind."

"Christ!" Wyatt swore.

The air was still bitter by noon, with a wind starting to blow from the northwest, but the sky was clear, polished obsidian. Both men labored, with the cold searing their lungs, unused to exertion. The snow, moist when it first fell, was crusting over.

"We're leaving a trail a mile wide," Wyatt said.

"No choice," Mallen said and Wyatt nodded, his face sour.

They camped short of the first ridge by five, with the sun low and pale in the west. The wind died as the sun went down, and the temperature was falling. Both of them worked through the short twilight cutting branches of pine, which they laid out on either side of the weak fire Mallen had built. By six both of them were in their sleeping bags. They shared a can of pork and beans Wyatt had warmed in the fire.

"How far you think we made today?" Wyatt asked, stuffing the remainder of the beans in his mouth and then tearing off the label.

Mallen pulled the bag up higher around his face. Temperature in the low twenties, he guessed. "Eight . . . ten miles, maybe. We'll get going by first light tomorrow."

Wyatt removed an envelope from his jacket pocket and tapped the contents onto a strip torn from the bean can's label. He rolled it and licked it. "Smoke?" he said, offering Mallen a drag.

"You never give up, do you?"

"Keeps me sane." He lit it from a twig and inhaled. "Better," he said.

Mallen laughed. "Better than what?"

Wyatt snuggled down in the bag. "Just better. End of day sort of thing. Master home from the shop. Dog brings slippers. Fire in grate. That shit."

"What kind of dog?" Half asleep, Mallen realized the stupidity of bringing up the past.

Wyatt looked into the fire for a long time. "Labrador," he finally said. "Black as me. He ate and farted and did damn little else except love the hell out of anyone within a half-mile radius." Taking one more drag, he flung the cigarette into the embers. "Let's make an agreement, Mallen—no chit-chat about the past. They didn't make it and I did. Natural selection of the strongest."

"You really that tough, Wyatt?"

There was a long silence with only the sounds of a light wind moving in the branches and the hiss of the fire. Somewhere down the ridge, a fox was barking.

At last Wyatt said, "No."

They were up at dawn and moving, Wyatt taking the lead and Mallen packing the sleeping bags and rucksack. It was less cold, with high cirrus screening the sun with a linen haze, and the wind was fitful; gusting one moment and dormant the next.

Wyatt did well, working over the country, seeking and finding the better path. By eleven they were to the second ridge and Wyatt called a rest stop—"Fifteen minutes only," as he dusted snow from beneath a young maple and sat down on the stony ground.

"It's going pretty good," Mallen offered, easing off the pack and sitting on it. Wyatt said nothing, working out the stale tobacco into the remains of the soup label. He added pine needles, licked the edge, and lit it.

Mallen's wound was beginning to itch. He stripped

back the bandage and examined the star-shaped wound. It had closed with a brown crust, but the center was reddish and weeped yellow matter. He squeezed it experimentally, and a drop of blood flowed, but nothing more. It needed washing. He resolved to clean and drain it that night.

"How's your head?" he asked, and Wyatt nodded.

"All right. Have a headache sometimes, and the left ear doesn't work." He offered the cigarette to Mallen.

Mallen shook his head. "Your left ear?"

"Yeah. Since that first night. I thought the hearing would come back. Let's go."

Ten minutes of hard climbing and they crested the ridge, which was a sheer, razorbacked escarpment. Wyatt took the Winchester and with the scope quartered the countryside before them while Mallen rested, digging snow from his boot top.

"Road down there," Wyatt said, handing Mallen the rifle. "Down there and to the right. Near the little hill with the scrub." He guided Mallen's arm.

The road was there, just visible through the trees and perhaps three miles away. Mallen couldn't see it well enough to determine whether there were any tracks in the tree-shadowed snow.

Wyatt led them down, working eastward along the razorback until the ridge petered out into a clump of pine. They swung downhill under cover of the trees, slithering and caroming off the bark to check their descent. The trees ended as the slope leveled off into a marshy meadow now frozen into a thin sheet of ice. Their entrance on the meadow startled a small flock of sparrows, which took flight.

By early afternoon they breasted a knoll overlooking a logging road. Ruts from heavy trucks gave it a washboard texture, overlaid with a thin layer of drifted snow. There were tracks of a horse-drawn wagon moving east, barely drifted over.

"Peace Division?" Mallen wondered, breathing heavily from descent exertion.

Wyatt scratched at the stubble of his beard. He ex-

amined the tracks through the rifle's scope and shook
his head. "I don't think so. One wheel on the wagon
has a wobble in it. See the way the track on the right
wanders a bit. Bad hub or a bent rim. Let's go."

They moved down to the track and examined it more
closely. Two horses, both unshod. "Definitely not Peace
Division," Wyatt said. "They'd use good horses with
shoes. This is some farmer's rig."

"Let's follow it," Mallen said.

Wyatt sighted along the road with the compass.
"Northeast," he said. "Not good. We leave tracks if we
stick to the road. As it is, we'd probably just be going
at right angles. Let's keep going north. After the last
ridge, we should be able to see down into the St. Lawrence Valley. Let's cross the road and try to leave a
minimum of prints."

All afternoon, they labored up a narrow rock-strewn
defile, mountains pressing in from either side. The trees
were all second-growth slash pine, springing up around
the stumps of trees burned by some holocaust years before. The skyline on the ridge before them would merge
with a small downward slope and yet another ridge,
higher than the last. They swore and sweated and stumbled, but they gained altitude.

By five they broke over the ridge. The last incline
was largely barren of trees and what scrub there remained was hunched over by the press of a northwest
wind. Before them lay a smooth gradient sloping down
through forest and meadows to isolated farms with
patchwork-quilt fields. Beyond there were villages and,
in the very great distance, the silver ribbon of the St.
Lawrence Seaway.

There wasn't much snow in the valley. Some of the
fields retained a green texture, but the rest were the
umbre and brown-grays of after-harvest plowing.

"Looks good," Wyatt said, wiping mucus from his
nostrils.

"Still a lot of miles. Come morning, we can work out
where we are," Mallen said. "I'm crapped out."

Wyatt said nothing more but laid the rifle against his

cheek and slowly scanned the countryside before him. He occasionally referred to the chart, making notes on the margin. He then took compass bearings and sketched them out on the chart. "We're here," he said at last. "See where the island is, in the St. Lawrence?" He pointed down at the chart. "Bears three five two degrees, which would put us on this line. And that agrees with that smaller ridge to the west of us."

"So that would put Ste. Sabine a little to the northwest." Mallen pulled off a glove and took the chart. "So maybe we have to pick something closer." He turned his back on the valley and moved toward the scrub pine. "Let's knock off. There's not much light left and we have to get a fire going."

Wyatt followed after him. "No fire," he said. "Not unless we go back down the ridge. It's too exposed."

"Bullshit," Mallen said, but realized Wyatt was right. And it would take them half an hour to work back down the incline into deep timber where a fire would be safe, by which time it would be too dark to collect wood.

Wyatt watched him steadily. "I said no fire," and Mallen nodded his assent.

They zipped their bags together under the overhang of a rock ledge, using scrub pine for a mattress. Dinner was nothing more than tinned milk and a can of ice-cold soup under flickering stars.

Wyatt rolled his evening cigarette and this time Mallen shared it. They smoked it in silence, listening to the wind whine over the ridge.

"It beats working for a living," Wyatt finally said.

Mallen took one final drag on the cigarette and tossed it away into the night wind, trailing a shower of sparks.

"Smokey wouldn't like that," Wyatt said. "Save our forests."

"They're not our forests anymore."

Wyatt snuggled down in the bag. For a moment their hips touched. Mallen edged away and there was a span when neither of them spoke.

The stars wheeled westward in their orbits, leaving

nothing to mark their passage. Mallen watched them, identifying the major constellations. Orion, friendly, faithful, and familiar. Three stars in the belt, with the outer limits marked by Rigel and Betelgeuse. Capella and the cluster of the Pleiades. Seven Sisters. Remote, clean. Wyatt was saying something.

"What?" Mallen asked.

"You think we'll ever get it back?"

Mallen propped himself up on an elbow. "Get what back?"

"The country."

"The radio says we never lost it. Just made an alliance for mutual benefit."

"Which is a load of crap," Wyatt said flatly.

"And everyone knows it's a load of crap. But the Russians did it beautifully. Made us partners. Produce food and technology for export. Select tough administrators and police. It was an easy transition for most people to make, the ones who lived through it."

"Some of us will fight."

Mallen sighed and lay back, his fingers linked beneath his neck, watching the stars. Beautiful clean stars. "Someday," he said. He fell asleep watching the stars.

Mallen woke to a gray dawn, rain mixed with sleet moving from the southwest. His stomach rumbled with hunger and he stirred Wyatt. "Dawn. Time to move," he said. He could smell the stench of both their bodies, with dirt and fatigue mixed together.

They moved north, over the ridge, easing their way down the steep slope, rain beating over their faces and saturating their jackets. Mallen, leading this time, took a final bearing on the island in the St. Lawrence before starting down into the forested area. "St. Anne, then," he said over his shoulder. Wyatt grunted behind him in agreement, both having agreed over weak tea and cold beans that Ste. Sabine was too far to the west.

They worked down through pine and elm, the remaining snow turning to slush in the warmer winds and dripping rain. The smell of pine resin was strong, as if it were spring. Mallen whistled tunelessly, something Anne had sung. Then he pushed it out of his mind . . . Rule One. "One," he said to himself aloud.

"One what?" Wyatt asked, behind him.

"Nothing," Mallen said. One nothing.

They came to the edge of the trees by noon, both soaking wet but pleased that they had made good time. Before and below them the fields ran down into the valley bottom, furrowed from the fall plowing and some still with the trash of corn husks and unharvested hay. Through the rifle's scope, Mallen could see draft horses grazing and in one field a herd of cows. Smoke lay in a thin layer from hearth fires.

"Domestic," Wyatt said. "What now?"

They sat down on the wet earth and Wyatt rolled one of his cigarettes, which they passed back and forth.

"We wait for night," Mallen said.

McKennon scanned the computer printout for the third time and crumpled it into a ball. He threw it into the far corner of the shabby room, then turned to the window. The rain was a slow, steady beat against the metal roof. He hoped it would be snowing in the higher elevations. Depressed, he stirred his tea and drank it.

Across the dead grass of the barracks courtyard, two Special Forces men were exercising horses. One of the men had thick Mongol features. He continually jerked at the bridle of a bay, forcing it to keep moving. Mc-Kennon could see the condensed breath of men and animals in the near-freezing rain. Lousy weather for a man on horseback, he thought. Brinkerhoff had denied permission for the use of 'lectrics. Horses it will be, he thought, grinding his heel against the pine floor.

On the wall was an ordnance map. He walked over to it and traced the line of infrared heat sightings over the last five days. Steadily north. Last night should have put them on the first ridge to the south of the Seaway, but the MIG-25 sweep showed nothing. There were two options open to Mallen, he thought: to keep moving north, across the St. Lawrence and then on into northern Canada; or, the one that had the most substance, to go north to the Seaway, then find a boat and move northeast into the Bay of Fundy. Mallen had been flying northeast, pushing for somewhere up in Nova Scotia, maybe beyond. McKennon puzzled on it for some minutes, drinking the dregs of the tea.

Four days left on Brinkerhoff's timetable. He picked up the phone and dialed a number. Baines's voice answered, sleepy.

"Baines here."

"McKennon. Tell Special Forces I want another sweep as soon as the weather lifts this afternoon. And one per hour tonight. Thirty kilometers north and south of their last position. And then all the way down to the St. Lawrence."

"Anything else?"

McKennon touched the chain on his neck, letting his finger trace along the meshed links to the coin that hung at the end. He pulled it out from beneath his jacket and looked at it, turning it over in his hand.

"Anything else, McKennon?" Baines repeated, sounding a little exasperated.

McKennon dropped the coin back beneath his jacket. "Yes," he answered. "You busy right now?"

"Nothing special . . ."

"Come up to my room. I want to discuss this thing privately."

The line was silent for a few seconds as if Baines were weighing something in his own mind. "Ten minutes," he finally answered and hung up.

Time's running out, McKennon thought, moving over to the desk. He sat down heavily, bent over the surface, his head resting in the crook of his arm. Brinkerhoff had patiently waited for this chance to get rid of me—just one screw-up and I handed it to him on a platter.

He sat upright, then pulled the coin out again, turning it over and over. How many times had he had a chance to sell it for almost anything he wanted? A gold coin in these times would buy anything or anyone, but he had stubbornly held on to it. Because of her? he questioned. Perhaps, but the memory of her face was fading from his memory, pushed back into the past, as was everything else.

The promotion to detective sergeant had been almost a complete surprise. Despite the department's ironclad seniority system, Crowell had passed over two senior officers and selected McKennon, a situation almost without precedent in the ranks of the Philadelphia Police Department. With it came a raise of $323 a month; not insubstantial, even in the stagflation-ridden economy of the middle 1980s.

McKennon had not discussed the promotion with his wife, holding back on the news until after the first increased paycheck. With subsequent paychecks, he would set aside more for the kid's education, with perhaps something left over to convert the screened sunporch into a den.

But this first check was for something special, a surprise strictly for her—something he had always wanted to give her and had promised her. It took a little squeezing, but a fence he knew sold it to him for just over seven hundred dollars, approximately half the true market value. McKennon had sparred with the man, never really making a direct threat. He just let out little hints about a nonexistent file he had on the man's Front Street jewelry store, with references to a mutual acquaintance serving hard time in a correctional facility. He watched the man carefully, seeing little gestures of nervousness, a staining of the man's armpits despite the coolness of the fall afternoon.

When McKennon had finally asked about the gold chain, Wessellkind had almost stumbled over his own feet, getting it out of the locked display case.

"Fifteen percent off," Wessellkind said, laying the chain on a velvet display pad. "At that price, Sergeant, I'm losing money." Smiling, perspiration beading his forehead, he looked up at McKennon, who was a head taller.

It was a gold double eagle, set in an 18-carat bezel

with a delicate chain attached. McKennon held it beneath the fluorescent lamp, inspecting the surface. It was in near mint condition.

"There are scratches," McKennon said. "Knock off a little more."

Wessellkind flushed, angry. "Uncirculated quality," he shot back, grabbing the coin from McKennon's hand. He set a jeweler's loup in his eye and bent down, his hand shaking.

Reaching down into his hip pocket, McKennon withdrew his wallet, letting it fall open on the counter. The nickelplated badge shone in the light of the lamp, and on the opposite side was McKennon's department identification card. Opening the flaps of the currency compartment, McKennon withdrew seven crisp bills and fanned them out on the counter.

"If you look hard," McKennon said evenly, "you can see the scratches. That must knock down the value a lot, Wessellkind." He pushed the bills across the counter toward the aging Estonian.

Wessellkind gave kind of a long sigh and carefully placed the coin and pendant on the velvet pad, taking the bills and slipping them into his pocket. "It is worth twice that," he said finally. "Twice that." He made a semblance of a smile and stood back from the showcase, his arms crossed. "But perhaps you can make some future . . . ah, payment; perhaps even just a favor."

"Such as?"

"I'm sure you'll think of something," Wessellkind replied. "Or better yet, forget something."

McKennon nodded, carefully depositing the coin and chain in his coat pocket. "For a friend—why not?"

He had given it to Barbara that evening, well after David and the mutt had been pushed off to bed. Pouring two drinks, he had come up behind her as she finished off the dishes. He set the glasses down on the drainboard, then slipped the chain and coin over her thin, elegant neck. She had known immediately what it was without looking. Turning, she grasped his face with her still-wet hands, covering his cheeks with soap suds and wet kisses.

"Oh, Mac . . ." she had said over and over, finally holding the coin up to the light. From that day on, regardless of what she wore, the coin hung in the cleft between her breasts. Even now, McKennon imagined that he could feel her body heat stored in the coin.

Three months later, she had worn it to the hospital. The smears had come back positive and there had been exotic treatments, qualified promises, and synthetic good cheer. But the bottom line, delivered to McKennon on a wet February afternoon, was that her condition was "inoperable and terminal."

"A promise," she had said. He had been watching a little launch push upstream on the Schuylkill River, keeping his head turned away from her. Tears were an indulgence he had not allowed himself since he was twelve. He saw the river blur and shut his eyes, not turning.

"What promise?"

He heard the clink of metal as she placed something on the enamel-topped nightstand. Someone paged someone else through a muted speaker in the corridor and, incredibly, to McKennon's thinking, there was laughter in one of the adjoining rooms.

"Just that you'll keep this for me. Let it be the last thing you part with."

McKennon had clasped his hands together on his chest, digging the nails of his right hand into the wrist of his left. He found that there was no control in his lungs or throat, as if they were paralyzed. But quite clearly he could hear the scream in his brain.

She was buried one month later. His semialcoholic unmarried sister moved in after Christmas to take care of the kid and the dog and McKennon. Except for the television's running twelve hours a day and an excessive liquor bill, it worked all right.

In May, McKennon flew up to Albany to attend a fingerprint computer seminar. As he calculated later, the first Soviet SS-18 warheads were impacting on SAC silos just as he was sitting down to a Holiday Inn roast beef dinner.

For five days McKennon sat in the hotel's laundry room with three other law enforcement officers, working steadily through a case of rye. One man, an older type from Cincinnati, stood up on the third day and said something about taking a piss in the corridor. They heard him through the door saying words of contrition to an imaginary priest, followed by a shot.

Surprisingly, Albany wasn't hit. Six months later, when the government was re-formed, McKennon joined the Peace Division. In accentless English, the Soviet major commented to him, "You're in on the ground floor of the new era, McKennon."

Baines knocked and entered without waiting for a response. Closing the door behind him, he leaned against it, his hands stuck in his jacket pockets.

"What's up?" he asked, in a bored voice.

"What do you think about the infrared sightings?"

Shrugging, Baines said, "Not my business, McKennon. But I think it's them. Problem is, most of it's dense cover. We try to drop a couple of troopers in there and it might turn out to be a disaster. They'd hear us coming. According to the body bags back at Warren, they got weapons."

McKennon nodded and sat down on the desk, crossing his arms, watching Baines's face.

"You think we should wait for them—let them come out into the open?"

Smiling, Baines shook his head ruefully. "You're a fucking comic, McKennon," he finally replied. "You know as well as I do that once they're in open country they can walk thirty or forty kilometers a day. We can't cover that with even six choppers, and Brinkerhoff was on the barrack commandant's ass this morning at radio check-in. He's pulling out the other chopper tomorrow and limiting my remaining bird to no more than two drums of fuel a day. You better get some horse patrols out before he limits them as well."

McKennon studied his boots for a minute. "You know about Brinkerhoff and me, Baines?"

"I've heard the story." Baines wiped his nose between thumb and forefinger, as if thinking. "I take it that one of you wins and one loses based on whether we get Wyatt and Mallen."

"That's where it stands," McKennon answered. "That and the fact that he's set a time limit. I've got four days left, or else."

"What's 'or else' mean?"

Walking to the window, McKennon looked out across the barracks' yard. It was raining harder now, flakes of wet snow mixed in and starting to stick.

McKennon turned back to meet Baines's look. "Let's look at it another way. If I get these two guys down to Albany, I can write my own ticket with Antonivich. Part of that ticket will be that I'll get Brinkerhoff's job. Shortly thereafter, I think Brinkerhoff might undergo some correctional therapy under my supervision."

Fishing in his pocket, Baines pulled out a walnut and, shelling it, popped the nut into his mouth. He raised his eyes to meet McKennon's but remained silent, chewing.

Tough bastard, McKennon thought. Baines was a professional soldier, and professionals didn't mix politics with work.

"Let's put it a different way, Baines," McKennon said carefully, working into another approach. "I win and I'll need a pilot in charge of Albany Air Sector. We get Mallen and Wyatt and you can have that job. Something else—fifty points a month, plus a fifty-ruble increase."

"You're getting pretty fucking generous with P. D. budgeting, seeing as how you don't have that job yet." Baines shifted, crossing his legs, and reached for another walnut. "And by my reckoning, McKennon, I give you less than one in four of getting that job."

McKennon inhaled slowly, held it, and exhaled. "You swing a lot of weight around here," he said softly. "You control the fuel, regardless of the barrack commandant's instructions. I've seen your orders."

Baines walked over to the washstand and tipped a small measure of McKennon's plum brandy into a glass, then drank it slowly but without interruption. He set the glass down carefully and poured another. "You got it right, McKennon," he said. "But I still gotta answer to Brinkerhoff. I'm not going to break my ass for you based on a few promises."

Drawing the double eagle out, McKennon tossed it to Baines.

Holding it up to the light, Baines examined it, then rubbed the surfaces of the coin between his fingers. "This real?"

"It's real. And if you can deliver Wyatt and Mallen, it's yours."

For the first time since McKennon had known the pilot, Baines actually smiled. "You know what I can do with even a quarter of this coin, McKennon?" He walked over to the window and held it up to the light, looking to the stylistic eagle poised for flight. "Just one chunk of this and I can buy a Langley green pass out of this asshole-strewn wasteland and get a Section Five in southern Mexico. Another half would buy a couple of horses, a dozen breeding cows, and a stud bull— plus a nice, clean mama to keep me warm." He closed his fist around the coin.

McKennon put his palm out. "I said *after* you deliver Mallen and Wyatt, not *until*."

Baines raised his eyebrows, with a bland face, and dropped the coin into McKennon's palm coin first and then the trailing chain. "You understand that I still work for Brinkerhoff, McKennon?" He hitched up his pants and zipped his jacket. "And what I do to help you is inside the limits of what I can get away with. In case we don't get them, I've still got to keep *numero uno* clean, understand?"

"Understood." McKennon slipped the chain over his neck and tucked the coin under his gray tunic. He moved over to the washstand and poured some brandy, then diluted it with water. Raising the glass, he silently toasted Baines and drank the mixture down. Too early, he thought. Too much pressure, and his stomach didn't take it well. Setting the glass down, he turned back to Baines and squared his shoulders. Tired.

"I want you flying ridge lines this afternoon. Work from south to north. Make it obvious. I want to drive those two *duraks* deeper into the St. Lawrence Valley. Also, get out horse patrols this afternoon. See to it that they cover every sector. If they have to split up, that's okay, but keep at least one Special Forces type on each element. These P. D.'s are lazy bastards."

Baines had his hand on the doorknob. "You got it. Anything else?" He opened the door a crack.

"Find them," McKennon answered. "Soon."

The rain persisted through the forenoon, coming sometimes in a rattle of sleet but mostly in a thin, pervasive drizzle. Mallen and Wyatt moved twice, trying to find a place with good drainage and a grove of saplings close enough together to form supports for the plastic tarp. They settled in a gully, using two saplings and the stump of a rotted maple for anchor points, and strung up the tarp. Lunch was a cold tin of meat that smelled rotten. They both ate, forcing the meat down, but Wyatt later vomited and ultimately both of them had a violent attack of diarrhea.

In the afternoon they both tried to sleep, zipping the bags together and huddling for heat, but the attacks of diarrhea rolled over them, forcing them to leave the bag and squat in the rain under dripping maples. Mallen thought briefly about wanting to die—and rejected it.

The rain quit toward dusk and they struck the camp, leaving much of the gear to pick up on the way back. Mallen kept the tote bag with the last of the food, and the Luger, Wyatt taking the sleeping bags and rifle. The bags were saturated with water and they both spent a good deal of time trying to wring them out.

"They'll take weeks to dry," Wyatt said, grunting as he twisted the fabric in his hands. "I say we leave them here."

"Suit yourself," Mallen said. "I'm taking mine. If

we're not under cover by dawn, we'll never live through another night."

Wyatt looked up at Mallen. "You think we'll make it?"

Mallen shrugged. "Yes," he said without conviction.

They moved out of the underbrush at dusk, striking down through a boulder-strewn meadow. The rain had quit and fog was forming in depressions of the field.

Orion was beginning to tuck beneath the western horizon when they came to the road. It wasn't much— one lane only, and carved from rutted mud. A thin glazing of ice covered the puddles. They listened for some minutes, then crossed into the next field, Wyatt cursing as he slipped on the embankment and slid into a rocky drainage ditch. The rifle was lost in the darkness, buried in weeds and ice-sheathed pools of stale water.

"You dumb shit!" Wyatt kept repeating, to himself, grappling around in the darkness.

Mallen climbed back down into the ditch, leaving his equipment on the crest. Together they worked by feel, searching out the ditch, foot by foot.

"*Jesus!*" Mallen grumbled. "How in hell could you lose a rifle?"

"Get stuffed," Wyatt said under his breath. "It's ten feet down into this ditch. Work more up to your right." Wyatt took hold of his shoulder and pushed him roughly in that direction. Mallen ultimately found it, but the scope was knocked askew and the optics were shattered. He was about to call to Wyatt when the black man, almost invisible in the darkness, loomed up before him and shoved his hand into Mallen's face.

It first struck Mallen that Wyatt had gone mad, until he heard the sound of horses' hoofs. Wyatt pulled him down and they lay still in the freezing water as four horsemen slowly cantered by, their forms silhouetted against the night sky.

13

They listened to the pounding of hoofs flailing the frozen mud until there remained only the sound of the wind and the hoarseness of their own breathing. Wyatt was shaking uncontrollably. Mallen scrambled up the embankment on all fours and listened. The riders were lost in the blackness, but he heard one man call to another and then the answer, though it was too distant to be understandable.

Wyatt joined him and together they moved in a loping shuffle across the open field, heading north. The field was rough, furrowed unevenly and littered with the stubble of dead corn stalks. Twice Mallen fell, cursing himself and Wyatt.

They rested under the lee of a broken stone wall, both completely winded. The pounding of Mallen's heart was bursting his rib cage, and he thought that it was more from fear than from running. He felt himself all over. His clothes were saturated with water and covered in slime.

"Jesus, that was . . ." Wyatt was panting, ". . . was close." His breath was a white steam in the blackness. "Cold. Fucking cold."

"Get up," Mallen said. "We've got to keep moving and get under some shelter."

"No. Here. We stay here." The wind whistled through gaps in the rock. Wyatt was unrolling his sodden sleeping bag.

Mallen estimated that the temperature was down in the low twenties and falling. The wind was probably fifteen, the wind-chill factor below zero. He pulled Wyatt to his feet and took the sleeping bag.

"Wrap this thing around your shoulders. We can't stay, because both of us will die from exposure, and if we don't die we'll be out in the open in daylight." He pushed Wyatt roughly toward the north.

They jogged together through the night, exhausted but both knowing that to stop was to sit was to die. Mallen took them across fields and then paralleled a dirt road, working toward the lower valley. Some time after midnight they crossed a blacktop road and turned west, running in the gravel along the side of the road. Every few minutes Mallen stopped and listened, then drove them on.

Regulus was down below the horizon and Mallen estimated that it was after two when they crested a small rise and looked down on a settlement of three houses clustered in a hollow. A light burned behind a drawn shade and a dog yapped insistently.

"Got to go around. We can't risk being seen," Mallen whispered, moving north across the ditch into an open field. It took them thirty minutes to skirt the houses and regain the main road. They could still hear the dog barking in the distance.

One truck passed them in the night. They saw the headlights from a great distance, growing larger, its beams sweeping the fields as it followed the winding road. Lying in a ditch, they waited until it passed. There were no markings that they could see, only the laboring of an ancient diesel engine and a rush of wind, and it was gone in the night, mud-spattered taillights nearly invisible.

"Not Peace Division," Wyatt said.

"Who knows?" Mallen answered, jogging toward the west. Three hours until dawn, he thought. He could feel the point of exhaustion getting closer and Wyatt was stumbling continually. They were both numb with cold. Large flakes of snow wet his face.

Mallen missed it, but Wyatt didn't.

"Mailbox," Wyatt said in a hoarse whisper. They moved off the road into a muddy lane and examined the box. There was a name marking the side, but Mallen couldn't read it in the starlight. The lane itself was narrow and flanked by withered shrubs on either side. No tire marks, he noticed. And no hoof-prints.

"This is it," he said, and they moved up the edge of the lane, keeping to the grass. "Keep the noise down. If there's a dog, we get out fast."

The farmhouse was set well back from the main road. No lights showed inside. The yard was strewn with a jumble of rusting farm machinery, their silhouettes in the half-light resembling prehistoric insects of gigantic size. More to the west, Mallen could see the shape of a barn and silo, black against the skyline. Wordlessly he led Wyatt to the barn, watching the house for any movement. Home free, he thought.

Inside, the barn was a coal-black haven filled with the smells and sounds of restless cattle. Mallen left Wyatt leaning against a stall door while he moved, arms outstretched, trying to find a ladder to the hayloft. He stumbled over a mucking trench and fell heavily, smashing his left arm against ragged concrete. The pain was incredible, and he bit his tongue to keep from shrieking. Even under the padding of the jacket, he knew that he had reopened the wound. He dared a match and saw the ladder less than an arm's length from where he lay.

"Over here," he whispered. Wyatt stumbled toward him, more zombie than man. "And watch out for the shit trench."

They climbed the ladder and heaved their gear into a corner. Mallen unrolled the bags and laid them out. "Get out of your clothes," he said. Wyatt didn't reply, already breathing heavily in sleep. Mallen nudged him awake. "Get your clothes off and get into the bag."

"Too fucking cold," Wyatt mumbled. "Cold."

"What the hell do you think I am? You'll warm up."

Wyatt fumbled off his clothes and crawled in. "Cold," he said, then was asleep. Mallen joined him. Home free.

Mallen watched the shaft of sunlight slide across the weathered planks, inching steadily toward the dark

corners of the loft. Around six A.M., he guessed. He
rolled over slowly in the warm but still damp sleeping
bag. The frame of the barn was massive and the posts
and beams, checked with age and dryness, rose above
him into the gloom. Bits of dust and straw drifted
through the single shaft of sunlight. Small, brilliant pin-
points drifted in the draft flowing between the chinks
of caulking. As his eyes adjusted to the light, he could
see well-developed webs in the recesses of the loft,
enmeshing flies of forgotten summers.

Wyatt was still asleep, the hood of his sleeping bag
pulled over his face. The bag moved in a rhythm of
labored breathing. A thin haze of moisture, condensed
by the cold, rose from his wet sleeping bag.

Let him sleep, Mallen thought. Christ knows what
had kept them both going this far. Sleep was like
treasure, to be hoarded up against future expenditures.
Mallen's body ached from the strain and exposure of
the last few days, but he luxuriated in the warmth of
the sleeping bag and the peace of rest. His mind cataloged things he should do: clean the rifle and the
Luger, which was in the haversack, and perhaps forage
for food. But as he tried to frame these thoughts, he
felt sleep overcoming his resolve. He picked up a
straw of hay and, placing it between his lips, drifted
back to haylofts in his youth. There had been secret
meetings of the White Mountain Scouts, resolves
scratched on slate with a nail, then sworn to by a band
of brothers. And the first cigarette. And the first girl.
Against his will, his eyes drooped and closed. He rolled
over and slept again, the straw clenched between his
teeth, grinding on its dryness.

Mallen awoke later, not knowing why. Mid-morning, he
guessed: the sun was still in the east, but higher. From
beneath him he heard the sounds of animals moving in
their stalls. But something had waked him, he felt. He
listened intently, willing Wyatt to make less sound,
though it was just a muffled rasp no louder than the
wind. He heard distinctly now the thing that had waked

him—footsteps. Someone light with quick steps. A pail clinked against the frame of the building. No sound, then footsteps again. Then the barn door rolling on protesting wheels. Heart pounding, Mallen unzipped his bag and moved to the grime-covered window. Jesus Christ, it was cold! He pulled the bag after him and fashioned a shawl with it, stooping in a crouch near the edge of the pane. A figure in a coat, with a blue stocking cap, walked across the barnyard toward the house. It could have been a woman or a kid in his teens, he thought. The figure paused near the step, transferred the bucket from one hand to the other, fumbled with the door, and disappeared into the house. Mallen, realizing he had been holding his breath, slowly expelled it and relaxed. Nothing more than morning milking, he thought.

Beyond the house and lane the land was a patchwork of barren white fields, dusted under a first snowfall. He couldn't see any other buildings, only a country road and telephone poles stripped of their wire, stretching off to the south like unused gallows. By craning his neck he could see the low foothills through which they had trekked.

His breathing fogged the glass and, experimentally, he huffed on it and drew a crude square. The moisture hazed and then froze in a tracery, and his finger felt numb. Goddamn cold, but it would hasten the formation of ice on the lake. Five or six more days of this and you could drive a truck across it. Unconsciously, he crossed himself.

"Pax vobiscum," Wyatt said. He was propped up on one elbow, the flap of the bag pulled up around his chin. Only the oval of his face was exposed.

"It dumped a couple of inches," Mallen said, sliding back into his bag. "Any tracks we left are covered. Likewise, we can't move until it snows again, unless it's at night and on the roads. Go back to sleep."

"What was that all about?" Wyatt nodded toward the window.

"Milking time. Someone came out and did the chores. A kid or a woman, by their size. No problem."

"Anyone else?"

Mallen shook his head and lay back, eyes half-closed. "Get some sleep. We'll think about what we do next later. How do you feel?"

"Like shit warmed over. Bad cold and the neck wound stinks. Feel pretty bum, massa."

Mallen rolled onto his side so that he could see more clearly. Wyatt's face was in the shadows. There was a sheen of perspiration on his face and a thin trickle of mucus hanging from his nostrils. Wyatt noticed and made a wiping motion.

"That bad?" Mallen asked.

"It's a lot worse than yesterday. Ache all over. Running a fever. At least the diarrhea stopped. But I don't feel too much like moving."

Their eyes met. Mallen put his hand up to Wyatt's face. It was a furnace. "Christ!" he said, almost involuntarily.

"Give it a day," Wyatt said. "Just one day. I'll be able to move then." They both knew it was a lie. Mallen felt his own body protesting; too much exposure to cold and the lack of food had drained his reserves. Overlaying that was the strain of being on the run without any letup.

"We'll give it longer," he finally said, averting eye contact. "The time it takes us to rest up works in our favor. The lake is freezing. Give it five days' minimum to be solid enough to support the Sperber. And it puts breathing space between us and the search. They've got to give up eventually. File some goddamn report and call it quits. The farmhouse has got food, heat. No telephone. Like they used to say, 'take five.' "

"Days?"

"Why not?" Mallen replied. "What's the big rush?"

"God, I could use it. Food too. If there's a cow down there, we could kill the mother and fry up some steaks."

Mallen snorted from the depth of his sleeping bag,

feeling rich. Beef would be something. His stomach rumbled in anticipation.

"You want to take a look at this?" Wyatt said more softly. "I can't turn my head enough to get a good look."

Mallen peeled back his sleeping bag and inched over. The bandage was loose and black with dried blood. He peeled it back gently, taking care not to open the wound, but this was unnecessary. The wound was open, oozing blood and a yellowish gray matter. More ominously, the skin around the wound was swollen, with streaks of swelling radiating up the neck and down the arm. The stench was nauseating. Involuntarily, Mallen wrinkled his nose.

"I forgot to use deodorant," Wyatt said. "How's it look?"

"So-so," Mallen replied, dropping the flap of the bandage. "It needs cleaning. It's infected."

"No shit. Never have guessed." Wyatt lay down, staring blankly toward the rafters. "We got anything to eat? Maybe some snow. I'm dry."

Mallen drew back the bag and pulled on his wet pants, which lay beneath the sleeping bag, then the jacket. He checked the window—the yard was vacant. Smoke rose from the chimney and whipped off in the wind, then curled downward in the lee of the building. He watched for several minutes, shivering. Once he saw movement past a window, but there was no other hint of life. Tracks led to and from the barn, but these were now blurring in the wind drift of the light snowfall.

Carefully he worked his way down the crude ladder. The lower floor of the barn was divided into two long rows of stalls, separated by an aisle and the mucking trench. A few thin spokes of sunlight fell across the broken concrete, but he could see little else in the gloom. Two cows moved restlessly in their stall and a scrawny piebald arched its neck out from behind the planks of a barrier and bared its teeth. The rest of the stalls were empty, long disused, a few containing rusted junk. He searched for and found a pail but discarded it, because it had rodent dropping littering the bottom. Near the sill of the door he found an enamel pan, probably a cat's, he thought.

The cow was nearly dry and protested, and he had forgotten the trick of pulling the teat, but eventually he extracted enough to half fill the pan with steaming milk. Carefully he made his way back up the ladder, salivating, unable to take his eyes from the pan.

They shared the milk in silence, taking turns. He had to help Wyatt, and there was a lot of spillage. They were both left with moustaches of white across the rims of their lips and a matting of white in the stubble of their beards.

Mallen saw the humor of it and started to laugh. Then, realizing that his voice would carry, he tried to suppress the laughter, just making it worse with choked snorts and then an open-throated cackle. He lay down and buried his face in the sleeping bag, shaking with the idiocy of it—of men winded and broken, sick and starving, fighting not only other men but the implacable, grinding weather. Still he laughed, his eyes burning with tears. Finally he controlled himself and looked up at Wyatt. But Wyatt was out of his bag, bent double, retching up the milk. Mallen, as he helped Wyatt into his sleeping bag, felt the intenseness of fever radiating from the coal-black skin and knew there was nothing he could do to contain it. With no more words, they both finally drifted back into sleep.

They slept through the day and the afternoon. Mallen awoke at dusk, hunger rumbling in his stomach. But his sleeping bag was nearly dry, and the warmth of it felt good against his naked skin. The loft seemed warmer now, retaining a little of the afternoon's heat from the pale October sun.

Wyatt still slept, the sleeping bag pulled up around his face. His breathing was coarse and watery and the bag rose and fell in jerky spasms as he coughed in his sleep. Even though he was used to it, the smell of decay sickened Mallen.

He tried to remember what blood poisoning or tetanus was like, and couldn't. People never had those problems before the war. Get a scratch and see the doctor. A shot in the ass and pills four times a day until the prescription ran out. Drain Wyatt's wound? That seemed a possibility. But he would need hot water and clean dressings. Deep down, Mallen knew that Wyatt's infection was critical, something more than rest and food would cure. And it wouldn't be possible to stay here forever; sooner or later a patrol would come.

In the failing light, he inspected his own wound. The old tissue was broken open and the wound oozed a bit, but it looked clean. Smelled good. The big difference. He patted the bandage back in place and rezipped the bag.

He planned on getting up soon to check out the house. He pictured himself waiting for everyone in the farmhouse to sit down to dinner and breaking through the door with the rifle. Or maybe it would be better to wait until morning and use whoever came to do the milkings as a hostage. And it would mean another twelve hours of sleep—something he still craved, either through exhaustion or because of hunger.

The wind had dropped and the stillness magnified each sound. He could hear the animals moving below. If they had been fed, he had slept through the coming and going of a person from the house. A rodent of some sort ran along a beam, the sound of its passage a drawn-out whisper. With the setting of the sun, the framework and roofing contracted, working against each other in small snaps of sound. And the wet, hollow rasping of Wyatt was a steady background.

Sometimes, in irrational moments, Mallen resented, even hated Wyatt, as he would being dragged down in the surf by a panicked swimmer. Yet he knew that the escape had been more Wyatt's doing than his own. Without Wyatt, would he have even made Canada? But even more so, it was the company of Wyatt, the feeling that he knew existed between them that had made the difference, some bond he couldn't put a name to.

He turned over, face down in the warmth of the down bag, wetness burning behind his closed eyelids, and finally slept.

"Levez-vous. Lentement."

Mallen came awake slowly, trying to push the sound away with his mind. He had been dreaming of food, of eating a huge roast of venison and handfuls of oven-hot bread.

"De suite!"

He opened one eye and squinted against the brightness of the sun, which lit up the loft's dust-smeared window with incandescence.

"Sortez vos mains d'abord. Tout doucement."

Mallen started to turn, to see the speaker. A woman's voice, he thought, then heard the metallic snick of a weapon's hammer being thumbed back. He froze. The voice, more insistent and amplified by the silence, spoke in French, but he could easily perceive the warning tone of the speaker. "I don't speak . . . *non parlez-vous Français.*"

A snort of contempt came from the darkness behind him. "I said get out of your sleeping bag. Hands first and very slowly. I have your rifle. Then wake the other person."

Mallen looked over toward Wyatt. The flap of the sleeping bag was pulled up, covering his face. Then he looked toward the rucksack, which contained the Luger. Gone.

"I have it," the voice said. A kid, Mallen thought. Not a woman, a kid! He kept his hands inside the bag and forced a yawn. "We're just passing through. Slept here last night. We're going soon."

"You're leaving here, but perhaps in a way that you didn't plan. I have training in weapons. Of all types. Lift your hands from your sleeping bag first. Unfasten the bag, and stand up."

"I have no clothes on . . ."

The explosion of the rifle firing was a shock wave

in the confined loft. He felt the passage of the bullet and the hot wind of the burning gases.

"Now!" the voice shouted. The lever action picked up another shell from the magazine in the silence following. Mallen could smell the intense tang of burned gunpowder, and blue smoke rose in the shaft of sunlight. Wyatt was awake now, struggling in the confines of his bag like a man drowning in a web of kelp.

The voice had a hint of panic, the unnerving edge of desperation. "For the last time, do as I say." There was the snick of the rifle's hammer being drawn back. Mallen realized that the Winchester would have been cocked as a new shell was chambered into the breach. The kid had lowered the hammer and recocked it for emphasis, which indicated more than a passing familiarity with weapons.

"All right, goddamnit. Jesus, be careful with that thing!" Wyatt had the flap open, looking out like a mole from his den. Confusion, doubt, fear were on his face, which was ashen and drenched in sweat. Mallen was arrested in movement, watching Wyatt, whose face was puffed up, skin swollen taut, eyes sunken in pockets of flesh. His lips were thick and cracked with fever. His mouth opened and he tried to say something, but it was just a croak.

"Get up," Mallen said. "He has the rifle." Wyatt nodded, but didn't move. "How you feel?"

Wyatt shook his head. "Nothing," he finally rasped. "Wiped out." He lay back, eyes closed.

The voice of a woman called from a distance. There was the sound of her voice again and then the creak of the barn door below, rolling on rusted bearings. "Paul . . . ?" the voice called.

Mallen pulled the bag open and stood up slowly, his hands lifted. The cold was shocking, and he felt his scrotum and penis drawing up into his body's cavities. "Can you get up?" he asked Wyatt.

"Je tiens les deux gars. Va-t-en à la cuisine et restes-y. Et pis charge la carabine."

Plainly, Mallen heard the woman below gasp and

then the sound of her running across the yard. A door opened and slammed in the distance.

"He told his mother to get a shotgun," Wyatt said. The voice was almost unrecognizable. He ended the sentence with a long, rolling cough, hacking up his lungs in bursts.

"Can you make it?" Mallen repeated. "It will be warmer in the house." Wyatt looked up and nodded.

"Both of you—down the ladder. Then to the center of the yard. You will wait there until I tell you to go farther."

The three of them came down from the loft, Mallen and Wyatt first, followed at a distance by the kid. Mallen caught a glimpse of him only once as he helped Wyatt with the ladder. Beyond Wyatt's body, incredibly hot to the touch, he saw a boy of no more than fifteen, standing legs spread and the Winchester leveled. Mallen had the impression of a thin face with hair the color of sun-bleached straw. The boy's face was rigid, expressionless.

They went across the yard, Wyatt and Mallen, naked and shaking in the wind. The sky was blue-white and diamond-hard in its polished brilliance. The intensity of the cold was of the kind that dispels any further hope of autumn. He stopped in the middle of the yard, holding Wyatt to keep him from falling. The door of the farmhouse opened and in the shadows he saw the small figure of the woman holding a shotgun. She nodded, allowing them to come toward her. The kid was behind them, footsteps crunching in the snow.

"Against the far wall," she said. "Sit down on the floor next to the stove. My son will soon get you blankets."

She stood well away from them, the shotgun held easily in her small hands. Mallen's eyes met hers for only a moment. They were cool, the color of glacier ice.

Mallen helped Wyatt down, Wyatt grunting in pain as pressure came against his shoulder. The skin around his neck, face, and arms was balloon taut, and the remains of the bandage flapped against his skin, the tape ineffective from sweat. "She'll get blankets," he said softly to Wyatt. Wyatt nodded, his eyes closed.

The boy came in, carrying Mallen's rucksack in one hand with the rifle held in the other, hand overlapping the grip and finger on the trigger. Like a dumb teenage kid playing cowboy. Mallen half smiled.

"It is not so humorous, Mr. Mallen," she said. Picking a yellow sheet of paper from the shelf over the sink, she pushed it across the floor toward him. "It says that you and the *nègre* have killed several men. From ambush."

The leaflet was badly printed, with columns in French and what he assumed was Russian. The number 75 was printed in large type across the bottom with the word *ochki*.

"What does it say?"

"As I've told you. For killing several men who were performing their duties. It says that you are dangerous. You killed them without warning. There is a reward of seventy-five points."

"Blankets first," Mallen demanded. "And get him into bed. He's got a bad infection."

She nodded, avoiding looking at their naked bodies, and left the room. The boy stood against the door, face impassive, the Model 94 leveled. Minutes were passing. Mallen realized that if he were to gain control, it would be soon or not at all. As if reading his thoughts, the boy tensed and, using a foot, pushed a chair between them. The barrel of the Winchester wavered, and Mallen wondered whether the kid was unstable enough to fire accidentally. Seventy-five points might mean dead or alive. He relaxed, leaning back against the wall, close enough to Wyatt to feel the heat of his flesh. A glance up at the boy showed that he had mirrored the relaxation.

"She's getting some blankets," he said to Wyatt, to break the tension. Wyatt nodded, keeping his eyes closed.

From deep in the house Mallen heard a door open, some mumbled words, then a door closing. The woman's boot heels echoed in a hallway and then she was framed in the doorway, edging around behind the table, keeping away from the field of fire. She tossed him two threadbare blankets. "That is all I can offer. We have no bed for the black. My grandfather is ill. He sleeps in the first-floor bedroom. The other rooms are upstairs."

"So he can use one of those," Mallen spat back angrily. "Christ, you see for yourself that he's sick. He needs warmth, a bed."

"Which he cannot have. My son will go to the garrison. I will guard you both until troops return with him. Paul will ask that a paramedic accompany them."

Mallen started to object, but she silenced him.

"No more," she said. "He'll have medical help by evening. You'll be warm and I can make tea for you. There are potatoes baking. Beyond that, we can offer nothing else."

Mallen started to rise. The kid brought the Winchester up and his expression hardened, more confident now, more in control.

"If you think I won't fire, you're mistaken!" He thumbed back the hammer.

Edging back against the wall, Mallen let his legs slowly unfold and slid down into a sitting position. He was intently aware that he was naked under the blanket and that the woman's eyes were boring into him. "Dammit," he said weakly. The situation was ludicrous. He looked up at her, for the first time really carefully. Thirtyish, a carefully molded face with fine bone structure. The eyes, like the boy's, were a blue you couldn't put an adjective to, but something you could swim in, sink in, drown in.

"I wasn't going to . . ." he began. Mallen lowered his eyes and pulled the blanket up around Wyatt's body, tucking in the corners under his legs. "I wasn't going to rush you," he finally said, keeping his voice calm. "But what you're doing—what happens when they get us—you want to live with that?"

"That's not our concern," she answered. "You have

to be held responsible for your actions. You've killed, haven't you?"

"It's not that fucking simple," Mallen shot back at her. "Registration papers. I didn't have registration papers, and they gave me electric shock treatments." He held out his scarred palms, showing the burn marks. "What in hell would you have done—waited around for a second dose? Wyatt and I had to get out. People got hurt in the process."

"Electric probes are no longer used," the boy said flatly. "They've been forbidden." He sounded as if it were gospel, as if it were accepted fact. "And I would know—I'm in training for Peace Division."

"So marvelous!" Mallen mimicked. "Then you know that we would have been sent down to the Albany Correction Clinic, understand?"

The boy sighed, shifting his stance. "Correction Clinics are for the reeducation of hostile attitudes. It's professional care, under the direction of psychiatrists." He said it pedantically, as if quoting from a textbook. "There are only a few who don't respond . . ." He dwindled off, as though he could not remember the right quotation.

"He's not Peace Division," the woman said. "Only in the Youth Education Division." She glanced sideways at her son, annoyed. "At any rate," she continued, "there is no more discussion. That is for you and your friend to settle with the division. Our duty is to hold you until they arrive."

"And there is a small matter of seventy-five points," Mallen threw out, watching her face for a reaction.

"And there is a matter of seventy-five points." She sat down at the small enamel-topped table and unbuttoned the coarsely woven jacket. "And there is the matter of my grandfather, who is sick. Without points we cannot obtain sufficient medication. That, too, is not your concern." She turned to her son and spoke in rapid French, her eyes still on Mallen. He nodded. As Mallen watched, the boy spilled out the contents of the rucksack on the table. The Luger rattled out, oil black against the white enamel. The boy picked it up, fumbled with the release, and dropped the clip. The rifle was leaned against the wall now, milliseconds away from the boy. Mallen tensed. It must be now, he thought.

She saw the look on his face and snatched the weapon from the boy, ramming the clip upward into the grip. "Luger model 1908," she said, bringing the barrel around in a sweep, leveling it so that only the bore of the barrel was visible. "My husband had one. And taught me to use it." Her thumb came up and moved the safety to the firing position without fumbling or even looking.

The rifle came up. Mallen caught the sudden flush on the boy's cheeks and their eyes met briefly. It had been that close, and the boy knew he had almost blown it. Mallen relaxed. "Your husband . . . ?" he asked, easing back, resting a shoulder against the wall. The stove was making a throaty growl, draft now wide open, starting to radiate heat.

She let her arm ease down so that the butt of the Luger rested against the tabletop but with the bore still a small, black mouth, gaping at him. "My husband will soon be here," she said without expression.

"My father," the boy said with no more emotion, "is gone. He was in Montreal when it happened."

Mallen looked down at his naked feet and shrugged. It seemed that so many had lost their lives that human tragedy had no more impact than discussing the weather. "I'm sorry," he finally said.

"Yes," she said. "So were my son and I. It wasn't a Canadian war."

Mallen gathered himself, trying to pull it all together. He felt humiliated, angry, numb, cold, that he had let Wyatt down—and himself. And yet pleading came with difficulty. "Christ, lady," he said. "We all lost. Everyone on this scorched planet lost someone. But that doesn't help us now. This man . . ." he thumbed his hand toward Wyatt's slack form ". . . and I can't allow ourselves to be taken. If we do, we're dead. Let us go.

We'll be out of here without anyone knowing it. Keep
the weapons, but let us . . ." He trailed off, knowing it
was no use and that he had sounded as though he was
a kid, begging.

He couldn't read her face. It gave off no hint of
emotion, just the calm, unflinching stare. Finally, in
answer, she shook her head. "It's all useless, Mr.
Mallen," She glanced down at the poster. "If we were
to let you go and you were caught, it would be very
difficult for us." She thought about it for a second and
added, "Very difficult for us." She turned to the boy
and whispered to him. He nodded, then pulled on a
weathered leather coat. Opening the door, he glanced at
Mallen with a quick look of hate that Mallen thought
impossible for a boy his age. How war changes, he
thought. Their eyes were still locked as the door
slammed shut.

"Where is he going?" Mallen asked. And knew.

"To saddle the horse. It will be a long ride. The
garrison is two hours ride from here." She unbuttoned
the old cardigan, letting it fall open. The room was
hot, and Mallen felt sweat forming between his shoulder
blades and beneath his arms. Partly from heat. Also
from fear, he realized. With the boy gone, it would be
a matter of only two hours until there would be choppers like mayflies on an apple.

Mallen turned toward Wyatt, keeping his movements
slow and deliberate, trying to gauge time and distance
and thinking of some way that would be possible. Wyatt
was semiconscious, perhaps asleep. He was slumped,
head cocked at an angle with his chin resting on his
chest. Streams of sweat rolled off his forehead, saturating the blanket with a stain of darkness. He kept his
head turned away from her, fussing with Wyatt's
blanket, trying to remember about the Luger. The more
he thought about it, the more it seemed possible. He
turned back to face her.

"I don't know your name," he said. From beyond
the house he could hear the barn door rolling open.

"Le Borveaux. Jeanne Le Borveaux. My son's name is Paul."

Mallen looked down at his naked feet, crinkled white from the cold and moisture of days past. He picked at a blister. "Well, ah, Mrs. Le Borveaux," he said, looking up, "I have to get this across to you before your son leaves. This man"—he nodded toward Wyatt—"and I did nothing. Nothing except try to save our own lives. Everything resulted from the Peace Division's coming after us." He looked down, flexing his toes and ankles, trying to work some circulation into them. "And I can guarantee you that both Wyatt and I will be dead by nightfall if your boy brings them back. Is that something you can live with?"

She let out a sigh. Whether it was compassion or impatience he couldn't tell. "I guess I would say the same thing in your place, Mr. Mallen. But I'm really not the one to judge. Paul thinks this is best. He continually tells me that the Division is changing, working more to help people. And you admit that you killed men."

It was more of a question on her part, something that he couldn't remember admitting to. There was just the flyer. He rocked forward on his feet, bracing his back against the wall, ready to move, yet trying to keep his voice reassuring, calm. A reasonable man am I, he thought.

Looking up, he met her gaze, the question still in her mind. His eyes dropped to the Luger. Barrel on. There was a tit on the extractor that would project above the flush black metal of the receiver when it was loaded, something his father had shown him when Mallen turned twenty-one; the Luger a gift. More than that —part of the rites of passage. "*Geladen,*" the old man had said. He had pointed to the letters etched on the protruding metal tit. "Means *loaded* in German. So you can see, even *feel* if need be, when there's a round in the chamber."

Mallen looked hard, squinting, but the muzzle was end on, the extractor not visible from this angle. And he couldn't remember whether it had been loaded when he stored it in the rucksack, but he didn't think so.

"Did you kill men?" she asked.

He squinted harder, as if trying to think of an answer. He still couldn't tell for sure, unless the weapon was turned away from him. And if it didn't have a cartridge chambered, it would take even someone experienced with a Luger at least a second to work the toggle, picking up a shell from the clip. Four steps across the kitchen floor. A dive across the table. Give it two, three seconds maximum. He tensed.

The sounds of the horse's hooves dancing on the frozen ground, and indistinct words the boy was speaking, calming the animal, came in. So it has to be now, Mallen thought. He rocked forward on his bare heels. "You know that the gun isn't loaded," he said casually.

He had said it so quietly, so matter of factly, that it didn't register on her at first. She started to speak and then paused, looking down at the weapon. No tit, he thought; no *geladen*. He was rolling forward on his heels, slipping on the bare flooring, careening off the searing stove, feet skewing across the planks in a clown's rush, with the woman desperately trying now to work the toggle upward and backward. He crashed against the table, mistiming his lunge and upsetting it against her. Then they were struggling and she cried for her son. Using what leverage she had, she brought the barrel down across his forehead. A flash of pain and then the explosion of the weapon going off within inches of his ear. Christ, he realized, she had somehow chambered a round. Bending her arm back, she bit him on the wrist, the shock and pain of it almost causing him to lose his handhold on the barrel. Footsteps pounded on the turf and then the Luger fell from her fingers and he scooped it up.

The boy was in the doorway, the rifle raised. Mallen stood behind her, the barrel rammed into her neck. The Winchester clattered to the floor and the three of them stood in shock, cold filling the room. The only

sounds now were the boy's rough breathing, the growl
of the stove, and the wind working under the eaves.

"Shut the door," Mallen said.

"Salaud, salaud," the boy hissed, tears spilling from
the corners of his eyes. *"Salaud . . ."*

"But a free bastard," Mallen corrected him. "Now
shut the door."

Mallen first locked the boy in the pantry, then told the
woman to stable the horse. While she was gone, he
crawled back into his clothes, which the kid had brought
in from the barn. They were nearly dry, and in the heat
of the kitchen he could smell the sweat and dirt of his
own body. Taking his blanket, he wrapped Wyatt's feet
in the threadbare wool. Before the woman returned, he
emptied the Winchester and the shotgun, leaving the
cartridges on the sill high over the kitchen window.
With amusement he noted that the shotgun shells were
the crimped cardboard type, the mouths frayed open
and the shot missing. They might have made a bang,
but nothing more lethal. Then he stood by the window
and watched her come back across the yard, head bent
against the wind.

Mallen's first priority was to get Wyatt into the
sack. "What's upstairs?" he asked.

"My bedroom, Paul's room, and a bathroom." Her
hands were in constant motion, working against each
other. "My grandfather lives in the lower bedroom.
He's very old and bedridden," she added.

He pushed past her, exploring the lower floor. The
parlor was a slightly blurred version of many he had
seen in his childhood: linoleum floor yellowed with age
and cracking along its seams, old furniture, a hooked
rug, an upright piano against the interior wall, sheet
music set out and dried flowers drooping from a glazed
vase. In front of the window, bathed in sunlight, was an
overstuffed couch. Mallen had the woman assist him
as he moved Wyatt into the parlor. Wyatt was semiconscious, his head hanging slack, then jerking awake.

"We'll get you food soon," Mallen said, tucking in

the two blankets. Wyatt's eyes opened briefly and he attempted a smile, then let his head sink back into the pillows.

"Just give me some time," he whispered. "Sleep . . ."

Mallen nodded, then stood beside Wyatt, listening to him breathe. Food and sleep; perhaps it would be enough. He turned, taking the woman by the elbow, and left the parlor, softly closing the door behind him.

She led him to the old man's room. He watched her move ahead of him, her hair now trailing in a golden swath, freed from the confines of her cardigan, long fine strands catching sunlight from the polished windows. He could catch her scent of soap. Something gut wrenching stirred within him.

The farmhouse was old, typical of those dotting the rocky fields of New England and the eastern townships of Quebec. Long narrow hallways were papered in faded flower prints, and furniture, generations old, glowed in soft maple warmth.

The woman opened the door gently and stepped in. The shades were drawn and the room was a dim cavern, dominated by an iron bed. She struck a match and, applying it to an oil lamp, carefully turned up the wick.

The old man was awake, but just barely. Under piles of covers his head stuck out like a turtle's, bald and with the flesh melted away, leaving sagging skin on a skull's frame. Scattered around the walls were faded photographs: men in uniform, a couple leaning against a 1930s roadster, families posing formally against a trestle table mounded with food. Over the bed were two flags on small staffs, crossed and thumbtacked to the plaster—one a Union Jack and the other the Canadian maple leaf. Both were faded, the reds gone to pink, the blues pale.

"*C'est-y qui, c'gars?*" The old man's voice was little more than a whisper.

"*Un Americain. Un criminel,*" she answered. "*C'est okay.*"

"What are you saying?" Mallen asked. He looked down on the man's face—the same eyes, blue ice.

"He was asking who you are. I told him."

She prepared the man's arm with a swab and alcohol, then drew an ampule from a small wooden box on the dresser. Opening a drawer, she took a hypodermic and drew off amber-tinted fluid from the vial, then injected it into the old man's arm, pinching his skin between her fingertips. Mallen could see that there was little of the arm that had not been scarred from the injections.

"What's wrong with him?"

She turned down the lamp and stood over the old man, holding his hand, massaging it carefully between her thin fingers. "A type of cancer. There is a name for it. All we can do is give him narcotics. The points would have brought many more months' supply. That and the food he enjoys."

"Whiskey," the old man said, showing a cracked smile. "What I need is a decent glass of whiskey." He pushed the covers away from his face and craned his neck, looking at Mallen in the half light. "She says that you're a criminal." There was just a slight trace of a French accent.

Mallen walked over and stood on the opposite side of the bed. The old man's face was gaunt, but there was a flush of color from the drug.

"I wasn't registered. They caught me and I got away." It seemed ridiculous to repeat the story.

He nodded in a ponderous way. His eyelids fluttered, the drug taking effect. "And now you're running?"

Mallen nodded. "Yes."

"Don't harm my granddaughter. Or her son." It was spoken softly, but it was a command.

"I won't," Mallen promised.

The old man muttered something else and then, as Mallen watched, his face relaxed, the wrinkles easing, the lids closing.

She blew out the lamp and lightly pushed Mallen toward the doorway. "He's close to ninety," she said in the hallway. "You see what you're doing to us?"

"I'm supposed to let you turn us in?"

She turned away from him and moved toward the

kitchen. "No, I suppose I can't ask that of you either. We'll keep your friend on the couch in the parlor. It's warm there. I only want you and your friend to leave here, as soon as possible." She paused in mid-step and turned toward him. For the first time he really saw her face, saw small lines around her eyes and mouth, the smooth texture of her skin, the fine down of almost transparent hair along the curve of her neck.

"Do you intend to kill us?"

He shook his head marginally. "Of course not."

"Then put that thing away." She nodded at the Luger tucked in his waistband.

"And your son? What does he do? I can't leave him locked in the pantry."

"He can stay with my grandfather. You can lock the door."

"There are such things as windows."

"He will do nothing if I tell him that you will leave us unharmed. Tell him what you want." She turned away and strode into the kitchen. He tried not to watch her hips moving.

They moved into the parlor. She spread a comforter over Wyatt. "He has a very high fever. I have nothing for that. If you want him to live, you have to turn yourself in. They would take that into consideration."

Wyatt opened his eyes. "Negative!" he rasped. "Don't do it, Mallen. Leave me here and get the hell out."

"I'm staying," Mallen replied. "Three or four days of rest and you'll be okay."

"You know that's bullshit. I can smell myself rotting. I'm wasted, and we both know it."

She started to pull the drapes, shutting off the sun. "Leave the drapes open," Wyatt said, turning on his side toward the window. "I want to see the outside."

"We'll have some food for you in a while," Mallen said softly, moving toward the door.

Wyatt shook his head. "You leave us alone, lady." He beckoned Mallen with a nod. "Sit here." He nodded to the floor.

Mallen eased into a squat next to the couch. Wyatt

had a stench to him and his breath was sour. It reminded Mallen of pork gone rotten. Involuntarily, he wrinkled his nostrils.

Wyatt managed a grimace. "You think I smell bad. Try your own armpits." He started a laugh that ended in a watery, rolling cough.

"I'll get you some more tea. She must have some decent food hidden around here."

Wyatt shook his head, still coughing. "No food," he finally said. "I couldn't eat it." The coughing subsided. "Look out for that kid, Mallen." Mallen nodded. "No, I mean it. You remember how tough a kid his age can get."

"Two days and we'll be out of here. I could get the plane down in her pasture."

"Fuel. She got fuel?"

Mallen nodded, lying. "Some," he said, compounding the lie.

"You'll make it," Wyatt said, eyes closing. "Stay with me just a day. No longer."

"I'm getting you out." Mallen didn't hear conviction in his own voice. He started to get up.

"Tell me about British Columbia, Mallen."

"Later on."

"No, now. I mean about what it'll be like out there."

Mallen sat back, pulling the Luger from his belt and laying it out on the rug. A hooked rug; she probably made it. The yard was aching white, the trees stripped of leaves. Beyond that was an open field with the stubble of corn stalks, shucks vibrating in the wind. A flock of starlings flew south, then veered west, altering their path as one, bodies glossy black against the sky. "B.C.? It's there. Open country. Mountains down to the sea. What else?"

"I mean, what's it *like?* The people, the land—what sort of feeling do you get?"

Mallen wished for a cigarette, for something to keep his hands busy. He found them unsure, and wondered why the hell he felt so damn worthless. Christ, if there was just *something* he could do. He looked out the window, avoiding Wyatt's eyes. "What's it like?" he said, trying to visualize. "Like I said, mountains running down to the sea. Deep inlets with butter clams so thick you only need to dig for a few minutes to feed ten people. Game everywhere. And inland, more mountains, the Monashee Range and the Rockies. Tremendous mountains, not like the stuff in the east. I've seen valleys in the spring with apple blossoms pink and white . . ."

"Lakes?"

"Lakes everywhere. Trout so thick you can pull them out with a bent pin." He told Wyatt about Howe Sound and the Fraser Valley, described places such as Big Bar Creek and D'Arcy, valleys with widely spaced farms, lush and grass rich. And then he fleshed it out with people, people who would want to know your name and waved as you passed on a road. And the high country. Mallen described the freshness of wind blowing down the canyons and the taste of glacier-fed streams.

Wyatt was breathing regularly now, his eyes closed. Mallen got up softly, taking care not to make a noise.

"It'll be nice there in the spring," Wyatt said.

"Yes," Mallen replied. "In the spring . . ."

It was past sundown, the sun gone, the twilight going quickly. Mallen moved the boy from the pantry into the old man's bedroom. From the old man's dresser he took an oil pressure lamp, pumped it, and touched a match to the mantle. It flared, then steadied down into a pulsing glow, as if the oil were of very poor quality. The boy watched every move he made, from the corner armchair.

"There's not much I can do, Mr. Mallen," the boy finally said. "You've got the weapons. I should have never left my mother alone with you. I should have known she wouldn't kill."

"I wouldn't put her down," Mallen replied wearily, sitting down on the edge of the bed. The old man stirred in his sleep, one thin bony arm projecting from a nightshirt held across his face. Mallen noticed in the lamp-light that the skin was almost transparent, the blue veins prominent like tributaries of a river flowing through snow fields. He looked back at the boy, which was in-correct. Something between man and boy. Pulling his hand back through his hair, he said, "She has a lot of courage, your mother." Mallen remembered vividly the Luger firing, the feeling of hot gas burning across his skin.

"I want you to understand, Mr. Mallen." The boy paused, drawing himself up, his hands holding the arms of his chair as if making a pronouncement from a throne. "I want you to understand that if you harm her—touch her—I'll kill you."

Mallen's beard was itching, the fatigue eating up his reserves. A bath, he thought. What I'd give for a bath. He looked back at the boy and their eyes met, the boy locking on, holding Mallen's gaze, wanting a commit-ment.

"It's up to you," Mallen finally said. "I don't want to harm anyone here." He nodded significantly toward the kitchen. "But I've got to stay until my friend is better—three or four days at the most."

"You're stupid," the boy said contemptuously, easing back into the folds of the chair. "That man is dying. Without a doctor, he won't last another thirty-six hours. But if you leave now, I'll wait twelve hours and then alert the garrison. There he'll have a chance. You can take yours alone."

Mallen shook his head. "That's not what he wants. And it's his life." Mallen found a bedpost to lean back against and looked up at the ceiling. The sight of wall-paper, though stained and brown with age, was a shock, as if there were still a civilization and normal people ac-cepted such things as a routine part of their lives.

"He's delirious," the boy injected. "He doesn't know that he's dying. You have to make decisions for him."

Mallen shook his head. "No, Wyatt knows he's dying. But he doesn't want to be taken by the Peace Division. He was one of them once. They want him badly." The boy shot him a look of pure astonishment. Mallen nodded. "You've got it. If they saved him from dying, it would be worse for him. I'm staying with him until the end."

"Why . . . ?" the boy started to question.

"It's not up for discussion," Mallen replied, cutting off the boy. "Our deal is simple. You stay here with the old man. No tricks. I can't bar the window, but if you escape you have to live with the consequences. It's your mother's continued good health for your cooperation."

Paul reached out and, taking a coverlet from the foot of the bed, pulled it over him. "I have no choice," he said finally. "But there's one thing you must promise— that you'll . . ." he groped for the word, ". . . that you'll *respect* my mother." Their eyes met for a long moment.

"You have my word on that," Mallen finally said, standing up. He pulled the door closed behind him, then locked it as an afterthought. Trust, he remembered, was a mutual affair.

Mallen and the woman ate in the yellow glare of the pressure lamp. She had made an omelette and baked potatoes. There was a plate of hard black bread, almost unchewable. Regardless, the meal was delicious. Mostly they ate in silence, her eyes never meeting his. Halfway through the meal, she rose from the table and went to a box set into the window that he had not noticed before. From that she brought a wooden bowl of butter and some maple syrup.

"It makes the bread edible," she said, sitting back down. He noticed that she had changed into a long, pleated wool skirt that fell to her ankles. The blouse was a flowered cotton thing, patterned with blue lilacs, which picked up the color of her eyes. And the sweater was something surely prewar, fluffy. He suddenly realized that she had dressed for him.

"You look nice," he said.

She shrugged. "We don't have to live like animals. I try to dress this way for Paul. It's a habit at our evening meal."

Mallen set aside the last potato. "Can you take this, add some milk and butter and mush it? I don't think Wyatt will eat, but I'd like to have him try."

She shook her head. "That's unnecessary. I've made him a custard. And there's tea brewing." She made up a tray and Mallen carried it into the parlor.

He was half awake, mumbling. Mallen was glad that there was little light. Wyatt's face was distorted with swelling, and his lips were badly cracked.

"Dinner. I've got some custard and tea."

Wyatt shook his head. "I couldn't touch the stuff. How about a steak? Mushrooms?" He laughed, hacking.

Mallen worked him up into a sitting position, Wyatt grunting in pain, then fed him spoonfuls.

"The woman made this?"

Mallen nodded. "Yes," he said. "Milk custard."

"Tell her I appreciate it. Ask her whether I can have some more ice in the towel." He nodded toward a soggy rag on the arm of the couch. "My head's splitting."

"She did this?" Mallen asked.

"Yeah. While you were with the kid. And took off the dressing and put on a clean one. Gave me some stuff that she says is like aspirin."

"How do you feel?"

"What do you think? I fade in and out. Some of the dreams are wild. People I haven't thought of in years. It's like a drug trip. Just want to sleep."

"I'll get some more ice for the towel." Mallen stood up, taking the plate and towel.

In the kitchen, the woman was standing beyond the table in half light, holding the Luger. It would be loaded now, and Mallen cursed himself for the stupidity of it all. Their eyes locked across the intervening space, neither saying anything until at last she lay the Luger down on the table.

"I think you should lock this away," she said. "I'll get more ice for the towel."

Later he took food for the old man and the boy. He had no way of telling time, only that it was three or four hours past sundown. An ancient Seth Thomas housed in a flowing walnut case rested on the mantelpiece, but it was dead, locked forever on twelve fifteen.

"You know what time it is?" he asked the boy.

Paul glowered back at him and bent down, forking up food to his lips.

The old man smiled, lips slightly parted to reveal yellowed teeth sticking up like slim gravestones from reddish-black earth. He displayed a watch, the nylon strap loose on the fleshless bone on his forearm. "Ten after nine. Or about. Paul tells me you flew here."

Mallen explained, omitting only where they had crashed and that the plane was reparable. And that they needed gasoline and time and antibiotics and an ungoldly amount of luck. Because he wanted, more than anything, for both himself and Wyatt to see another spring.

The old man smiled again and extended his hand. "Colin Le Borveaux. French father—a Québécois, actually, and an immigrant Irish mother. Who left me with a taste for both cognac and Irish whiskey." Mallen took his hand. The grip was cool and surprisingly strong, like a fragile-looking prosthetic device, slim but with the advantage of leverage. The old man noticed the look on Mallen's face and darted his hand beneath the covers to withdraw a rubber ball. "I squeeze the hell out of it. Can't walk, can't control my own damn bowels, but I got hands left. I keep them strong." He squeezed the rubber globe, compressing it.

Mallen set the tray on the bed table and helped the old man into a sitting position. For the next ten minutes, he talked about growing up in New England, helping the man fork food into his mouth, wiping his lips. Le Borveaux was right—his hands were strong, but the coordination was gone and the fork had to be guided. Mallen felt no self-consciousness about helping him, just that it was a necessity that both of them recognized. Mallen felt a stirring of empathy, of identification with Le Borveaux: helpless, tired; thoughts of death; terminal fear. He finished forking in the last bit and wiped the old man's chin. "Do you get a shot now?" he asked softly.

"Shot of whiskey? Damn, I could use that. But the other stuff, no. I keep off it until things get too rough. Jeanne normally gives me one injection a day, which keeps the wolves from tearing up my guts. Goddamn crap! Nearly addicted to it now." Le Borveaux edged around from his one side to the other, a process that seemed both painful and endless. "Side gets tired. So I lie on my back and my ass gets tired, and then I try the other side. Don't bother to get old, Mr. Mallen, its not what it's cracked up to be." He eased his head back into the pillow. "Peace Division or Special Forces on it?"

"Both," Mallen replied. "Man called McKennon picked me up, interrogated me. But it looks like he's got assistance."

Le Borveaux nodded. "Peace Division," he said, yawning. "Typical cops. Cop mentality. But the Special Forces are something else. Most of them probably professional soldiers—the kind that always live to fight another day. Most of them mean bastards. All nationalities."

The old man turned to the boy. "Get me a glass," he said. "One for Mr. Mallen as well." The boy started to object and the old man glared at him. *"As I say,"* he snapped. He turned back to Mallen. "You'll take some rum?" He didn't bother to wait for the response, leaning back on the pillow. Mallen could easily visualize how he would look, stretched out in a coffin, fleshless skull against velvet.

Paul moved to the closet and took down a bottle from the shelf, along with two pewter mugs. Besides the ordinary wearing apparel, Mallen could see a uniform of sage green, brass buttons going green with age. A sword hung in its scabbard from the back of the door.

"Twenty-first Canadian Rifles," the old man said proudly. "Verdun and a few other places people have forgotten. And we thought then that it was the end of the world." He turned to the boy. "Hurry it up, Paul."

The boy turned away from the closet reluctantly and poured the amber fluid into the mugs. Returning to the bedside, he handed each of the men a mug and laid the bottle on the bedclothes. Mallen met his eyes but found only guarded neutrality in the boy's expression.

"Here's to you," the old man toasted, "and here's to me, and if by chance you don't agree—ta hell with you and here's to me." He laughed once, a kind of cluck, and drank.

"To you, then," Mallen said, smiling. He sniffed and drank, the rum very sweet and hot on his tongue. It tasted slightly of beets. "What about the rest of Canada? Do you have any idea what cities were hit and how the country is now?"

"Who in Christ knows? They tell you in the standards that it's a wonderland: everyone happy, producing food, flowering in a fuckin' classless society. Everything they say is in Technicolor, Mallen. Leaves you with the impression that where you live is the only goddamn bum place to live. Like *you're* the only one who isn't doing his job." The old man drank again, head half raised, held the liquor in his mouth, swishing it around from cheek to cheek, then swallowed. He dropped back on his pillow, blowing out his breath. "Jesus, that stuff is about the only reason my heart keeps ticking over. Local freeseller fellow peddles it—claims it's made from Rumanian sugar beets—five points the bottle. And has the damn gall to call it rum."

Mallen took another sip, already feeling the alcohol racing in his bloodstream. The stuff had to be very high proof. "Look," he said. "I want any kind of idea you might have about conditions. What areas to avoid, what you need in terms of travel passes, and what cities are still hot."

Le Borveaux made a face, compressing his lips. "You don't understand yet, do you," he said. "There is no travel. And there is no news, other than what they want you to hear. A travel pass in this Peace Division district probably isn't worth a shit in the next one. You're looking at a whole new system of little feudal states,

Mallen. Peace Division has nominal control, but it's really run by Special Forces."

The boy, silent until now, spoke. "It's not," he said. "Special Forces will be disbanded. The pacification phase is nearly finished. It's only men like this that give them reason for being."

The old man scoffed. "Paul, Paul, Paul," he said, shaking his head. "Because some idiot stands up in a classroom and feeds you that crap doesn't make it true." He turned toward Mallen. "Paul thinks the great Leninist dream is going to work: a world-wide socialist state. If you can believe it, that's the reason an insane war was fought and probably close to five *billion* people died. For that one single goddamn reason. But what happens? The only ones with arms were to be Special Forces, like the boy said, to be disarmed eventually, once pacification was complete." He grimaced at Mallen, the smile sardonic. "You ever heard of an army giving up its arms voluntarily, Mallen? Christ sake, no! Instead, they're consolidating their strength, recruiting, setting up their own system of taxation—even withholding distribution of food and clothing so that they can demand and get what they want of the population."

"What about the Soviets? Aren't they controlling the situation?"

The old man laughed. "What Soviets? You think so many of them survived? And from what Paul tells me, they're still fighting the Chinese. The nuclear weapons are finished now, thank God. It's artillery now and rifles tomorrow and the last men will die chucking rocks at each other. Some brave new world, Mallen."

The boy came forward into the circle of light cast by the oil lamp. "It's men like you," he said, looking at Mallen intently, "that gave us this war. And it's men like you that help continue it—fighting and destroying, looting, totally unwilling to help rebuild." He stepped closer, facial muscles taut. "And it's men like you who give reason to Special Forces. When you, and men like you, are finished, the Special Forces will be disbanded or sent to the Chinese front. It's then, Mr. Mallen, that we'll rebuild in peace. Only then!"

"Which is what your fairy books tell you, Paul," the old man shouted. "And I keep telling you to get out of it. You don't have to be in the Peace Division. Eventually, you'll be forced to join the Special Forces. It's the way things are going." His voice was rising, cracking. "You understand?"

The boy turned away and flung himself into a chair in the far corner of the room, drawing a coverlet over himself. "It's you that understand nothing, old *papushka*."

Le Borveaux's face was strained, with lines of pain around his mouth and eyes. On impulse, Mallen reached for his hand and gently squeezed it. The response was immediate but weak.

"Keep on going, Mallen," he finally said. "Fight and run. It's better than just sitting down and waiting for the world to grind to a stop. This is my house. Stay as long as you have to. I understand about the other man—the fact that you have to be with him even if it's useless. You wouldn't be much of a man if you left him to die alone."

"He helped me when I needed him."

"Like others have helped me," Le Borveaux answered. "You don't have to explain. And Mallen, if you want the truth, it's only the love and respect that we hold for other men that makes it a civilization. Without that, man's simply trash on a dirty planet." He looked up and gave a half grin, half grimace. "The booze doesn't do me much good. Send Jeanne in. She'll give me hell, but she understands." He reached up and gripped Mallen's wrist. "Alberta or British Columbia, Mallen. Make it to there and you're home free. It's free of contamination and the rumors are that it's a free-sellers land."

"No organized government?"

The old man grinned back at him. "None," he said. "None, from what I hear. It's worth the effort, Mallen."

*   *   *

Mallen had the dishes washed when she returned. As he wiped the plates, she retrieved a kettle from the stove and poured water through the tea strainer.

Mallen lowered himself into a chair, rocking back on the legs, huffing at the heat of the dark liquid. "He's quite a man, your grandfather."

"To me he is." She paused, picking up shreds of the tea leaf that edged the rim of her cup. "It was a filthy thing to do, letting him drink liquor."

"How was I to know . . . ?"

"How could you *not* know? A man his age with cancer? Can't you see what you're doing to us?"

"It's not something I can control. I have him . . ." he nodded toward the parlor where Wyatt lay ". . . to think of."

She ignored his explanation. "If you're caught here, or even if you escape and then are traced back to this farm, it will mean that my grandfather will have no more drugs. Paul will be punished—I don't know. We could easily lose what little we now have."

Mallen sipped at the cup. The tea was more like a brew of grain and bark—bitter, with a strong aftertaste. "I'll leave as soon as I can; that's all I can promise."

He looked up from his tea to find her watching him intently. In a way, he thought, she was beautiful. A little hard and unsmiling, perhaps overly thin. with sharp features, but in her own way handsome.

"There's something that I have to bring up. It's not pleasant."

"It's your dime." He caught her look of puzzlement, realizing that it was really an American expression, one probably forever dead from the language. "I'm listening," he said, setting the cup down and rocking forward.

"Do you want to—to have me?"

She had said it so conversationally, it stopped him cold. "No, I hadn't . . ."

She handed him a worn key. "To my bedroom," she said. "You will lock it from the outside and I will bar it from the inside. That way neither one of us will be troubled." She stood up, smoothing her dress. "I have scissors, Mr. Mallen. That is all I have, but I'd use them if you tried to force your way." She led him upstairs and paused in the doorway. "There's a kettle of water heating on the stove if you desire to bathe. Since you have Paul locked in my grandfather's room, you might as well use his." She gestured toward a door on the opposite side of the hallway.

She looked so fragile to Mallen, particularly in the candle light, her features softened, the eyes hidden in shadow. He had a momentary vision of her brushing her hair, head thrown back, stroking a brush down through the long, golden mass of wheat-colored hair. Her respiration now was more rapid, the sweater a tight constraint to her breasts. She backed into the doorway, still facing Mallen, her hand groping for the doorknob. Unconsciously, he put his hand forward to touch her face, but she closed the door quickly, shutting him off. He heard the bar fall into place. In the stillness of the house, the sound was as loud as the pounding of his heart.

In the kitchen he stripped off the dirt-encrusted clothes, laying them aside for washing tomorrow. He found a bucket beneath the sink and, storklike, stood on one leg and then the other, sponging off the dirt with hot water and something that passed for soap. The wound was closed again, a bright pink pucker of flesh with a blackened crust along the seam of the puncture. He dabbed at it with a rag, not wanting to allow the water to soften the closure. It was still itching, a good sign, he thought.

Finally finished, he stood naked next to the Atlantis stove, drying in the radiant heat, letting it soak into his frame as an ultimate luxury, something he wished his body could store. But he had to keep turning, like a pig on a spit, keeping the heat moving over his flesh. If I ever have another place, he thought, I will have two stoves, one on either side of the room, to have some uniform standard of heat. He pictured it in his mind: A tightly chinked log house. Stoves, maybe brick fireplaces eventually. He would add to it as the years went along, enlarge the place, add rooms. But there would be heat in every room.

He was swaying with fatigue. Not wanting to leave the heat for the coldness of the upstairs, he took a rug from the parlor. In the darkness, he listened to Wyatt breathe. A machine to process air, he thought—that's all the lungs were, and these of Wyatt's were breaking down, filling with liquid.

At the door of the old man's room he could hear nothing. He unlocked and opened the door. The lamp was a pinpoint of orange. He could see the shadow of the boy, asleep on the chair. Closing the door softly, he relocked it.

He spread the rug next to the Atlantis and rolled up in it, feeling the latent heat of the iron eventually seeping through the rug. He smelled the wood smoke from the banked embers. And fell asleep.

He woke at dawn, the kitchen chilling. In the hall closet he found a dirty greatcoat and wool trousers. Pulling these on, he returned to the kitchen and, using the remaining embers, fired the stove with wood from the bin. The pump refused to pull up water, so he primed it with water from a pitcher. Finally, he was rewarded with a thin trickle of rusty water and then a full flow with every stroke. He filled the kettle and set it on the iron plate of the Atlantis.

The weather beyond the ice-glazed windows was still clear. No new snow, but the sky to the west had long, thin streaks of cirrus, and he doubted that the day would last without flurries. Perhaps enough to cover new tracks; but there was Wyatt.

Wyatt lay almost motionless, his respiration shallow, like a dog panting. Mallen jostled his shoulder, but he rolled over, facing the back of the couch, coughed, and then steadied into a more regular respiration rate. Mallen left him to sleep.

She was awake and dressed when he knocked at her door. Without comment, she pushed past him in the hallway and made her way down to the kitchen. He sat behind the table, watching her move economically.

"Four more days and Paul will be expected back at the garrison," she said at last, breaking the silence between them. "And you might think of letting him out of the room. There is wood to split and the milking." She kept her back to him, taking dishes from a rack and stacking them on the stove. "How is your friend?" She turned to him, smoothing down her apron.

"Not better. He's still sleeping."

"Will he want food?" He realized that her lips had a slight gloss, as if she had used a neutral shade of lipstick. And her hair was combed out. She looked younger than she had yesterday.

"Later," he said. "He may want food later. I'll get the boy."

"Paul . . ." she said over her shoulder. "He's not a boy. I think he would prefer not to be called one."

Paul was awake, moving inside the room. Mallen listened at the door for a moment, then quietly turned the key in the lock. He opened the door quickly, without knocking.

Paul was standing with the closet door open, pulling on a sweater. He turned and looked at Mallen in surprise and shut the closet door.

"Your mother needs you to do some chores." The boy nodded and started to push past him. Mallen took his arm, restraining him, gently forcing him to turn. They were face to face, the boy almost as tall but pounds lighter. "No cute ideas, Paul."

Paul pulled from his grasp and moved quickly from the room. Mallen could hear him briefly arguing with his mother, and then the kitchen door slammed. Brushing aside the curtains, he watched Paul stalk across the barnyard, pull back the rolling door, and enter the barn.

"He'll be all right," Le Borveaux said.

Mallen turned to find the old man propped up. From beneath the mattress Le Borveaux withdrew a thin wooden cigar box.

"Help yourself," he said, lighting one. The smoke

was pungent, oil blue in the streaks of sunlight that entered between the slightly parted curtains.

They smoked together in silence, the only sound that of the woman moving in the kitchen. The old man took one final puff and then carefully flicked off the glowing tip into a saucer and, wetting his finger with spittle, snuffed the remaining ember.

"How's the black man?" he finally asked, sliding down beneath the covers.

"About the same, I guess."

Le Borveaux readjusted the pillow and settled back. "Saw a boy die in France," he said. "Come to think of it, saw a lot of boys die. Nineteen sixteen, seventeen. Seems like a century ago. But this particular kid died like Wyatt's dying. Without even basic medicine there's nothing much you can do." He took the dead cigar and replaced it between his lips, sucking on it.

"This plane of yours—will it fly?"

Mallen shrugged. "With some repairs and some fuel. A gas line was chewed up. I'll need flexible tubing, some hose clamps. But the more important thing is getting fuel. Reasonably high octane."

"Premium gas, you mean?"

"The same thing."

The old man pulled on the cigar, making a dry sucking sound. "Gasoline," he said, drawing the word out, "I got plenty of. You don't live out in the country without some kind of a store of gasoline." He pointed vaguely toward the barn with the dead cigar. "There's a barrel with maybe thirty gallons left in the shed. The rest of the stuff you probably need is around the workbench. Otherwise, you might have to cannibalize the car."

"Car?" Mallen couldn't believe it.

Le Borveaux nodded. "Car. It's an old Peugeot, a sixty-nine, but in pretty decent shape. Second car in my life that I actually bought brand-new."

"I thought—heard that all the cars were confiscated."

"Correct. All the ones they could find they confiscated. I stacked brush all over it and left it for nearly a year in the south pasture in a clump of trees. Saved it for an emergency." He rolled the cigar between his fingers, thinking. "Shit, Mallen—God knows what kind of emergency. Just that I was damned if I was going to give away something that I worked hard for."

"This thing run now?"

Le Borveaux looked at him for a while and then smiled. "Mallen—you're not *taking* it. I'm *giving* it. My own free will. Probably a state offense if Jeanne ever tried to use it. And for me, about the only ride I'll ever get is in a horse-drawn hearse, if that." He shook his head. "No, Mallen, it's yours. The car is parked in the shed now. Paul knows how to start it and he warms it up about once a week."

"You're sure you want me to have it?"

"*My God,* Mallen—how many times do I have to tell you? Use the damn thing any way you want. It'll give me some pleasure to know that you've got half a chance of getting clear. Send me a postcard from wherever you go—that is, if they ever get some sort of postal system going." He snorted and flung the cigar toward the fireplace. "Better yet, Yankee man, send me a case of Bushmills."

"I . . ." Mallen made a helpless gesture, trying to frame some kind of gratitude into words.

"No thanks necessary." Le Borveaux made a throw-away motion with his right hand. "No thanks necessary. Just a favor."

"Name it."

The old man sighed. "Look, Mallen. Paul's father wasn't worth much—a womanizer. There wasn't much love in their marriage." He pulled on his nose. "I see Jeanne dressing up like I haven't seen in two years. There something going on between you two?"

"Nothing." Mallen tested the litmus of his own beliefs. Nothing real, his mind echoed.

Le Borveaux stared at him for a long time, to the extent that Mallen felt uncomfortable. "Then I ask you to keep it that way," the old man finally said. "Understand this: Paul is a little frightened of you, maybe even hates you in some way. But he also admires you. I see him watching you, see that he sometimes duplicates your mannerisms. In short, Mallen. keep it clean and keep it simple. The boy hated his father, knew like any kid of thirteen would know that his old man was fooling around. Little things; a kid sees them when even an adult doesn't."

The old man worked his way into a semireclining position supported by his spindly arms and elbows. "What I'm saying, Mallen, is that the kid is very protective of his mother. Do like I told you, don't mess around. As long as it stays that way the boy will be all right. But cross that boundary and I can't predict what his reaction would be. You understand?"

Mallen stood up and moved toward the door. "Understood," he answered. He looked back, but Le Borveaux had already sunk back on the pillow, his eyes closed.

14

McKennon scratched absentmindedly along the scruff of the Alsatian's neck. The dog sat, eyes closed, leaning into the man's hand, growling occasionally in pleasure. Before him on the desk was a scattered pack of index cards detailing Mallen's background, the interrogation, and as much as McKennon could piece together of the escape. In a separate stack of cards was the background information on Wyatt, but Mallen was McKennon's primary interest. Intuitively, he felt that Mallen was the leader and it was a guessing game now, one that neither Wyatt and Mallen nor McKennon could afford to lose.

The dog, now ignored, spread his forelegs and slid into a reclining position, felt the cold planks beneath his belly, and, thinking better of it, heaved himself up and resettled nearer the stove. He whined once, wanting the ritual afternoon walk with McKennon, but, seeing no response, lay his head between his paws and drifted into sleep.

The bare room was cold and meanly furnished. Beyond the desk, an iron-framed cot, and shelves crudely built into the corner, the room was a shell. There was a smell of wood smoke and disinfectant. Lane, the desk orderly, had said that it had been a barracks, built in the forties.

McKennon had a headache, more from tension and lack of sleep than from drinking, though he was draining a full liter of brandy per day. The erosion of power was almost complete. Most of the garrison knew of the breach between him and Brinkerhoff, he thought, and of the time limit on finding Mallen and Wyatt. With only a few days remaining and nothing even vaguely hopeful in the last four days of searching, his position of power had dissolved. Now, at dinner, the others avoided his table and he generally ate alone. But he still commanded three long-range horse patrols and one chopper. And, surprisingly enough, Baines had stuck with it, flying two and three sorties a day.

He pushed back his chair and went over to the window. Still clear and no new snow, both good factors for tracking. But if Mallen had holed up, as he suspected, it also worked against the time limit, because Mallen would not—could not move, unless there were falling snow and bad weather to cover his trail.

The barracks yard was beaten down into a mixture of ice, packed snow, and horse manure. As he watched, a young trooper spread wood ashes along the path. Besides two ancient diesel trucks, it would be strictly horse patrols and choppers for the balance of the winter. The 'lectrics were useless in this stuff.

From a pile of wood he selected two short logs and fed them to the stove. The iron shell was shimmering with heat, but the poor insulation and single-pane window bled off what little warmth there was into the outdoors. He lit a cigarette and studied the wall map. Section by section, he had covered the smaller villages, the outlying farms, and buildings that were known to be still standing. But still he had been able to cover only a third of the territory that he thought Mallen and Wyatt would cross. And if he were wrong? It was more than possible.

He flicked the butt of the cigarette with accuracy into the asbestos sheet that insulated the stove from the flooring. Horseshit, he thought. If they're dead or gone, I'll never know. But if, as he believed with growing conviction, they had moved down into the eastern townships of Quebec to find food and shelter, he had to keep sweeping with the patrols, moving steadily south toward the border. With a pencil he blocked out the coordinates covered by yesterday's sweeps. Now he was beginning to feel the press of time against his back. He would have to go more rapidly, splitting each patrol and avoiding hamlets of three houses or more, for he felt that Mallen could not hide his presence in a small community as easily as he could in an individual farmhouse or barn.

McKennon worked in silence for another twenty minutes, circling areas for today's and tomorrow's sweeps and listing the map coordinates assigned to each patrol. Finished, he leaned back in the chair. The dog, hearing him move, rose in anticipation and came to him, slowly sweeping his tail in tentative strokes. The dog, nameless and generally uncared for, was a permanent fixture of the barracks. McKennon had never inquired what the dog's name was, for in his own mind it was Beggar. Pouring himself a half cup of plum brandy, McKennon lit yet another cigarette and worried the dog's ears with the flat of his knuckles. The dog responded with something of a rumble, bending his neck in pleasure, eyes locked on the man's face.

"Beggar. You old Beggar," he said to the dog in a soft voice. The dog's fur was velvet beneath his fingertips as he expertly worked around the perimeter of the ears and neck, then finally pushed the dog away, very gently.

"I gave my son a dog like you," he said, and the dog sat down, facing him, ears erect. "He would have been fourteen this fall," McKennon added unnecessarily. He poured another half cup and looked across the fields beyond the courtyard, avoiding thinking. If that was possible.

Mallen helped the boy bring in firewood in the midafternoon. Hidden behind high cirrus, the sun had no more substance or warmth than a pale china plate.

They moved, each carrying armloads, from the woodshed to the kitchen stoop, staking the cracked and dry maple to the depth of a cord. The boy did it economically, mindlessly, without conversation. Twice they saw rabbits, which Mallen pointed out.

"There are no more shells for the shotgun," Paul

said. "Not until next session. They give me two per month. I reload the shells with lead balls for the deer. Three I got in the last year." He walked ahead of Mallen as if the older man would contaminate his presence. "Besides," he said, "the rabbits are no good for food; some kind of sickness."

Mallen helped him muck out the stalls and feed the horse. It was warmer in the barn, out of the wind, and somehow comforting—the scent of manure and feed and the myriad smells that city people somehow are never comfortable with. Mallen remembered an uncle who had a dairy herd of twenty head and claimed he could smell a barn for five seconds and tell whether there was even one diseased cow—and then what the disease probably was.

At last they both sat down on a stack of lumber, winded and sweating. Paul glanced sideways at Mallen, dug into his coat, and produced a leather pouch. "Tobacco," he said. From a pants pocket he produced rough pulp paper and put it down on the plank between them.

Mallen raised his eyebrows.

"My father's," the boy said. "It's old. You might not find it any good."

As Mallen rolled a cigarette, he wondered whether it had been the boy's idea or his mother's. The stuff was rough cut and dry, crumbling when you touched it, but it still had flavor.

"It tastes fine," Mallen finally said, blowing out an abortive smoke ring. He tapped ash into his cupped hand. "Your training," he asked. "What's it like?"

Paul twisted stalks of straw between his hands, keeping his eyes on the floor. "We learn language. Training with weapons, the operation of equipment." He threw the straw away. "Some political stuff."

Mallen started to frame a question about politics, then realized that it was an area bound to generate hostility between them. "What kind of equipment do you operate?" he said at last.

The boy stood up and walked back and forth, his

head bent down, kicking at the straw. "All sorts. The 'lectrics, of course. Diesel- and alcohol-fueled power-generating sets." He looked up at Mallen. "You flew in your air force, didn't you?" The boy's face was not accusatory.

"Transports," Mallen answered. "Two- and four-engine stuff."

"What's it like to fly?"

Mallen thought about the dumb part of it—sitting in stale cockpits for boring hours, flight lunches that seemed composed of equal parts of cardboard and rubber. But then he remembered what the sun was like as it came up out of the Atlantic on a transoceanic flight, or the feeling of flying alone on top of a cloud deck. He ground the cigarette out on a plank and settled back, both hands clasped behind his neck.

"I don't know. Like flying," he finally said. He re-crossed his legs, shifting his position.

"Only that?"

Mallen looked at him carefully, then thought about it. "More than that, Paul. The first time you fly—I mean actually pilot an aircraft—something either clicks or it doesn't. If whatever it is clicks, you have to fly. You make all kinds of stupid decisons that affect your life, just so you can fly. I was going to be a farmer. Loved the land and the independence that goes with it. I came from three generations of farmers. But then one day— I guess it was about my sixteenth birthday—one of my uncles gave me a ticket for an introductory ride at the local pea-patch airport. Took my camera, because I thought the neatest thing would be to get a photo of the farm. Afterward, I realized that I had never even taken the camera out of its case. Couldn't even remember what we had done, except for this *feeling,* the click."

"I'd like to fly some time."

"You never flew?" The horse thumped against the flooring, the sound hollow and impatient.

"Once," Paul said, "with my father. We took a plane. Two engines, I think, from Montreal to Toronto. But we sat in back. I don't remember much except that he bought me a soft drink." He stood up, moving away toward the feed bin. With both hands he reprovisioned the horse's feed bucket.

Watching the boy move, Mallen felt vaguely defeated, as if he had almost touched Paul's mind but somehow, inexplicably, had missed. "Your dad—what was he like?" As he said it, he realized that it was a stupid thing to have done, to have brought up things from the past. He was just trying to maintain contact with the kid.

The boy kicked at straw, moving it into a little pile and then pushing the pile with a foot toward a broken bale of hay. Paul shrugged. "He didn't do much for us. Away most of the time, traveling. He said it was business, but I think he had—somebody—he liked in Montreal." He shrugged again as if he felt it was unimportant. Turning back to Mallen he suddenly asked, "Were you married?"

"No. Not quite. Once, almost . . ."

The kid nodded as if he understood. "Do you like my mother?" He turned to face Mallen, his expression blank.

"Yes," Mallen said. And as he said it, he saw furrows appear on the kid's forehead. "She's been kind," Mallen amended. "Without her, Wyatt . . ." He paused, his mouth open. From the barnyard came the sounds of horses, shod hooves muffled somewhat in the thin layer of snow, but unmistakable.

There were five of them—two in the sage green of Special Forces and the other three in Peace Division gray. All had AK-47s. Mallen watched from a gap between the barn's planking. The Special Forces' mounts were better cared for, with saddle blankets trimmed with piping and division seals picked out in gold thread. As he watched, one of the Special Forces men, a Mongol by his features, looked directly at the barn.

Mallen became intently aware of three things: the Luger and rifle were unloaded and in the pantry, his and the boy's tracks were a maze of footprints between the barn and the house, and his own life expectancy now had finite limitations. Grabbing Paul, he covered the boy's mouth, holding him close. At first Paul struggled, but then the fight went out of him and he relaxed, slowly shaking his head against the pressure of Mallen's hand.

The Mongol and one of the P. D.'s dismounted, the Mongol, crouched and running, starting to circle around behind the barn. The other man, Caucasian and older, face pinched by the cold, headed for the house. The remaining three horsemen sat slumped in their saddles, too tired or too bored to dismount. As did most soldiers, anywhere, they took no initiative, waiting only for a command.

Mallen turned slowly, holding the boy against him, watching for the movement of the Mongol between the cracks. But the man was good. Mallen had expected him to circle the barn, but instead he had reversed directions, keeping low and running on the balls of his feet, soundlessly in the soft snow. Less than two feet away, on the other side of the planking, Mallen heard a bolt drawn back and released, chambering a round in the automatic weapon. A shadow passed close to the crack and the barn door moved a fraction as the man pushed against the edge with his boot. Over the nervous stamping of the animals, the noise was nothing.

Mallen sank slowly into a crouch behind some hay bales, dragging the boy down next to him. It would be only seconds before the Mongol rolled open the door, and then even fewer seconds for his eyes to adjust to the gloom.

The thin slit of light became a stripe and a space large enough for a man to enter. But the Mongol had flattened himself against the outside planking, presenting no target. Only the vented muzzle-blast deflector showed—that and the man's fur-trimmed booted foot as it pushed against the inertia of the door.

There were suddenly shouts in the yard, hard accents, and a foreign language, Slavic sounding.

Paul, surprising Mallen with a sudden twisting of his body, tore away Mallen's hands. "Get your head down!" he hissed. "They're telling him to use a grenade!"

There was a cry from the yard and then voices—a feminine one arguing, then those of the men, shouting something back to her, half angry, half irritated. Mallen could hear her shouting again, this time in French. From only feet away, the Mongol raised his voice in a question and she replied.

There was a space of seconds when nothing happened, but then, quite suddenly, the Mongol stood fully exposed in the frame of light. "Get out here," he commanded.

Mallen could see the man in the slit of vision between the bales of hay: medium short and thick, heavily muffled in a green wool forage coat heavily trimmed with fur. There were hashmarks on the sleeve—possibly a noncommissioned officer, Mallen guessed. There seemed little point in resisting. He took a deep breath, preparing to stand up. Paul was face down in the straw, his hands covering his head.

"Out here now, *májibynk!*" The Mongol raised his AK, muzzle toward the roof, and squeezed off a short burst, the sound deafening, the muzzle flame white-orange in the darkness.

She was on the man, pushing him over from behind, kicking ineffectually with heavy booted feet. From behind her, the men were laughing, shouting at her and at the Mongol in a mixture of French, English, and Slavic. Mallen caught the words "kick his balls" and the words were then overlaid with one man's rumbling laughter.

"*Paul, sors de suite!*" she screamed.

The boy stood up slowly, never glancing down at Mallen, moving carefully. "*Dis lui . . .*" he said with contempt. "*. . . de mettre son fusil au cran de sûreté.*" He crawled over the bales and walked carefully toward the light, his hands behind his neck, fingers clasped together.

The Mongol was in a crouch now, his weapon

leveled. She left first, then the boy, followed by the Mongol.

Mallen gave it ten seconds and then crawled to the crack. All the men were dismounted now, stretching and stomping to restore circulation. She led them into the kitchen, the boy following and the Mongol the last to enter. In just the few seconds that Mallen had had a clear view of her, he had realized that she was wearing outrageously oversized boots, probably those of her husband, and that their size would roughly match the footprints of his own boots in the snow. She's covering for me, he thought with amazement.

They were gone again in an hour. Two came from the house first, then two more. The tallest one, with the pinched face, lingered in the doorway. He made an ineffectual grab at the woman but she pushed him away, laughing. The other men guffawed, one of them shouting that the man had an incestuous relationship with his right hand. She laughed again, hands on hips, elbows back, straining the shirt across her breasts. Then she gave a twist of her hips, a gesture both comic and provocative.

They yelled their approval and left, two by two, with Pinched Face drawing up the rear. He turned just before the end of the lane, making a ring with the fingers of his left hand and thrusting the index of his right hand into the circle. She laughed and returned the gesture.

Mallen waited for long minutes, then returned to the house. The kitchen still smelled of horses and gun oil, sweat-dampened clothing and coarse tobacco. She was washing cups in the bucket.

Mallen took one last look from the doorway. The patrol had split at the main road, both parts being out of sight. He closed the door and stood on the hearth, warming his back, chaffing circulation into his hands. She hadn't even turned to acknowledge his presence.

"Where's Paul?" he asked uneasily.

"I hid Wyatt in my grandfather's closet. Paul's helping him get resettled in the parlor. His wound is suppurating badly. I blamed the smell on my grandfather's illness."

"You could have easily turned us in."

"The thought occurred to me," she answered. "I felt I had to leave the decision to Paul—he has the most to lose." She turned away from him, stacking the plates and cups on a shelf. "He covered for you from the very first."

"But why?"

She flexed her shoulders forward in a gesture of indifference. "Does it matter?" she answered mildly. "I doubt that he would be willing to explain."

Mallen salvaged the tobacco from several stubbed-out cigarettes, rolled it into a home-made, and lit it. "The patrol—did they give any indication of where they were searching?"

"They didn't say, and I didn't press them. Fishbeck, the older one, is a French Canadian. I've met him once before at Midsummer Barter Fair. He said that they had only two more days before they were to return to the garrison. I think he meant that they would be calling off the search after that. Beyond that, he just asked normal questions—whether we had seen strangers in the area—whether we had seen a small plane. I think they suspected nothing."

"The Mongol was suspicious!"

"I couldn't tell. He doesn't speak to the other men much. Paul told me that he's always that way."

He stood up and pulled on his jacket. "Your grandfather told me about the car and the gasoline. Before it's dark, I want to check it over. That and get some things for the plane."

She wheeled around. "You're not taking it! If he gets much worse, I could at least have a way of getting him to the clinic in Quebec City."

"Jeanne, it was a damn close thing this afternoon. Sooner or later there'll be another patrol. This guy McKennon isn't the kind to give up. With the gasoline and the car, I can . . ."

"Take it *all*," she screamed back at him, smashing a

cup into the washing bucket. "Take everything—car, fuel, food, clothes—*everything!* We're literally risking our lives for you, and all you want is more."

He came over to her, wanting to touch her face, to hold her. Instead, he kept his arms at his sides. "You understand my position?" he asked gently.

Her face was contorted, on the edge of hysteria. Mallen carefully backed away, to sit on the edge of the table. "No," he finally said, "you don't understand. But your grandfather does. Every day I stay here increases the danger for all of you. With the car I can take both Wyatt and the fuel. There's a place he knows of in Ontario. I'd maybe have a halfway chance of getting him there alive. If the weather is decent, I'll leave tomorrow."

She turned away from him; stood with her back to him, shaking.

Embarrassed, frustrated, Mallen tried to think of something to say to calm her. At last, he stood up, working the fastenings of his jacket, pulling on his gloves. He turned for the door.

"Gregory . . . ?" She had turned to face him, wiping her hands on her skirt, composed.

"What?"

"Yes. I do understand. Take the car. It's his to give. And don't go tomorrow. Your friend shouldn't be moved. It would kill him. Another few days won't matter."

Mallen lifted his shoulders fractionally and dropped them. "I'll talk it over with Wyatt," he finally said. He opened the door, then looked back at her.

"Stay," she said almost soundlessly. "Please."

He found the barrel of gasoline cradled between sawhorses behind the door of the tool shed. A brass tap on the drum supplied him with a sample—mostly water at first, but as it ran, the color changed to pink. Smelling it, he recognized the pungency of gasoline. The clear fluid had just been condensation.

Toward the back of the shed, under a low, cobwebbed ceiling, he found the Peugeot. Despite the accumulated dust on the body and chicken droppings spattered across the hood, the engine started easily. He checked the gauges. Decent charge in the battery, and the gas gauge registered full. Shutting off the ignition, he left the keys on the dash as he had found them and scrounged around on the disused, cluttered workbench. He found two rolls of vinyl electrician's tape, a few hand tools and—best of all possible finds—a number of lengths of tubing. Comparing them to the sample section he had retained from the RF-5, he found one just slightly larger but close enough in size to work.

The hose clamps took longer. Nothing on the bench or on the overhead racks. He checked under the hood of the Peugeot, but the only ones he found were in the vacuum system of the windshield-wiper system and of the wrong size.

As he searched, he kept thinking of Jeanne and her reaction. She was right, of course. Wyatt couldn't be moved. A few days wouldn't matter. But there was something in the way she had said it, as though she had been frightened he would leave. Shaking his head, he put it out of his mind.

He was about to give up when he found a wooden box filled with junk. He overturned it onto the dirt floor, expecting nothing. But there, heaped together with the guts of an electric iron, rusty nails, and assorted nuts and bolts, was a bracelet of hose clamps linked together by wire. Twisting the wire open, he compared the sizes to the tubing sample. Six of them were a near perfect fit, only slightly corroded with rust. Taking the best four, he worked for another half hour, scouring them with a wire brush and lubricating them. As he worked, he whistled softly to himself, something from a Beatles' album, except that he couldn't remember the words.

"You thought I'd turn you in at first, didn't you?"

Mallen turned. Paul stood just behind him, holding a steaming cup.

"I didn't hear you come in." He wiped the excess grease from the hose clamps and dropped them into a plastic bucket, along with the tools, hose, and tape. Skidding around on the stool, he heaved his shoulders. "I think you're right. A couple of hours ago I figured that you and your mother would blow it."

The boy set the mug down on the workbench. "Cocoa," he said. "Prewar. One of the P. D.'s gave me a packet."

Mallen raised his eyebrows, half smiling. "For me?"

Paul stood back, jamming his hands into his jacket. "I figured you might like it. I can always get more."

Mallen sipped at the near-scalding liquid, making appreciative noises. It was bad—a bit stale, but still with the essence of chocolate. "How come?" he finally said. "Seventy-five points, and all that stuff."

Shrugging, Paul moved toward the bench and inspected the contents of the plastic pail. "I don't know," he said, almost to himself. "Partly that Mr. Wyatt is so sick. It would be hard on him to be moved." He picked up a pair of pliers and scissored them open and shut a few times before dropping the tool into the bucket. "Partly also that it would get my mother into trouble." He glanced sideways at Mallen as if judging his reaction. "Anyway, I didn't. I guess I want you to make it," he finally said. He rattled the bucket. "These the parts you need?"

Nodding, Mallen smiled. "They'll do, I think. Nothing the Federal Aviation would have ever approved, but close enough."

There seemed to be a shyness now to Paul. Mallen watched him move around the shed, picking things up and dropping them. He kicked a deflated soccer ball across the dirt floor. "My father played soccer. Did you?"

"Football," Mallen replied, running a finger along the broken ridge of his nose. "Never did me any good. Zigged when I should have zagged."

The boy smiled politely, then switched it off. "You like Mr. Wyatt a lot, don't you?"

"I guess." He thought about it. "Yes, a lot."

"My great-grandfather says he'll die. You think so?"

Mallen took a great breath and blew it out. "I guess, Paul. There's not much I can do for him. It's gangrene plus some kind of lung infection. I can only hope that his body will fight off the infection somehow."

The kid nodded. "But if he dies—you'll have to bury him?"

Mallen swirled the remaining cocoa in his cup, then finished it. "Yes," he replied. "That's something I didn't want to think about." Easy to block unpleasant things from one's mind, he thought. Maybe that's why we survive; we reject the unthinkable.

Paul moved toward the door but turned back. "I thought about it," he said. "There's an area of ground near the largest oak north of the house. It's consecrated ground. My great-grandmother is buried there. I asked my great-grandfather. He thinks that it would be all right to put Mr. Wyatt there if—if it happens." Pulling his cap down around his ears, he opened the door and stood there for a moment looking out across the fields, then turned back. "If you want," he said, "I'll take proper care of it in the spring. Plant grass and stuff. Maybe some flowers."

"Thanks," Mallen said softly. But the door was already closed.

Mallen sat in the gloom of the shed for a long time, first listening to the boy moving away toward the barn, the rollers on the door creaking, then the silence that followed, broken only by the sound of the wind and his own breathing. He thought a lot about Wyatt: what his life had been like, where he had grown up, the friends and enemies he had made. The frustration of not being able to do anything gnawed at his stomach, leaving a hard emptiness within him.

"Fuck!" he said aloud, startling a chicken nesting beneath the car. From a corner he picked up a spade and shuffled out into the bitter afternoon.

As Paul had said, there was an oak and then a solitary headstone protruding from the same snow. Pacing off a long rectangle, he started to hack Wyatt's grave out of the frozen ground.

Mallen, the woman, and the boy ate in silence by oil lamp. Before dark, Wyatt had awakened briefly, refused food, mumbled something about rain, and pushed the plate out of Mallen's hand, spilling food across the pillow. Mallen brushed it off as best he could and pulled the blanket up.

"How is he?" Jeanne asked.

"No better. Maybe no worse—I can't tell. Mostly now he doesn't seem to recognize me or where he's at."

"You'll have to stay two or three more days," Paul said suddenly, as if he had been rehearsing it. "The Hungarian corporal said that the search is finished tomorrow but that it will take them some time to get back. They're working the foothills, then they'll move back east along the valley and down to the Seaway."

"You sure? And that's the end of the search?" He watched Paul's eyes carefully, unsure whether to believe him.

Paul nodded. "Positive! They were talking about the fact that the officer in charge of the search is being pulled out of it for disciplinary reasons. Something political, the corporal said."

Mallen leaned back in the chair. Just like that, he thought. McKennon had lost and he had won.

The boy was talking rapidly now, laying out what had been bottled up inside him. "If you want," he said excitedly, "I can help a lot. I go back to the garrison in three days, but the training session lasts just a week. When I come back, I can bring stuff that you need. Passes, tools maybe. Even sulfa drugs. I can help fix the plane . . ." His face was flushed, smiling.

"You're saying that you'd help me?"

"I have friends in the administrative section," the boy snapped back. "What I tell them to get me, they'll get. And I can repair diesel trucks."

A quiet descended on the table, Mallen watching the boy as if he could interpret his motives.

"I'm not questioning your skills, Paul. Just that I wondered *why* you'd want to help me."

The smile faded. Another few seconds of suspended animation and Mallen was thinking that he had erred badly, made the insinuation that Paul had some other unspecified motive.

The boy stood up quickly, almost knocking over his chair. "I don't *know* why! Does there have to be a *why?*" He threw his napkin down on the table and slammed his way out of the kitchen.

He looked at Jeanne. "What in hell did I say wrong?" Mallen swore, turning toward her.

She stood up and started to clear away the dishes. "Nothing you said was wrong. Except that you implied that he wasn't trustworthy. That he might somehow use going back to the garrison as a means of trapping you. He offered you help and you slapped him. Other than that—there was nothing wrong." She scraped the dishes, her back to him.

Mallen pulled his hand through his hair, annoyed. *Dumb, dumb, dumb.* The kid had been sincere, and with only a few words Mallen knew he had soured it. "He was ready to pull the trigger on me a couple of days ago," he said defensively.

She worked silently for many minutes, cleaning the dishes, stacking them up on the drying rack. From the pump she drew a kettle of water and set it on the stove, then turned back to him. She hung up the towel on the stove's drying rack and threw her head back, raking the strands of hair together with her fingers.

"He's trapped between boyhood and manhood, Gregory. Can't you remember what it was like? Regardless of what he might have said to you, he loved his father in that blind way any boy loves his father. Perhaps he sees you as a replacement. Maybe he's tired or unsure of trying to be the man of the house. Maybe he just wants a man's love. Do you see?"

"Yes—but he has to understand that I can't risk anything . . ."

She turned on him. "Mallen, just what do you think

we risked for you and Wyatt this afternoon? You think *that* was easy? Pushing off Fishbeck's hands under the table—the words those men said that were so foul they sickened me. And having to laugh at it, knowing that Paul was watching everything. It was a humiliation that I'll remember—that Paul will remember."

Mallen put his head down on his arms, staring at the oilcloth's pattern, blurred in its closeness.

"I didn't . . ." He couldn't find words to finish the sentence.

There was a long silence. She opened the feeder on the stove, dropped in two small sections of wood, and closed it. Walking over, she stood behind him. She didn't touch him, but he felt the pressure and movement of her body against the chair.

"Growing up is not simple, even in the best of times," she said quietly. "He even talked to me of asking you to stay. There is a farm about four kilometers from here, abandoned. He could probably find the papers necessary to give you a new identity. He was going to bring it up."

"I can't . . ."

"I know that and you know that, but he doesn't," she replied. "Paul thinks that it will finish with the Special Forces, that eventually they'll be pulled out because there will be no use for them. But we both know that won't happen. It will go on and on and on." She sighed. "Give me the key to the pantry. We're finished with this talk."

"I'll say something to him in the morning." Like what? his mind responded. How do you take back something like that? He stood up and unlocked the door. While she rummaged through dusty shelves, searching for something, he rechecked the Luger and Model 94 Winchester he had stored on the top shelves. Must clean them tomorrow, he thought. Letting things slide.

She had found whatever it was. He relocked the door and sat down, yawning. Tired, he thought. Sleep in the kid's room tonight.

She set down a glass on the table for him and filled it with an amber fluid; then one for herself.

"Peach liquor," she said, sipping. "May you have a long life."

"There seems to be a growing probability that I'll see fifty." He drank, tasting the sweet but pithy liquor, actually more of a distilled wine.

"My father taught me to make it," she said. "Taught me to box and to fix things. Taught me about the Canadian north and more about our history than any school ever did." She raised her glass toward Mallen, letting the light catch the sparkle of the liquor. "Taught me how to make this as well."

"A versatile man, your father."

"A forty-year-long railroad man," she said. "But a very good man—a man who cared for and loved everything and everyone around him."

"You lost him in war?"

"No—years ago. He was killed in a train derailment."

"To your father, then," he said softly, "and to you." Mallen sipped and set the glass down, watching a drop of liquor run down the side of the glass, catching the light like a cat's eye. He reached across the table and covered her hands with his. She looked back at him, her eyes in shadow, and carefully withdrew them. There was a very long silence between them.

"I'm going to try to make it to British Columbia," he finally said. He took back his senseless hands, clumsy wooden things, and wrapped them around the wine glass. "The plane is down on the shore of a lake in Maine and it needs fuel and some repairs. I need a map of this area, if you have one."

She stood up, pressing her skirt down against her legs, smoothing it. Her footsteps echoed in the hallway, then there was a murmur of voices from the old man's room, the closing of a door, and the opening of another. She came back into the kitchen and drew her chair around beside him. "This was my father's," she said.

"He hunted every autumn in Maine for deer—and fished there in the spring as well."

The map was American and to a small scale, showing topographical features in fine detail. It was much worn and used, with the creases reinforced by clear plastic tape now gone yellow.

"We're here," she said, leaning next to him. He could smell more than just the smell of a clean woman; the scent of ginger and almond. Her shoulder brushed his and he leaned away, subconsciously determined just to leave it alone, but something stirred within him, not exactly identifiable.

He traced their route backward, referring to the aeronautical chart with the crudely noted bearings in the margin. Back along the dirt road, through the sloping fields, and up into the foothills. His finger followed terrain contours, over timbered slopes, through a valley and then the series of ridges where they had camped. He laid out rough bearings, transferring the azimuths on prominent features to the geodetic chart. He found the highest ridge from which he and Wyatt had first seen the St. Lawrence River Valley, then went back through the corrugations of the Tumbledown Mountains of Maine. The last bearing he plotted rested over the pale blue of a lake shaped in the profile of a sitting cat. *Christian's Portage,* read the finely italicized letters.

Jeanne bent across his arm and peered closely at the detail. "You could use this logging road," she said, her finger tracing a broken gray line.

It might just be possible, Mallen thought. The road, if still passable, skirted the far shore of the lake, across from where the Sperber lay hidden. Working back, it intersected another road that lay to the south of the lake and curved around into a track that ran east-west, possibly the same road he and Wyatt had crossed on the second day of their trek north. The road with the wagon tracks, he thought. At least it would probably be passable. It was a long route, but in the Peugeot, at an average of fifteen miles per hour—how long? He examined the legend of the map, looking for a mileage scale, and was shocked to find that he and Wyatt had come fewer than twenty-five miles in a direct line, actually less.

"How long does it take ice to freeze solid in one of these lakes?" he asked.

She paused for a while, playing with the pencil, and said, "A week. Less, perhaps, if the lake is shallow and exposed to the wind. In weather like this, just days. You're planning to drive the car across it?"

He studied the route a second time, ignoring her question. Tracing it with his blunt fingernail, it seemed possible. He rolled another cigarette, thinking. "Have you been to this lake?"

She shook her head. "No, I don't remember it. But my father was there several times. He said it was good fishing, not too deep."

"This road, then. Have you been over any part of it?" He tapped the stained paper.

She poured them both more of the peach liquor. "Once or twice, in the fall foliage season. Then in the spring when we harvested sugar maples. A lot of the land was forest reserve. No one said anything. Several of the neighbors would work together. The children were allowed to pour maple syrup in the snow so that we could eat it like . . ." she sought the word ". . . like taffy."

Listening to her voice, he smiled, thinking of what it must have been like. The last of winter. Ice breaking up in the lakes and streams. Rabbit tracks. The lower elevations starting to green up. And set against this, the almost ritualistic work of sugaring.

"You're laughing," she said, surprise in her voice.

"Not at you, not at anything." He turned toward her and touched her hair, because he had a compulsion to do so. She stiffened, not moving, and slowly turned away. Mallen withdrew his hand. "That didn't mean anything."

"Then why did you do it?"

"I don't know—you're beautiful, I'm tired. The wine . . ." He made a waffling gesture with his hand.

"How in hell can I explain? It was something I've wanted to do since . . ." He left the sentence unfinished, useless.

She stood up and put her chair back in place with finality, as if she had closed off anything that might evolve between them. For a few minutes, she moved around the kitchen putting things away. She finished off the last of her wine and, after placing the glass in the soaking bucket, started to leave the room.

Behind him, she paused, placing her hands on his shoulders.

"I think . . ." She said the words hesitantly, as if she had to phrase it exactly right, ". . . that in my best of all worlds, I want you to stay. But I know that's impossible. Paul's sometimes—erratic. And terribly jealous. Eventually there would be patrols or someone from the locality who would report you. Undoubtedly, they have pictures of you." She sighed. "I want you to stay, but I now fully realize you can't."

She hesitated for a moment, shifting her weight, leaning against his chair, working her fingers into his shoulder muscles. Mallen could feel the closeness of her, the warmth of her body. He kept his hands together on the table, toying with the burned-out cigarette, looking straight ahead.

"Sometimes," she said, "I think that I love you. But then I think that we're both just terribly lonely. Or tired, or bored, or frightened. Something like that, but not exactly. As much as anything, a long, continuing emptiness. I can't identify my emotions anymore. And death—always more death. Your friend is dying and my grandfather is dying and all of us carry some lasting effects of the war. After so much death, even more.

"And one day soon," she continued, "you'll be gone. And I don't want to hope for anything more than I already have." She bent down and kissed the back of his head. "Whatever you do, wherever you go, I wish you well." She turned and left the room and he listened to her footsteps moving away.

Mallen rose and went to the window, smearing the

condensation with his fingers, then peering into the night. His eyes slowly adjusted to the darkness and shapes took on substance in the starlight. God give her some sort of peace, he thought. And give me enough strength just to keep going. It was a sort of prayer, the closest he could come to. He hadn't heard her. She touched him on the back with light fingertips.

"I have a fresh towel and some real soap for your bath. The water will heat."

He turned and kissed her very hard. She didn't move, standing stock still, not responding. Mallen felt that he was sliding down a smooth, glassy hill, pleasantly out of control and not caring. He buried his face in the hollow of her neck, feeling her heart's beat, tasting the salt of her skin with his tongue.

She stood for a long time, not moving, and finally pushed him away gently, her fingers splayed against his chest. "I can't," she said. "I don't know why, but I can't."

He dropped his arms, and as she turned away he saw tears streaking her face.

Mallen sat up for another hour, getting slightly drunk on the peach liquor, trying not to think of her, or McKennon, or the days behind him and the days before. Sponging off with soap and hot water, he stood awkwardly in a shallow backing pan that caught the drippings, feeling absurdly like a turkey. Wrapping a blanket around his wet body, he stood for a long time near the window and cursed himself for playing the walk-on part of a fool. He had a final glass of liquor, then blew out the lamp and groped through the hallway into Wyatt's room.

His breathing was shallow, the skin hot and dry. Wyatt stirred under his fingertips and rolled over, waking.

"What's . . ." he mumbled.

Mallen stooped down. "It's me. How you feel—any better?"

"Tired. Ache all over. I keep having crazy dreams.

Like about dying." He tried to lift his head, looking up at Mallen in the darkness. "Can you stay longer, Mallen?"

"I can stay the whole fucking winter, you dumb spade. The patrol told the kid they were giving up in a couple of days. So just relax and get some sleep. You need anything?"

Wyatt coughed, a racking dry cough from inelastic lungs. He spit into a rag. "Water. Just get some water."

Mallen brought him back a pitcher and poured a glass, but Wyatt was asleep, so he left him rasping in the darkness.

Jeanne had told him that he could sleep in Paul's bedroom. He had looked at it this afternoon—a boy's bedroom, to be sure. The photos were of men in uniform, the books, manuals of arms. Its sterile neatness had depressed Mallen.

Climbing the stairs, he thought of the boy. Maybe he ought to lock the door. But that seemed to be a violation of the growing trust he felt between the two of them. The kid could have blown the whole thing this afternoon, but he hadn't. He dimissed the idea.

As Mallen turned the corner of the landing, he was startled, heart suddenly thudding. Jeanne stood at the top of the staircase, her nightgown a smudge of indistinct white in the darkness. Taking him by the hand, she led him to her room and shut the door softly.

In the light of a guttering candle she held him, rocking a little as if unsure or unsteady, holding him very hard against her with both hands clasped behind his neck. He kissed her, gently at first and then harder, so that the round buttons of her nightdress were painful against his chest.

Leading him to the bed, she blew out the candle and dropped her gown in the darkness, the sound of its falling not more than a rustle of wind. He pulled her to him and her fingers brushed aside his blanket and traced across his shoulder, down his back, along his hips.

Without thinking of what he was saying, not knowing

how he would say it, he told her in scraps of phrases the words that had been stored in his mind: that her eyes were incredible colors and her hair was the shade of sun-bleached wheat.

She had lain her head across his chest, her hair a flowing stream, and he could feel the wetness of her tears on his skin.

"Just hold me for a long while," she whispered. "For a very, very long time."

In the early hours of dawn, with gray displacing black in the curtained frame of the window, they finally made love, desperately, holding to each other as if caught in a siphoning whirlpool, afraid to drown alone, yet terrified to drag the other down. He told her things he wanted her to believe, himself believing them. And she said she believed and that it was impossible, sometimes answering in French, the tears salty on her lips. In her final release, she called out his name, strongly, as if he were very far away.

Afterward, as she slept, he held her to him and tasted her hair and her breasts and her neck, and felt her heart beating steadily.

He finally drifted easily into sleep but woke again, his heart hammering, as hoofbeats pounded down the frozen lane.

15

Mallen was to the window in two strides, but the pane was opaque with frost, and he scratched frantically at the glazing with his nails without effect. The hoofbeats were getting fainter and then were gone. One rider, he thought. The kid.

Jeanne was fully awake, sitting up with the quilted comforter pulled over her breasts, loosened hair falling in a cascade over her face and shoulders. "What is it? What's wrong?" Her voice was thin, frightened.

"That little bastard!" he spat. Running from the room, he took the stairs in five stumbling leaps, insensitive to the cold on his naked body. The little bastard, he thought, examining the pantry door. Two of the three hinge pins were missing and only the third, the center one, which was corroded in place, had prevented the door from being forced open. A large screwdriver still lay on the floor in front of the door and there were gouges in the wood where Paul had tried to force the center hinge plate.

Mallen took the key from beneath the now-cold wood stove and unlocked the door. The Luger and Winchester were still there.

Her plan? he questioned. She and the kid had worked it out, but he knew that was wrong—wrong because of the way she had held him to her, her face wet from tears. But the idea kept swimming back to him like a hungry fish nibbling at a fly. *"Shit!"* he cursed, driving his fist into the wall. "Shit, shit, *shit!*"

Her cry startled him, the sound echoing through the empty house. She cried again, this time, his name.

She was in the parlor, hunched down on the floor, dressed only in a blanket, her arms cradling Wyatt's head, her fingers struggling with the tape that bound his mouth. Wyatt lay on his side, naked, his hands and legs tied by heavy cord. Mallen could not see movement of the chest from breathing, or feel a pulse on Wyatt's throat. His skin was cold and wet, the texture of thawing meat.

Mallen pushed her away roughly. "Get some hot water on," he rasped at her and bent down, easing the tape from Wyatt's skin. Somehow he knew that Wyatt was alive, though barely.

The last layer tore away, exposing Wyatt's mouth, and he opened his lips, his tongue just exposed and swollen. His eyes squinted against the light, closed, and opened again.

"He's gone," Wyatt whispered.

Mallen nodded, slipped a pillow under Wyatt's head, and, pulling the blankets from the couch, covered Wyatt's body.

"I know," he said. "We'll get you back in the sack, get some hot soup into you. We've got a couple of hours leeway. The old man has a car. I'll get our stuff together and we'll be out of here."

Wyatt had closed his eyes. "Not me, buddy." Mallen had to bend down to hear him. Wyatt's voice was nothing more than mouthed exhalations, lips forming words with no sound behind them.

"I'm getting us out," Mallen insisted, knowing that they would not make it farther than a tank of gas, an hour of time, a box of cartridges.

Wyatt was shaking his head. His mouth opened, tongue starting to stick out, but he coughed, and it was as if the effort had been too great, too painful, his face contorting in the effort. No sound came—just the feeble convulsion of his chest and the fetid exhalation. His Adam's apple bobbed, swallowing, and he opened his eyes again. "You get out, Mallen. I'm warm now, jus' want to sleep." He closed his eyes again. "I tried to get to the hallway to warn you, but no good . . . he came,

Mallen . . . torn up, crying. Mad enough to kill you—crazy."

Mallen could feel Wyatt's muscles relaxing, some heat now in the skin. From the kitchen he heard Jeanne pumping up water, the sound of wood being fed into the firebox, the squeak of the firebox door closing.

"Okay, now," Mallen said. "Okay." He brushed Wyatt's hair back from his forehead. A little insane, he thought, as though trying to make him well, as his mother had done when Mallen was young and terribly sick with a high fever. Brush the hair back and stroke the temples. "Okay, now," he repeated.

Wyatt opened his eyes fully. It took him a while, as if a great deal of effort was involved. "Not okay, bullshit artist," he said distinctly. "Gone . . . long time ago, except I wanted to say adios. Watch . . . your . . . ass, man." He relaxed under Mallen's hands, his eyes closed.

Grabbing Wyatt's shoulders, Mallen squeezed down hard, terrified, angry, shouting into Wyatt's face, "You bloody bastard, you aren't flaking out on me. Damn you, *no.*"

Mallen, kneeling, pulled Wyatt's head and shoulders up onto his lap, leaning over him, trying to transfer life and heat from skin to skin, body to body. He gripped Wyatt harder, squeezing down with his arms and chest, his lungs convulsing, his voice rasping into Wyatt's ear that he wasn't going to fuck up everything now—just when they were leaving. Goddamn it to hell, when there was a fucking British Columbia and it was there and in spring it would be . . .

Jeanne came in, took a blanket from the couch, and put it around Mallen, but he didn't notice, bent over, holding Wyatt's cooling body to his chest, his face contorted. For a long time he could feel the beating of Wyatt's heart, until finally he realized that it was only his own.

Jeanne waited for a while, then came to him, prying his fingers from the hold on Wyatt's shoulders, easing

Wyatt's head to the floor. She covered Wyatt's face with a towel for lack of anything better, as Mallen remained rigidly hunched over, staring at the floor. The blanket itself was too short to cover Wyatt's long frame, so she left the feet exposed, naked and still bound.

"You've got to get going," she said carefully.

"Your son caused his death." Mallen's voice was quiet, distant, as if distracted. He ran his fingernail along a crack in the floor, absently picking out dirt and stale wax.

"It was my fault," she said. "He heard us. It would never have happened if . . ."

Mallen nodded. "If," he repeated. He noticed that he was shivering uncontrollably.

"Get dressed," she said. "I'm putting together a bag of food. You'll find some clothes in my grandfather's closet. Perhaps a little loose, but they'll fit, I think." She reached down and took his arm, pulling gently upward. "It's time to go. You can do nothing else for him."

He stood up, pulling the blanket around him. Lead clouds in a steel sky beyond the window frame. Bits of long grass projecting up through the snow, bending in a new wind. Absently he cataloged the scene in his mind as something no more and no less than a winter's New England day. He turned to her, taking her shoulders in his hands, looking into her face, his eyes unfocused.

"Your son caused Wyatt's death," he said again, softly. "Was it something you both figured out?" He shook her gently in a lazy sort of way, as if she were a heavy package with unknown contents.

"No, god, Mallen." Her eyes were shut and she tried to move forward, to put her face on his chest, but he pushed her away.

"Was it?" He was shaking her harder now, fingers gripping into her flesh. She just shook her head, eyes closed, tears streaming down her face. "No, no, no," she whispered. Her head was flopping back and forth now, all resistance gone, the low sun catching glints of refined gold from her hair. "It was us," she sobbed. "He heard *us*, Gregory."

"Then goddamn us both, lady," he said with a tired anger, knowing now that she wasn't lying—knowing the reason all along, but unwilling to face it. He released her and she dropped where she stood. Lying there, she curled into a tight ball, sobbing, bare flesh blue-white in the cold.

He turned back to look at Wyatt, stretched out on the floor, mounded by the khaki blanket. "I loved you, you dumb bastard," he said, his vision blurred. "And there's only one thing left I can do for you."

The old man lay there, propped up, a grease-stained down vest thrown over his shoulders. He was half awake, his head nodding. Beside him on the covers was an empty syringe and the box of ampules. He opened his eyes with effort, the lids fluttering, and held up a stalklike wrist, peering farsightedly at the watch.

"Two hours you've got, Mallen. Not more than that. Probably less." He said it pedantically, like a school monitor announcing the time limits on a test.

Mallen swept his hand through the closet, finding heavy working pants and denim shirts. In the back on a peg he found a leather jacket, worn but with a heavy wool lining. He grabbed them and sat down on the bed, pulling on the pants. No undershorts, no long underwear, and it would be cold now—colder at high altitudes. It ran through his mind, as every man perhaps remembers from his childhood, that the standard mother's admonition was to wear clean underwear, in case you had an accident. He realized that his mind was seeking the trivial, trying to deflect the impact of Wyatt's death. So let it, he thought.

The old man was talking very softly and slowly, just beyond Mallen's shoulder, as if it was a secret. "Fox doesn't shit in his own hole, Mallen. Gave you food and a roof. Told you just one thing, Yankee man . . ." He sneezed on the intake of breath. ". . . told you to leave her be. You had to bed her, didn't you? Couldn't wait . . ."

Mallen was gritting his teeth, trying to push both

the old man's words and the nagging of his conscience out of his mind. He pulled on a shirt—loose but good. Belt. Socks drying in the kitchen—spotted some on the closet floor and picked them up. No good; thin with holes where there should have been toes; probably the old man's. His boots were on the stove's hearth, now cleaned and dry, with a fresh dressing of mink oil. He stood up, getting ready for the last thing he had to do before going. Wyatt.

"You came here, Mallen. I gave you the house. Jeanne and the boy shielded you and the black. And this is the way you repay . . ."

"I don't give a good goddamn, Le Borveaux!" Mallen screamed back at the old man, his voice cracking, Time, time, time, he thought. Something of which there was always too much remaining or too little left of. He had blown it—laying around, when he should have organized everything for this moment. The car, gasoline, food, clothing. He pulled on the jacket, ripped it off after seeing a sweater on an upper shelf, then got them both on. Boots now. Then Wyatt then car then lake. *Go,* his mind shouted. Get gone.

"Don't," the old man rasped. "Don't go. Not yet."

He was half out the door when he turned back, anger raging within him. Mallen gathered all the frustration in one great breath, wanting to spit out a stream of invective, a summation of the hate and sorrow and fear he felt trapped within his chest. But looking back at Le Borveaux, the frustration burst with the puny force of a soap bubble broken on the wind. His enemy was time and McKennon, not this derelict, broken old man grimly clinging to the edge of life. Mallen expelled his breath in a long sigh and answered. "One minute is all I've got."

Le Borveaux was lying back, his face hidden in a cave of the pillow. In profile, Mallen could see only the old man's silver-stubbled chin and throat and the slow, labored heaving of the covers as Le Borveaux's lungs gasped for air.

"I don't want us to part like this," the old man

finally said. He lifted his face with great effort and, seeing Mallen still there, dropped his head back on the pillow. "What I said, Mallen, I didn't really mean. You're hearing an old fart whimpering, looking at death and not proud enough to accept it with some dignity."

Mallen nodded. "I understand." He automatically looked at his wrist, forgetting there was no watch. "I have to go, Le Borveaux. I'm sorry as hell. But she was—is—a lot more important to me than what you said." He thought for a second, then finally understood that what he had admitted was the truth. "The fact is, I love her. No excuses, but a lot of regrets for the trouble this will cause. But it was simply that I loved her." His voice trailed off, knowing that what he had said was inadequate.

Le Borveaux made an effort to sit up, but he could make it only part way, supported on spindly elbows. "I know," he said. "I understand as well. I saw it in your face from the first. And in a way I wanted it to happen—you and the girl. She needs someone. In better times, it would have been all right."

"Except for the kid . . ."

Anger momentarily flashed across Le Borveaux's face, then became a hard, neutral expression. "Paul? Put yourself in his place, Mallen. The girl's room is right above this one. We could hear you both. Everything. The boy was wild. There was nothing to stop him. But give him credit for a sense of honor. He acted in anger, but he acted for good reason."

Mallen nodded. "I suppose . . ."

"Suppose nothing! You would have done the same if you had been him, Mallen. Chalk it up to lost faith in fallen idols." He hunched forward, the tendons standing out in bas-relief against his shriveled neck. "One thing I ask of you, Mallen."

Time was like a block of ice in the sun, melting away, irretrievable. "I can't stay longer, Le Borveaux. I've got to get the hell out."

"Top drawer. There's a set of Richeloffs. Both red and green. I want you to take them."

In the bureau Mallen found a small, transparent plastic box containing two miniature syringes, each with needles already attached but protected by translucent polyethylene tips. The syringes were identical in size except that one was filled with a pink fluid, the other with green. Holding them up to the light, Mallen could find no markings. As a gesture to placate the old man, he dropped them in the breast pocket of his shirt. "What are they for, Le Borveaux?" Mallen zipped up his jacket, anxious to terminate the conversation.

"You've never . . . ?" He stared at Mallen, unbelieving.

"Quit wasting time. I don't have the damnedest idea what they are."

Le Borveaux avoided Mallen's stare. "They're called the Richeloff set, after the company that made them, I think. Just about the last thing the government of Canada did following the war. They were offered free—millions of them. Kind of the last gasp of the welfare state." He gave a hoarse cough, something that might pass for a laugh. "Puts some meaning into the expression 'from the cradle to the grave.' "

He leaned farther forward, intense. "Understand this, Mallen. Lot of folk couldn't take the idea of dying slowly from radiation sickness, or they had lost their kin and didn't want to stay behind. The pink stuff has a narcotic in it that tranquillizes you. But there's a delayed-action nerve drug in it. Your heart just stops ticking after about two hours."

"Christ!"

"He's there, waiting for you, Mallen. Don't know what the final days were like where you were, but people suddenly got religion. Heard stories of people meeting in parking lots, all going together with somebody leading them, sermonizing."

Mallen didn't realize it, but he was staring at the old man, frozen in time, unable to move.

"The green stuff," Le Borveaux continued, "counteracts the effect of the pink if it's taken within an hour. Understand that a lot of people knew they had taken massive radiation. Hair falling out, diarrhea, respiratory infections—they knew they were the walking dead. But most people couldn't get up the nerve to take the pink. So then Richeloff brought out the green syringe, then even packaged them as a set. The green stuff is an antidote, if you care to call it that. It's sort of a psychological sop so that the process is reversible in the event you have second thoughts. Makes it easier to take the pink, knowing there's time to think about it and some way out. But there's a narcotic in the pink, Mallen. Smooth and easy, like sliding down a chute to paradise. Once they took the pink, damn few people changed their minds. Damn few."

"There's no fucking way that I'll . . ."

Le Borveaux cut him off, his voice cold and metallic. "Shut the hell up and listen, Mallen. Paul thought he was doing right. To get you. Understand, he loved you in a way, Mallen. Thought of you as he would of a god—something to fear, but also something to worship. You were totally unlike his father, that worthless chicken turd. Had no time for Paul or Jeanne, no ambition, no guts. Just drink and pussy snatching. But that doesn't change things. What Paul's done is ultimately to expose the fact that Jeanne hid you and Wyatt, a state offense of the worst sort. I'm telling you direct, Mallen. You can't let them take her."

"Christ sake, Le Borveaux! You expect me to . . ."

Le Borveaux was staring at him. "You heard me! If she stays here, it's over. They'll squeeze Paul for the truth and it'll come out. You've got to take her with you. And if there's danger of capture, you've got to give her the pink Richeloff."

Mallen felt his body teetering, drained of blood. "I can't . . ." He left the sentence unfinished.

"You *will, by God!* because you don't understand the system. They wouldn't shoot her, no sir! Waste of precious state resources and not enough of an example. No, they'd send her to one of the Special Forces recreational centers instead. Places for Special Forces enlisted men, where they can suck up vodka for free and whores are *dva ochki,* two points, Mallen. Except that a woman convicted of a major offense against the state is free. And the men are encouraged to use her—a lot. Sort of a special thing; prove your manhood and at the same time your loyalty to the state by punishing the state's enemies. Jeanne couldn't last." He took a long breath and let it out slowly. In a steadier voice he asked, "You understand me now?"

Mallen withdrew the box from his breast pocket and looked at it, then repocketed it. Despite the thickness of his shirt, he felt the box through the material. "I understand, Le Borveaux. But I'll never use it. We'll make it."

"Somehow," Le Borveaux finished. "I know you will, Mallen. I know you will. Never doubt that." He smiled; more of a death's-head grimace. "Good luck, then, Yankee man. And shake my hand." He stuck out a bony claw.

Mallen shook it. "Good luck to you—Colin. You'll be all right?"

The old man nodded down at the syringe and ampules. "I'll be all right. Four score and then some." He nodded toward the syringe, which caught the low, horizontal rays of the winter sun. "With some help."

Embarrassed and with nothing he could say, Mallen backed away and turned for the door.

"Do as I've told you, Mallen," the old man called after him. "And, as my mother said, . . ."

Mallen turned briefly toward him, hesitating in the doorway, looking back at the wasted shape beneath the rumpled blankets.

". . . as my mother said, Mallen, 'keep the faith.' "

"I will," Mallen replied. Because it was the only possible answer.

It was bitter, cold biting through his jacket, the wind picking up granules of ice and blowing them in sheets across his face and body as he dragged Wyatt through the snow. As a last, insanely desperate act, he had laid Wyatt down in the kitchen and listened for a heartbeat, then even held a brass cartridge beneath Wyatt's nostrils, looking for moisture. None.

Where she was, he didn't know, didn't think. As if he had entered his own private hell.

After scooping the drifted snow out with his hands, he laid Wyatt down in the grave. It was too short, the body fitting only diagonally, corner to corner. Mallen found it impossible to look down. Almost immediately, the snow granules, rasping across the frozen crust, began to cover Wyatt.

"I'm sorry," was the only benediction Mallen could think of.

She came up behind him. He didn't turn, but knew it was her. She didn't touch him but held a potted plant out to his side. It had one bloom, a fragile tissue of red, already withering in the cold.

"I thought you might want it for him," she said. "I have the car running. Don't be long." She turned away and walked toward the shed.

He started to cover the grave with snow, then realized that the plant would be a marker for them, and he wouldn't have that. He put the plant down on Wyatt's chest, forced himself to look at the face, then covered it with loose snow, letting the wind finish the work. "Like—adios," he whispered.

Jeanne was waiting by the shed door, now open, the condensed exhaust of the Peugeot drifting upward from the opening, then torn off in the freshening wind. She had an old army coat, presumably her grandfather's, with lieutenant's bars still sewn to the epaulets but tarnished almost black. She wore stretch ski pants from some other era, along with fur boots and a bulky sweater. Beneath a wool watch cap her hair was drawn up into a bun, only a few errant strands framing her face.

"It'll take you there," she said flatly.

Over his heart, Mallen felt the presence of the box. "If you want it that way," he answered, almost too casually, knowing that she would have expected his objection. "Give me a hand with the drum," he said, cutting off conversation and pushing past her into the dark interior of the shed. She had backed the Peugeot up to the sawhorses that held the drum and had roven a sling of manila rope around the drum. He released the handbrake and pushed the car farther back, the trunk already opened, until the bumper touched the sawhorses. He heaved, just barely able to unseat the barrel, but not moving it over the lip of the trunk. She appeared on the opposite side of the car, took the other lead of the rope in her hands, and, without acknowledging his presence, joined him in heaving. The increased pressure pulled the drum upward out of the crotch of the sawhorses so that it teetered for a second and then fell heavily into the trunk.

Mallen circled the car, moving toward the driver's side, but she was already there, pulling the door closed and locking it. He shrugged and moved to the passenger side.

"Let's go," he said.

She drove with the intensity of complete concentration, flicking expertly through the gears, pushing the Peugeot to the edge of control on the icy roads. He watched her, saw the complete immersion of her mind and body in the task, and kept silent, thinking. As had the albatross of the ancient mariner, the box lay against his chest, pressing down against his heart with unnatural weight.

She broke the silence first. "I heard you talking. Not much of it. But the walls are very thin."

"And?"

"I'm not sure what Colin said, but you have to know only two things. Paul was not wrong in what he did. You know that and I do as well. We were responsible— for what happened."

She downshifted and slid through a rutted corner, applying the accelerator. The car bottomed out, fishtailed, then was straight and accelerating. She shifted quickly, glancing down at the tachometer, and shifted again into top gear.

"More important," she continued, "I am taking you there. I know the way; you don't. But then I'm coming back."

"You can't."

"I can and I will. Just as you couldn't walk out on Wyatt, I can't walk out on that sick old man. Nor can I walk out on my son."

Mallen glanced across at the speedometer, watching it climb through eighty kilometers per hour. They flashed by the rusted, burned-out hulk of a truck, through a curve without slowing, and onto a long straight section, climbing in an easy grade toward the foothills.

"If it were possible, would you risk coming with me?" he asked.

She threw him a sideways look, then concentrated on the untracked road with its fresh dusting of snow, marked only by the ditches on either side. "With nothing else to consider, of course I would. But I don't have that option. So don't talk of it."

From the set of her mouth, he knew she was closed to discussion, but he couldn't leave it alone.

"You can't come back," he said evenly. "They'll accuse you of . . ."

"I will come back," she said, cutting him off. "And we won't talk about it. You've said too much already."

She headed south along the road that he and Wyatt had used, spinning the wheels through the slick, untracked snow. Mallen looked for hoofprints, but realized that the boy would have gone the opposite way, north, perhaps cross-country.

"How long?" he asked. "How long will it take Paul to reach a phone?"

She was bent forward, her face tense as she studied the road. She downshifted, ignoring him, taking a depression in the road at full throttle, cresting the rise on the far side with the tires howling through the snow and finally biting on the underlying dirt. "Two hours," she answered. "From dawn. The district political supervisor has a hand-cranked radio, but it sometimes doesn't work. If not, then it will take him another three-quarters of an hour to the barracks. They'll use helicopters."

It was only then that he noticed that she had laid out all his equipment in the back seat: the Luger and Winchester, the spare parts, his knapsack, and a string bag filled with canned goods. He half smiled, noticing that one of the cans was a small tin of paté. Gourmet survival. On the floor he found an unlabeled jug of the home-made brandy and took a long slug, feeling the fluid heat his throat. Better now, he thought. Just relax and wait.

He lay back in the seat, trying to ease the tension from his body. Ten, maybe fifteen minutes would be all it would take to slip the rubber tubing over the fuel line and clamp it. Another five to fill the tanks, assuming they could get the car within walking distance. But almost unconsciously he found himself gripping the edge of the seat, willing the car forward. The tires must be bald, he thought, because the car barely had traction on the steeper pitches, and from the map and his own experience, he knew that it would be uphill most of the way, perhaps with drifted snow in the protected gullies of the road.

"If they come with helicopters, they'll follow the car tracks, you know," she said.

He nodded, thinking, then pressed his foot harder to the floor, trying to make the Peugeot go faster. As it was, the thing was barely under control, slithering and tail-wagging through the flat corners. "Paul knows where the lake is?" Half question, half statement; it had come out before he had time to stop the thought from surfacing.

"If you mean did I tell him, the answer's no. He knows only what you told him. A lake in Maine."

He looked across at her, but she was without anger in her face.

"I didn't mean it as it sounded." But he knew his voice had betrayed him.

"I . . ." She started to say something but hesitated, thinking. A row of fence posts whipped by, a black bird of some sort resting on a strand of wire, rocking in the wind. "I can't tell you," she said finally, "how I feel. But I know that Paul did what he did only out of anger. And perhaps out of a jealous love for both of us. The two are sometimes very close to each other. You have to accept that."

Mallen started to object, then realized she was right. They, Wyatt and the boy, the old man, Jeanne, himself—even McKennon—were casualties of a war. Surviving was too far from living to allow the normal emotions to work. Except, he realized, that he had regained the ability to feel love, where before there had been nothing.

"Wyatt . . ." he started.

"Wyatt died," she interrupted sharply. "You did what you could for him, but he died. He would have anyway. But he wouldn't want you to think about it now."

He nodded. "I wasn't blaming Paul. Just that I wanted to say that Wyatt—he was something. Special." He thought about it. Something special.

They passed through a collection of farmhouses set beside the road, a house and shed to the right and barns on the left. Mallen caught just the quick flash of a face framed in a window as they passed. A small child was playing in the yard, balling snow up into irregular mounds. Looking up, the child smiled, waving a stick. Mallen found himself lifting his hand in return, the automatic American gesture, but it was too late and they were past. He glanced back, as if trying to retain the memory, but the car was over a low hill, accelerating downward, and then it crested the next rise and downshifted, braking hard for a turn. He looked back once more and saw that there were power or telephone poles marching away to the north through white, open fields. Too late, but then he remembered that the wire had been stripped by looters a long time ago.

The map lay between them. He studied it for a moment, trying to guess how far they had come and in how long.

He tried repeatedly to work it out in his mind but

found his mind slipping into irrelevant patterns. It was just a simple equation, a schoolboy question in algebra about time and distance and moving bodies.

Time: He squinted at the hard brightness that was the sun, obscured by low, flattened layers of clouds. Perhaps an hour since dawn, probably less. The speedometer gauge was calibrated in kilometers, bouncing between fifty and eighty.

Distance: He guessed that the farm and the Megantic Barracks were roughly equidistant from the lake, say, fifty kilometers. Except that his fifty kilometers would be over snow-encrusted roads, and McKennon's in a straight line by air.

On a mental blackboard Mallen constructed a neat drawing of a farm, a barracks, and a lake. He drew arrows with sharp points and labeled them, and colored the lake blue.

Question: Does McKennon intercept Mallen before Mallen gets to the lake? Or does McKennon just get to the lake first and wait? Who wins the prize? Answer: All or none of the above.

Mallen leaned his face against the cold glass of the window, avoiding even preliminary calculations. None of it could be rushed. She was driving well, confidently. The repairs would require time. Beyond that, it was luck.

They were trending uphill now, out of farmland and into upland pastures, then into forested patches. Pine and maple closed in on the road and Jeanne was usually in second, the engine straining and wheels spinning. Suddenly the graded road ran out and they were on a rutted lane, heavily drifted. On the first corner the right-hand fender clipped a rock outcropping on the shoulder's edge and she fought the wheel, just barely keeping it under control.

It became worse. The road was corrugated with frozen ruts, and rocks jutted through the snow. Jeanne tried to hold forty kilometers per hour, but the suspension was bottoming out and the tank of gasoline in the trunk slammed from side to side against the body panels.

"Hold it down," he said, just as they slid into a ditch, throwing snow across the hood in a wave of white surf breaking.

By the car clock, it took twelve irreplaceable minutes of heaving and straining to get the Peugeot back on the road. As he had thought, equations of time and distance were for blackboards and not for real life.

During the last ten minutes, Jeanne had been quiet, keeping the speed down, accommodating to the road. They were much higher now, into the foothills, with only occasional meadows in the monotonous patchwork of forest. The bend in the road had been gentle, swinging through a grove of birches and over a small rise. Before them, fewer than thirty yards away, were two men with horses, one still mounted and the other by the side of the road defecating. They both wore the green uniforms of the Special Forces. The horses were breathing hard as if winded, their coats steaming in the mottled sunlight.

The mounted one had undoubtedly heard them coming. He was already unslinging a carbine, spurring his horse around in the road to face the car. The other, staggering in the snow, getting his pants up, had a stunned expression on his Mongol face.

"Keep going!" Mallen screamed at her, working the toggle of the Luger. Without hesitation, she shifted down and floored the accelerator.

It was as if in slow motion: vivid impressions, extraneous things capturing attention; the slow, comical movements of the Mongol, wading through snow knee high and then stumbling or, more likely, falling for cover, face down. The horse, moving sideways, head lifting to the constraint of the reins. The side window sliding down under Mallen's frantic efforts, taking too long, despite his efforts to wind the knob.

The mounted one had the carbine leveled in firing position, the sling wrapped around his elbow. Mallen saw the muzzle flash and felt the impact as a bullet spanged off the hood. He took a snap shot, knowing as he pulled the trigger that he would miss, and saw the man's teeth flash and the carbine swinging as they passed for a shot that was going to be point blank, and Mallen squeezed again, framing the whole of the man's body in the opened window. The trooper fired high, the weapon locked by his finger's convulsion on full automatic, tearing out a torrent of sound, his body propelled backward by the Luger slug's impact. Turning, Mallen saw the horse rearing and the man falling backward over the saddle.

And they were past. In the rear window, Mallen looked back and saw the mounted man being dragged by his horse into dense brush, one boot still caught in its stirrup. The Mongol was now in the road, kneeling, and as Mallen watched, three closely spaced shots thudded into the Peugeot, taking out the rear window and spraying splinters across his arm and face. Jeanne was in a turn now, face set rigid, oblivious to the destruction, and he took one look and caught a last glimpse of the Mongol firing a fourth time. Then they were blocked from view by the trees.

Before them was a long winding road, rising slowly through a valley, with a ridge in the far distance. The sun, still low and occasionally visible through the deck of clouds, made intricate patterns on the snow through the overhanging limbs of birch. The tracks of the two riders were clearly visible, heading north at what must have been a good pace. He had the temptation to keep going—to try to outpace the Mongol. But there would be no assurance that a car would be faster than a horse, and the man would be back there, tracing them, keeping his distance, waiting for a clear shot from cover.

Jeanne's face was in a kind of shock, small beads of perspiration forming above her lips. She was driving well, pushing it hard but not panicked. Mallen saw her eyes flick up to the rearview mirror and he half turned his head, but the bend in the road behind them gave them protection.

"Stop here," he said, and she slowed immediately, tapping the brake to keep from skidding. Snatching the Winchester from the rear seat, he opened the door before the car was stopped. "Wait for me over the next rise," he yelled at her, and rolled out of the door, jarring his back as he stumbled and landed in the ditch. She was still stopped, looking at him through the opened passenger window, starting to say something, and he smashed his fist up against the fender, infuriated. "Get the hell out of here," he hissed. She said something he couldn't hear, but a question, then turned, her face white with either anger or terror, and ground the gears. The wheels spun momentarily and then the Peugeot pulled away, throwing a thin white roostertail of snow from behind the tires.

He realized now that he had almost no hearing—just a hiss in his brain as high wind in the trees. The Luger's blast, confined to the car's interior almost inches from his face, had deadened his hearing. Great asset, he thought, for the hunter. Or hunted.

Mallen worked the lever and watched the finger of brass be plucked from the magazine and chambered, the breech sliding home, hammer cocked. He eased the hammer down to halfcock and waited, settling as deep into the ditch as possible. As an afterthought, he took handfuls of granular snow and dusted his coat and hair.

The Mongol didn't come as Mallen had thought he would. Nothing for a minute, and then two and three. The Peugeot was gone around the bend. Jeanne would be well over halfway to the crest. He tried, frustrated, to listen for any sound, but he heard nothing other than the pounding of his own heart.

Four, then five minutes. About. He inspected the ditch, then the trees around him. And the road. No movement, except limbs swaying and rubbing together in the light wind. Occasionally the sun broke through, flooding the grayness with hard light and shadow, then disappearing behind fractured clouds.

More minutes. Nothing—and he realized that it had been dumb. For some reason the Mongol had not followed, and all he was doing was lying, cold and stiff, in a ditch, wasting minutes that were irreplaceable. The snow on his hair was melting from body heat. He felt a trickle of icewater shiver down his scalp and blot into frigid dampness beneath his collar. He tensed, about to get to his feet.

Then Mallen saw him in the shadows on the far side of the road—a figure moving low to the ground and then gone, lost in a swaying, complex mixture of half light and partial darkness. Mallen looked harder, believing that it had been his imagination. His position in the shallow ditch was exposed, and he pressed his body down against the snow and held his breath, vainly trying to listen for sounds he couldn't hear.

And then he saw him again, or at least saw movement, abreast of him now and moving in the direction the Peugeot had taken. The Mongol's back was to him now, but there were too many trees between them for a clean shot, particularly without the telescopic sight. Mallen thumbed back the hammer.

The Special Forces trooper was good. He moved erratically, spacing his runs and using the cover well. The snow, even in the deeper patches, could have been no more than shin deep; in areas exposed to wind it was shallower. The man paced himself, lifting his legs high in the deep areas, running low and bent over, and hugging natural cover in between. It was as if he were performing a drill from a textbook on field maneuvers: automatic weapon horizontal, away from his body, head low, knees always bent, elbows out to deflect the errant branch. It spelled training and experience.

Why the Mongol had not used the horse worried Mallen. It had seemed the logical thing, staying back, shadowing the car, using the animal's energy instead of his own. It was as if the Mongol knew something that Mallen didn't, and it made no sense. To Mallen.

The Mongol was well past him now, twenty-five yards or so along the road, hugging the scrub and trees on the opposite side of the road. In watching him, Mallen had seen him look back only once, and then briefly, as just a reflexive gesture. The intensity of his attention was forward, beyond the bend of the road, which Mallen could not see.

That Mallen was temporarily deafened explained it. That and the fact that the Mongol was on the far side of the bend, giving him better scope on what lay beyond. Just ahead, Mallen caught a glimpse of the Peugeot, partially obscured by birches. Jeanne hadn't understood that he wanted her to drive to the ridge on the skyline, not just the first little mound. The Mongol had known, probably just by hearing, because the sound of a car climbing a grade would be heard a great distance in the closed valley.

The Mongol was belly down now, working the cover to best advantage, the carbine cradled in his arms. He was working down toward the road, still a hundred feet or so behind the Peugeot.

Alternatives spurted through Mallen's mind, none of them workable. Charge the man? His sphincter muscles constricted at the thought of a magazine of lead tearing through his own gut. Diversion? To what end? Eventually, same bullets, same result. If the scope had been undamaged, he might have had a clean shot, but the open iron sights were an unknown.

The Mongol was down to the border of trees that edged the road, crouching down behind a Siamese pair of birches. He fumbled with his pack, the carbine leaning against the tree. Mallen could see little puffs of condensed breath that the man made, the sure, practiced movements of his hands, as of a craftsman who knows his tools and uses them well. The pack was off his back now, opened, the man's gloves held by his teeth, his hands working quickly.

And then Mallen saw that he had no choice. The Mongol was fitting a rifle grenade to the muzzle of the carbine, and it would be the Peugeot as his target. From where he was, Mallen couldn't see the car clearly or tell whether Jeanne had abandoned it. But the Peugeot was everything—fuel for half a continent.

He lay the barrel of the Winchester in the notch of a

limb, keeping his movements slow. The hooded blade sight aligned with the notched V and he placed it on the edge of the Mongol's left shoulder blade, allowing for a three-inch drop over the one hundred-odd yards. Lung shot. Irrational thoughts. No license to hunt men. God, he's not the one I saw before in the barnyard. This one's a child. Mallen inhaled, expelled half his breath, and squeezed, just as he had for deer and woodchucks and paper targets; always the surprise when the weapon fired; and then the aftershock and the momentary hesitation before chambering another cartridge. But this time he had no time for hesitation. The man, unscathed, was turning.

Mallen was already up and moving when the Mongol finally saw him. He tried for a snap shot with the rifle held at waist level and he had a clear view of the Mongol as he turned more to face Mallen, crouching slightly, raising the weapon, firing. Mallen knew that he was a dead man still running, running into the ten-yard lethal radius of a fragmentation grenade.

The concussion was enormous, a torrent of pressure and hot gas throwing him backward. The shock wave raised a cloud of white snow, and severed branches rained down around him.

Mallen fell heavily on his side, rolling as he did, and frantically levered another round into the action, then fired in the Mongol's direction. And another round was chambered, with the spent cartridge arcing back in the sunlight, and he fired again, working the lever yet again.

Nothing. No returned fire, and no movement in the trees. He got a sideways glance at the Peugeot, but it was empty, the door open and a seat belt trailing across the sill.

Lifting his head, Mallen wiped the snow from his face, quartering the trees before him, looking for the Mongol. Shreds of bark hung from the twin birches, as if they had been stripped by a hurricane. On the ground were bits of canvas and clothing, odd pieces of wreckage, what was left of the man.

The Mongol, or what was left of him, was on his

back. There was no doubt that he was dead. Mallen turned away and tried to be sick, but all that would come up was a thin drool with the bitter taste of bile. The grenade had been deflected by a tree limb and had fallen back. The pock-marked depression of broken earth was not more than a yard from the Siamese birches where the man had stood.

Mallen scavenged the backpack, finding one more grenade and a foil-wrapped pack of rations and cigarettes, plus four banana clips of shells for the carbine, which lay useless on the ground, its stock splintered and breech jammed open. And next to a tree, Mallen found the guts of a black box oozing transistors and capacitors, and the severed stump of a whip antenna, out onto the frozen ground. Mallen didn't have a doubt that the Mongol had used it.

Jeanne was coming back down the road, face pale. Mallen looked back at the man—no, really, boy, and turned to meet her, not wanting her to see. The thought kept going through his head that McKennon would now know exactly where to look.

16

Brinkerhoff called just as McKennon had expected, early enough so that the orderly was forced to awaken him. Undoubtedly under Brinkerhoff's instructions, the orderly had yelled through the still-silent hallway, and men, waking from the night to the full light of a winter's dawn, knew that McKennon was now a hostage to Brinkerhoff's whim.

As McKennon walked down the hall, he saw men looking out at him, expressions neutral, even slightly embarrassed, as if they were watching a man on the way to his execution. Glancing back, McKennon found no sign of recognition on their faces, as if he had already ceased to exist.

The orderly, a slight Dutch kid with a caved-in chest, had his back turned, fussing with a samovar of tea. "It's the commander," he said, not turning.

"Time's up," Brinkerhoff said, without prelude. "You got anything yet?"

"The patrols are not all in yet."

There was a pause—the sound of a pencil tapping, clearly heard, as if Brinkerhoff were using a conference phone. Another voice in the background said something. Brinkerhoff gave a sharp laugh—more an exclamation—and said, "So you have nothing, right?"

"Not yet." McKennon, even in the cold of the orderly room, felt the heat and dampness of sweat saturating his armpits. The orderly, setting down his own cup of tea on the desk, eased his butt down into a chair and flicked his hand through a sheaf of papers, a witness only through circumstance, embarrassed, perhaps—but more likely remembering the words for the retelling over breakfast rations to an interested audience.

"Not ever," Brinkerhoff said flatly. "Not fucking ever, McKennon. I want you down in Albany by tonight. Tomorrow at the latest. We're going to have a full review set up for tomorrow evening."

"No one else could have done any better," McKennon objected. The orderly had stopped leafing through the pile, his face averted but obviously listening intently.

There was static on the line and then it cleared. McKennon could hear the pleasure in Brinkerhoff's voice as he said, "No one, McKennon? I suppose that's something we'll never know." There was complete finality in his statement. McKennon started to say something, but the line went dead.

McKennon pulled his robe more tightly around him, retying the belt. From a shelf he took a cup with a walrus crudely painted on it and filled it with weak tea, then walked to the window. He had to use both hands on the cup to keep his shaking from spilling the tea.

It was a dawn indefinite in color. Flat, dense stratus clouds banked up on the eastern horizon with cirrus higher up, foretelling a cold front and probably snow. But the weather would be good enough for a chopper flight, and there would be no excuse to delay it.

McKennon, not unlike a man seeing his fortune erased in a market frenzy, kept pushing his mind away from the consequences of failure. He thought briefly of Brinkerhoff, then forced his mind to back away from it, examining instead the patterns of frost on the window, the winter-stripped elms in the courtyard, the sounds filtering down through the barracks quarters above. Absently he fingered the gold coin on the chain around his throat, thinking of the inscription on the bezel, then pushed that away too, sipping at the tea.

"Get hold of Baines," he said aloud, still staring at the barracks yard. No response from the orderly.

He turned. "I said get me Baines. He's probably down in the maintenance shed. I want him in my room in ten minutes."

The orderly still didn't respond, but McKennon saw him nod absently and scribble on a pad.

Baines took more than twenty minutes. McKennon was fully dressed, fuming, pacing between the window and the closed door of his room, unwilling to face the rest of the barracks. The dog watched him intently, thumping his tail occasionally, as the man passed from one side of the room to the other.

Baines finally entered the room, without knocking. "You wanted me?" His face was red from the cold, a leather cap pulled down over his ears, expression neutral.

"You're taking me down to Albany."

"You're asking me, or telling me?"

McKennon sat down heavily on the cot, all the anger, all the exasperation gone out of him. "Don't harass me, Baines. Brinkerhoff says to take me down today. We both know what that means."

Baines shrugged, a little embarrassed. He sat down next to McKennon and pulled out a plastic flask from within the folds of his jacket. "Decent rye," he said easily, taking a sip and passing it to McKennon. McKennon nodded and took one, then another pull on the container.

"You gave it a good try," Baines said. "Outguessed them most of the way." He took the flask back, took a sip, and replaced the cap. "You had it right, too," he said, getting up. "At least the way I see it."

McKennon looked up. "Right about what?"

Baines picked up McKennon's small canvas bag of clothes, hefting it under his arm. From the courtyard below, they could both hear mounted men assembling in a clatter of hooves on frozen ground, the shouts of a man with a deep, bellowy voice yelling in Russian. Baines walked over to the window and looked down and nodded. "One of the split patrols, Yasev and Reiss, called in twelve, fifteen minutes ago. Poor conditions. Couldn't understand them too well, according to the radio operator."

"What of it?" McKennon asked, his heart suddenly pounding.

"Nothing definite." Baines belched into his fist and turned for the door. "It was Yasev—the Siberian kid with the lisp. Can't speak Russian for sour owl shit, but said something about a car. Two people in it. Then something like Reiss killed. Sounds like Mallen and Wyatt to me."

"Where was Yasev—what sector?"

Baines lifted an eyebrow, then smiled. On the wall map he punched a finger in the eastern sector, about seven kilometers below the old border. "About there, McKennon. But if you're talking about ordering me to fly you out there, forget it. Brinkerhoff called the C.O. You're off the search."

"It's him," McKennon snapped. "Goddamn Brinkerhoff—it's Mallen out there. And if I don't personally get him, Brinkerhoff will have me hanging from a meat hook in two days." McKennon started to rise, but Baines pushed him gently backward onto the cot.

"Ease off," Baines said, not smiling. He backed away toward the door, the canvas case under his arm. "Weiner says you're under close arrest. They won't reissue your weapon from the armory. Weiner even insisted that you were to wear handcuffs, but I talked him out of it. Too damn cold in the chopper."

Baines fished around under his jacket, digging down with his free hand until he pulled out a small Browning 9mm pistol, and tossed it onto the cot next to McKennon. "Damned if I know where you got that thing, but if you stick it under my chin when we're airborne, I sure as shit am not going to disagree with your plans. Just remember, McKennon, it's your neck. Keep mine out of it."

"I won't forget this . . ." McKennon started to say, but Baines opened the door, paused, and looked back.

"You *better* forget it, McKennon. I'm bringing Muller with me as escort guard. He knows nothing about this, and it better stay that way. But he'll do what I say if things get tight. Take off from the pad in about five minutes." Baines slammed the door behind himself.

Mallen drove this time. Dangerously fast, bottoming out in the ruts. Jeanne clung to the dashboard, bracing herself as the chassis swayed erratically over the rutted road. He was hitting forty down the straight stretches, the shadows and sunlight a flickering kaleidoscope of light across the windshield. A blur of pine and then an open grove of leafless birches, up a grade with the engine howling in first gear and the rumble of the unsecured barrel of gasoline banging off the walls of the trunk. Then he was back into second and third, accelerating with the pedal on the floor and touching fifty.

The illusion of speed was terrifying: trees whipping past and the body swaying, nearly out of control, slewing into corners, slamming off rocks. One mistake, he thought, and he could roll the car, blow the gasoline, and it would all be over in a flash of flame. Mallen felt that time, like the trees constricting the road, was an ever-narrowing tunnel, limiting options, removing possibilities, running to an almost predictable end point.
the patrol—that he was dragging her into something

He thought about it, as he had since the clash with the patrol—that he was dragging her into something in which she had no part, and the old man had to be wrong. "You've got to get out of this," he said. "Now. I'll leave you beside the road. It'll take you no more than five hours to walk back. If you hear anything coming, just hide in the brush. And if you're caught, say I forced you."

She didn't reply, looking straight ahead, her knuckles white on the plastic cowl.

He didn't want her to leave him and yet he did. *"Now!"* he said, slowing. "They can't tie you to me. Paul doesn't know about your coming, and the old man will cover for you."

She still didn't reply, but in the periphery of his vision he coud see her shaking her head. "I'll see you through this," she finally said. "I owe you at least this."

"Damn it, you owe me nothing."

She turned to him, her eyes brimming. "Mallen," she said, "I'm going to get you to the lake. Don't argue. Let me pay my own debt in my own way."

He put the pedal to the floor, clutching down for the long grade that rose to the final ridge. It seemed they would never crest the hill, the tires alternately biting and spinning, the rear end of the car grinding up through the ruts. Twice she had to get out and heave against the fender to get the Peugeot moving. Mallen had reset the car's clock to seven o'clock, just after the thing with the Mongol. Now he did not dare look at the hands, knowing that time was eroding. He pictured helicopters lifting off, turning south, and men armed with automatic weapons. He listened for the sound of choppers, but the howl of the tires and transmission was so great that he would not have heard them until it was too late. "Keep going," he said through clenched teeth, trying to force the vehicle up the hill by sheer will power.

Cresting the rise with the smell of the clutch burning, Mallen eased to a stop before the descent. Before them, to the south, the lake lay dull and monolithic. Ice ran from shore to shore with no breaks. From this elevation he could pick out the details of the lake and its catlike shape. On the far shore he searched for men or movement, trying to identify the Sperber. Nothing. But if there were men already there, he had no choice. There was no place left to run, and only the faint promise of flight.

They descended, slower now, looking for the road that led to the south shore. Twice they saw rabbits and also the tracks of deer. In places exposed to the south, the snow had melted, leaving the road bare, with good traction, but in shaded areas the snow still lay heavy, purple white in the morning light. At one point Jeanne reached over and held his arm, her grip tight, yet said nothing.

They almost missed it, seeing only a faint depression through the bush. Not more than a twitch in the road, the access way led off to the east, overgrown with the brush of two years. Mallen stopped, backed up, and downshifted into first, taking the washed-out gutter as fast as he dared, hoping not to get bogged down. The exhaust system hung up on the ridged gutter, but he rode the clutch, pulling the Peugeot clear. Worse, far worse, than the road had been, the lane was one track wide, badly overgrown, and guttered by erosion.

"Less than a quarter-mile now," Jeanne said, the map spread across her lap.

Mallen had to stop twice to clear fallen saplings from the lane. The second time he saw a grossly deformed beaver, which gnawed fearlessly at the base of a birch. The beaver finally flicked its tail and waddled off, unconcerned with the strange creature but prudently cautious.

Mallen fished out one of the Mongol's cigarettes before getting back into the Peugeot. Last time for everything, he thought. Last time at school, last time in a city you know you won't return to, last kiss with a woman you know you won't see again. And all those things mark the passage of time toward the grave, not easily recognizable, but there.

Oddly enough, he felt as though he were a man about to start, not to finish, having a pause before the task, thinking how it can best be done. He recognized that he had done his best, regardless of mistakes, and that it was impersonal time and circumstance that would work either for or against him. He quickly lit the cigarette, the tobacco rich and black like Turkish. The woods were achingly silent, the wind blocked. Through the leafless trees he could see the sky, more overcast now with multiple layers of cloud and high cirrus moving in from the northwest. The sun was dull, still there as a disk but now a shape of light rather than a point of warmth. The few remaining leaves of birch and maple hung lifeless like convicted thieves. He looked up at them and then to the sky beyond. If he could obtain that—the sky. One last puff and he threw the butt at his feet, stepping on it. A thought struck him, something from Robert Frost, who had so loved this country: "And miles to go before I sleep."

The frozen lake spread before them on the last turn, stretching like a dull lead plate from east to west. The Peugeot took the final grade with gravel and snow spewing away from under the tires and he let it go down the final grade, not trying to control the speed but just steering to keep it upright. He braked on the beach, just touching the foreshore, which was mounded with irregular slabs of ice.

Mallen got out and tested the ice with his own weight, bouncing violently, stomping on the slightly roughened surface. The sounds of his testing were clear, solid thumps, with no indication of the hollowness of thin ice and no shifting beneath his weight. He paused, looking around. Nothing lived. No single bird or animal moved, but the sky was darker now, the sun truly obliterated, and the trees were beginning to sway in a rising wind. It was definitely colder.

"You have to leave," he said. "Go back along the lane."

"We discussed that. There isn't much time. Will the lake take the weight of the car?"

"We can try," he said, making no promises.

Muller sat in the back seat of the chopper, chewing a large chunk of jerky, his face empty of emotion. Across his lap lay an AK-47. On the seat next to him rested a rucksack stuffed with black bread and sausage. He acknowledged both Baines and McKennon with a hesitant, disinterested pause in his chewing, meeting their glance, then nodded and resumed grinding his jowls.

"Get in," Baines said. "And knock the goddamn snow off your boots."

McKennon ignored the directions, climbing into the right-hand seat and pulling up the canvas travel bag behind him. He shoved it in the back next to Muller's rucksack.

The mounted patrol had already left—twelve men, with a truckload to follow. Except that the truck wouldn't start despite the swearing and pounding it took from the old Pole in charge of the two vehicles. One man was on the hand crank, swinging the balky engine over as the Pole poured raw gasoline down the throat of the air intake. It had caught once, but the driver had failed to pump the throttle quickly enough, so the engine had stalled and backfired. The Pole lay down a haze of Slavic blasphemies, stomping around in the snow with eight onlookers laughing.

Baines kicked his boots against the skid and climbed in. Strapping his seat belt, his hands traveled as an organist's over the stops as he flicked switches, set levers. He pulled a T-handle and the engine fired immediately, picking up revs. The long rotor blades began to cut air, swinging faster, wiping out sound. Playing with the console, Baines would not be hurried, touching each gauge, tapping it, moving back to the radio to set in frequencies.

McKennon fumed, stamping at the metal floor with his booted feet. "Let's get this thing moving," he shouted at Baines, who ignored him, tearing off a piece of black tobacco from a plug in his jacket pocket.

"You tend your knitting, I'll tend mine," he shouted back. "Always in a hurry. This engine is cold. I give it too much throttle too soon and it could pack up on me—throw a rod—whatever. You that anxious to see Brinkerhoff?" He threw McKennon a significant nod, his eyes rolling back in the direction of Muller.

Baines picked up a headset and handed one to McKennon, showing him where to plug it into the panel. The big ear muffs cut the sound of the engine and rotors to a tolerable background roar.

"Pofff—you hear me okay?" Baines's voice was clear, professional, with just a touch of Dixie.

"Yes. Loud and clear." McKennon turned and looked at Muller, who stared back and smiled, exposing a mouthful of partially masticated meat. Muller had no headphones.

"This being transmitted out?" McKennon tapped the radio panel.

"Nope. Only when I key this mike switch on the cyclic." Baines put his gloved thumb over a white button on the top of the stick and punched it twice, producing two electronic clicks in McKennon's earphones. He keyed it once again, holding it down.

"Megantic Barracks, this is chopper P. D. Four—you read?"

Blurts of electronic hash . . . *loud and clearly*. Slavic inflection.

"I'm ready for takeoff. You want me to divert on my way south to check in the general area of report?"

Different voice—this time older, in a heavy Germanic accent. *Baines, this is Weiner, barracks commandant. I repeat my instructions. Proceed direct Albany. Report abeam Rutland on this working frequency. You are not to divert. We have two helicopters coming up from Montpelier.* There was a pause. *These orders are directly from Commander Brinkerhoff. He's been informed of developments and has taken direct control of the search.*

Baines turned to McKennon, his thumb off the mike button. "Heavy-handed bastard, isn't he?"

You understand exactly, Baines? Weiner transmitted.

"Understood," Baines replied.

Baines eased in throttle, the howl of the engine rising, blades turning faster until they blurred to a translucent disk. Then he slowly rotated the pitch control. The chopper eased off the ground, turning slightly into the gusty wind and gaining altitude until McKennon was looking down on the faces of the men in the courtyard, their bodies foreshortening with the change in perspective. One man waved, his gap-toothed mouth open, like a small boy seeing off a train. Baines tucked the stick slightly forward and the nose tilted downward, the chopper picking up forward motion.

They swept out of the compound, clearing the walls, gaining altitude and speed rapidly. Almost immediately, McKennon could see the troop of mounted men off to his left heading south overland, about two kilometers away. They were strung out, cantering, the horses and men fresh.

McKennon tapped Baines on the arm, motioning toward the patrol. "Can you monitor the frequency they're using?"

Baines didn't answer but instead referred to a thumb-marked card that he withdrew from behind the sun visor, then passed to McKennon. "Don't have enough hands. You look."

McKennon found it and dialed it in. There was a cacophony of noise, men talking in three languages—ribald jokes and commands, complaints and static.

Slapping at the control with his glove, Baines reduced the volume. "Undisciplined bastards. Think they'd settle on one language." He squinted at the sun's glare as they rose above the lower cloud deck, then pulled a battered pair of sunglasses from a case and fitted them on with one hand. "Where to, McKennon?"

"Start with the sector they had the report from. We'll follow tracks from there."

Shifting the wad in his mouth, Baines eased over into a shallow bank, turning south. "Don't forget, McKennon, I'm doing this with a gun in my side." He gave a flat smile, eyes searching the terrain ahead. "And regardless of how it works out, I get the coin."

"That's the deal," McKennon replied wearily.

The chopper was in level flight now, moving rapidly south. McKennon tried to relax, blanking out the thought that if he didn't find Mallen and Wyatt almost at once, he would eventually have to face Brinkerhoff. Baines was sticking his neck out a long way, and there was the matter of fuel—enough for a direct flight to Albany plus only another forty minutes for the diversion. Yet he was sure that it was them and that from the air, with a fresh trail to follow, it would be simple. The thought crossed his mind to wonder how long it would take the choppers coming up from the south to reach the area. He studied the map, spanning off the distance with his fingers. Baines, glancing sideways, answered his question.

"About one hour fifty minutes, maybe two hours with this headwind. Relax, mister. We'll be there in twenty minutes." Almost jovial, Baines turned in his seat and slapped Muller's knee. "Good ride?" he shouted back at the man. Muller nodded, chewing bread, mumbled something in German, and said "Good." It might have been nothing more than his appreciation for the black bread he was now eating, crumbs littering the front of his jacket. "Good," he repeated, and Baines turned back, mumbling in his headset, "Dumb bastard."

The land was rising beneath them, the open patchwork of fields now giving way to clusters of trees. They cleared a small ridge, dipping down into a small, intermediate valley. Before them rose worn-down mountains, smooth and featureless but heavily forested.

McKennon, almost lulled by the drone of the engine, missed the first part of the transmission, not from the patrol but from the barracks base station. He clamped the headset tightly between his hands, trying to pick up the rapid, insistent voice, but the operator was speaking Russian and he couldn't translate it quickly enough.

Baines had a pencil out, quickly copying in a scrawling script the key phrases and coordinates, then switching frequencies. He called in English, then shifted into Russian.

McKennon was picking up words; *"Le Borveaux,"* "political supervisor," but little else. He caught the anger in Baines's voice, the urgency of his tone. After another brief exchange, Baines slammed the power switch to the set off. His face white with anger, he pounded his fist on the console.

"What was it?" McKennon demanded.

"Kid called in from the District Political Supervisor's office—place on Route 181. Said that Mallen and Wyatt probably have got a French car the kid's father or grandfather owned illegally. Their plane is still in one piece up on some lake. Plus they got fuel and they're armed."

"So?"

"So *shit*. . . . I told them we're close enough to pick

the kid up. He thinks he knows what lake it is. We could be waiting for them. They told me not to divert, fuckin' cabbage eaters. Weiner can't reach Brinkerhoff on the phone and says that the orders stand."

"They could refuel and be gone by the time the choppers from Montpelier get there!"

"Yeah, I understand that, McKennon. How dumb do you think I am?"

McKennon drew the Browning and laid it in his lap. "It's my ass, like you said, Baines. Route 181 is just off to the right. How long to get to the supervisor's house?"

Baines was grinning. "About . . ." he glanced down at the map, chewing hard, ". . . about six, maybe eight minutes."

McKennon leaned against the Plexiglas door, the automatic raised slightly. "Then do it, Baines."

The chopper banked sharply in the early morning light, picking up revs as Baines brought the power up to redline. "One other thing that should please you, McKennon," he said into the headset. "Weiner's instructions to the patrol are that he doesn't care if the bodies of the fugitives are warm or cold."

"You set?" Mallen asked Jeanne.

She nodded. "Let's get it over with." Awkwardly, she crossed herself.

He backed up the Peugeot a few more feet, then engaged the clutch and rolled toward the ice, the lake a dull, flat plain before him.

They had taken what precautions they could, unsnapping the seat belts and leaving the doors ajar on the slim hope that, if the car plunged through the ice, there would be some slight hope of survival. It had occurred to Mallen that a man might survive as much as five minutes in freezing water, but that implied that there was a warm, dry place for recovery. Which there was not.

The wheels crunched over the cake ice bunched on

the shoreline and then they were on the lake, skidding slightly but safely over the humped ridges.

At first he grossly overcorrected, but then as the Peugeot gained momentum he found that just a light touch to the wheel and hand brake would control the car. The speedometer crept up, building to thirty kilometers per hour. He suddenly realized that he had been holding his breath and expelled it, then felt the tension in his forearms and the quiver in his thigh. He tried to relax, yet found that he couldn't. There was always the knowledge that he could hit a thin section and the car might break through.

Somehow, he realized, Jeanne was more under control, although neither of them had talked since they rolled onto the ice. She pulled a cloth-wrapped package from the rear seat and unwrapped it, then broke off sections and fed small bites to him.

"You like fruitcake?" she asked, offering him more.

It was good but dry. "No more, thanks," he answered. "Ice seems firm enough, doesn't it?"

"Firm enough for the plane?"

A good question, he thought. The plane was lighter, but most of the weight was on the main landing gear, rather than being spread out over four wheels. "I think so," he finally answered.

The surface of the ice was good, he thought. It was mostly glaze ice but with some scattered patches of granular snow, as though it had thawed and then refrozen. With the wind blowing out of the northwest, getting airborne would require very little room, though he would have to taxi across the lake directly downwind before turning into the wind for his takeoff roll.

"Can you fly in this weather?" She motioned at the cloud deck, now well consolidated and much darker in the northwest. Out on the lake, without the protection of the trees, he could feel the car occasionally being rocked by hard gusts.

"It looks turbulent, but my only worry will be icing up of the wings. With luck and some time, I can get above the worst of it."

"How far can you go on the gas you have?" She motioned her head toward the trunk.

"Six hundred miles on the main tanks. With the two spare cans I have, another four hundred."

"And after that? What will you do for gas?"

"Steal some. Barter for it if I can. It's not an immediate worry."

She was looking straight forward, speaking almost in a detached voice. "Alberta," she said. "A thousand miles would put you in Alberta, I think." She looked over at him then and said, "And then British Columbia?"

Mallen only nodded. From the corner of his eye, he saw her look at him for seconds longer, then turn to watch the shoreline coming closer.

He had cut across one corner of the lake, across the haunches of the catlike shape, up toward the backbone. To his left was the shoreline where the Sperber lay hidden. He watched for an identifiable feature, trying to remember how the lake had looked as he had set up his final approach. He was beginning to think he had overshot the area but then saw the set of twin boulders. Brief thought of Wyatt, coffee together in that first dawn, the leaves still falling; a whole train of memories. Nudging the wheel, he steered for the shore, backing off the accelerator.

The Sperber was untouched, the slash pine camouflage still green and unwithered. The mud that Wyatt had spread over the top surfaces of the wings and fuselage was gone, probably to the earlier rains, but that made no difference now with the ground covered by snow. White on white. Mallen pulled in parallel to the leading edge of the wing and then reversed, backing toward the fuel filler cap on the left wing root. The dash clock showed eight twenty-three, so it had taken him at least two hours, and likely more.

He had planned to siphon the fuel directly from the drum into the tanks, but the height differential was wrong. Without comment, Jeanne helped him wrestle the drum level, propping it up with the spare tire. He turned the tap and gasoline flowed, cloudy at first with flecks of dirt, then pink and clear.

"You make what repairs are necessary," she said. "I can at least transfer the gasoline."

He paused, only for the briefest of seconds, looking at her. Small, intent, determined, she conveyed confidence, somehow projecting it in spite of the ludicrous, oversized army coat. I can't leave her, he thought. Can't. Won't.

"Jeanne, come with me. You can't go back. You know that." He reached for her arm and she drew it away.

"You don't have time to waste. Paul's surely notified them by now. There's no time left." She backed away from him, her eyes not meeting his, then looked up, her face set, eyes hard. "Mallen! Show me what to do."

He brushed the snow from around the filler cap, blew the remaining granules away, and screwed open the fitting. "The bucket," he said. "Get the bucket and fill this tank. Don't worry about spillage—it can't be helped. Just do the best you can."

As she started to fill the bucket from the drum, he collected the tools and fitting from the back seat of the Peugeot, then slid under the Sperber's fuselage. The wind was bitterly cold now and it was painful, numbing to work without gloves. He slid the length of rubber hose over the aluminum tubing and then taped it, making the connection tight. Next he fitted two hose clamps and screwed them down. Another plus. The hose fitted well—a little large, but the hose clamp made up in compression for the gap. Other side of the line: tube, tape, and clamps. Twice the screwdriver slipped and he skinned his knuckles, swearing. But then it was done. He replaced the inspection panel and tightened it. The line would hold. Of that, at least, he was sure.

Jeanne was still pouring in fuel. He squeezed her arm in passing, unsure of what he could say, and started to remove the brush from the wings and fuselage, half conscious now of sound, listening for the whack-whack of chopper blades. So close now to making it.

He opened the canopy: smells of hydraulic fluid, sweat, fake leather. Charts in the right-hand pocket. Not now, he thought. Head northwest, keeping under the cloud deck. He'd sort it out once he was airborne. He flicked on the master electrical switch. Nothing. The gauges lay dead, needles not even registering a quiver. He felt panic slide up his back, wrap his chest cavity, tighten on his heart. Twice more he snapped the switch, with no reaction on the panel. The battery was dead.

Jeanne was still pouring fuel from the bucket into the wing tank, spilling some but not much, steadying the bucket against the buffeting of the wind. He was about to say something just as the tank overflowed.

She looked up. Her eyes were smarting from the fuel fumes, and he noticed that her coat was wet, almost saturated along the sleeves from spilled gasoline. "It's finished," she said.

He took the bucket from her and threw it into the trunk and then screwed the filler cap back onto the wing tank fitting.

"It's not finished, Jeanne," he said. Mallen took her hand, pulling her against him, wrapping his arms around her. "In two minutes, with some luck, we'll be airborne. And in six hours we'll be six hundred miles to the west of here. You can't stay. They'll eventually find out, probably from Paul, that you willingly gave refuge to Wyatt and me. How would you explain lying to the patrol? Without capturing Wyatt or me, they'll crucify you as a consolation prize."

She was shaking from the cold, burying her body against his, her face pressed against his chest. "No," she sobbed. "I can't. You know I can't. My grandfather . . . I owe him what you owed Wyatt. I couldn't run out on him. And Paul—he'll never . . ."

Mallen turned away, letting go of her, knowing that there was only one way to do it. Without his support, she stumbled and fell to the ground, a tragicomic figure,

a little girl in an army coat, hair spilling out from beneath her watch cap.

Ignoring her, Mallen slung the packs of food into the
luggage hold of the Sperber and stuffed the Luger beneath the front seat cushion. He was thinking now of
wind direction, and half wondering but knowing that it
would make no difference as to whether the lake would
support the plane. It would or it wouldn't; there was no
other option.

He moved the Peugeot out of the way, leaving it on
the foreshore, then came back to her, pulling her up
by the shoulders.

"Get in the plane."

She was whipping her head from side to side. "No,
Mallen. I can't go with you. It's not a choice I have."

"Damn it, lady, I'm not going to argue with you.
Whatever the hell you want. If you're dumb enough
to believe . . ." He pushed her toward the aft cockpit.
"Look, the battery's dead. I can't get this thing going
by myself. You've got to help. The fuel feed line is dry.
I've got to prop the engine over. And you've got to
catch it with the throttle when the engine fires. Do that
and you're finished with me."

He half helped her, half shoved her into the aft cockpit. She was objecting, shaking uncontrollably, tears
streaming down her face. "Greg, you understand. I love
you, if that means anything. But . . ."

He took her face in his hands, turning it up toward
his. And kissed her. Taking the watch cap off to let
her hair flow unrestrained in the wind, he kissed her
again. "I understand, I understand," he whispered
against her face. "Whatever happens, I understand."

He took her hand and placed it on the throttle, then
moved it back toward her. "That's closed position."
Then he moved her hand forward under his. "That's
full open. When the engine fires, move it up about a
third. Then when it's running steadily, pull the throttle
slowly back to a smooth idle. You got it?"

She looked and nodded, something like shock in her
face. Her mouth opened and she started to say some-

thing, then closed it, biting down on her lower lip. "I'll try," he heard her answer.

Mallen set the brake up hard, flicking on the master switch and the magneto. No time to show her that. He pulled out the choke and positioned himself in front of the prop. Pull. He turned it through its arc, feeling the stiffness of the oil, molasseslike, dragging on the pistons.

Pull five more times, with not a cough, a kick. *Pull.* The smell of raw fuel came now. The mechanical pump was primed, pushing fuel through the lines, filling the carburetor bowl and lifting the float. Vapor was getting past the venturi. The valves were like little robots, blindly opening and closing in the black recesses of the engine. *Pull,* you sucker. Fire, you *bitch. Pull!*

It fired and died. From beneath the cowl, raw gasoline dripped, fractured in the wind, and blew away atomized, staining the snow. If the electrodes on the plugs fouled with fuel now, it was over, he thought. Goddamn plugs. He reached around into the depths of the cockpit and closed the choke, snapped off the magneto.

"Open the throttle all the way and hold it open. The damn thing is flooded."

She looked up, intent, and nodded, moving her hand forward.

He thought he heard something—more than just wind moaning through the tops of the trees. A snow squall was sweeping down the lake, picking up surface granules, flinging them before the suddenly violent wind. Big fat flakes blinded him, plastering his jacket, stinging his eyes. He listened more intently.

The sound again. More than just the wind, but it couldn't be—not yet.

Mallen pulled the prop through again and again, rapping his knuckles on the sharp edges of the blade. Five, six, seven. Mags back on.

"Set the throttle about halfway," he shouted against the wind. Her hand moved all the way back and then slightly forward.

Pull. It fired and coughed, fired again, and picked up into a scream, cold metal rotating against cold metal. She brought the throttle level back, the revs falling to a steady rhythm. Her face was shining—triumphant, radiant.

He sprinted around the wing, back to the cockpit before she could rise. She looked up at him and threw her arms around his neck, drawing his face down to hers.

"Oh dear God," she cried, "I was so terrified that it was all for nothing—that the engine wouldn't start." Her face wet against his, tears and melting snowflakes merged on her reddened cheeks.

He kissed her hard, wrapping his arms around her body, trying to distill everything he felt and hoped for into one brief moment. And he knew that without her there would be no point in going.

It was almost as if she sensed what was coming, because she drew away from him. "You've got to go now. And so do I." She started to grip the canopy sill, pulling herself up so that she could get out onto the wing.

Very firmly, he held her shoulders, pushing her back into the seat, not letting her move. He had to convince her, he thought. Because, despite what the old man had said, it had to be her free will and not just his own mandate.

"Jeanne!" He tightened his grip on her shoulders. "Jeanne—hear me out. Know this—I love you in every way possible. I'm not positive that I'll make it to western Canada, but I know that I've got a good shot at it. And you have to come with me."

She was shaking her head, tears streaming down her face. "Mallen. Don't make it more difficult for me. I can't . . ."

"There's no other choice. You can't go back. That patrol back there on the road—they had a radio. Regardless of what Paul does, McKennon will send in patrols to this area. If you tried to drive back, they'd pick you up. And despite Paul, regardless of what he said, there would be enough evidence to convict you of harboring Wyatt and me. And if that happened, they'd . . ." He thought of what the old man had said but couldn't bring himself to say it—even to think of it.

Jeanne was staring up at him, as if she finally understood the magnitude of what was happening. He saw it in her eyes.

She quit struggling and slumped back into the seat. The wind lifted her hair, blowing it back across her forehead. Flakes of snow were accumulating on her eyebrows and hair. She sat still without speaking for long seconds, then looked back up at him. "I heard you both talking. But I thought it was only about Paul."

"Jeanne, your grandfather made me promise that I would take you with me. He said you wouldn't be . . . safe if you stayed."

She gripped his wrist, her nails biting into his flesh. "I've heard the stories. But they wouldn't . . . I mean, Paul would protect me. They'd listen to Paul. And Mallen—I can't leave my grandfather. He's so old and sick and there's so little of his life left. Without me, he'd . . ."

"Dammit, Jeanne," he yelled at her, feeling frustration and rage seething up at him. "Can't you understand that Paul is not going to be able to protect you—that if you go back, you may actually endanger him. Right now he's clean; he did his duty. But if they put you under interrogation, it might look like he had been helping you." Mallen, tormented, looked for logic and reason, but found only jumbled scraps of ideas. He reached down and took her face between his hands, turning her head gently to face his. "Jeanne," he said softly, "your grandfather is an old man. He's near death and he's in pain. This is the one and only thing that he can give to you—release. He wanted you to come with me, even though he knew that there was great risk. If you deny his giving this gift, you leave him nothing—not even death with dignity. As for Paul . . ." Mallen felt the pain in her eyes, felt what she must be feeling now. "As for Paul—we can't blame him. It was anger, and we caused that anger. He'll make it through all of this. And I think—know—that he'll eventually understand."

She had clamped her eyes shut, arms crossed and hugging herself, rocking in the agony of decision. "I don't *know,* Mallen—I can't even think."

Standing outside the shelter of the cockpit, he heard it first—the deep, unmistakable beat of an engine, overlaid with the whump of rotor blades. Still far off, he guessed; the sound was reflected and intensified by the low clouds, just as fog will amplify the sound of a distant ship. He looked down at the panel. The oil pressure was good, but the oil temperature was barely off the peg. The amp meter was flickering at a high rate of charge, and fuel pressure was now steady. He carefully eased the throttle back and the engine fell to an easy idle, just ticking over.

He assessed the risk. Two or three minutes to taxi downwind across the lake and then turn into the wind— say a total of four minutes' exposure on the ground. Once airborne, they could find plenty of stratus and snow showers to hide in. This particular chopper could be just hunting in a general area. The Special Forces kid could only have narrowed the search area, not pinpointed it. But if Paul had spilled his guts by now, they would be looking for a lake in the area, and that narrowed the focus to Christian's Portage.

Mallen turned back to Jeanne and pulled the seat belt tight, then snapped the shoulder straps into the quick-release mechanism. She was struggling against him, almost frantic. He grabbed her jaw, forcing her face upward toward his.

"Decision time, lady," he shouted into her face. "They're here—there's a bloody chopper just over that ridge. If you stay, I stay. Eventually they'll get us. The old man will have died for nothing, and Paul will probably get burned for helping you. The only alternative is to fly out of here together—and it may be too damn late for that."

Her eyes were wide, terrified. Then she too heard the chopper. It was close, distinctly just one machine, but running at high power output, as if it was not searching but heading directly toward the lake.

He pointed, squinting at the blurred image, partially obscured in the snow shower. Just briefly visible, the chopper disappeared behind a low hill, then turned away from him, sweeping the area between the road and the lake.

"They're leaving," she started to say.

"They're not leaving," Mallen snapped. "They've picked up the access road, and if they can spot the car tracks, it'll be less than two minutes before they'll be hovering fifty yards away, pouring shells into us."

His mind was leaping from one idea to another, seeking alternatives, but there was only one option. "I've got to draw them off with the car, because if they spot this plane, even one or two tracers will turn it into a torch. If I can get to the opposite shore, I'll have cover. Eventually, they'll have to set that bird down and I'll have the advantage. It's the best—the only chance we've got."

"I'll drive . . ."

"No! Once I draw them to the far shore, I want you to stamp a path through the snow so that the landing gear doesn't get bogged down. Once I get back, we'll have damn little time. Undoubtedly, they've got troops coming overland." He paused, thinking. "But one thing you haven't answered . . ."

She reached up and wiped snow from his face, but it was more of a caress. "I'm going with you. Wherever it may be."

He thought of the old man and the promise extracted. Reaching down into his shirt pocket, he withdrew the Richeloff set and placed it in her lap. "If I don't come back . . ."

She took the box and looked at it in revulsion, then flung it away into the bush. "You'll come back, Mallen. And I'll be here when you do. Just leave me the Luger." She reached up and kissed him.

They both heard the sound of the chopper growing louder, far down the lake.

17

It was the small one, the chopper with the yellow tail. Coming in over the eastern horizon, just skimming the trees, it faltered in its direction and then banked, screaming straight down the center of the lake.

Mallen was already sprinting through the snow. He scrambled into the driver's seat and hit the ignition, pulled the gear lever into first, and headed for the ice, tires spewing snow and frozen clods of sand.

In his mind there was no question that the Sperber was well hidden. If they saw the car first, there was little chance of their seeing the white on white of the aircraft against the snow. But he cursed himself for the delays, time that could have ensured a margin of safety. Wasted seconds, minutes, days had accumulated like bad debt.

The chopper was halfway down the lake, slowing, beginning to ess in sweeps back and forth from the center line. It was obvious that they hadn't picked up the tracks of the Peugeot's crossing on the intermittent patches of snow. Watching the Klistov, Mallen had to admire the pilot—flying in hard, gusting conditions, sometimes half blind. The man was good. Very good.

He was up into second and then into third, aiming at the far shore. By ducking his head down, he could watch the chopper, converging but drawing ahead of the interception point. It was essential—critical—that they see him, but the chopper was now abeam, essing out toward the far side of the shore. "Christ, they missed me," he thought, astounded. Well past, the chopper banked back toward the center line of the cat, along the backbone then to Mallen's side but well past him. He was on their blind side now, and their eyes would be forward, looking for the tracks. Mallen braked to a stop and waited, offering himself up as bait, knowing they would return.

As he watched, the chopper reached the cat's-tail end of the lake and wheeled upward, bleeding off air speed and banking back, this time along Mallen's side of the lakeshore. It was like a baying dog, overrunning the scent and then doubling back, now sure of the kill. He had blabbed that to the old man, hadn't he? With the kid taking in every word. "Down on the shore of a lake in Maine," and that's where they had come. With the transmission from the Mongol, they had picked the right one.

Sure he was finally spotted, Mallen dropped the gear lever into low and accelerated along the shoreline, heading toward the opposite shore. It was either that or let them spot the plane.

Grinding up through the gears, Mallen flung the Peugeot across the shore, pounding over ridged slabs of ice and frost heaves, axles bottoming against the chassis on the rough terrain. The snow squall had passed, leaving a flat light with no shadow, just a bland, neutral wash of gray to the landscape. No time to glance back—the wind behind him—and only the slimmest possibility of another squall offered the hope of reprieve.

He caught a glimpse of the chopper out of the right-front window. It was coming in low and fast, angling ahead of him for the interception point. Mallen flicked the wheel, steering out onto the ice. The tires caught for a second, keeping traction, but then the Peugeot broke loose in a wheeling slide, turning end for end. Above the howl of the car's engine, he could hear the mounting blat of the chopper's exhaust and the flat stutter of automatic weapons fire. He felt it as a physical presence above him, the pressure of the wind thrown downward by the blades—the sensation of standing within feet of railroad tracks as a train passes, with its pressure surge and unbelievable noise. Then it was past, and the Peugeot was still in one piece, still moving, but sideways, uncontrolled.

He pulled the hand brake and reversed the wheel. The Peugeot slithered sideways and caught hold, stabilizing in direction and accelerating.

Down at the east end of the lake the chopper was turning in a leisurely arc, gaining altitude. Mallen headed for the opposite side of the lake, estimating the distance at somewhere between a mile and forever, but desperately trying to draw them away from the Sperber. As a pig on ice, the Peugeot had no stability, no sure direction. It was as if he were caught in a nightmare, trying to windmill his arms and rise above the snapping dogs, but moving too slowly and without control or hope, sinking back toward them.

And yet, incredibly, the Peugeot was gaining speed, tires biting into rough ice and snow, the weight of the fuel drum helping the traction. He eased the wheel straight, flicked through second and third gears, saw the needle climbing past fifty and sixty. Glare ice was beneath him now, and he felt the car fishtailing, backed off the pedal, came onto rough ice again, and went into fourth with the accelerator to the floor doing sixty, seventy.

There was no hope for a shot with the Winchester. Jeanne had reloaded it, but it lay beyond reach in the back seat. Eighty now, and the car was lurching, unmanageable, without control. He chanced a glimpse to the east. Yellow Tail hung in clear air, nosing over for a run, the speed perceptibly lower, taking time for an easy kill.

Before him, the shoreline was closer. Trees, individual things were now magically growing taller as he closed the distance. He picked the nearest point and edged in more pressure on the accelerator. He saw bushes now, and a shoreline littered with rough humps of stone and small stunted trees.

The chopper came in on his side, closing fast. From the corner of his eye Mallen saw fountains of ice chips spraying across the lake, like rows of white flowers suddenly blooming. The Peugeot and the flowers merged, the windshield exploding in a crystalline burst of shards. He felt the frame shudder violently under jackhammer blows, then the scream of shearing metal, his own: sound without end, all in one brief instant of time.

His face was numb, vision blurred. The trees and shore were ballooning up in a white blur. He sensed the car sliding sideways but had time only to bring his hands up in front of his face as the Peugeot hit the shore. It lurched insanely and then straightened, bottoming out, but started rotating in the opposite direction, rolling. He stabbed at the brake just before the frame hit a boulder, snow mantled and half concealed in a slash of pine. The shock of the collision was taken up by the front end, bursting the radiator in a cloud of steam. The Peugeot tried to climb the boulder and half won, horsing up at a thirty-degree angle. Then, as in the vacuum that follows a shock wave, there was relative silence, just steam hissing from the guts of the engine and the creaking of overheated metal contracting in the cold.

There were only seconds, and he vaguely grasped that, holding it as the central thought—the only thought—in his brain. Decode and read *seconds. Move,* his mind screamed. He pulled the rifle from the seat and tumbled out of the car, crab walking on the frozen, snow-covered ground, his vision blurred and aftershock numbing his senses. He saw points of light swimming across his retinas like incandescent red and green gnats moving away from the center of focus. He tried to follow them and was amused that he couldn't. Look and they weren't there, moving away like a school of fish or a swarm of flies. Gone. Coming back.

He remembered. Chopper. Mallen stumbled to his feet and almost toppled, reaching out for something to steady himself but finding nothing. Got some feet—pair of feet—move feet! He heaved himself in the direction of the brush, inertia the only saving grace. Panting, he fell heavily in the scrub and crawled over the spiky branches, swimming uphill through foliage.

The slashing of the weapons fire and the reverberations of frozen earth soaking up the impact of high-velocity shells came again, tearing up great gouts of dirt just feet behind him. The chopper passed very low in a rush of wind and sound, pulling back out over the lake then rearing up, the pitch of the rotors changing as it slowed to hover.

Mallen lay between two stunted pines, panting, trying to focus, feeling the earth whirling beneath him, in the sensation of spinning on a piano stool and suddenly stopping. He tried to coordinate his sight, concentrating on one point, his hand, trying to get the damn thing stopped. Blurred. He realized that he was bleeding. His vision was clearing, but, touching his forehead, his hand came away covered with blood. He gently felt with his fingers, touched something that sent a raw shaft of pain tearing through his nerves, then probed more gently and carefully extracted a needle-thin stiletto of glass. The flow of blood increased in volume and he blotted at it with the sleeve of his filthy jacket. He closed his eyes and then opened them again, looking at his hand. Ten fingers slowly merged, separated and then remerged into five. His head was ringing, starting to ache, but he was at least in one piece—slightly shopworn, frayed at the edges, but functional.

The chopper was hovering at low altitude over the center of the lake, more than a quarter of a mile out, slowly swaying from left to right like a dull insect, indecided where its prey lay. The light was hard, but even still, Mallen could not distinguish how many the chopper carried, seeing just forms within the bubble of Plexiglas.

Up to the west, another snow squall was sweeping down, the second advance wave of the coming storm. Visibility would be reduced to nothing, a situation that could work either for or against him, depending on the brains of the man directing the attack. McKennon? Mallen had no doubt about it.

He mopped at his forehead again and saw that the bleeding was less. Body shutting down protective circuits, he thought. Capillaries constricting, the bitter cold helping. He leaned his head against the trunk of the tree, closing his eyes momentarily, wanting to rest.

How long now since he had left her in the plane? An unbelievably great time; in reality, no more than a few minutes.

He watched the aircraft, fascinated, unable to understand why they would waste the fuel, decreasing their range. He knew that choppers used a disproportionately high amount of fuel in the hover mode, so it argued that they were gambling on getting him now, on the ground. If they had even one spare man, it would be logical for them to drop that man as a flanker, but the damn thing just hung there, as if from an invisible string, just beyond range. And then it came to him. The chopper was hanging out there, swinging like a fat target in a carnival shooting gallery: knock it down and get the teddy bear on the top rack—which is what McKennon would be testing for. He wouldn't know whether Mallen had a weapon, and he had to find out whether Mallen would go for the prize or was out of dimes.

The chopper moved in slightly closer, perhaps to less than three hundred yards' range, and Mallen assessed the risk. Still too far out for an effective shot and Yellow Tail was moving all the time. If they watched carefully, they would be able to spot his muzzle blast, yet the likelihood of his scoring a vital shot would be remote. He felt down into the jacket pocket and counted the thin fingers of brass. Four. Five more in the magazine. One up the spout for a total of ten. It was not nearly enough to waste even one round on a doubtful target. Let McKennon think that he was dead or weaponless.

The snow squall was much closer now, he estimated; five minutes, maybe less. Chopper or not, he would head back on foot across the ice. What lay to windward in the storm might be less restrictive in visibility, and obscurity of vision was his only hope. He squinted, trying to see the Sperber, a mile or less across the lake, say seven minutes at a hard trot. He couldn't see the outlines of the aircraft, but he could see what he thought at least were the twin boulders. So he would keep the prevailing wind on his face, perhaps just a bit to the right. The direct line would pass well downwind of Yellow Tail.

God, it was cold. Bone-searing cold, and the wound in his forehead was beginning to throb, the initial shock wearing off. He groped for a cigarette and came up with the empty, crumpled pack. Given a choice, he would have traded a cartridge for a cigarette. He smiled, remembering that Anne had said that smoking was just a continuation of infantile oral gratification, and why didn't he suck his thumb instead. Better for life expectancy. But then again, Mallen didn't feel that lung disease was his present terminal expectation.

They couldn't stay out there forever. Sooner or later, McKennon would begin to press, in a flanking movement, he guessed. Perhaps the chopper would drop one man to the west and another, if they had spare cannon fodder, to the east, or maybe one up the middle, if there were a total of four, with the pilot hanging out of range. A couple of fat flakes stung his cheeks, melting, predecessors of many. Let it come, he thought. Welcome, snow. Insanely, he hummed a bar of "Winter Wonderland."

McKennon's voice came to him, carried on the wind and distorted by amplification, but still unmistakably McKennon's.

Mallen . . . allen . . . come . . . ome . . . out . . . ta.

The sound echoed around the lake, deadened by the falling snow, blotted up by the trees. Still no move by the chopper except the hypnotic swaying.

Mallen lay his head down on his arm, the flakes accumulating, building up on the sleeve of his jacket, on the wooden stock of the Winchester. He watched two of them slowly merge together in one droplet and run in a microriver down the cheek of the stock. How long? Visibility still good enough to see the chopper. The squall was lighter than he thought. It had looked like a solid wall, but now he was less sure. It was more dense

for seconds, then lighter, as if coming in waves. Have
to move soon. Very soon.

The chopper was suddenly obscured in a snow shower
and the tone was changing, picking up the beat. He
imagined that it was coming closer and thumbed back
the hammer, tensing. But then he caught a glimpse of it,
farther to the east and low, moving fast. Time to go, he
thought, picking himself up. A body he didn't know,
numb and protesting, reluctantly obeyed.

He stopped, only for seconds, beside the dying
Peugeot. It was bleeding the remains of a dirty brown
fluid from the burst radiator. The driver's door was still
open and a tinny, insistent buzzer nagged at a nonexistent driver. The drum of gasoline was still intact and he
turned the tap fully open, denying them the remainder
of the fuel. As an afterthought, he picked up a tire iron
lying next to the drum and shoved it under his belt.
Then he headed north, into the wind, onto the open ice.

The snow was much heavier now, sweeping horizon-
tally in a blurred smear of white. It was difficult for him
to look into the wind, and he squinted his eyes, grimacing. His face had lost all feeling, a mask of dead skin.
Traction was minimal and he repeatedly slipped. He was
moving, and in the right direction, but at a lot slower
pace than he had planned on.

The chopper's engine, just a faint drone, grew louder.
He couldn't see it, but he had a rough idea as to its
direction. It seemed to be going inland or west and it
matched Mallen's concept of McKennon's strategy—
dropping two flankers in a pincer movement. Only one
choice now, he thought. Get across the lake, and quickly. It would be the least likely place they would guess
him to move toward.

He turned away from the wind, unable to take the
numbing cold but still moving backward, toward the far
shore of the lake. As he walked, he wiped the snow
from his face, flicking away the moisture that blurred
his vision. There, back along the border of trees that
ringed the lake, he saw a movement of green against
white. Instinctively, Mallen dropped to a prone position.

The man hadn't seen him yet and was moving in a running crouch toward the Peugeot. Flanker number one was squat, possibly overweight, but moving with the complete confidence that comes with disciplined training. The man wore a coat, the hood thrown up. A weapon, which Mallen couldn't identify but was irregular enough in shape to be an AK-47, was held easily in the man's hands, off to his side, the barrel forward, for a broad field of fire.

A snow shower momentarily obscured him, and the next Mallen saw of him was as he hunched down next to the Peugeot, squatting in a duck walk, weapon held at chest level, advancing around the rear end of the car.

Mallen brought the Winchester up, both elbows against the ice, guessing at the distance. Somehow, before, he had missed the Mongol with what should have been an easy shot. The cartridges were old, the gunpowder probably unstable and therefore erratic. He sighted on the man's chest, held his breath, and squeezed.

In that same instant, the man turned and ducked, loosing a long burst traversing an arc toward Mallen.

Bullets whined overhead and ricocheted off the ice; the sounds of insects on a summer's afternoon. Something plucked at his jacket. Working the lever, Mallen chambered another shell and pulled down the sights toward the man's groin. The man was crouched down near the rear fender, changing clips and bringing his weapon up. Mallen fired, and a nano-second later the man on the shore fired, a pink-white muzzle flash growing to an irregular point of white light blossoming to a ball of yellow white flame—and the rag clown of a figure cartwheeled before the blast, tumbling through the air, end over end. The flames were leaping high over the Peugeot as the shock wave of the explosion rumbled down the lake and back, a muffled crumping sound, dulled by the falling snow. Mallen felt no elation. In exchange for the man's death he had exposed his own position, and out here on the ice there was no cover.

Working the lever again, Mallen chambered another

cartridge and waited. Except for the yellow flames and a greasy black cloud of smoke whipped away by the wind, there was no movement along the shore.

Glancing down to the west, Mallen studied the shoreline. He could just hear the faint, slow beat of the chopper's rotors, but not the sound of the exhaust. There was a possibility that the chopper was on the ground, dropping off number-two flanker. Visibility was poor, as in trying to see through multiple layers of gauze. Then Mallen saw him, or thought he did—just a movement, a darker shape against the white background. The range was an unknown, and Mallen was not even sure that the movement was a man, but he fired three quick shots, spacing them through a small arc, leading in the direction the figure had been moving.

No returned fire. Mallen waited for a few seconds, chambering another cartridge, realizing that it was the last in the magazine. Reload and then move, he thought. How many cartridges left? Fingers numb, he dug into his jacket pocket and pulled them out, three of them dropping on the ice. The chopper's exhaust was loud now, picking up in volume, moving right to left.

He fumbled one of the shells into the magazine; then tried to pick up the others from the ice but he couldn't grasp them, kept knocking them about, letting them slip from his fingers. Stupid goddamn fingers, more like wood stumps on creaky hinges. A little insane with the frustration, he laughed—felt like a kid with a carnival claw machine, trying to pick up the phony gold fountain pen.

With no warning, no real perceived increase in sound, the chopper swept over him, no more than twenty feet away and moving fast.

They didn't see me!

. . . didn't see! his first thought—prayed, but then knew that it was the only possibility his mind had allowed him to accept. The chopper flew on for another second and then pitched up into a turn, momentarily was lost in a snow shower, but then reemerged, revs picking up into a flat pitch, heading back for him. He wanted to run, hide, bury himself in the ice and then, very suddenly, felt the nakedness and impotence of the prey, alone in an open killing ground and under fire.

From less than a quarter of a mile away the chopper was an apparition, disappearing then reappearing as it flew toward him through successive curtains of snow, its rotor speed picking up into a much higher whine with the distinctive whistling that comes of blades working in ground effect.

There were three shells on the ice at his feet, but he had no time to get them. He scrambled into a sitting position, clamping down on his mind to restrain the panic, bracing the rifle and then raising it, finger taking up the slack in the trigger mechanism. One chance, he thought. Two at the outside. Adrenaline was pumping through his body and he suddenly felt hot, complete, vital.

The angle of the chopper's approach was a bit off, farther to the north than he had anticipated. He swiveled rapidly on the seat of his pants, leading the target, allowing for the deflection, and then squeezed.

At some subprimitive level of awareness, Mallen knew that he was being transformed, that fear and instinct for survival were now barriers he had bypassed. Even as the Model 94 hammered against his shoulder, he knew that the bullet would hit where he wished it, as if muscle and mind had combined to guide the slug of lead at will. He heard himself screaming, but it was the scream of an animal at bay, turning back to attack the hunter.

The pilot of the machine bucked under the impact, one arm suddenly flung out in a defensive gesture, the canopy starred and then shattering, chunks of Plexiglas tearing away and spraying into the cockpit.

"Yahhhhhhhhh!" Mallen screamed. The sound was buried in the howl of the chopper's engine, but Mallen was not aware of anything except the machine's ballooning, swelling in his sights. Mind-eye link assessment, computation of trajectory, commands transmitted through nerve bundles to tendons to flesh. Lever down again, action picking up a cartridge, lever slamming home, and then squeeze. One hundred fifty grains of lead left the muzzle at over eighteen hundred feet a second, blurred for a millisecond in the flat light, then mushroomed into the oil cooler of the Klistov.

The chopper thundered by him, close enough for Mallen to see the rivets and smears of oil, the blur of faces in the cockpit. Mallen wheeled, expecting the thing to crash, but the chopper climbed, yawing insanely from side to side, just on the thin edge of control.

About a quarter of a mile away the Klistov finally slowed to a hover, then started to drift backward, the tail wagging under erratic rudder control. The engine exhaust noise rose to a howl, like the scream of a dying prehistoric animal, and beneath the chopper a tornado of wind-blasted snow and ice was hurled out in a roiling wall of white.

Screaming in frustration, Mallen jacked the lever one more time, the empty brass case spinning past his face. He laid the sights on the exposed fuel tank and squeezed the trigger. The firing pin snapped into an empty chamber.

In a fury, Mallen smashed the empty Winchester on the ice. From beneath his belt he drew out the tire iron and started to run after the chopper, following a drunken course, slipping and falling, insensitive to the pain. The wound on his forehead was bleeding heavily again and he brushed at it irritably, surprised that there was no feeling. Dimly, he understood that there was no point in it, but he was beyond rationality now, a madman fighting back with a stick of iron, screaming against the wind and the noise of the chopper's engine, fragments of words, curses, and triumph.

But it didn't crash. Somehow the pilot kept the thing airborne. Erratic, the chopper was a machine gone berserk, doing things that no aircraft could do, pitching up and then diving, wallowing, each oscillation more extreme.

Mallen was closing the distance. As he ran, he

shouted at the chopper in a voice he didn't recognize as his own, *"Crash, you sonovabitch . . . BURN!"*

Another squall swept across the ice and the light was gone to a pale, flat gray, the snow plastering against his face, wind gusting so hard that Mallen actually felt himself leaning into it. Momentarily he lost sight of it, so paused and turned, searching for the machine, knowing it was very near and getting nearer. To his right, the chopper burst through a snow shower, heading directly for him, moving fast and just feet off the ice. He had time only to draw his arm back and heave the bar at the canopy, the violence of the throw unbalancing him. He fell heavily on his side, feet tangled, feeling the wind and the sound of the chopper passing him with the roar of an avalanche. Half turning, looking behind him, he saw the chopper pitch up, its tail rotor smashing into the frozen lake in an explosion of metal and spewing ice. The thing skidded sideways on the crumpling fuselage and then the main body of the chopper settled heavily like a tired animal, almost in slow motion. The main rotor blades shredded and then disintegrated, breaking off, hurtling outward in end-over-end cartwheels. The thing slid on, a cacophony of screeching metal and violently dying machinery. There was one final rumble—a dull explosion in the guts of the machine—and then the chopper was nothing more than an inert pile of wreckage, semi-immersed in a bed of shattered ice, water beginning to rise through the cracks in a spreading pool.

"Dear God almighty," he thought. "I won." Exhausted, Mallen stumbled the last twenty yards. The Klistov was unrecognizable as something that once flew. It was junk; a collection of torn sheet metal and buckled tubing. Oil, gasoline, hydraulic fluid oozed from the mangled engine compartment, creating an iridescent slick on the thin layer of water.

The pilot was dead, or so near to it that it didn't matter, pitched over onto the controls, his neck at an impossible angle, face merged into the shattered instrument panel. His left hand was rigid, still gripping the collective. Blood dripped from beneath the sleeve of his jacket, spattering into the water below the sinking chopper and adding to the seeping wastes of the wreckage.

McKennon was in the right seat, semiconscious, with rivulets of red running from both nostrils. He sat upright, still strapped in the seat, nodding as if carrying on a mental dialogue with some private voice. Mallen could get no closer than thirty feet to the wreckage. Cracks, still opening under the stress, radiated out, and the pool of water was expanding as the chopper sank lower, water already lapping the accordioned belly of the fuselage.

"McKennon!" Mallen yelled. No movement, just the nodding. There were no weapons in the cockpit, only banana clips and the trash of some unidentifiable food littering in the aft passenger area. Mallen's chest was still pounding so much that he could hear the beat of his heart in his head. But he was starting to collect his thinking, realizing that he had won, that there was more of a future than just another second in his life. How many minutes had passed since he had left her? There was no way of telling, except that it had seemed an eternity but had probably been less.

"McKennon!" He had to go, he knew that. But he couldn't drag himself away, mesmerized by the sight of McKennon slumped in the shattered cockpit, sinking into icy oblivion. Mallen was suddenly convinced that he had won, but the victory was meaningless without McKennon's acknowledgment of it.

"McKennon!" he shouted again. "You hear me? It's Mallen."

The figure stirred, his hand rising, pushing slowly away at an imaginary obstacle. He then moved his head, turning it toward Mallen, all in slow motion as if it cost him a great deal of effort. He finally opened his eyes and looked toward Mallen as if he was an irritation, something that had disrupted his thinking.

"David?" he asked, trying to focus, his eyes squinting. He suddenly choked on something and started to cough, spasms of pain racking his face. His hands grabbed at his chest as if he was trying to contain his own body from exploding, and he thrashed against the shoulder strap in a fit of agony.

Standing there on the ice, listening to McKennon hack his life away, feeling the vibrations of ice breaking away beneath the shattered wreck, Mallen quite suddenly realized that McKennon had been the enemy, yet an enemy now defeated and dying. There was no pleasure in this, he realized. The fight was finished and he was only gloating over the vanquished's grave. Each irreplaceable minute was a minute less of safety, a minute closer to danger, but he couldn't tear himself away.

The seizure of hacking had subsided and McKennon had raised his hands, looking at the red smears of blood on his palms, not really understanding the significance of it. He hacked once again and half spit, half drooled a reddish-black glob. His head was beginning to sway from side to side, as if trying to focus.

"Help me," he said weakly. He had his eyes open now, looking toward the man standing on the ice.

"Get out of that thing!" Mallen yelled. "The release —snap open the release!"

McKennon widened his eyes, eyebrows raised, like a bleary drunk just coming to, and stared at Mallen. He then looked across at what had been Baines and then down to the cockpit floor, already immersed in swirling water. "Mallen . . . ?"

A tongue of ice broke off and the airframe lurched sideways, rolling drunkenly to the left. Water washed over the canopy sill, spurted up through ruptured access plates, through control cable fairleads.

"Mallen," he said distinctly, "help me."

"Unbuckle the belt. The *belt,* McKennon. Then get out and swim!"

McKennon released the latch, using both hands, then crumpled sideways against the dead pilot, unable to move any farther.

"Out!" Mallen was screaming, hearing his voice echoing back in a mocking parody of itself.

Pushing away with both hands against Baines's body,

McKennon slowly straightened upright, coughing again. He collapsed back into the contour of his own seat, sucking heavily for air, trying to bring the racking of his chest under control. His face was ashen; radials of pain were etched into the creases of his face. He finally stilled the convulsions and rasped, "Legs dead. No feeling . . ." He turned toward Mallen. "Caught up finally . . . knew . . ."

The water had submerged the cockpit floorboards and was lapping at his ankles, but he didn't seem to notice. He raised both hands to his throat, then yanked down once, then twice. An object came away in his fist. He looked at it, first on one side and then the other and, satisfied, lifted his arm and tossed it awkwardly across the intervening gap. It landed at Mallen's feet and skidded away on the ice.

"Yours," he said. "Use it . . ."

The thing landed within two strides of where Mallen stood and he scooped it up, turning it over in his hand. It was a thick gold coin, an old U.S. double eagle, valuable enough to buy almost anything. It was still warm from McKennon's body heat.

The tail rotor suddenly cocked upward as the airframe started its final plunge. McKennon lifted his hand, finger extended in profane salute. "Luck, Mallen . . . Next time . . ."

As the angle became more acute, McKennon tumbled forward against the controls, then the chopper heaved sideways and then down. In less than ten seconds it was gone, leaving only fragmented ice and a slick of oily scum swirling in a shallow vortex.

For a long time, incalculable in measurements of such units as seconds or minutes or lifetimes, Mallen stared at the pool, hypnotized, unconsciously backing away. The slick erupted with a burst of bubbles and then a glut of oil ruptured the surface, spreading outward.

At last, Mallen turned away and headed north, toward the shore.

*　　*　　*

He had crawled a long way, much farther than he would have thought possible under these conditions and with the wound. His gloves were saturated, his knees frozen, and his leg throbbed with each movement he made. Paul Le Borveaux rested briefly against a birch and allotted himself thirty seconds before moving on.

He had seen the chopper crash just minutes after he had been wounded, and he knew that no one—neither McKennon nor Baines—stood in Mallen's way. Just himself. There wasn't a great deal of time left, and he knew it He first readjusted the leather strap of his carbine, slung across his back, and resumed crawling.

It took him another four minutes to make it to the top of the shallow rise, but from there, he realized with a surge of relief, he would have to go no farther. The rise gave way to a steep bluff overlooking the lake, giving him a free field of fire. From here he could command the lake with the carbine.

Paul picked a shelter formed from two fallen logs, knowing that here there would be some protection from the brittle wind gusting in from the northwest. Dragging himself over the nearer log, he used the remaining stumps of branches as handholds. The top of the log was coated with snow and the bark beneath was rotten, causing him first to slip and then to collapse. The pain from his wound shot through his body like a hot iron, and he saw waves of red and black as he clenched his eyes shut, but they gradually subsided, leaving a residue of dull, pounding pain.

Gritting down with his teeth to stifle the agony, he carefully lifted his left leg with both hands, repositioning it straight out in front of him. Using his pocket knife, he slit the fabric of his pants and examined the wound. He guessed that it had been a ricochet, a bullet glancing off the ice, deformed and tumbling but with still a great velocity. It had ruptured his flesh, just below his groin, but the bullet was still inside him. Feeling carefully, he touched a hard, alien lump at the back of his thigh.

The instructors had shown him how to apply a tourniquet. But the wound was just a few centimeters beneath his groin and there was no room for the belt to grip. It had repeatedly slipped out of position, regardless of the tension applied on the winding stick. As a compromise, he decided that he would hold the arterial pressure point, releasing it occasionally, to lessen the possibility of gangrene.

Many things still to do, he thought: make sure that the barrel of the carbine was clear of snow or obstructions—and keep warm. Those were the important things. He could remember the Polish sergeant pounding in the importance of those two points—*Keep your weapon dry* and *Preserve body heat.*

A wave of giddiness swept his mind; his vision was spinning. He knew that he had to remain conscious for just minutes more. Eventually Mallen would have to move his airplane out onto the ice, and it would be in this direction—downwind. He knew that much. Planes took off into the wind, just as ducks did from a pond. Mallen would taxi downwind to obtain the maximum takeoff space, and Paul knew that the carbine would have the range. Again, he thought, it was just a matter of minutes, then he could build a fire and take steps to care for himself.

Trying to focus on something, trying to retain the clarity of his purpose, he concentrated on Mallen. It had been easy to hate him in the early hours of the morning, when he had heard them through the thin ceiling. Paul had at first awakened as he heard Mallen's footsteps in the hallway, opening the door and then closing it. Then there were steps on the staircase and whispers; then footfalls again, and a closing door. A long silence followed, and Paul had almost drifted off into sleep. But then their voices came again—and the metallic creaking of bedsprings, and her final gasp. For minutes, and then hours, he had lain awake, his imagination wild, loathing for both of them growing into an intense knot. It had been betrayal of the worst sort, combined with the filth of sex.

He had heard men in the barracks joking about it. The dirt of their description, how women coupled with men. To Paul, it was something that animals did; a savage, blind act with no love. He had heard the men in the barracks joke, describing the things that they forced the whores to do, and even the cost of it, as if it were something you bought the way you did food or boots.

Mallen had betrayed him, broken his word, yet Paul realized that he had liked the American. Something in his manner was tough and hard and coarse, but there was compassion. He had seen Mallen's response to the old man and to Wyatt, known that there was something more than greed and self-interest.

Thinking back, he remembered their talk in the barn. He had felt something with Mallen, a sense of *being* with someone; an acceptance. It was a quality that Paul hadn't found even in his own father or with the other cadets, and he had held to it, reliving the brief contact. And he had thought of Mallen's description of the plane, what it would be like to fly—how he could extend his mind out to move through three dimensions.

But then Mallen had betrayed him.

Paul realized that he was very tired, as though he had run a great distance. But with the tiredness came an easing of the pain and a certain warmth. He closed his eyes and counted to fifty, forced them open, then breathed rapidly ten times, trying to clear his mind. He glanced back across the lake and guessed that it was snowing less now, but somehow the light was failing— darker, more overcast. He closed his eyes again, counting to thirty. Watching was unnecessary, he thought, because he would hear the engine of the plane, wouldn't he?

With dull curiosity, he frowned, watching the snow stain brownish-red around his left leg. His finger had slipped from the pressure point, but he hadn't noticed. He quickly wound the spruce branch tight on the tourniquet, slowing and then stopping the flow. Stupid, he thought; fingers so cold they've lost feeling. *Keep your weapon dry and preserve body heat*. He giggled, a little giddy, imagining that he could somehow scoop up the blood he had lost and save it, keep it warm by filling his pockets with it.

Paul also thought of his weapon. Keep it dry. He lifted it from the place it rested against the tree and examined the breech, blowing snow away from the action. It seemed particularly heavy and difficult to hold.

Mallen and Wyatt were never coming, he thought. His airplane engine must be broken or something. Mallen. Tried to remember what he had looked like. Couldn't think of anything they both had talked about except flying. Very stupid, he thought. Mallen was dumb to betray me, because I wouldn't have given him away—proved it. But different now. Things changed.

He felt it was warmer now. Possibly the fallen trees gave him more protection. And there was no real pain to speak of, just more like a shadow; a suggestion of discomfort. With sudden clarity, he realized that the combination of blood loss and cold was lulling him into lethargy. He would have to build a fire, not only to keep warm but to guide the chopper crews to his position. Couldn't last through the night, he thought—but wouldn't have to. McKennon had said that the choppers would be here soon enough, and the troops coming overland would probably arrive by mid-afternoon.

From his jacket pocket he withdrew a handful of dried apple slices and chewed on them methodically. They were tasteless, but he imagined the energy they would replenish his body with and thought of the warmth flowing back to him from the sun to the tree to the branches to the fruit.

The sound came to him, blown down on the wind. Not a chopper or truck. Lighter and higher in pitch, much like the sound of a small gasoline generator. He pulled himself upright, looking out over the lake.

It was Mallen's plane, perhaps five hundred meters away, taxiing downwind, the exhaust driven before the wind in a white plume. The plane was like nothing Paul had ever seen before—a thin, graceful fuselage and enormously long, delicate wings. Although it was dirty and smeared with washed-out streaks of mud, he could see the glossy white finish, banded with stripes of red and blue on the outer surfaces of the wings and tail.

By comparison, he could only equate its grace with the hawks and herring gulls, birds that soared effortlessly, their wings unmoving, spiraling higher and higher toward the cloud bases. He had also watched them, lying with his back against the warm earth as they angled their way along the ridges, riding the invisible cushions of wind that curled upward over the summits. To Paul, it had been the very essence of freedom—the act of free flight.

The plane was taxiing rapidly, slewing a little from side to side in the gusty wind. As he watched, he could see more detail: the numbers on the side of the plane, the blur of the prop, the reflection of light off the canopy.

As it drew closer, he had to shift his sights, lowering the aiming point to compensate for the decreasing distance. Within one hundred meters of where he now lay, the plane swung through a half circle and poised, engine picking up in pitch to a high wail, hunching forward on its landing gear in that last moment before flight.

It was even more graceful from this angle, he thought, a reminder of a time when he was younger, before the war had happened. He had seen a bird poised for flight on a fencepost and had aimed and fired with his father's .22, not really meaning to hit or to kill, but just for fun—to startle the bird. But he had fired and the bird had taken flight and faltered, died in midair and plunged to earth, lifeless. He could not even pick it up to bury it—a mass of black silk feathers and bright arterial blood, the body still warm to his touch.

He found that he had closed his eyes; his mind lapsing off into images and dreams. The plane was still there, its engine rising in pitch. There was a small shudder as the brake was released, then the thing started to roll. He couldn't remember whether the selector was on single shot or automatic, but it didn't matter. It would be impossible to miss.

Paul tightened his finger on the trigger, the sights

centered on the cockpit. Tightened, but he couldn't pull hard enough, as if the trigger were frozen. He found his vision blurring—impossible to see properly. Couldn't control his lungs or his reflexes, as if they were locked, unwilling to take commands. Biting his lip, Paul wiped the film from his eyes and tried again, but his finger had no strength. It seemed like an impenetrable barrier beyond which he could not pass.

The plane accelerated slowly, wind blasting the snow into a vortex of white. Paul caught glimpses of it, awkward at first, bound to the ground and ungainly. But then the tail lifted and for a few seconds the plane seemed part of neither sky nor ice, balancing delicately on the landing gear as fragile as the time of its brief transition between the two elements.

And then it was airborne—first paralleling the ice, gaining speed. As he watched, the landing gear tucked up into the belly of the fuselage and then the plane began a long, slow climb, finally banking to the west as it cleared the trees.

For several minutes he studied the sky, watching until the plane was no longer visible. For still longer he stared, hoping to catch a glimpse of it, a reflection of light from its canopy, the cruciform shape etched against the storm's cloud bank. But it was gone.

For a very long time Paul lay with his cheek against the stock of his rifle, his eyes closed, listening to the wind. Still things to do, he thought. Build a fire. Warmth.

Opening his eyes finally, he looked out over the sights of the carbine to where the plane had been. First inhaling, he gently squeezed the trigger, just as he had been taught to do. The carbine shattered the quiet, spewing out a long stream of tracers against the empty sky, the butt hammering against his shoulder. He held the trigger down until the firing pin fell into an empty chamber, the clip exhausted.

Paul Le Borveaux smiled, then released the weapon, letting it clatter off the log, falling muzzle first into a drift. There was a faint hissing as the heat of the barrel vaporized the snow. "Go with whatever God there is, Mallen," he said, half aloud.

Exhaling slowly, Paul lowered himself into a comfortable position between the fallen trees, then worked for a long time, patiently stripping bark from the trunk of the log, scooping a hollow in the snow down to the bare ground and lighting a fire. Carefully, he added twigs and then the broken-off stubs of small branches. The blaze finally took hold and he fed more wood to it, building the strength of the blaze.

As he tended the fire, he ate the remainder of the apple slices and avoided examining the reasons for what he had done. Perhaps he could come back here in the summer to fish and to think about it, but he knew now that besides the sense of loss, there was a much, much greater sense of gain, the same feeling you get when you have given a valuable gift.

He relaxed now, tucking both hands beneath the front of his coat and rolling over onto his back. It would be just a short time before they would be here, and the smoke from the fire would guide them. Warm from the blaze and his stomach full, he drifted back to a summer when he was very young, when she allowed him to play on the upstairs landing that overlooked the fields.

There was a cat that was his own and the two of them played with a ball of string, unraveling it, then winding it up again, only to repeat the game. From the stairwell hung Japanese wind chimes that made thin, delicate sounds as they stirred in the summer's breeze. And he had always loved the evening light; the merging and blending of colors through the stained glass of the landing's window.

For a second, his mind cleared and he opened his eyes. With difficulty, he focused on a snowflake that lay on his collar, perfect in six-point symmetry. And then he closed his eyes, waiting.